FOREVER

THE CONDUIT CHRONICLES

ASHLEY HOHENSTEIN

WORDS TO FOREVER LIVE BY

I asked my closest family and friends to share their favorite quotes.
The words they *FOREVER* live by. This is what they shared.

Some people come into your life for a reason, for a season or
Forever!
-Sheryl Mattera

When you know better, you do better!
-anonymous

The more you learn, the more you realize you don't know.
&
Earth is not a platform for human life. We are not on it, we are a
part of it. It's health is our health.
-Emma Coito

Remember to be gentle with yourself and others, love your life!
-Peggy Malnar

Figure out your purpose, because if you know your purpose...The
how, what, where and why will take care of themselves.
-Dave Nelson

Always choose love, even when it doesn't make sense, your heart
knows the way.
-Stephanie Marazzo

Eat good food, drink good wine, brush your teeth often, so if your
friends come over your breath will be fresh.
-anonymous

You can absolutely do anything you put your mind to. (Lived out by
Jayden Powell)
-Christina Powell

Make your heart the most beautiful thing
about you.
-Michelle Scheuermann

Fill your time with the things that make you fulfilled, the things that
fill your soul with goodness...People, places...Soak it all in...Put
yourself first
-Kelly Bidwell

Life is not being rich, being popular, being
highly educated or being perfect. It is about being real, being
humble and being kind.
-Lindsey Nelson

Of all the paths you take in life make sure a
few of them are dirt.
-Krisanne McCullough

Trust God for everything and in

every situation.
-Kay Parks

Accept what is, let go of what was, have faith in what will be.
Sometimes you have to let go to let new things come in.
-Dave Bidwell

Do not remember the former things, nor consider the things of old.
Behold, I will do a new thing, now it shall spring forth; shall you not
know it? I will even make a road in the wilderness, and streams in
the desert.-Isaiah 43:18-19
-John Mattera

Maybe it won't work out. But maybe seeing if it does will be the
best adventure ever.
&
If your path demands you walk through hell, walk as if you
own the place.
-Jen & Jeremy Pearce

I have been blessed to be surrounded by a supportive and loving
community through this challenging journey. Their wisdom has
helped me through some of the greatest hurtles in my life (and I'm
not referring to my writing career). It truly takes a village to
navigate this world. Some of them may be your biological family,
but many more will be your chosen. Love fiercely! Be Generous!
Choose Vulnerability! Inspire the light you wish to see in the world
and reflect the beauty you see in others!

This book is dedicated to the three people who have been my biggest fans since day one! Jen Oloff Lewis, Alicia Beckham and Michelle Bonea. Not only are the three of you my greatest cheerleaders in my writing career, but you are also amazing friends.

I am also dedicating this book to my fantastic editor Ella Medler. She has been with me through a lot of life. Not only is she incredibly talented as an editor, but she has shown me so much love and grace on this journey.

I literally couldn't have done any of this without you guys!

PART I

"What the fuck just happened?" I looked at Vosega. "How the hell did we just lose them?" We'd been tracking Esther, Clive and the Oracle all night, then suddenly they were gone. All traces of their whereabouts vanished.

"I don't know, son."

I was agitated. I wanted to snap back at him, tell him to not call me son—*not now, not ever! But what fucking good would that do?* I turned to Helia. "Got any ideas? You guys were hunting dragons, right? You must be able to sniff out these assholes."

Tete growled above our heads. "I guess that's a no." I looked around for the closest thing I could punch. A tree trunk would work nicely. My fist hit the wood, and it splintered into a million pieces. Olly had saved me and Yessica, only to become a captive herself. Worse than any prison I've been in, she was caged in her own body. Aremis had given me the Cliff's Notes version of the events leading up to tonight while I followed him to the Haven they'd been camped out at nearby. Everyone was certain that was the safest place for Yesi while she recovered, and a suitable base while we tracked down the enemy.

It seemed Yanni had been taking possession of Olly when she

was weakest. The gifts she'd been absorbing were too much for her to handle; she'd been having blackouts. These episodes made her vulnerable to possession after a séance they had performed with some quack job named Moira in Australia.

"We all want them back," Medusa shouted down at me from the gargoyle's back. "Get it together, Healey! We don't have time for your bullshit."

"My bullshit?" I glared at her. "You don't even know me, you stony bitch!"

"Your reputation precedes you," she shot back.

"This is not what Miss Ophelia would want," Aremis interrupted.

"That wasn't Olly." Sparkle's voice cracked when she spoke.

Shiva began speaking, and Borte quickly translated. "Shiva says he agrees with the spunky one. Ophelia was absent."

"Do you think she can never be returned to her body? Moira could return to her body," Oya added.

"Why does that even matter? Olly is in there somewhere, right? Do we just give up and let Yanni win? What about Viraclay? You guys aren't worried about him?" I looked at the faces of several Conduits I knew and many I didn't. Ophelia had somehow brought this ragtag team of misfits together.

Ying was the next to speak. "We wish to see both Miss Banner and Viraclay returned safely." His beautiful wife stood by his side nodding in agreement.

I closed my eyes and rubbed my forehead vigorously. The image of the fireball raining down on all of us consumed my mind. It was déjà vu from the night Hafiza fell, but this time it was my Olly managing the firepower. We had all scattered, barely avoiding the carnage. Anyone or anything left in the basin had been incinerated. That meant that Di and Rand were gone. Another pique of rage shot through me as I recalled that Clive the hobgoblin was so close. That monster had ordered the hit on my family. I looked at Vosega; I hadn't even had a chance to tell him what I discovered from Oracin, the pixie. *That felt like lifetimes ago now.*

The night's events were racing through my head in rapid succession. After the bloodbath, Aremis led me and Yesi off to the Haven where I left her with a Conduit named Mikkel before we caught up with the others. I was sure we would get our hands on what was left of the Nebas that were here tonight and finish this! *But here we are...*

"We should regroup. Devise a strategy before pursuing them at the compound," the Khan suggested. Of course he would want to go back to the Haven. That was where Yesi was. Come to think of it, *how well did I know this Mikkel character?* My skin crawled with anxiety. I wanted to be there, but I needed to be here. I needed to save Olly. She was the one who saved me. None of the others would've risked their necks on my behalf. *Fuck!* I kicked the tree. *This is all my fault. If she hadn't been trying to save me, she wouldn't be a captive now.*

Winston shook his head at my outburst and agreed with Genghis. "It seems likely that is where they will take them. Master Elias would want us to be calculated in our approach. We must also recover the Rittles."

"But where did they go? We were in a caravan on our way here. How did they just disappear?" I could see I was outnumbered. I was the raging bull, and these people were attempting sensibility.

Sparkle looked at me empathetically. "I don't know, Lucas. We did kill several of their entourage. Maybe they were able to move faster with half the men." She had a point.

Vosega's arm gripped my shoulder. "Lucas, my son, no one is giving up. We will find them." He paused. "We will find her."

I looked around at their resolved faces. I needed the numbers if I was ever going to see Ophelia alive again, so it was time to be a team player. Yessica was going to have to walk me through this one—thank God she was alive. *Or thank Olly, rather. It is thanks to Olly.*

I thrashed in my chains. "Ophelia!" Deep down, I knew it was no use. After all, it was she who had imprisoned me. But I was aware it was not really her; it was Yanni wearing her beautiful skin. I saw it in her eyes. They were black as coal. Evil and calculating. I had looked into the soul of a monster, not my dearest Olly. *But she had to be in there, right? Somewhere?* If I had known the episodes I witnessed could have led to this, I would have done more to spare her. The first time I saw the possession I should have done more. *Why did I not do more?*

The door opened and I turned to see Aurora standing in a long white robe. It was sheer. You could see her shape through the fabric. White was no longer becoming of her, now that I knew she was the traitor. I looked away, assessing my surroundings better. We must be in Chernobyl, *but how did we get back here so fast? Had I been incapacitated during the travels?* My mind could not recover the memories that would explain our swift travel. More duplicity. The resources she could orchestrate were vast. Maybe it was a Convening, magic from the Pierses.

I had not had much time to consider what her treachery actually meant, the true depths of her betrayal. There were too many moving pieces, so many questions, and devastating realizations were just below the surface of my understanding.

I wondered who had survived the battle in the basin. The last thing I saw was a massive fireball looming above us all before Yanni, Esther and the Oracle escaped with the Rittles and myself as a captive, and my Olly, lost as a prisoner in her own body. I clenched my jaw in rage. *How can this war be won with the greatest Ramalan we have ever known aligning with the enemy?*

"Viraclay," she said gently as she approached me cautiously. Although we both knew there was nothing I could do in these shackles.

"Is she okay?" I blurted out.

"Ophelia?"

"Indeed," I answered through bared teeth. She most certainly knew who I meant.

"I am afraid I cannot say. She is indisposed. Yanni appears to have taken management of her faculties." The Oracle now stood inches from my face, but out of reach. "I have never seen such a thing. Esther is a body snatcher, but possession…that is a new occurrence for me. And I must admit it has been some time since I have experienced anything new in this world."

My mouth went dry. The image of Aurora slicing Di in two to save Esther flashed across my mind. None of this made any sense. *Why would the Oracle side with her longtime captors?* Di risked her life to release Aurora from her captivity centuries ago. Rand's decapitated body, lifeless on the ground. The last of my family dead. His disheveled state just before his murder was haunting me. He just rambled on when Olly and I found him wandering through the trees. There was nothing I could do to save him. *How did he get out there? What had happened to him?*

"I see you attempting to connect the dots. Please do not bother. It will all become painfully clear in due course. But to bombard you with all the details in this moment, while you are still fretting over Ophelia and reeling from the night's events, well, I am afraid too much would be lost on you, and I do hate to repeat myself." She came in closer still. I could feel her breath on my skin. "Just know this: You have been a fly in my web since the day you were born, Elias. I warned your parents, but they did not heed my foreboding— I had no choice but to take drastic measures."

The thought had already occurred to me, but to hear her say it aloud made me ill. My face went cold and sweat pooled on my forehead. I was going to vomit. The bile crept up my throat, acid stung my nostrils. I swallowed hard. I would not give this beast the satisfaction of witnessing the effect her admission had on me.

She laughed knowingly. "Oh, Viraclay, you are just as stubborn as your father." Aurora turned around. Her hair brushed my cheek as she flitted away. "I will return after I have given you a moment to collect yourself."

My shoulders slumped forward. Something felt like it died within me, seared away by the terrible knowing that my parents were murdered by a dear friend, that I had been toyed with for the entirety of my existence, and that Ophelia may be lost forever.

ESTHER

*H*e stood in front of me. His mannerisms, his eyes, even his scent was faint but wafting in the air. I'd been watching him as we made our escape as he had been watching me— I felt his eyes upon me, my soul restored by his presence. Now here we stood in my chamber, alone for the first time.

"Esther, I have missed you." It was not his voice, exactly. Ophelia's vocal cords didn't match my Yanni's, yet it was him. Every cell in my body yearned for him and ignited when it heard his commanding tone. I had felt his soul return from the River Tins multiple times, but I never could have fathomed this.

"My beloved." I nearly whispered the words. He cleared the gap between us and took me into his arms. But they weren't his arms, yet they felt like his arms. I collapsed in the embrace. "I knew you would come back to me," I whispered in his ear as I swept the wild curly hair from my face. I closed my eyes so I could imagine that I was being held by Yanni's true form, not by this ridiculously sad borrowed sack of flesh. He pulled me in tighter. His hands moved across my body, sensually, seductively, until they worked their way up to my face. He cupped my cheeks in his palms and pulled me back to look at my face. I couldn't open my eyes. I didn't want to see the girl's face where I wanted his to be. With my eyes closed, I could visualize Yanni's chiseled features.

"Open your eyes," he demanded. I did not comply. "Open your eyes, Esther!" More authority in his request. His hands moved to my scalp, where he took hold of my hair with both his fists. "Look at me!"

I obeyed reluctantly. There they were, Yanni's deep coal black irises staring into my soul. He put his mouth to mine and kissed me hard, without restraint. There were hints of his flavor in my mouth and it consumed me. I began to work my tongue around his feverishly. He gripped my hair tighter, causing searing and exciting pain to erupt all over my body. I kissed him more forcefully, exploring every corner of his mouth. Yanni released one fistful of my hair and began working his hand down my back until he was able to cup my butt in his palm. He squeezed firmly. I responded by biting his lip. A moan interrupted the silence between us. *Was it he or I?* It did not matter.

He yanked my mouth away from his with the hand that still held the fist of my long black hair. I opened my eyes, forgetting for a moment that the face that met mine would not be the one I adored. Instead of Yanni's olive skin and dark features, I looked at the face of Ophelia Banner. My stomach turned. He sensed my disappointment, but did not waver.

"I am taking you to bed." With that, he threw me over his shoulder and tossed me onto the large chaise in the center of the room.

My head felt muddled. I tried to open my eyes but they weren't there. *My eyes weren't there!* I tried to move my hands to touch them. *They have to be there!* But my arms, my hands, my fingers were absent—I had no sensory capabilities. *Am I in a coma?*

What is the last thing I remember? Think, Olly, think! I demanded. We'd caught Esther, then something went wrong...terribly wrong. Aurora killed Di, then it all went dark. No, not dark. I was captured. Piece by piece, realization after realization washed over me. I was captured in my own body. Yanni had seized my body. It all happened so fast, *but where am I now? In the recesses of my conscious-ness?* I felt around for anything of substance, a thread of something to grasp onto. Still, there was nothing. I was trapped in my own mind. Panic gripped me. *I am trapped in my own mind!*

"We have to get them," I said as I threw my filthy clothes on the ground. Yessica looked on after me as I ranted. "We can't waste time trying to figure out who's in charge and who should call the shots. We need to just go get them. Whatever it takes."

The shower water was hot, but it couldn't wash away the anger, the frustration of being blindsided by—of all people—the Oracle. *How do you fight against someone who can see the future, see everything?*

"I hope they are making plans to leave this Haven. We can't stay here," I shouted.

I was so engulfed in my emotions I didn't notice Yessica in the shower with me until I felt her smooth skin and round breasts up against my back. *Is this real?* It didn't seem real. Worse, it didn't feel right to be this happy when I had just seen Ophelia abducted by the enemy. But I couldn't resist this moment. It had been nineteen years since I'd seen Yesi. Now I was holding her naked body. I had to have her.

Her lips brushed past my ear. "I know there is so much going on and so much to consider, but that is exactly why I cannot wait another moment to be with you. It could be our last."

She didn't need to explain anything to me; I was already hard and ready to take her. I picked her up into my arms, cradling her perfectly round ass in my hands. It felt like we'd been together like this only yesterday. It felt like home.

She moaned gently in anticipation. But I had no intention of making this quick. I pushed her back against the shower wall, stabilizing her so I could use my free hand to fondle every inch of her that my mouth wasn't already busy with. I traced her nipple with my tongue and her breathing got heavier. Her arms around my neck squeezed a little tighter. I slipped my fingers between her thighs, and I felt the warmth that I'd been missing, yearning for, and thought I'd lost forever. She was wet. Her body trembled with every touch, every twist of my fingers or flick of my tongue.

I could have gone on like this for hours and been satisfied, but Yesi took a handful of my hair and gently tugged. "I want you inside me." *Who was I to keep a woman waiting?* I took both her thighs in my hands and spread her legs forcefully, pushing her higher up against the tile wall before sliding inside her.

OPHELIA

There was nothing but darkness for what felt like an eternity. I was adrift in the deep chasm of nothingness, no form, no sensations, only ethereal thoughts passing through, and even those were hard to grasp. Thoughts about the dragons we had just escorted to The Cathedral. Thoughts about the Summit and the death of many good souls when the Nebas infiltrated the huge Haven. Thoughts of the hairsy charm and my tether to Lucas that led me straight to him, only to be in this predicament now. Thoughts about my mother and Lilith being held and tortured by the Nebas, specifically by my father Nestor.

Then a light flickered in the distance, small at first, until it grew and engulfed me, whatever I was. Suddenly, my sense of smell came back. There was the scent of strawberries in the air. Tingling consumed by body and my proprioception returned. My vision came in blurry and then slowly focused until I could make out my surroundings.

Where am I? I stood in front of a string of doors. One was cracked open, the rest were shut. Each door was a different color and made of a unique material. The first one was forest green. It looked like it had been painted and repainted several times, drips of paint had dried and been covered with another layer visible on its surface. It had a glossy finish. Soft shadows filled the grooves, and a kerosene lantern hung from the mahogany wood frame. The golden light from the flame flickered and romanticized the ambiance of the entire picture before me.

My eyes moved to the next door, to the right. It was made of copper, tarnished around the edges but polished like a new penny everywhere else. The door hung in a large oak frame that was ornately carved with flowers and suns and moons. I had never seen anything like it before. I could've stared at it for hours, examined every detail, but my curiosity got the better of me.

My eyes trailed to the third door. A crimson red, round and encased in an iron frame. Three candelabras jetted out of the iron infrastructure, one on either side of the door and a third above it. The candles were the same crimson as the flawless circular door. A large, intimidating knocker with the face of a grotesque gargoyle was mounted in the center. The gargoyle's eyes seemed to move, examine me just as I examined it. *Or is that my imagination?*

And for the first time it occurred to me: *I must be dreaming. This is a dream. It has to be.* The doors were erect in the middle of nothing, but it seemed perfectly normal to have them there, the type of felt sense you only have in dreams.

I looked at the final door, the one that was ajar. It was black, jet black. I wouldn't have been able to make out the seam between the frame and the door if it wasn't open. A purple light glowed on the other side. I stepped closer. *Perhaps I could take a peek inside.*

"I would not do that if I were you," a familiar voice warned behind me. I turned around, only just realizing that I hadn't taken in all of my surroundings.

"Rand!" I ran to him, so relieved to see him in his right mind. He was standing by a river of rainbow colors. It was tranquil, yet somehow fierce in nature. I threw my arms around his neck, he gently swept me off my feet and into his comforting embrace. His scent filled my nostrils, his long curly brown hair tickled my cheek. This felt so real. *But how could it be?* The reality of the last time I saw

Rand came rushing back to me and I had to choke back a sudden and intense sob. He was beheaded by the hobgoblin Clive. Rand had been so out of his mind, it was disturbing, and then he was just gone. My heart shifted to hope. Perhaps we were able to salvage him, save him before the Nebas could set fire to his body. Tears started to stream down my cheeks.

Rand put me back on my feet, pulled out a handkerchief and dabbed at my face. "Surely, Miss Ophelia, we can save the tears for another time. I am here now."

"So, you're alive? We rescued you." I was trying to scan my brain for my last solid memory, but I couldn't retrieve anything after Di being slaughtered by… My thoughts trailed off. My memories were foggy because I had started to feel the onset of an episode. Then it just went dark. "Where are we, Rand? What happened?"

His eyes said it all. He didn't want to be the one to break the news to me. "Sit. It is best you sit."

"I am not sitting." My breaths became shallow, quick. The light-headedness was coming in fast. "Okay, maybe I should sit."

A chair appeared just behind me and Rand sat me down.

"Am I dead?" I blurted the question out, unable to contain it any longer.

"No, my dear." Rand stroked my hair with his hand. "I don't believe so."

I put my head between my legs. "Good, because it would seem unfair to still be able to have panic attacks in the underworld. Unless this is hell. Am I in some sort of hell?"

I sat back up, searching my surroundings for some answers. On one side of me were the four doors, on the other side was the vibrant colorful river. Everything else in the space was there, but wasn't, like the sensation in a dream, the knowing without the seeing that something is.

"We are in a purgatory. In between the River Tins and the Gates of Consciousness."

"That's the River Tins?"

"The one and only." Rand used one of his eccentric hand

gestures, as though he was generating a great reveal. I had to laugh, because it was something so familiar, so comforting in a completely disorientating way.

"Rand, how did I get here? How do I get back? Are you in purgatory too?" He could be saved. I knew he could be saved. I had seen it. Only flame would disperse his life force from his body in a mortal way.

"I could not just leave you, lost and afraid in this space."

I shook my head. It was too much to take in. I couldn't wrap my brain around it all. My head felt like it was going to explode.

Rand knelt in front of me so he could meet my gaze. "I had only just immersed my toes into the stream when a voice said 'Wait. She will need a friend.' So I stepped out of the river and have been waiting for you here on the shore. Then you appeared like an apparition."

Relief washed over me, because it was true. Seeing Rand brought me some solace. But then it occurred to me. "By waiting for me, you prolong the reunion with your Carissa."

His eyes said it all. I had spoken his truth. He took my hand in his and squeezed it gently. "Dearest Ophelia, we will get you home."

ESTHER

It was beyond words, lying here beside my Yanni. I gently pulled the messy red hair from around his face. It was bizarre, looking at Ophelia's body but feeling Yanni's presence. I inhaled deeply and a waft of his familiar scent filled my nostrils. *But it couldn't be his scent, could it? Did one's smell follow their spirit?*

I traced Ophelia's hips with my index finger. I preferred the love of a man's form; there was no denying that. But Ophelia was beautiful. Her long curly red hair covered most of her back where she lay. I sat up to get a better look at the body I would learn to love because it now possessed the other half of my soul.

Yanni rolled over to face me. "Beloved?"

"I am trying to get familiar with your new skin."

His smile widened and I saw a hint of the grin I used to adore. "Do not let me stop you. I liked your first exploration."

He swept my long hair out of my face and over my shoulder while I leaned in to kiss his soft pale belly. Ophelia's skin was milky white where the sun had not tinted it. I slipped my right hand down between her thighs and pulled her legs apart. Yanni moaned softly and I felt my own body spark with arousal. My lips slowly journeyed down to his navel, which I traced with my tongue. I sat up to reposition myself when a small tan spot caught my eye. My head swelled with bewilderment. Tingling ran down my spine.

Yanni quickly noticed the shift in my demeanor. He sat up. "What? What has happened?" He followed my gaze. I put my hand on the birthmark that caught my attention. A patch of skin that was slightly darker than the rest of Ophelia's leg, located on the inner right thigh. I knew it well. I would recognize it anywhere. It almost resembled half of a heart.

He looked up at me, disbelief in his eyes. "What does this mean?" He reached down to my inner right thigh and put his palm over my identical birthmark.

After Yesi and I had properly enjoyed our reunion, I was ready for more answers. I didn't know who was in charge of the rescue mission. I would've preferred that I have that authority. But there was no way this group was going to authorize me with any leadership. No, it was better to make nice with the likely candidate: the great Alchemist.

I set out to find him while Yessica and Genghis were spending some quality father daughter time together. Yesi would want to clear the air, heal wounds, and start a new foundation. She was a better person than I'd ever be. I had no desire to build bridges with Vosega or Oya or any of the others.

The moment I thought it, I reconsidered, because there was an exception. I wanted to apologize to the Tallus family. I never got to do that with Nandi. If I had gone to her, to explain what had really happened—the agreement Huan and I made to keep each other safe while we searched for answers—if I had told her the truth, maybe she'd still be alive. Now that she was gone and I played a part in the death of another Tallus family member, I regretted my silence.

But where do I start? The whole family was here. If they didn't want to hear me out, they could just kill me. *Maybe that was their plan all along?* If it were me, I know I would want revenge. And here I was seeking the patriarch. *What a way to find out.*

I found Ruit in the yard with Jezebel. I hesitated. Maybe I was going soft, but I'd overheard Aremis tell Sparkle it had been seventy years since the Soahcoit had seen each other. Yesi and I spent a fraction of that time apart. It felt intrusive to impose on their reunion. *Or perhaps it was the perfect time to apologize to both of them.*

My conscience got the better of me. *Yeah, I am definitely going soft.* I turned to head back into the house. I'd insist on strategy later, after the burial rites. Tete had informed me that there would be a farewell ceremony for Di and Rand in a few hours. I was antsy to get out of this Haven to make sure that Yesi was safe. Maybe even head in the direction of Chernobyl. But I wasn't a lone wolf anymore and I needed help. *I hate needing help.*

"Lucas Healey, stay. We have much to discuss," Ruit insisted before I slipped back into the house.

I turned around to face him once more, and Jezebel gave me an affirming smile as she passed.

"Do we now? I have some ideas for storming the compound." *Way to apologize, Lucas,* I internally berated myself. *I am a coward.*

"That will come later. It is true your knowledge will be helpful in our tactics, but for now I want to clear the air about something, and I need to better examine your chording to Ophelia."

My mind flashed back to the moment Fetzle shared the hairsy charm with me and Olly. Selfishly, I was smug about having one more tie to her, one more connection Elias didn't have. I never could've imagined it was the thing that would save my life and put hers in danger.

"Walk with me." Ruit passed by and I stepped in line with him. "How are you doing?"

Odd question if he planned on killing me. I hated small talk, but I could give him this, couldn't I? "Better in some ways and worse in others."

"It must be a relief to have Yessica back in your arms."

"Indescribable, really," I admitted.

"Trust me, I understand."

I bet he does.

"It is time to clear the air about some things. We all need a present mind right now if we are going to be victorious."

He had my full attention.

"I was also abducted by the Nebas, as you well know. But I escaped four years ago, and I did not go to my family. Do you know why that was?"

"No. I know they were beside themselves." Huan had told me as much.

"I knew they were too. I had even heard whispers that my son Huan had taken up with the Nebas before his death. My son was my best friend. If he had joined the Nebas after my disappearance, it was to discover what happened to me. I knew this, yet I still did not disclose my whereabouts, or that I was no longer a captive. I was aware this put him in danger, danger that he would not be in without my absence. I would find out later that he died in their service. I have a theory about how I woke from my state, and it revolves around the timing of Huan's death. Do you know when he died?"

Guilt stung every cell in my body. I knew exactly when he died. "Thirteen years ago."

"Curious. That means my theory is incorrect. I had pieced together an incorrect timeline based on what little I knew. I was sure I woke when I felt his strokes leave this earth, that the loss of my son was enough to puncture any curse." Ruit wiped tears that were spilling over from his eyes. "The timing does not match. I woke just before Alistair killed Cane and Sorcey. I followed him for six months before he went to the Haven in South Africa and murdered them. Had I gone to him straight away, I could've prevented their murders."

This was a perfect moment to apologize. But instead, I deflected, again. "Did you know about the Oracle?"

"No, I had no idea that she was treacherous. I was held captive for many years with the same strange serum that kept your Yessica asleep and out of your reach, and that disabled you. After I woke, by the luck of the strokes, I kept myself undetectable with a series of incantations very similar to your shield. In many ways, it was for my family's protection, but selfishly, it was also so I could move in the shadows and play my part in the impending war. After I realized what Alistair had done to the Krauses, I did everything in my power to stop him from achieving the composition of the Loktpi I witnessed him take in China. I laid the groundwork for Elias to visit the tribes and discover The Cathedral. And I left clues for Nandi to find the Sorcerer's Stone before Alistair did. I was so occupied I was not even there to stop Rand the night he killed my grandson. I made a choice, and it cost my daughter as well as my grandson their lives. The hand that killed them is just as much my hand as the one that wielded the weapon."

We walked in silence for several paces.

"I loved Huan. He was my friend in the darkest time of my life. Killing him took the last ounce of humanity from my soul." I had never said that aloud before.

"I believe you." He stopped and made eye contact with me, comforting me with a hand on my shoulder before turning and continuing to walk. "I also believe his death is what ultimately led to my grandson's demise. Huan dying seemed to confirm to Alistair that I was there, alive and waiting for rescue. He chose darkness, seeking what he believed was the light—me. Sometimes we hurt those we love the most in unconscionable ways."

We walked in silence again. I'd hurt many people in deplorable ways. I tried to forget most of them. Numb it out, rage it out, blame it out, justify it—ignore entire periods of my life. But it was always there hiding under the surface, waiting to ambush me and remind me of all my failures and trespasses—remind me that I wasn't a good person.

Ruit stopped walking to face me once more. "We make decisions every day. Some are good, some are terrible, some have seemingly no repercussions, while others rock the foundation of the world. We were painted with the ability to alter our strokes and the strokes of those around us because we are all connected. I must believe there is a reason why I made the choices I made, some unforeseeable outcome that will make all of the atrocities that fell in their wake worth it. Whether there is or isn't, we have to forgive and accept, otherwise those ghosts haunt us and influence future opportunities in subtly toxic ways. I stayed away from my family far longer than I needed to out of shame and guilt. I built a wall of seclusion, and more people got hurt. Tear down your walls. You have been forgiven—you always were. The last one to set you free is your own hand."

My eyes welled with tears. Ruit was granting me a forgiveness I wasn't certain I could even give myself. He'd said what he needed to say, and I didn't know what to say after that, so we stood in silence. I let the tears fall and the Alchemist held space for me to surrender to the pain I'd been ignoring.

When the tears dried up and I composed myself, he spoke again. "Are we in accord with one another?"

I nodded.

"Very well. Now, the next order of business. Tell me about the incantation that binds you and Ophelia, please."

I repeated the story as I remembered it.

"Interesting," Ruit mumbled under his breath as he began to assess me physically.

"What's interesting?" As he circled me, it felt as though he was sizing me up like a lion does an antelope.

"This incantation that connects you to Ophelia… I have only seen one other example of it in my lifetime. In fact, it may be the same charm. It's Pierses magic in its original form. Created by someone long lost to our time. It is called a Gattilak charm."

"Fetzle said she got it off a Poppit."

"She may have, but a Poppit didn't create this charm. What did she call it?"

"A hairsy charm." I even scoffed at the name when I said it because I knew it couldn't be the real moniker. *Sweet Fetzle.*

"Fitting for how she chose to use it. Binding you and Ophelia with the Pierses relic through your hair."

He'd stopped circling me, which was good because I was about to lose my shit. "Okay, so what are you looking at? I don't even have the charm. Olly does."

"She doesn't have the charm anymore. She is the charm. The magic and all of its properties are now part of her being. True Pierses magic in the flesh. It's remarkable."

This was the first I'd heard of this.

"What do you mean?"

"It would seem she absorbed it, like she does everything else around her. The bond it created between you two, that allows two individuals to pinpoint each other's whereabouts, is now part of her gifts."

I was trying to calculate what kind of implications that type of energy could have on Ophelia in the long run. I was coming up short. I didn't really understand what was going on. "What does this mean for her? How do you think this will affect her?"

"Honestly, one cannot know. I believe it is part of the reason why she has been having blackout episodes."

"Because she is becoming consumed by this original Pierses magic? You don't think it's because she was being possessed by Yanni?"

"Yanni was only able to take possession of her because of the episodes. According to Aremis' account."

I remembered that's what Aremis had told me, but he didn't mention this Pierses shit. "So, this Pierses magic is hurting her?"

"Perhaps, or perhaps it's all the gifts she's absorbing. I know the object you call a hairsy charm has many more properties to it. I intend to find out what those are."

"Will you let me know what you find? Are you detecting something with the charm around me?"

He nodded.

"Then we have to see if this magic you see around me can help at all, right?"

"Certainly, no stone left unturned."

"Anything, if it helps her." I examined his demeanor, and my shoulders relaxed. He wasn't placating me. He was going to do everything in his power to help save her. "We should talk about our strategy for storming the compound. And we should leave this Haven. We've been here too long."

"In due time."

I opened my mouth to object and Ruit put his hand up.

"I have created massive protective wards around this Haven. No one will be able to disturb us within these walls until our time here has come to a close. I have also closed all Rune channels of communication between Viraclay and Ophelia and my family."

"Rune channels?"

Ruit exposed a symbol tattooed on his body. "It's a very exclusive form of communication that I created for my family and the Oracle exploited. It cannot be trusted right now. I hope to access them again when the time is advantageous for us to strike."

How do I get my hands on one of those, I thought. Then Ruit covered it once more and continued.

"There needs to be mourning. We all must enter the next stages with a clear and present mind. I am collecting information, and with your permission, I would like to syphon a small extract of the energy that binds you two."

"Yeah, whatever you need, but I think we need to act now. Esther has some pretty lethal tricks up her sleeve, and now with the Oracle..." I shuddered as I remembered The Vice. "There is no telling what they will do."

"I assure you, there will be no time wasted. My sense tells me Ophelia is safe as long as she is occupied by Yanni. It is Viraclay we need to concern ourselves with."

I supposed he was right.

"I will come to your chamber just before the burial rites, to extract a sliver of that magic."

I wanted to say more, to insist on hastier actions, but I couldn't bring myself to dispute his points. Ruit was smart, calculating, and powerful as fuck. For that, the man got my vote and deserved some respect.

"I'll be there."

"Very well." Ruit moved swiftly past me and was almost to the house when he called back to me. "My sense tells me that it may be a good time to call upon your troll friend. She will play an important role as all of the events unfold." Then he was gone.

A smile spread across my face. It would be good to see Fetzle. The smile turned into a guttural laugh as I considered how delighted Fetzle would be to see Yesi.

The door flew open. The Oracle stood over us, looking at me, then over to Yanni. She did not bother to hide her disgust. "Are you finished with your reunion?" she spat. "We do not have time for these trysts. They will be coming for both of them, in haste. I can see it."

I got to my feet and Yanni came to my side, as though together we could avoid Aurora's tyranny. We both knew better. It was ironic that my father had been murdered for being a villain when in fact, it was his captive that could unleash true terror. I had seen it multiple times.

"Of course. I am assuming you will not need me to persuade the Nebas to comply with your next plan of action." I seethed a little inside. I had built this compound. It was I who manifested the momentum it would take to conquer the dominion over those that would oppose us and the human world. But Aurora, the Oracle, would see to it that she alone sat on the throne.

"Of course. I don't need your help. I am the Oracle. There is nowhere for anyone to hide. They will all submit, especially after we vanquish Ruit and his small clan of merry men." She walked over to me briskly, pointing at Yanni. "She is the key. I need her to complete my transformation. Between her and the captives I will be able to harness the greatest Sulu power the world has ever known."

"This form no longer belongs to Ophelia. I told you, Yanni is back—"

The crack of her hand across my face shut me up.

"You do not tell me a thing, child. You do not command the gift of foresight. Whatever this is," she looked Yanni up and down, "is convenient and clearly a gift from Chitchakor. This changes nothing. The Sulu is the key."

My face burned where she struck my cheek. I showed no emotion, but Yanni knew. He placed his hand at the small of my back. *From evil things spawn evil things*, was all I could think. My father's maleficence begot Aurora's rage. I couldn't blame her for hating the world that would see her as a captive for centuries and do little to help. The Pai Ona were righteous hypocrites as far as I was concerned. They deserved her wrath. They would get mine for murdering my father and taking my Yanni's form from this earth. I looked down at the slightly exposed birthmark once more. We would have the rest of our long lifetimes together to discover what the mark meant. For now, we needed to prepare for the certain battle to come. I had more to fight for than ever. I would not lose my beloved twice.

"Come, both of you. We will see how well you channel the Sulu's gifts."

We both stood naked and sweaty from our reunion.

"Put on clothes and meet me in the courtyard." The Oracle headed toward the door. "Be quick with it. There is much to attend to before our enemy descends upon us."

We both picked up our clothes. I pulled my dress over my head as Yanni put on his pants.

"I will need to bring a little style to this body," he said as he picked up the top.

"That reminds me. I found something of yours." I walked to my vanity, where I had put his ring. "You can start with this."

I placed the ring on his finger.

"Where in Malarin's name did you find this?"

I didn't want to remember where I found it. That day was the worst day of my life.

"Some things always find their way back to us." I kissed his forehead. "Like you, my beloved."

*S*he had left me alone in the room for hours with nothing to do but replay every moment I had ever engaged with the Oracle. Now that Aurora stood inches away, her back to me, I was stuck somewhere between bewilderment and rage. I saw the Rune on her shoulder, confirmation that she was the other traitor. It had always been her. Rand had discovered the truth before he died; that was why he felt nothing was safe. *How could it be when the enemy has infinite sight?* My mother and father had loved her. They treated her like family. *What kind of monster betrays family?*

"Sweet boy, there is a lot to consider."

She was in my head—not reading my thoughts, but she knew the questions I wanted to ask. Perhaps I would ask them in the near future.

"I know you have much to examine and deliberate over. It is exhausting, no doubt." She turned to face me. "So please, before you give yourself an aneurism trying to discover my motives and the part I played in all of this, answer a few of my questions. We can make a game of it. You answer one of my inquiries and I may answer one of yours."

I said nothing. *What answers could I have for the all-seeing Oracle?*

She approached slowly, methodically, and I was struck once more by her similarities to Olly. They were subtle, but there. I had to shake them off because it brought a sting to my heart, a deep grief that would distract me from navigating this predicament as best I could. I also recognized something I had never seen before—a resemblance to Esther, the way they both used body language to seduce and toy with their prey. The mark of a true demon. Maybe she kept it hidden until now, or perhaps we were all fools with blinders on.

"Do you remember that prophecy I gave you when you were a wee boy?" She was close enough to touch once more—that is, if I was not chained to the wall.

"Where is Ophelia?"

"Ah, ah, ah! You must answer my question first, per our agreement. Do you remember it?"

We could both ignore each other for all I cared.

"It was scribbled onto a small piece of paper. I know you kept it for years, folded up in your wallet."

If she knew that, *why is she asking?*

"You lived and breathed by that prophecy. It has been one of the most influential things of your life since you first heard it; is that not true?"

I stared blankly back at her. "Is Olly safe?"

"See, this is exactly what I am referring to, child. Your obsession with your Atoa. I do not think it is entirely healthy. One must seek their own way in the world. Sometimes that means bending the rules or changing them completely. Do not blindly take what another says as all-knowing and unchanging. The world tells you that you are here to love one soul, to be complete with the company of a single being. Alas, now the world is full of Poginuli since this war began. And are they not satisfied with the new love they have created? My point is that if we rely on what others tell us as truth, we give them our power. Nothing should influence you more than your own purpose."

Was she insinuating that the prophecy was not true? Had Ophelia been right all along, when she said we needed to create our own fate?

"I made my way," she continued. "I had to. I rewrote my entire story. I never let myself be led by my heart exclusively. When Cadmael died, I carried on. I did not crumble."

I cocked my head, realizing there was so little I truly knew about the woman I had trusted my whole life.

"How did he die?"

The question stopped her in her tracks. She looked through me with an icy stare. *Has she always been this dead inside?*

"It does not matter how he left this world, only that he did and I survived. Nay, I say I thrived in his absence."

This is thriving to her? Aligning with the Nebas, betraying her closest friends?

She got close to my face again, all pretense or facade wiped from her expression. "What did you do with the prophecy, boy?"

I said nothing.

"Bring in the girl!"

Suddenly, Ophelia was standing in front of me. But it was not my Olly. She wore a tight black leather suit. Her hair was swept back into a slick bun and her expression was flat. Her eyes were what haunted me the most—coal black, soulless. Not Ophelia. Yanni.

The Oracle walked over to Ophelia. "I have no problem killing her." Yanni raised an eyebrow as though he was vaguely intrigued by the threat. "Then you will have no chance of getting her back."

I said nothing. *What am I to do?*

"Or I could pick this body apart piece by piece." Aurora pulled a blade from her thigh and put it at Yanni's throat.

I did not have time to evaluate how serious she was about her threats. *Besides, what could this information change?*

"I burned it."

"You what?"

"I gave it to Olly and after the Summit. We burned it. It was time to change our fates."

Aurora laughed a shrill, callous laugh. "You gave it to the girl and then you burned it. Why would you do such a thing?"

"It was just as much hers as it was mine."

"How is that new fate of yours working for you?" Yanni laughed with her. My stomach twisted and my head grew hot. This was all too much. *How has it all gone so wrong?* "I had enchanted that prophecy. It was one of my dearest creations and you simply burned it." Aurora shook her head.

That made sense. It explained the explosion that occurred when we threw it into the flames. "Enchanted it how?"

"I suppose my secret makes no difference now that you have destroyed the device. Such a shame." She shook her head again. "I have been dying to tell someone how ingenious it was. It was a tracking device of sorts. I knew where you were, without using my gifts, at all times. Brilliantly disguised as the prophecy you held onto like a childhood token. I did not even have to tell you to carry it with you always. You simply did. It was the perfect tool until you burned it in China."

"But we did not burn it in China."

She gave me a double take. "Did you not?"

"No, we burned it after the Summit. As I said."

So, it became useless to her after Olly had it in her possession. Curious.

"My turn."

"Oh, dear boy, you already asked a question." She smirked. "My turn."

She came around to my side and grazed my Rune. "Tell me, does this still work for you?"

I had tried to utilize the magic of the Rune when we arrived here. No one answered my communications. I could not reach them.

"I do wish to get a message to Ruit."

I focused my attention into the Rune and felt nothing, again. "You have your own."

"It would seem the great Alchemist isn't taking calls from me right now."

"Apparently all lines are down." I could give her this answer.

"Interesting. So they have truly left you alone." She turned and made a gesture to Yanni, who quickly left the room. My heart hurt as I watched Olly's vacant form leave my sight. "Tell me, boy, why would they do that?"

I had been pondering the same question. *Have they really left me alone? Without my efforts to challenge the Nebas and end this war, would it all fall to ruin?* Everything my father had fought for, died for—gone, with one false step. Shame and guilt swept over me.

The Oracle stuck the knife she held in her hand to my neck. "So, you believe they have forsaken you?"

I peered into her callous eyes and saw a flash of something. *Fear maybe?* She knew different. She was trying to see what I sensed. Her vision had her afraid. That was good, very good.

OPHELIA

Maybe the dead can have anxiety.

"Calm yourself, Miss Ophelia. You will put yourself into a fit and that will not serve either of us." Rand was right. I knew he was right.

I stared at the River Tins as it rushed by, a flurry of color and texture, flowing and transforming simultaneously. Then I turned to the doors. "Rand, what are the doors here for? You called them the Gates of Consciousness."

"I made an assumption. A great medium once told me that we each have a door. A threshold into the living, from the dead. She called it our Gate of Consciousness."

"Was it Moira?"

"I am sorry?"

"The great medium. Was her name Moira?"

"Oh. No, it was Helene Smith."

"Shit, it was Moira."

Rand looked at me as though I was losing my mind.

"It's a long story, but Helene goes by Moira now. We had an encounter and that's why I'm sitting here with you today. I absorbed her bag of tricks." Recognition sparked across his face.

"I see. That is how Yanni was able to gain possession of your body."

I nodded. "But how do you know that?"

"As I said, I stuck my foot in the river before I realized your state. There is a perception in the water, a vastness. I got a sense of what had just happened, and a very clear voice told me to wait for you."

"Whose voice?"

Rand just shook his head.

"So, one of these doors should be mine?" I pointed at them. "The open one?"

He shook his head. "I am afraid I do not know."

"Then why did you stop me?"

"I know I can be a little eccentric, but I am no fool. It will be best if we discover what or who is behind those doors before you enter into a situation we know nothing about. I am rather fond of you, my dear, even now as I enter the afterlife. Let it be a dead man's final wish, this deep desire for you to succeed."

I couldn't imagine my life without Rand. I stood up and hugged him. He wrapped his arms around me and brushed my hair with his hand. It was then that I realized sensations felt different, numbed, muted—off.

Rand stepped back and my arms fell to my sides. "I do not wish to cut a cherished moment short, but we also do not know how much time we have. Will I be called into the river? I dare say I do not know."

I just nodded, afraid that if I opened my mouth, the tears would begin to fall and wouldn't stop.

"Let us retrace the events just before you arrived here. Do not leave out a single detail."

I sat back down, willing myself to maintain my composure. I needed to search my memory while I still had Rand here to help me solve what was going on and discover how I could get back to reality.

I traced my recollections back to before we ambushed Esther in the basin. We were successful. We had them trapped. But then it all went so wrong so quickly.

"Rand, what was wrong with you?" I stared into his eyes for answers. Did he remember what had transpired, how he had held Aurora with a knife to her throat, spouting gibberish?

"I was tortured with a device called the Vice. It scrambled my brain so that I could not cohesively put my thoughts into words and warn you and Elias about what I had discovered."

"But you still were aware of your actions? Why, then, did you attack Aurora?"

Rand hung his head low and shook it in dismay. "It was always the Oracle and her henchman, the hobgoblin, Clive. Aurora has always been the puppet master, playing us all with her story of captivity. Alas, we were all fools, pawns in a fiendish scheme that the Oracle has been plotting for longer than we may ever know."

"I don't understand. That makes no sense." But the image of Di's beautiful body being sliced in two seemed to confirm it. "She killed Di," I muttered the words, remembering.

"I only have pieces of the puzzle, my dear, but I will share all that I discovered. Because if you are able to restore your place on earth, I am afraid there is a battle coming that will be like none we have ever known, and the warrior at the helm of this siege is none other than the greatest Ramalan of all time."

LUCAS

I looked in the room that Ophelia had shared with Elias.
The bed was made. For the first time ever, the thought of
them sleeping together didn't disgust me, or enraged me, rather. It
wasn't that I didn't still love Olly. That wouldn't be fair to her—that
would imply our bond wasn't real. But it felt more like I loved her
like a sister, that I hadn't realized that before because the absence of
Yesi distorted everything. I was so grateful that Yessica had the type
of heart that could understand that, in the wake of her perceived
death, I fell in love with another woman. I told her everything after
we made love this morning. Every detail I could muster, every
feeling I felt, and she received it all with grace as I knew she would.
I couldn't have handled it the way she did, but somehow that only
made our love that much sweeter. She was the best of both of us and
I just tried not to fuck everything up all the time. Yessica expressed
an excitement to get to know Olly, if ever there came a time, and I
hoped there would. That woman was too good for me. *Shit, they
were both too good for me.*

I brought my attention back to the task at hand. I could smell
Olly. The scent was stronger under the bed. I walked over and

39

reached under the box spring. There was a bag. I pulled it out and recognized it as Ophelia's. *Is it rude to sift through it?* Maybe I would find something of use to us, besides the medallion I needed to call on Fetzle. *Maybe Nandi's journal is still in here.* I had a twinge of guilt but ignored it—she wouldn't mind.

A few shirts, her personal journal, a dreidel... *That's odd*, I considered as I spun the thing on the nightstand before returning it to the bag. Her sweatshirt smelled the most like her. I pulled it to my nostrils and took a big whiff. Floral and nutmeg, home sweet home, then folded the hoody and placed it back with her other things. I saw a glimpse of something shiny. I knew I could count on my girl. *It is my medallion!* Of course, Olly would keep it somewhere safe. I plucked it from the bottom of the bag.

I thought about the last time I saw Fetzle, how she'd helped me interrogate the pixies who led me to Oricen, who ultimately told me about Clive the hobgoblin. Fetzle doesn't know Yessica is alive. She also must be told about Ophelia. *Has Olly contacted her? Does she know I've been a captive? Or worse, does she think I'm dead?*

I let excitement buzz through me again. I wanted to see my old friend. I wanted her to see Yesi. I pocketed the medallion, practically ran down the hall, and swooped Yessica into my arms. She nestled in and hugged me softly.

"Lucas, I love you."

"I know you do. I love you too. I have a surprise for you."

Her eyes opened slowly as she looked up at me. "A surprise?"

"I thought seeing an old friend might raise your spirits." She looked at me curiously but didn't ask any questions, just dutifully followed my lead.

I held her hand as we walked outside and toward the largest tree on the grounds. She was exhausted. Whatever the Nebas were poisoning us with was still heavy in her system. She wasn't complaining but I could sense it. It worried me. I decided right then and there that I would bring it to the Alchemist's attention. If anyone could help her, it would be him.

We stopped at the base of the tree and I knelt down, excitement coursing through my veins.

"Ready for this, baby girl?" I looked up at my wife and raised my eyebrows.

"You bet!" Yesi smiled at me in that way that made my heart skip a beat. She knew exactly what we were doing now.

I put my hand with the coin in my palm on the exposed roots and said "Twopledom." I didn't even get the second sound out before the tree began to vibrate. Fetzle's voice came through before she manifested in the trunk. "ItsthatsyousLucas's? FetzlesfriendsLucas's?"

"Yes, Fetzle, it's me."

She barreled out of the tree, stumbling forward and almost crushing us. I quickly pushed Yessica out of the way and behind me.

"Hey, big girl, watch it, will ya?" I laughed at her exuberance.

She picked me up and swirled me around while shouting, "Fetzlesthoughtsyousgone!   Fetzlessososad!   FetzleswilltellsstinkyOphelias!"

My heart sunk at the mention of her name. Fetzle was going to trade one blessing for more bad news. The she-troll abruptly stopped when she realized Yessica was here too. She nearly threw me aside and leaned down to get close to Yesi's face. "Fetzleseesghosts. Fetzlemustsbesick!" Alarm replaced the joy. "Fetzlesmustbedeads!" She put her hand to her throat as though to see if it was still there.

I stifled a laugh, but Yessica couldn't. "No, Fetzle, you are very much alive, sweet friend."

Fetzle fell to the ground and the earth shook. Yessica took the opportunity to wrap her arms around the troll's barrel chest and hug her.

"Fetzleissohappysheswillcrynow." A big gooey tear dripped from her right eye as she gently held Yesi with her finger and thumb. I thought I might cry. Instead, I walked over and joined the moment, leaning into my wife and dear friend. The gelatinous tear soaked into my shirt as I held my girls, and I felt a strange buzzing energy take over my body. A surge of tingling and a sudden jolt of my gifts overwhelmed me for a moment. I took a sharp inhale and, for the first time since we had escaped our captors, I felt like myself. I chuckled internally. *Maybe the Grinch had a heart after all.* Apparently, I was quite affected by love these days.

We stayed there for a long time. When Fetzle finally sat up, I knew it was time to tell her everything. She listened in silence as I relayed the events of the last few months as I knew them to be. I explained all I could about the abductions and the captivity—how they drugged us and how Olly saved us. When I finished with the battle in the basin, Fetzle's face had stiffened. I wondered what was going on in her head.

"FetzleandLucas'smustgetsViraclaysandstinkyOpheliasback! Fetzlesisthequeensnow! FetzlepromisesstinkyOpheliasthatshe-troll-swillhelpsthePaiOnas."

"You're the queen now?" I looked at Yesi, who looked back at me with the same amazement. "A guy gets abducted for a few months and shit goes crazy."

"FetzleuniteshertroliageafterNebashurtsLucas.   Fetzle-saysnomores!"

"I don't know what to say, Fetzle."

Fetzle got to her feet. "Fetzlelovesherfriends," she declared. "Fetzlethinksweshouldgetsthembacks!"

"Yes, of course, Fetzle," Yessica agreed. "And your friends love you. We are formulating a plan."

"Fetzlesplanisgoesandgets'em!" She started toward the tree.

I scrambled to get ahead of her. "Hey, I am with you. But Yesi is right. We have to make a plan. Can we count on you when the time comes?"

Fetzle squinted her eyes, clearly not sold on the waiting part. "FetzlewillfollowLucasandYessicasassoonastimesareright!"   She patted me on the head. "Fetzlethinkstimeshouldberightssoon. Fetzlewillgethersarmiesready."

She moved past me.

I turned and followed her as she went to dissolve back into the tree. "Okay, Fetzle. We promise to let you know when it's time. Not a moment sooner or later," I tried to make my point.

"Fetzlelovesherfriends, evenstinkysOphelias." Then she began to disappear into the tree.

"I missed you, Fetzle," I called out, and her trill laughter met my ears and warmed my heart.

ESTHER

"Curse this body!" Yanni looked defeated. He had been trying to channel the Sulu's gifts for a few hours now but to no avail. "I can feel the power surging through this body. I just cannot seem to harness it. The best I can do is elevate some metal objects." He turned to a sword he was holding in midair across the courtyard. "The Oracle might end up killing me at this rate. She's already threatened."

I kissed his cheek gently. "Shhhh!" I scolded him. "She will not kill you. This body is too valuable. Do not worry about the gifts, my beloved. They will come. How in the strokes could you be adept at such things without previous knowledge?"

"But the Oracle… She grows impatient."

"Never mind her. She has been impatient for centuries. This will prove to be a great advantage, and she will be grateful. But until then, she will do what she does best—demand more." I nibbled at his ear. "How did you manipulate the fireball in the basin?"

"That was by chance. Viraclay's pet had already conjured it. It just fell from the sky."

"I see." I bit a little harder on his lobe. "No one else needs hear that."

He nodded.

"I will conquer this body. I will bend it to my will."

"I have no doubt. When this body is consummated, nothing will hold you back." I took his hand in mine. It was strange how quickly I was getting accustomed to his new form and its touch.

"The idea of consummating with Viraclay sounds dreadful. Will it come to that?"

"It must, for us to be together forever." I said matter-of-factly, because I knew it had to happen. "For now, I must call upon the remaining Nebas. Aurora wants to announce the power exchange tonight." I pointed to the floating sword. "That parlor trick should suffice."

The Oracle would take over leadership tonight. It was time for her to make her grand debut, and I was the privileged opening act.

❀

EVERYTHING WAS IN PLACE, just as the queen had requested. We had lost most of the Nebas that fought at the basin, with the exception of Astrid, Claudia, Rasputin, Calypso and Mutu. It was a small price to pay to leave with the Rittles, Viraclay, and the Sulu. I thought for certain we would be caught by the Alchemist and the Pai Ona survivors, but Clive utilized one of the Rittles for a hasty escape. I could not tell you which object or how he did it. But he seemed impervious to their defense enchantments and had at least some intimate knowledge of their abilities. I would need to bring that to the Oracle's attention. My red silk gown clung to me perfectly. I felt sexy, I felt whole, and strangely at ease with handing off the empire I had built to new leadership. *Is it really new?* It would feel new to the Nebas. In reality, it had been centuries of the Oracle staying a step ahead of our enemy.

I adjusted a wrinkle in the dress on my upper thigh, and I remembered the birthmark. Chills ran down my spine. I didn't want to think about what it might mean. Aurora must know, but if that was the case, *then why has she not told me that the Sulu and I share some sort of connection?*

Calypso knocked on my door. "Mistress, they are ready."

"I did not give you permission to interrupt me in my chamber!"

"Sorry, Mistress, I…"

"You infuriate me!" I swept past her and quickly made my way to the balcony.

"Claudia, Astrid, open the doors." I nodded in both of their directions. "Let the games begin," I mumbled to myself. I could feel the Oracle's eyes on my back. I preferred her pulling strings under concealment but I always knew this day would come. After my father's execution, Yanni and I floundered. I was lost. My father had been my whole world after my mother, Shatki, died. Without him spearheading our course, I couldn't see straight. Everything in Delphi was a blur. I couldn't even remember why we made the choices we had. All I knew was that I wanted revenge. I wanted those who ordered his execution to pay dearly for their judgements. I needed to see those who tore his body to pieces and threw the vehicle of his soul into a fire burn themselves. I desired carnage but had no idea how I would execute such a feat. Aurora found me and Yanni in the shadows.

I remember that night well…

⁂

WE WERE IN SIEM REAP, Cambodia. At the time there was little to the town on the outskirts of the ruins of Angkor Wat. Yanni and I had found some sense of solace in the streets of the ancient city. Clive appeared first, always on guard, a faithful servant to the Oracle for centuries. I never knew of a time, aside from her years as a captive in Delphi, that the hobgoblin was not at her side. *Where was he all those years?* But as soon as I considered the question, it seemed to slip away.

Hobgoblins cannot verbally converse with Conduits, so he held out his hand with an envelope. Yanni took the letter. In delicate script, it read, *An invitation from the Oracle*. The messenger could not give us any further information, so he slipped away into the night.

"What do you think this is? It must be a trap." Yanni had yet to open the envelope.

"It may be, but we will not know unless we see it through."

The note was concise.

Meet me at the base of the Baton at sunrise. We have much to discuss. Dare I say, we have a common enemy.

"A common enemy? Who could we loath that the revered Ramalan would despise? And why would she come to her captors for help?" Yanni crumpled the paper in his hand. "It is a trap so that the Pai Ona will have cause to smite us from this earth as they did your father."

"I hear your concern, my beloved. I honor you as I honor myself. But consider you this, the Oracle was in our captivity for over seven hundred years. No one came to her rescue. Instead, we watched with our very own eyes as Conduit after Conduit visited the Oracle of Delphi, participated in the Sulu ritual, and left her in her prison." My words registered and a light ignited in his face. "We may not be the ally she desires, but we are the only other Conduits who feel jaded by the righteous Pai Ona."

Meet we did, and that was when the Oracle divulged her hatred for the Pai Ona. She wanted them to suffer as she had suffered. It was our shared abhorrence for those who turned a blind eye to her pain, while I hated the Conduits that took my father from me.

Yanni was suspicious, as was I, he wanted to make sure we were not being double-crossed. "So? We share an enemy, but we were your captors. My beloved is the daughter of your greatest assailant. How can we be certain you will not betray us?"

She laughed maniacally. "You were just as much a pawn of Apollo as was I. I pity you, that you think you had a choice. Fools, the two of you, obeying Apollo as he attempted to carve out a pathetic piece of power from this world. I can show you true power.

Together we can burn down the entire world and rebuild it to our taste. They won't even smell the smoke until there is no escape." The Oracle moved closer to me and brushed my hair away from my face. "Tell me, child, do you fancy yourself a queen, a leader?"

"I have commanded many."

"Aw, you see, there is a difference between commanding and manipulating. I can teach you. Your father," she paused as though she had to choke out his name, "Apollo, he had little vision. A disdain for the dilution of Conduit magic into the mortal world. What I speak of is world domination. Conduit, human, every creature ever painted…bending to my will. To our will."

My blood boiled as she dismissed my father, but there was more. Because as I looked at Yanni, I realized we would either be on her side or no side. There was never a choice, not really. I took my beloved's hand. "We will join you, on one condition."

"That is?"

"Never speak of Apollo again," I hissed.

We never again spoke about my father, from that day to this. But we spoke about our enemy and our revenge every day since. It was what had brought us here. Her sight had proven to be the biggest advantage we had. Making the move before the enemy could, finding allies that would otherwise slip through the cracks, and ultimately her ability to stay aligned with the Pai Ona, specifically the Kraus family. The distinction of Nebas, a term that was coined by my father and meant "pure stroke," became the cornerstone of the Oracle's plan. The man she loathed set the foundation for the backs of the Conduits she would rise on.

❀

"MISTRESS, EVERYONE IS HERE," Astrid interrupted my reverie. I looked down on the mob of Nebas who had either been living in the Chernobyl compound since the siege of The Cathedral, or those who had more recently arrived when they discovered they could no longer live in ambiguity. Viraclay's little transmission had finally forced those who would have stayed in the middle, expose their side. I was grateful for it.

"Comrades, it is good to see that so many of you have decided to take the stand. No longer can we wait out our enemy, killing them off one by one. No, the time has come for us to unite with our vengeance. We have stayed one step ahead of the Pai Ona for centuries. Have you ever wondered how? Were the strokes simply in our favor?"

The crowd stirred. A wave of muffled questions and theories moved through the room.

"The strokes have served us well, but it was an ally that we have had in secret who has changed the tides in this war on multiple occasions. A queen in the Conduit world, revered and respected for her abilities that have gone unmatched."

I paused to let the mob draw their own conclusions.

"We will not fail. We cannot fail. Victory is literally in our grasp. We know every move the enemy will make."

The voices were getting louder, with intermittent cheers.

"I present to you your queen, your leader, the power that makes us invincible to our enemy. The Oracle!"

I stepped aside as Aurora stepped up to the banister to address everyone and bask in the awe and reverence of her people. I leaned against the pillar behind me to watch the spectacle.

The mob was a mixture of disbelief and enthusiasm.

"My dear subjects, my devoted Nebas. I have worked hard and long to bring us to this moment of glory. Not only do you have my gift of sight, but I also present to you the Rittles." Claudia and Astrid were both wearing gloves as they held up several of the weapons in the Rittles arsenal. This caused the crowd to explode into an uproar of cheering. Aurora raised her hand, and they immediately went silent. She had their allegiance, and she hadn't even had to implement pain. I chuckled to myself. *Yet.*

"I also present to you the Sulu! She is our puppet, ready to kill all who oppose us."

Yanni looked back at me before facing the crowd and lifting his hands in the air, simultaneously elevating the Rittles with a gift he could barely manage. The gesture created a frenzy and the Nebas began chanting in unison.

"Hail Queen Aurora! Hail Queen Aurora!"

LUCAS

he Haven was quiet. For there being so many residents within these walls, there was virtually no audible evidence. We were all just waiting for the burial rites that were about to take place in the next hour. I sat staring at Yesi;. She was still weak. The drugs she'd been on for years were taking their sweet ass time getting out of her system. I had left a note for Ruit in his room, asking him to consider treating her when he came to see me this evening.

A knock at the door startled me, I was so lost in thought. "What?" I cleared my throat. "I mean, come in."

I turned to see Ruit standing there with a slighter man behind him. It wasn't his son. I didn't know who he was, and it made me uncomfortable having a stranger in my room.

"I got your communication, and I brought a salve that may help her come to her senses quicker." The two men walked toward the bed cautiously.

"Who's that?" I nodded to the stranger.

"This is the gatekeeper, Susuda. He is like a son to me." Ruit moved aside and let Susuda come forward.

"Am I supposed to know who that is?"

"I am a good friend of Miss Olly. Ruit tells me you are as well." He moved a step or two closer. "We met in the vehicle."

"In the van?" *What the hell is he talking about?* The only other thing in the van was that monster. It hit me like a slap in the face. *This was the monster—somehow.* I immediately shifted positions and hovered over Yessica's body. "What the fuck are you thinking, bringing that thing in here?" I accused Ruit.

Ruit stepped forward. "Lucas, the gidim you witnessed in the van is the kind, docile man you see before you. When he is not in the confines of a Haven, he takes his cursed shape. But you and your wife are safe. Susuda only wished to make your acquaintance to assure you that he would do everything in his power to rescue our mutual friend, Ophelia Banner."

Susuda nodded confidently behind him.

I didn't know how I felt about the new guy yet, but I could figure that out later. I eased my posture slightly. Ruit trusted him and he cared about Olly—two things I had to take into consideration. "What's in the salve?"

"A few herbs and some sand from the Namib desert, blended with black willows bark. It will syphon out whatever is in her system faster."

"What do you think they were poisoning us with? It was some strong shit, to mask a bond between Atoas."

"I have my suspicions. Has she been sleeping like this all day?"

"No, the exhaustion comes and goes. She was up a little while ago. We met with Fetzle and that seemed to take it out of her."

"The she-troll? How were you met?"

Why is that any of his business? "Good. She was happy to see us." I took the small jar from his palm. "Where do I put it?"

"On the back of her neck."

I lifted her head slightly and she moaned gently.

"I know, baby girl. This is going to help. Or at least, it better not hurt." I said that more for Ruit than Yesi. The salve was smooth and silky on my fingers. Yessica's neck was hot to the touch.

"That should be plenty. Reapply in an hour or so," Ruit instructed. "What are her symptoms, besides lethargy?"

I put the jar on the bedside table and adjusted myself to face them again. "She seems to have a fever, possibly some memory issues, and I would say lethargy is putting it nicely—she went comatose when they applied the poison."

"You saw them apply it?"

"Yeah, on her neck. What could do this to a Conduit?"

Ruit looked past me in thought. "There are very few things, I assure you. May I place my hands on her chest? There is a symptom I must confirm. It will only take a moment."

"Don't get handsy." The warning was more of a formality. I didn't really think Ruit had "handsy" in him.

He placed both his hands on her sternum above her breasts, then turned to the beast man. "Do you hear that?"

The gatekeeper nodded.

"Hear what?" I looked at both the men, expecting an answer. "What the fuck? This is my wife."

Still, they said nothing.

"Ruit."

"Lucas, I believe your wife... You..." He paused like he was not ready to say what he was thinking out loud. "All of the captive Pai Ona, including myself, have been poisoned with dragons' blood."

"Come again?"

"Why did you kill my parents?"

"Finally, the question you have really wanted to ask."

This was only one of a million questions in my mind. I doubted I would ever learn the answers to most of what plagued me.

"They loved you. My mother spoke about you as though you were her sister."

"Oh, dear Sorcey. She always was a soft-hearted fool. Both your parents were, really. That was ultimately the problem." She combed through her long red hair with her fingers as she nonchalantly leaned against the adjacent wall from where I hung. "Leadership takes a degree of callousness. You must be able to make difficult decisions that could cost casualties. In my experience, victory almost always requires some sort of sacrifice. Your parents were too altruistic for true leadership."

I rolled my eyes. *She was wrong.*

"What, you do not agree?" Aurora began to braid her hair. "Dare I say that is why you are in this predicament. Thank the strokes you have no better sense than they did."

"You are a monster. We will never be in agreement."

"A monster? I will not argue with you, but I was not always this way." She looked beyond me. "But that was not the story you asked about; you inquired about your parents. It was fortuitous that Alistair came to Esther to seek the whereabouts of his cherished grandfather, pleading for his release in the exchange for the Loktpi. Huan had just been killed. Almus still slunk in the shadows looking for clues, but Alistair, he was pointed in his search and had nothing left to lose. Esther told me of his offer. I conceded to releasing his grandfather, a bargain I never intended to fulfill, but he was too much of an imbecile to consider that. I did not know then that what I would seek was the murders of your parents. Alistair shared his Rune, and we devised a plan for him to reconstruct the Loktpi. Later, your father contacted him about the Summit. I wasn't ready for the Summit to occur; it was all happening too fast. I needed to finally get rid of your pesky parents and their notions of uniting the Pai Ona once and for all. I was growing impatient for Alistair to deliver on his side of the bargain. I realized—why wait for the Loktpi when I could just take it from the weakling in my coterie? With this new agenda, I no longer needed the reconstruction. The strokes fell in my favor. Tell me, dear boy, why would the painter let your parents fall if it was not clandestine?"

I could not speak; the anguish was too close to the surface.

"Just things to consider, would you not agree?" She brushed her long braid over her shoulder. "When your father contacted Alistair, I knew it was my opportunity to strike. With the Loktpi, and of course my familiarity with the Kraus compounds, we easily accessed the South African Haven. I distracted them while Alistair dismembered them and burned their bodies. It all happened so quickly and efficiently. I had intended to murder you too, but Rand's unexpected visit threw a wrench in that plan."

"You killed them to prevent the Summit?" I said it more to myself.

"Among other things. It was mostly an ideal opportunity to eliminate two Conduits who I knew I would eventually have to face as things unfolded."

"But why wait until then? Certainly, you had many opportunities to betray them over your vast lifetimes together."

"Viraclay, there is so much more to the strokes than you can possibly understand. Your parents were required to set into motion many things before I could rid myself of them. For example, I needed you to come to pass...the sweet miracle that you are." She came over and caressed my cheek. "I warned your mother against it initially, but as their choices came more into focus, I was able to understand the value. It made me uncomfortable to have so many gaps in my vision at first. The unknown has that effect on my gifts. Alas, it became clear as day that you were a precursor to the Sulu. I may have let them see many more days if it weren't for your mother's knowledge."

"What knowledge?"

Just then the door opened. "Is it time for me to start my investigation?" Esther wore a long black velvet gown that made her look exceptionally devilish. "I brought the weapon we found on him in the basin." She held the Dirk of Inverness in her hand.

"Oh, yes. This weapon intrigues me. It feels familiar, although I cannot quite place it." Aurora examined the hilt. "He is ready for your interrogation. We are finished here."

But we were not finished. "What knowledge did my mother hold?"

"For another time. We have much to discover about these Rittles you delivered and very little time to do so." The Oracle clapped twice. "Do good work, Esther." She flitted out of the room, and I was alone with Esther.

"Where did you get this special trinket?" She tossed the Dirk from one hand to the other.

I just stared past her.

"I asked you a question, Viraclay." She knelt down in front of me. "Don't be rude." She drew my face to hers with the benign edge of the blade. "Where did you procure this Rittle?"

Still, I said nothing, I hoped my expression said it all—I would not be cooperating.

She flipped the blade so that now the lethal edge pressed against my cheek. I had only seen what the Dirk did to a Consu. I had no clue what it would do to me, an Unconsu.

"What does it do?" She smiled wickedly. "Maybe I need to just find out for myself."

The pressure on my cheek increased. She would pierce my skin in a moment and that would be it. After all of this, after all we have gone through—it would end like this.

I closed my eyes and saw Olly's face. I focused on every detail I could remember. Her smile, her rich hazel eyes, her strawberry curls.

Olly, I love you.

$\mathcal{R}$and was relaying his findings and how he had tracked down Clive just before he was captured by the Nebas. His investigation first led him to believe that Ruit was behind Sorcey and Cane's murders when it became clear he was still alive but not in contact with his family. Rand had tracked Alistair and consequently Ruit's whereabouts across many continents and countries, discovering that Ruit had been frequenting the same villages for many years—generations, really. But the years immediately prior to the murders of Cane and Sorcey, Ruit was witnessed in the villages just before or after Alistair's arrival.

"What I suspected proved to be true, by your account with Ruit and his memories. The grandfather was detouring the grandson while he determined his motives. Thank the strokes for that!" Rand shook his head. "Can you imagine how this could have all been so much worse?"

"Worse than losing you?"

"Far worse, my dear, trust me. I do not understand the motivations behind the Oracle's treachery, but her intentions are something far greater than we yet know."

I couldn't argue with that.

"I kick myself. Did you know I had Alistair under surveillance for two years before I took his life?"

"I think Elias mentioned that."

"I never followed him on his travels. If I had, it is likely I could have connected the dots sooner. I just thought he enjoyed obscure holidays."

I put my hand on his shoulder. "You did exactly what you thought was right. There is no telling what following him would've done. It wasn't a safe time to be out and about. It's still not."

"I supposed you're right, sweet friend. I am exactly where the strokes intended me to be." He continued. "After retracing Alistair's steps, I returned to where I started, in India. Rajahish, the leader of the Bhil village that Alistair and his family frequented, and I had become quite familiar. Unlike most of the leaders, he was far more cooperative with my questions, and we became close. He helped me connect with Elias just before the Summit, he'd had a premonition of Elias needing my help. In fact, he'd had many premonitions about me and Elias and Alistair. He was a very astute man.

"The siege of The Cathedral made everything more tense for the keeper of the portal, essentially the keeper of the keys, as the strokes would have it. Rajahish was eager to assist me in my investigations, as he felt that without the gatekeeper, his job was that much more perilous. He didn't want to fail his ancestors by letting the portals fall into the wrong hands. Both of us felt that the accomplice in the Kraus murders would likely also have one of the unaccounted-for keys."

"Huan's, Ruit's or Alistair's?"

"Exactly! So, when I returned, he had a curious episode to tell me about. Just before Alistair died, a woman with wild red hair and an odd companion came to him and inquired about a great fortress that Rajahish's great great-grandfather once spoke of. The leader of the Bhils was cordial to the queer pair and denied knowing of any such fortress, and bid them on their way."

"The Oracle? She was doing her own investigation while Alistair was trying to decode his grandfather's journals and assemble Nandi's Loktpi."

Rand nodded. "The pair returned, this time a day before the siege at the Summit. Rajahish described that this time, the woman wore the token that he knew to be Alistair's Loktpi around her neck, and when she turned to leave, he saw the symbol he had seen on Alistair and Ruit many times before on her left shoulder."

"The Rune."

"So, she had a Loktpi since Alistair had died?"

"Yes, or rather before. Since she was not there the night he died."

"But why?" I was asking when I heard a disturbance in the water behind me. Rand's eyes got big. I had no idea what to expect, but there was no use in putting off the inevitable. I turned to face whatever was coming next. A stabbing pain shot through my heart.

"What are you doing here?" I was staring at Zavier, my grandfather.

He ran to me and took me up in his arms. "That's my door, the green one." He kissed my cheek. "I never imagined I would get the opportunity to hug you. Not in this form."

I melted into his embrace. I didn't know him well, but something about him was comforting, especially now. He was my grandfather, and I'd watched him die only weeks ago. Another casualty of this war. After his death, I found a letter he'd written me asking for forgiveness for both himself and my grandmother Lilith. They had made the impossible decision to abandon my mother in the hopes that it would keep her safe from the monster who I now know is my father, Nestor.

"I am so sorry," he whispered in my ear. "I am so sorry."

"I know. I forgive you. There is really nothing to forgive." Tears began streaming down my cheeks.

"I tried to warn you."

"I couldn't get to my mother in time, but thank you for coming to me in my dream. I know the Pai Ona will stop at nothing to save her, now that they know she's been taken." Then the memory of the séance flooded back to me. "But I never discovered—what did Lilith do? Did she have something to do with my mother's abduction?" That made no sense, since she herself was tormented and hexed by Nestor. I visibly shook at the thought of him being my father. My grandfather pulled me back to look in my eyes, searching for answers. "You said that my grandmother had done something," I nudged him, hoping he'd remember the incident.

"Not your grandmother Lilith," he said, his cadence made me uneasy..

Time seemed to slow down as I tried to process what the alternative was. "Do you mean Nestor's mother?"

Zavier nodded solemnly. I looked to Rand, thinking he must know who Zavier was referring too, but he looked just as bewildered.

"Aurora. The Oracle is your grandmother, Ophelia."

My knees buckled. Both men caught me before I fell to the floor. "I-I-I don't understand."

"Sweet child, there is much to tell."

LUCAS

*Y*esi seemed to be doing better with the salve. I was so grateful. And Ruit's energetic biopsy didn't hurt; *who knows what is going to come of that?*

Yessica held my hand while we stood waiting for the rites to start. I wasn't exactly friends with either of the Conduits we were honoring tonight. But friends or not, no one could deny that the world suffered the loss of a great warrior with Aphrodite's death. Rand, on the other hand—he and I had always been at odds. It happened after the last open battle when his Carissa had died. His son Caleb and I didn't see eye to eye on the next course of action. I may have been a bit harsh and inconsiderate, but more lives were at stake. Rand never forgave me. However, Yesi and Olly loved him. It only seemed right to respect their love for him.

Yessica was fortunate enough to be here to honor him in her own way. Ophelia wasn't, and it killed me to think about how frightened she must be. How devastated she must feel by the betrayal and the loss of her friends. *Can she feel anything while she is possessed by Yanni?* There was no way to know how terrified she must be.

Here I was, finally at peace in many ways, having been reunited with Yessica, only to trade places with Olly. If this was all part of a fated plan, the creator had a real cruel sense of humor.

It wasn't common anymore to perform any kind of burial rites. Mostly because those who passed were often killed without anyone else knowing until they were realized to be missing. Before the war, if an accident were to occur and someone were to turn to dust— *what kind of accident that would've been, hell if I know.* I guess they happened though—the remaining family members would honor their deceased by releasing their ashes into a stream or river. It signified the River Tins.

We didn't have a river or stream handy, so I was interested to see how they modified the ritual. There were other pieces to the rites, but that was about all I had gathered from the whisperings between the survivors. I saw Ying gather their ashes and, as he did, he smudged his cheeks with what was left on his hands.

Is that part of the ceremony? I guess we would find out.

Everyone was gathered outside. It was dusk and the colors in the sky were impressive. Yesi and I were beside Aruna. Yessica kept stealing glances at me. Each time, her smile melted my heart. It was as though I'd never lost her. It was like she'd always been here, waiting for me to return to her. Her long black hair fell in front of her face like a thick curtain. I tucked it behind her ear and kissed her cheek. *Damn, she was sexy.*

"They are beginning," Aruna whispered, diverting her attention to the smaller circle of Conduits in front of us, her husband in the central role. Ying stood on a small pillar, making him slightly taller than the others, his face smeared with the ash. To his right stood Aremis, to his left Ruit, and directly in front of him Winston. All three of their faces were also covered in soot. A man I now knew as Thracian was just outside of the circle. I wondered what his part was.

Ying began to speak. "Our brothers and sisters have returned to the dust, to be swept up by the River Tins and cleansed by the waters. When we enter the River, we are no longer separate, but part of the whole, the original strokes. We reconvene with those we have lost. Although we may be in different forms, our strokes are familiar as they flow in the infinite circle."

On a table just in front of Ying lay two large piles of ash. He reached down and took a heap of one of the piles into his hands and raised it above his head. "Aphrodite, the great warrior and facilitator of love and connection. We were all blessed by her strength and her courage. Di was fiercely loyal."

Someone wept aloud at that statement. I looked around to see it was Lucia.

"The strokes take her back to her Walthrup, to be cleansed." The three other men put their hands up above their heads and Ying distributed large handfuls of the ashes into their open palms. "If you desire to wear your grief and honor those fallen, please step forward to bear the mark." Vosega moved quickly into place, putting his palm on the remaining ashes on the table, on the remnants of Di, and smudging his face as tears raced down his cheeks. One by one, between sobs and with reverence, everyone got in line to pay their respects. I wavered. When Yesi moved to the line, I conceded and decided to participate. I was the last one, as everyone else held each other and cried openly with ash-stained faces.

I followed Yessica and wearily looked at the remains of Rand. *Will I participate in his too?*

Once I was done, together, the men chanted. "May her strokes be cleansed and one with the River Tins." They continued to chant as a stream of water appeared about four feet from the ground. I realized that was the purpose of Thracian being so close. He provided the stream. The water followed him, and he walked around in a circle. One by one, they each released their handful of ash into the circle of water that flowed around them. When Winston released his, each of their hands were empty. They just stared at each other. I saw tears streaming down Aremis' dirty cheeks. The others stayed stoic.

Ying repeated the same sequence of events as he honored Rand. "Rand, the wisest and the most perceptive of us all. His wit was unmatched, his humor distinctly his own. Rand was cunning and true to his friends."

Who decided what to say about these two anyway? I guess both statements were correct, but what about those of us who didn't exactly see eye to eye with everyone? I guess these sorts of ceremonies aren't for us. I shrugged it off. As I looked around and felt Yesi's grief, it occurred to me that I'd shut down, cut people out of my life and somehow disassociated from true connection. I was operating from some robotic broken space, where I couldn't even feel true sadness for the loss of life. I took Yessica's hand firmly in mine. *What have I become to survive her loss? Was I always this callous? Am I savable?* Tears welled up in my eyes. When Yesi saw the emotion on my face, I felt a sense of relief wash over her. She must be afraid I wasn't savable either. The tears came and they came in force.

I thought about Rand, how he had saved Olly multiple times. How he had taken her under his wing. How even his suspicions of me were not unwarranted. I was moved when I realized some of the tears I was shedding were in fact for him. When Ying called for the mark, I stepped up quickly behind my father.

I didn't care what anyone else thought, what I looked like. I felt a touch of something I had not let in in years. I felt compassion.

One by one, the ashes were placed in the water. When Rand's portion was concluded, Thracian commanded the water to follow him as he moved out of sight. I wondered where he'd put the water? *Does it matter?*

Ying stepped down and bowed, and everyone else bowed back. When I caught Yessica's stare, I saw so much relief and pain contorted together that I lay my head on her chest and wept openly with her.

"Mistress?" Astrid appeared behind me.

"What is it?" I hissed. "I am busy with dear Viraclay." I pulled the blade away from his cheek and turned to face my distraction. "Do you know what this is?" I pointed the blade at her. I was growing more and more irritable, and her intrusion did nothing to ease my nerves.

Astrid shook her head.

"It is a Rittle. Which means it is not just a knife, but in fact has other abilities. Do you know what those might be?"

Again, she shook her head.

"Well, I was just about to find out from Elias here before you interrupted me. So I guess that means you will bear this burden for me instead." I swept the blade across her cheek. Shock befell her face, but I couldn't see any other immediate effect.

"Mist…" Then her speech cut off and I realized something more was happening. A moment later it was obvious Astrid was frozen. I circled her, laughing.

"This is a useful weapon." I looked at Viraclay with amusement. "You've been holding out on me. It has stupefied her. How long do the effects last?"

He said nothing.

"You will answer me, or I will see what it does to an Unconsu next."

"I do not know. I never stayed long enough to know the length of its debilitation. But she will eventually resume control of her body."

"See? How hard was that? We can be cordial, Viraclay. And in the long run, you will save dear Olly from any unnecessary pain. I will bring her in to be my test bunny if you cannot find it in your heart to cooperate next time." But I was bluffing, and I was fairly certain Elias knew that. I no more wanted to hurt Ophelia's body than my own, not with the soul it held. Still, Viraclay was far more likely to be informative if he felt she was in danger. And so, the circus went on.

The Oracle wanted me to record the abilities of each of the Rittles we had in our possession. The Dirk had been found on Elias, so he knew the particulars. But I was not certain how knowledge-able he would be concerning the other items. Clive used his abilities, whatever they may be, to disarm the Rittles. I found it very curious that he had so much comprehension of them and their faculties. I would need to find a way to ask Clive what he knew of the Rittles, a nearly impossible task since only the Oracle could exchange with him. I had to find a way to convince her that the information he new was valuable.

There was a twinge of something in the back of my mind. *If Clive was so familiar with the artifacts, then was this not just a waste of my time...a fools errand...a distraction. But from what?* I pushed the thought aside, it made no sense, the Oracle needed me.

"Claudia!" I called for one of my least favorite pawns. She had somehow worked her way up the rankings as those who held my previous confidences had been picked off by the enemy.

"Yes, Esther." She entered the room quickly, eyeing Astrid's unnatural state warily as she made her way to my side.

"Bring me another Rittle."

"On it." She turned to leave.

Viraclay looked up at me. "I told you, I do not have familiarities with any of the other items."

"Make it one that looks painful." I slipped the Dirk in its sheath and placed it on the only furniture in the room, a small wooden table.

"Very well, if you desire to waste your time with an inventory I cannot make, that is your prerogative." His head relaxed into an uncomfortable-looking position. "Tell me, how did you sway the Oracle to your side? Was it because her people betrayed her? Is that why she killed my parents?"

I chuckled to myself. "The Pai Ona certainly proved to be less virtuous than they would like to believe. Can you blame Aurora for seeking vengeance?"

"My parents… they were a part of this travesty?"

The truth was that neither Sorcey nor Cane ever visited the Oracle of Delphi Temple. They were two of the loudest opposers of Aurora's captivity. My time at the temple was foggy at best, but I was certain I never saw their righteous faces. Viraclay didn't need to know that. "No one is who you think they are."

Just then Claudia returned. This time she held a long sword. "Oh, that looks like fun!" I clapped my hands gleefully. I was enjoying this exploration. It was keeping me amused. A welcomed feeling compared to the nagging questions that were mounting every time I thought about Ophelia's identical birthmark. "Should I call the Sulu in now? Or should we test it on Claudia first?"

OPHELIA

I was in shock. Zavier, my grandfather, had dropped a bombshell on me. The Oracle was my grandmother, and Rand had confirmed she was the traitor all along. Rand stared at me warily as Zavier explained that in the River Tins all is revealed that has ever been. In that revelation, he saw that Aurora had committed many atrocities and that she is in fact, my blood.

"There is someone you must meet, dear granddaughter, someone who can elucidate so much more."

Rand took my hand in his. "Don't you feel like the girl has heard enough for now?" He squeezed it tighter. "Will any of this help recover her to her body?"

Zavier looked at Rand in such a way that I almost thought they might fight. "Do you not believe I care for her?"

Rand shrugged flippantly, "You hardly know her."

Rand, my ever-vigilant bodyguard, was trying to protect me, even now. "It's okay, I can handle this. Whatever it is. Whoever it is," I assured them both.

"I know you can." Zavier nodded in reassurance. "We do not know how much time you have with us."

"Maybe forever." I shrugged.

"No, your strokes have not ended, not like this and not on this day," Rand replied vehemently.

I put my hand on his shoulder, and he immediately disarmed. "I can do this. I can handle the truth."

Rand nodded. "Of course you can, my dear. You are exceptional in all ways."

"Tell me, Zavier, who is Nestor's father?"

"It is I, the villain of this story."

I saw Rand's body stiffen and his face harden as he watched someone approach me from behind.

"But you cannot believe all you have been told," the unfamiliar voice insisted.

"You will need more words than that to convince me," Rand hissed.

I turned to see a tall man with dark black hair and a calm demeanor, almost suave in nature. Rand stepped in between us.

I looked to Zavier. "Can I be harmed here?"

"I do not know. But no harm will come to you on my watch."

I placed my hand on Rand's shoulder and gently moved him aside. "Hear that, Rand? I'm safe."

"From this fiend, no one is safe."

"Who are you?" I looked him over curiously. There was a vague familiarity about him.

"Hello, Ophelia. I am your grandfather, Apollo."

My knees tried to give again. I grabbed hold of Rand's shirt to steady myself. *This just kept getting worse.*

Apollo stepped closer, peering into my eyes. "You look so much like her."

"Like who?" My voice was shaky. Rand was still stiff with rage.

"Aurora," Apollo answered. He reached his hand out and took my wrist to steady me completely. "You are stronger than anyone who has ever existed, child. You can handle this." His eyes stayed locked into mine and his assurance gave me a peculiar sense of peace. "I have watched you grow into the incredible woman you are. You have all her tenacity, but with the tender heart of your grandmother Lilith."

Zavier nodded at Apollo, agreeing with his assessment.

"What?" was all I could mumble, in shock as I was with these revelations.

"You will keep your distance," Rand asserted, glaring at Apollo's hand on my wrist.

"I will not harm her. You now know of the Oracle's treachery. Surely you can assume there is more to my story. I only ask for the grace to share my truth, what I know." Apollo looked to me to disarm Rand once more.

"I need answers, Rand…please."

His shoulders softened and he took half a step away from me. We both had to admit that if Aurora really was the monster she turned out to be, Apollo may also have a different role in this war.

"You have been dead for hundreds of years. How have you been watching me?"

"The River Tins share all that ever was, but not all that could be, for those strokes remain to be seen. Each time a new soul enters the Tins, more is revealed from their perspective, lens, and life. We can only see the full story of those who have entered. Until then, there are gaps and inferences to be made. And although I have been gone, there are ways around death, as you well know. After all, here you are and there Yanni goes, parading about with your form."

"Yanni, your son in law!" I accused.

"Yes, the very one." Apollo rubbed his brow and ran his hand through his long hair. "I steered them astray, but to explain what really occurred during those years at Delphi would take days, perhaps even months. And I dare say, I do not entirely understand what truly befell upon me during that time. A shadow—"

I interjected. "You're going to blame years of torture and captivity on a shadow? You have got to be kidding me. Are you guys buying this?" I looked at Rand and Zavier.

Zavier pleaded, "Please listen, Ophelia. You can trust me. I have seen what he speaks of."

Rand gave Zavier a stern look, but his admission seemed to further relax his stance.

"I blame no one but myself for what has become of my children and my descendants, make no mistake of that." He put his hand on my cheek. I fought the impulse to pull away, but something felt familiar. "I came to you when you were just a baby. I wanted to do something to protect you. I had already failed my wife, my daughter…" His voice trailed off for a moment, then he continued. "The Soul Seed gave me a few precious moments with you. I knew you were special, even at merely a few days old. I held you in the hospital room while Eleanor slept. I absorbed your joy, your wonder. I felt the exchange between us, even then."

"What is your gift?" The question came out as a whisper, because somehow, I already knew the answer.

"I absorb the emotions around me and compel others to speak their deepest truths."

My soul went numb and icy cold all at once.

"I absorbed your gifts? So, they were never mine… It was always your curse!"

Apollo took my hands in his. They quivered as tears streamed down my face, realization after realization filing through my thoughts like a marching band, loud, disruptive and undeniable.

"When I felt our exchange, I knew then more than ever you would not be safe in this world without protection, some safeguard from absorbing every gift you came in contact with as an Unconsu. I pleaded with the Star Seed to enchant you with a Palladian charm. She conceded, sealing you from absorbing any other gifts. That was until you ran into Elias. As the painter would have it, no charm can circumvent the power of an Atoan bond. Slowly but surely, the charm dissolved, and you were once again able to absorb every gift you encountered."

"I don't even know what to think."

"Deep breaths, Miss Ophelia. Take some deep breaths," Rand coached me.

"I have so many questions..." My voice trailed off as I felt a strange sensation tug at my consciousness.

Yessica decided to stay in the room while I went to the meeting. Strategy has never been her thing, and she needed rest.

There was a large congregation of Conduits in a central room of the Haven. I didn't know them all, but they seemed to know me. Dear old Dad approached me first.

"How is Yesi? Is she recovering?" He put his hand on my shoulder. "We all will miss them very much. It's alright to grieve openly, my son."

Aw shit, I did an internal forehead slap. He must be referring to my unusual emotional outburst. I knew that wouldn't go unnoticed. I chose to ignore his comment about grief. "Yesi seems to be okay. So, what's the plan? Do we have one?"

"Let's make introductions first. After all, many of these Conduits have just risked their lives to save you."

I guess the formality was necessary, but it felt like a waste of time.

Vosega did the honors. Getting out of the mountain had earned him a few new friends, I guess. "Helia, Sparkle, Tete, Medusa and Thracian—you have met these five." He then pointed to Oya to his left, and slightly beyond her were Borte and Genghis. The last three didn't care for me; it was apparent by their expressions. But I waved, not to taunt them but to say thank you because they were the last people I expected to come to my rescue.

"How is my daughter?" Genghis asked solemnly.

"Better."

Borte looked peeved, like Yessica's reappearance was a nuisance and consequently my fault. She could kiss my ass.

Vosega continued. "You know Aremis, Lucia and Winston, Ying and Aruna, and I know you're familiar with Stalt." Aremis smiled gently. Winston held tight to Lucia and didn't bother with any welcoming gestures. He probably blamed me for the abduction of Olly and Elias. Ying bowed slightly and Aruna waved. Stalt surprised me completely.

"Any son of Vosega's is a son of mine!" He took my hand and pulled it across his chest, in a manly hug of sorts.

I turned to Vosega and he smiled a knowing smile—the old man had his own explaining to do. He proceeded with his introductions.

"Mikkel."

The Frenchman gave a soft wave and said bon jour. We had met briefly when I left Yesi with him as we unsuccessfully tracked Esther and Olly.

"Friedrick Olmsted and Shiva." I had tried not to stare at the giant blue Ancient sitting in the corner. I'd never met an Ancient; I didn't know what was considered rude. I wasn't usually intimidated by many things, but I'll be damned if I was going to get on the wrong side of Shiva the destroyer.

Borte spoke next. "Shiva says he looks forward to fighting beside you to win this war."

I liked his spirit. "Me too. Go good guys!" I raised my fist and Shiva nodded assuredly.

Dear old Dad interrupted the exchange that had now gone cold. I appreciated him for that. "I believe you know the Tallus family."

"I've met Ruit and Jezebel." Ruit nodded. *But what did I say to the rest? What could I say?* I tried to gage their perception of me, but they were keeping it close to their chests.

Ruit gestured behind him. "This is our son Almus and his Atoa Inca." They didn't move or make a sound. "This is our adopted son, Susuda."

It was now or never. "I have never been good at this… I'm sorry. For my part in the deaths of Huan and Nandi, I am so sorry."

Almus bowed slightly. "All is forgiven." He looked at his father. It was obvious the show was more for him than me, and I wasn't offended.

Ruit took the lead and Vosega stepped back. There were many powerful Conduits in this room, and they'd chosen their leader. It's always nice to keep leadership simple, follow one person's orders. Too many hands in the pot slows things down.

"Now that the formality of introductions is over, let's get down to business, shall we?"

I liked how Ruit led so far. I respected Ruit. I don't know that I'd ever respected anyone besides Cane.

"I propose we take two strategic plans of action at once. Almus and his companions were initially charged with the enormous task of determining a venue for the final battle to take place in. One that gave us, the Pai Ona, an advantage against our enemy. They successfully narrowed the search down to two locations—Death Valley in Russia and the Solomon Islands."

I interrupted, "I don't mean to be an asshole, but what does this have to do with getting Olly back? We are up against the Oracle now; we need to be putting all our resources towards getting Ophelia back."

Ruit continued. "That brings us to our second action point. How do we destroy Chernobyl without putting its captives at risk, so that we may liberate our friends?"

I stepped back, aware that I was stepping on Ruit's toes and I needed to keep my shit in check. *Ruit can handle this*, I reminded myself.

He continued. "We must set in motion both plans at once, for several reasons. First, we are dealing with the Oracle. The more we diversify our actions the less she will be able to pinpoint our next moves."

All right, I liked that train of thought.

"Secondly, when we crush the hornets' nest, they will be ready to attack. We must be prepared for that. We will then have to lure them to where we want the battle to take place."

The nods in the room made it clear everyone agreed with this strategy. I had to admit, it made the most sense. You wouldn't bat down a hornet's nest without having somewhere to get away from the angry swarm.

"We need to call on the bidding," Mikkel suggested. "Recruit others to help us carry out both missions at once."

"Who made the bidding, Mikkel?" Ruit asked politely.

"Ophelia and Viraclay." I could tell he didn't understand why Ruit asked, and I didn't either. I'd never participated in a bidding before.

"A bidding can only be called into action by those who requested the oath." That created a stir among the group. "We can utilize the commitment of the bidding when we recover Ophelia and Viraclay." His confidence in the statement made me respect him even more.

"How in the strokes will we arrange all of this? We can't overcome the Nebas compound and ready a prime location for a war to play out. That is out of reach, even for the great Alchemist," Thracian sneered.

"I don't usually agree with Mr. Pessimist over here, but seriously, Ruit, there are only twenty-four of us. We have no idea how many Nebas reside in Chernobyl, but it has to be more than we have here," Medusa argued.

"Not to mention, they have the Rittles and a volume of the Pierses," Tete added. "That's bad shit, man."

"And a possessed, homicidal Sulu." Borte snorted.

"We do not have the authority to call on the bidding, but we aren't without allies. Each of us knows a companion or two, or even several, who would come to arms to assist Viraclay. That is our first task: to accumulate as many Pai Ona as we can to destroy Chernobyl. We will need our friends with strong defensive gifts. Those who do not possess such powers will be equally important in readying the battle grounds," Ruit explained.

The mood of the room shifted slightly with his direction. He was a good leader.

"How will we contact them?" Aruna's voice cut through the chatter of everyone else. "We don't have the time to seek them out."

"Leave the communications up to me, my dear. You just decide who you trust and who might have the courage. I will have the how figured out by morning."

The room erupted into several side conversations. I turned to leave, because it occurred to me I had a total of two people I could trust. One was in a bedroom down the hall and the other was being held captive by our enemy.

I stopped when Ruit spoke once more. "There is something else." I had wondered if this was when he would mention his suspicions about the poison. Everyone hushed. "I believe the captives are being poisoned by none other than dragons' blood." It got eerily silent.

No one said anything for a long minute, probably in the same shock I was at that statement. Aremis broke the silence. "We transported all the living dragons to Cataphet. They are safe in The Cathedral."

"It would seem that not even the Sovereign of the Dragons knows of this kin, or perhaps they have a supply from the time of the dragon slaughter."

Genghis asked the question I needed to know. "Well, it is curable, is it not? You are restored, as is Lucas." He couldn't even look at me.

"There is an antidote. I saw them administer it," I interjected, realizing I hadn't even told Ruit that part. Ruit scrutinized my statement, but he didn't respond to it directly.

"It seems the longer you are under the elixir, the more difficult it is for the poison to dissolve from your system. And if it is as Lucas says, and there is an antidote... I assure you I will do my best to discover its origins. There is reason to believe that the Nebas have been obtaining captives, to what end I do not know. If my suspicions are correct, it will be integral that we storm Chernobyl in a more delicate way. I will be relentless in discovering the cure to the dragon's blood. We are going to need the captives in full form as soon as possible."

The room erupted again in whispers and strategy talk. Ruit walked over to me casually. "You failed to mention an antidote before."

"I only just remembered. Seriously. Shit, I didn't mean to keep it from you."

"All is well, but we will revisit this."

I nodded and excused myself as Tete approached with more questions. I would let the buzz calm down and return when we were back to strategizing.

I entered the courtyard cautiously. I didn't wish to break any concentration Yanni may have harnessed. Aurora stood in the opposite archway to me, leering at my beloved as though he wasn't doing his absolute best to familiarize himself with the arsenal the body of Ophelia Banner possessed.

It would be wrong of me to claim I didn't see the value in him learning his skill sets faster. There was a battle brewing. It was coming and, because of the Oracle's faulty visions as of late, we had no idea when exactly.

Yanni stared at his hand with fierce focus. Small sparks flashed in his palm. My heart lit up for him. *Progress!*

"Enough!" The Oracle stepped out of the shadows. "If this is all you have learned, I am sorry to say this is a sad day indeed."

I followed her into the center of the courtyard. There was no point in being quiet now.

"Did you see the flame in his hand?"

She laughed. "Flame? You call that a flame? Aremis conjures fireballs. That was a flicker at best."

I stepped beside him. As she approached, I felt an urge to move in front of him. Defend him from her onslaught of insults and demands. But Yanni would never condone that. He had lived under the thumb of Aurora's rule for just as long as I have. He knew how to handle himself, but since his return I found myself more protective of him.

"I am advancing every moment I spend in this body, Oracle."

She scoffed and waved him off. "Never mind you and your disappointment. I had a vision." Just then, Clive stepped out of the east wing. "I am sending Clive to tend to it. The Pai Ona who faced us at the basin are dispersing into two factions. The Alchemist and Lucas will move in one direction, Aremis and the gatekeeper in yet another direction."

"Can you see their destinations?"

She shook her head. "But it seems most pertinent that we follow Ruit and Lucas. They will be the quickest to strike. Lucas' rashness will push him to move with haste. Therefore, he is the most likely to slip up."

"Are you certain his affections still run as deep for Ophelia, now that he has his Atoa back?"

"Dear child," Aurora stepped closer, "sometimes I worry about your wits. Whilst holding his beloved, he could not refuse his connection to the Sulu through the bond that the troll wove between them. He is still greatly connected to Ophelia." She looked over Yanni with disgust.

"Why don't you use the same mechanism that you did to extract the location of Ophelia to find Lucas?" Yanni asked. He did not understand the measures we took to torture Lucas into helping us. I took his hand in mine, ready to object to the same tactics.

I thought back to how Aurora found the tether in the first place. It was in the strokes that she could sense the Pierses magic coming off Lucas. Her visions had always told her he had an important role to play in seeing her destiny realized, but it wasn't until she saw the wisps of Pierses magic in his aura that it became clear as to how. The troll had bonded them with a charm that Aurora found in the binding of the Pierses volume she received. She gave it to Walthrup, Aphrodite's Atoa, as a thank you for their assistance in her rescue.

Walthrup was murdered by an unknown assassin who was believed to be seeking the ancient power of the Pierses. The Gattilak charm, as it was originally called, had multiple faculties, but one of the most prominent gifts was a soul tie. Aurora quickly consulted her volume of the Pierses and found a way to distort the connection and see it.

"It is no use. The connection that ties them is to the soul. Ophelia's soul is not here, fortunately." She stepped closer and caressed Yanni's cheek. "I already looked for the tether and I would have easily tortured you until the end of your life if I thought it would assist us. Alas, that is not at our disposal."

My whole body stiffened at her admission. It was not surprising, but she also knew what that would do to me and to him. Aurora wanted me to know that she would go to any lengths, and that having Yanni back meant nothing to her unless she could utilize him. The only fortuitous stroke was that she still felt the Sulu was the key to her ascension to power, so I concluded she was bluffing.

"How is Clive to track them?" I changed the subject.

"From the basin, of course. It will take him time, but he will succeed. He is skilled." She smiled at her pet, and he returned the gesture. I never fully understood their bond, but it didn't matter. Clive had proven to be useful on multiple occasions. Which reminded me...

"Clive has intimate knowledge of the Rittles."

"Does he?"

"He used one to transport us here. How else did we arrive so quickly, in a blur I cannot entirely remember? He disarmed the hex that made them impossible to touch."

She turned her back on me and walked toward the east wing. "He has many means. Whether he has knowledge of the Rittles or not, it makes no difference. He is better utilized in the hunt."

"But couldn't my time be of better use, if Clive already has the information to catalogue their faculties?"

She continued to walk away, repeating herself. "He will serve us better as a tracker."

I went to object when another thought occurred to me. "What about the Rune? Can that assist you?"

She instinctively touched the mark on her shoulder. "The Alchemist has done something to shut down the channels. As far as I can tell, he has used the same mechanism to also interfere with Elias' Rune, leaving Viraclay utterly alone. It was an interesting and callous move on Ruit's part. I have more respect for the man now."

He was very cunning and calculating. There was a reason for this strategy. We would certainly discover it when it was too late. "So, we have our next plan of action."

"It would seem we do. In the meantime, you will discover how the Rittles may best serve us, I will scour the Pierses for a Convening that may give us an advantage, and you…" She glanced at Yanni over her shoulder. "You will not fail me. You will learn how to operate the Sulu."

He nodded and the Oracle and the hobgoblin left through the east wing. I needed to help Yanni, in any way that I could.

My mind was tormented with thoughts, terrible realizations.

Aurora's treachery explained how the Nebas always seemed to be able to find us. How they breached the summit, entered Hafiza—chased us around the globe. My stomach flipped again. It was getting harder to hold back the visceral reaction.

I closed my eyes and concentrated on soothing my nerves. The door creaked open, and I could hear the sound of quickly moving footsteps until I could feel their proximity. It was Esther; I could smell her.

"How does the Sulu work?"

When I did not answer right away, she took hold of my hair. It was long, unkempt, and she had a solid handful in her fist.

"Viraclay, I haven't the patience for you." She pulled harder and I felt the roots tear from the follicle in places. "How did your pet utilize the others' gifts?"

"Esther, I know no more than you. Ophelia is extraordinary."

She put her lips close to my ear. "Ophelia is no more. My beloved takes her place."

I opened my eyes and looked into her dark soul. "Then perhaps Yanni can tell you how to wield the Sulu's gifts. Certainly, he must be more equipped than an Unconsu."

Her eyes said it all. Yanni could not. *What does that mean for Ophelia?*

LUCAS

I was waiting in the central room with everyone else at dawn. I didn't have anyone to contact, so I was just there to satisfy my curiosity and see what the next plan of action was, while crossing my fingers he had found a cure for dragon's blood. Yessica held my hand and waited with anticipation. She had many people she trusted and who trusted her. This would be an opportunity to contact them, learn if they were still alive and ready to help. After the last meeting, I explained Ruit's plan, and she created a list of those she wished to reach out to.

Ruit entered the room with Almus on his right and Susuda on his left. The three of them carried two weird-looking boxes each. *This ought to be good*, I thought.

"As most of you know, I created the Runes that I share with my family and the old channels that Elias used to produce a mass communication to the Pai Ona when assembling the Summit. This is neither this nor that. It's an entirely new device that works in a similar fashion.

"I believe this will serve us in two ways. The Oracle does not know of its existence. This will make it harder for her to see what's happening. She is far more effective with her sight when she knows what she should be looking for. In addition, it will be effective at articulating a message to each individual you wish to contact, and on their end, it will be evident the message is coming from you," Ruit explained.

"I will demonstrate." Almus stepped forward. He set down one of the boxes and held the other in his hand. I hadn't seen it up until that point, but one of the eight sides had a hole. Almus inserted his hand in there. Nothing exceptional happened but Sparkle lit up with excitement.

"Wow, I heard you loud and clear, like you were inside my mind, while literally standing there." She continued to smile. "It was kind of creepy actually."

Ruit had set down his own boxes and took hold of the one Almus had just used to show us that it worked. "You put your hand in the hole. Once inside, think of a single person you desire to contact—only one. Once you have them clearly visualized, project exactly what you wish to say. Everyone may project a little differently, some with more words, while others may use more images to convey their message. In this way, the device acts very similar to a Rune. There are two key components: being clear on your recipient and being clear with your message. The disadvantage is that you can only contact one Conduit at a time. I had just enough resources to create these six boxes, so it may become tedious and time-consuming waiting to get your messages out. I apologize for that."

"Where are we asking them to meet us? Will everyone come here?" Aruna asked.

"I think we should discuss this. There must be a larger, more accommodating Haven than this," Winston insisted. "We could not comfortably host many more than we already have here."

"Where would you have us go?" Thracian looked at Winston expectantly.

"I think we should return back to The Cathedral," Susuda said plainly.

I'd never been, but the look on many of the others' faces said that that wasn't exactly what they had in mind.

"The Nebas infiltrated The Cathedral. They have a Loktpi," Aremis explained. "However, while returning the dragons, we went back several times without a problem or an enemy in sight, and that was before the gatekeeper returned to his station."

"The Loktpi means they can get into any Haven. There is no exception," Susuda agreed. "May I continue, Father?"

The gatekeeper looked to Ruit for permission and the Alchemist nodded.

"I returned to The Cathedral while Ruit created these new channels. I explained to Cataphet that we had reason to believe that a dragon is being held captive and their blood being harvested to sedate the Consus. This infuriated the Sovereign of the Dragons, and she has sworn an oath of vengeance."

"So the dragons will fight with us?" Helia asked.

"She did not say that, but she was enraged at our now-common enemy." Many small conversations picked up in the room. Susuda continued. "What is more is that upon request of my father, I brought it to The Cathedral's attention that Aurora was able to enter with the Loktpi and her devious intentions did not alert the wards. The Cathedral and Cataphet explained that the Loktpi let her in, and the hobgoblin Clive masked her intentions. To that point, they have now properly secured the Haven from hobgoblin trespassers. Therefore, we are safe to return."

Ruit and his family were just full of surprises. Part of me was antsy to get on with storming Chernobyl, but a bigger part of me was in awe and respected the way Ruit was governing this group. He was calculating, merciful, patient and full of ingenuity. I trusted him, a bizarre feeling for me, since I rarely trusted anyone. There was a confidence in his leadership that brought me peace.

"With this new information, all those in favor of returning to The Cathedral say aye."

It was a resounding yes in the room. I was excited about this new development.

ESTHER

I don't know what was wrong with me. The thing I enjoyed most was leaving me feeling dry and lackluster after only a few hours. For the first time since I could remember in my vast lifetimes, I was finding torture and interrogation tedious. All I could think about was Yanni. I desired nothing more than to be near him. Occasionally, I would hear something calamitous occur in the compound, and I knew it had to be him practicing with his inherited gifts. It just made me yearn to be closer to him.

I walked toward our chamber. I was hopeful that he would be waiting there and that we could share in some time alone. When I saw the door cracked open, I realized that was not the case. Even worse, I knew the caller was Aurora.

When she heard me approach, she began her tirade, "You have failed at controlling anything more than the manipulation of metal, and Esther has failed at accruing any further intel from Viraclay regarding the Rittles. How are we to achieve victory with your shortcomings at every turn?"

I stepped into the room, my irritation growing with every passing second. "I am so sorry to have disappointed. How much time do we have until the Pai Ona descend onto the compound?"

This was both a legitimate question and a dig at the Oracle because I knew from her tone that her visions were malfunctioning and that was the real origin of her anger. *She did not like to be blind like the rest of us.*

She kept her jaw clenched as she replied. "It's the Alchemist, I know it! He has made a mess of my sight." She reached for the closest thing and threw it against the wall.

But before Ruit reappeared, her sight had been faulty because of the Sulu, or so she thought. It was becoming more apparent that her glitches were rooted in something bigger than she first theorized.

"It will come back. Patience." I walked past her and took my place beside Yanni. He had pulled Ophelia's wild hair back into a low, tight bun and replaced the black suit she wore with a pair of leather pants and a matching bandeau top. It looked good on him.

"I do not have a set time for their arrival, which means their plans are forever shifting. Which gives you a chance to learn how to use this body and take advantage of the power. You will do better."

"I will do better," Yanni agreed.

"And you, Esther." She approached me slowly, and if someone didn't know how wicked she could be, they would think it was in a gesture of goodwill or affection. But I knew better, which meant I also knew I couldn't show the lioness any fear. She fed on fear. "You will discover what these Rittles can do the old-fashioned way." She caressed my cheek with the back of her fingertips, until they met my ear, which she gripped tightly. "I do not care how many casualties it takes to uncover their gifts. But Viraclay remains unharmed for now. We may need him as collateral, should we get in a bind. Or there may come a moment when consummation with this one is required." Her nails dug into my lobe, and I could feel the blood trickle down my neck. "Am I clear?"

"Of course."

She released her grip and turned to leave. "I will be spending some time with Viraclay, then he is all yours." She disappeared. *What does she hope to get from him?* He had been a pawn in her plan his entire life. *What information can he have that she doesn't already know?* Perhaps it was more of a pleasurable taunting, slowly divulging to him all the ways in which she had played cat and mouse over the years.

I slipped over to the door and shut it behind her, relief washing over me. I had time alone with my beloved.

He sprawled himself on the long chaise I had in the middle of the room, his legs spread and ready for my intrusion. I kelt down, to worship his body as a good lover should, and when I got to my knees, I remembered that I had brought something to ask him about. I adjusted myself so I could reach the baton at my back.

"Oh, it's going to be one of those trysts," Yanni purred at I adjusted myself between his thighs.

"Possibly." I winked at him. "But before we begin... Do you remember this object?" I handed it to him.

"Is this the staff we picked up in India? Where Vivienne met her demise?"

"It is."

"I know no more about it now than I did then."

"Have you no access to Ophelia's memories?" Ophelia had been there the day that Nandi and Vivienne had died. I wondered if she would have any insights as to what this weapon was.

"I am afraid not, beloved. I am only inhabiting the skin. Her memories, mind, and soul feel absent. Out of my reach. That is why I cannot learn how to use this body and its gifts readily."

She very well may have the knowledge I seek, but those secrets went with her soul to the River Tins. "So, it is different than when I possess a body. Where the soul is there to watch me utilize their form. Since they are there, the gifts lend themselves to my disposal effortlessly. The rest of the body's faculties, speech, taste, touch are all beyond my control."

"It appears to be different."

"May I take control, feel what I can sense?"

"You know I hate that, but if it gives us insights, by all means." He closed his eyes, and I put my hand on his cheek to seize control of his gifts. It was like nothing I had ever encountered before. It was emptiness. A fog lingered in the abyss, and there was a tinge of something in the space, but not tangible.

"That is peculiar," I said as I pulled my presence away.

"I have never possessed a body before, but it does feel strangely vacant."

Thinking of vacancies made me uneasy. It reminded me of how I felt when Yanni left this world. I set the baton beside him on the chaise. "Where were you? When your body failed to exist?"

"In the dark. I was in the dark. There was nothing. Until a door appeared, and I went through it. Suddenly, I was in a basement, in a circle of our enemies, fighting for space in an unfamiliar body. I had a moment of inhabitance and then it disappeared. But the door stayed there, and I was able to open it, peek back inside this world. The opportunities were sparse until the moment I seized a weakness in my host. My memories are foggy at best, shrouded in shadow and etherealness." He stroked my hair with his hand, and I lay my head on his lap.

"I felt you, every time your soul crossed over. I felt you."

"That does not surprise me. Our strokes are one and the same."

"It would seem."

We sat in silence for a moment.

"Why did you not enter the River Tins?" I was worried for my beloved.

"I have wondered the same. Perhaps there is no place for the wicked on the banks of the River Tins?"

I inhaled sharply. "We have been wicked. Led by the wicked, while leading the wicked. You believe the painter has forsaken us?"

"I will not know until I enter the threshold of death once more."

"Until *We* enter," I corrected. I thought about my father, wondered where he might be after death. I thought about my mother. She was certainly in the River Tins; she was a good soul. I thought about the lives we'd taken by our own hand. And I attempted to make clear the actions that made us deplorable to begin with, the captivity of the Oracle, but the memories continued to evade me. *When was the last time I put this much attention to that season of our lives?* It's been centuries.

Yanni pulled my face up to look into my eyes. "We have this moment now. That is all that matters."

He was right and I was going to take advantage of it. I placed the baton on the floor then began to unbutton his pants. A wave of anxiety stopped me as I began to tug them down past his hips. *The birthmark, my birthmark.* I needed to ask the Oracle what it meant. But if she knew and had kept this knowing from me, she would be unlikely to elucidate now.

Yanni lifted my chin with his fingertips. "Where are you right now, Esther?"

I shook off my misgivings. "Nowhere but here." I couldn't fool him, but he didn't object.

"What information did my mother have?" I asked again.

Aurora was sitting on a delicate chair a few feet in front of me. Today she wore a pale pink gown. It reminded me of the fallen Aphrodite. I had seen her parade in something similar once. *It suited her far better.* After hours of this ruse, where she would ask a question only to toy with me and dance around whatever I asked in return, I had given up on acquiring any real information.

"I have been considering sharing a very curious phenomenon with you, Viraclay. You see, since you told me about the day when you gave the prophecy to your dearest, I have been plagued by mysteries I have no answers for. As you can imagine, that is rare. In fact, the last time I remember this many holes in my vision was just before the fall of Atlantis at the last Katuan Trials. For thousands of years, my sight has been flawless. Then you meet your Atoa and she develops extraordinary gifts. Now—and I do not relate this to you in jest—I am experiencing holes. What is more, this did not start immediately after you met Ophelia, no. In fact, the malfunction began after the fall of Hafiza. How else could I have mastered that siege so gracefully?"

I did not bother looking up. There was no use in engaging with her.

She continued. "So, I ask myself, what changed? Her powers began to develop…but there must be more, because she comes in and out of my sight." Aurora took my chin in her hand and pinched it hard as she lifted my face. "You must have some theory. You may be naive, but you are far from stupid."

Whatever game she was playing, I was not going to participate. I had had enough of being threatened by Esther as she catalogued the Rittles. Enough of being exploited by the Oracle. At least with Esther I was receiving valuable intel from time to time. I was curious what the Rittles were capable of just as much as she was. Whether she knew it or not, she was feeding me all the information I would ever need to know about the invaluable artifacts. It was difficult for me to imagine how I would utilize the details I was collecting, but the strokes were always changing.

Aurora let go of my face and my head slumped forward once more. Sometimes letting your enemy believe you have given up is the best strategy.

*B*efore leaving for The Cathedral, we were called to one last meeting by Ruit. I entered to hear Mikkel giving his opinion about our priorities.

"We must discover where we will hold the last battle. Ophelia and Elias' capture does not change the objective," Mikkel said.

"Olly's capture?" I scoffed. "Possession is now the same as abduction?"

"That is not what I meant, Lucas," Mikkel argued.

"It is not going to solve anything, arguing over technicalities. The truth is, we have lost them both and that should be our first priority—to recover the Sulu and Viraclay." Winston asserted.

"For the first time ever, I agree with you, Winny."

"We cannot simply waltz into the Nebas compound at Chernobyl. That is why we did not storm it to recover you, my son." Vosega put his arm on my shoulder, and I had to fight the urge to shrug it off. I was still uncomfortable with our blossoming relationship. "Olly would want us to be reasonable, now more than ever."

"What's reasonable about this situation?" Sparkle asked.

"Olly is possessed by that crazed maniac Yanni, Viraclay is a captive of Esther, and Aurora has somehow been manipulated by the enemy. Reasonable appears to have long since passed us. We are flying straight towards ludicrousness," Helia added.

The room suddenly erupted with a dozen different conversations, everyone with their interpretation of what was happening and what we should do next.

"After much deliberation and a few more facts coming to light, I feel we need to adjust our strategy." Ruit's calm voice sliced through the buzz of conversations like a sharp knife. Silence followed in its wake. *The man had presence, I had to give him that.*

"We have gotten further confirmation from some of the allies you have contacted that appears to confirm the Nebas have captives. We can assume from our last interaction with the Sulu that Ophelia is lost to us, possessed by our enemy. They now have all of the Rittles and the Oracle on their side. What's more is that Aremis informed me that he has made a promise to the dragon Napitae that he must honor. It is pertinent that we stay in good standing with the dragons in order to maintain an alliance that will likely change the tide in this war. When I reached out to Cataphet to inform her that many would be returning to The Cathedral shortly and that another party would be seeking the grounds for the final battle, she generously shared that the battle must take place where the world ends. We are in a quagmire of questions. Where to have the final battle? Does anyone know where the world ends? How do we recover Ophelia and dispel Yanni? How have the Nebas manipulated the Oracle such as they have? With so many cards stacked against us, it seems we should seek answers and allies before we seek revenge."

"You're saying we should just leave Olly with that monster taking over her body? Who knows what the fuck he is doing in there?" I voiced my greatest fear. I trusted that Ruit would have more sense than this.

"Lucas, I understand your angst, but we need to understand what is happening to her before we end up on the losing end of her abilities."

Ying interjected. "How do we find the answers?"

"Who among you will continue to vet the locations for our final stand, where the world ends?"

Winston and Lucia stepped forward, followed by Shiva, Friedrick, Aruna and Ying.

Stalt stood and took his place beside Shiva. "I trust the Alchemist, but more than that, I trust what the Sulu and Viraclay started. I trust that they would want to see it through."

Mikkel moved to stand beside Stalt, as did Thracian.

"If this is what I have to do to help Olly, this is what I will do," Thracian conceded.

"Tete will help find answers, but there must be more to do than this shit!"

Ruit turned to Aremis. "We need to be in the good graces of the dragons. Not only do we need Cataphet's blessing to occupy The Cathedral, but my gut tells me that our journey with them is nowhere near its end. When the time is right, and when I can be certain, we will need them to help us understand how to restore the captives who have ingested their blood. Tete, will you accompany Aremis to The Cathedral, along with my family and Susuda? Lucas and I will be traveling to Australia."

Wait What? Why the fuck am I going to Australia?

Almus interjected before I could get a word out. "Father, we will not leave your side."

"I am afraid you must, my son. Your mother and Inca would do best to align with Cataphet and the other dragons. Build alliances with Susuda as best you can. Someone must be there to greet our allies and continue to send out invitations to take up arms."

"I will go with you, Aremis." Sparkle locked her arm into his.

"And I'll be damned if I leave you to your own devices, Tete." Medusa gently punched the shirtless man in the arm.

"Once settled in The Cathedral, we need everyone to learn as much as they can about the Rittles so we know what arsenal they will be carrying. Scour the libraries, chase the rumors, and discover the facts. The rest of you will attend me and Lucas on our errand in Australia."

I looked around at my dad, Oya, Borte, the Khan and Helia. They weren't objecting. Maybe they knew something I didn't. "I give up. Great Alchemist, what's in Australia?"

"I hope the answers as to how to recover Olly to her body."

ESTHER

The Oracle returned to our chamber after her dealings with Viraclay, requesting Ophelia's body for an errand. Yanni didn't hesitate to comply. But I was growing more and more uneasy. Something was amiss. I had felt it ever since I found the birthmark. Aurora knew something that she wasn't telling me.

I was uncomfortable, absentminded in my work, yet I continued to chip away at the endless task of discovering the use of each Rittle. *Which also felt like a huge waste of my time, she was distracting me from something, but what?*

Nevertheless it has been a day of successful findings. I looked over the Rittles I had investigated so far. The most curious of items was the globe, a crystal ball that would immediately expose an untruth. I could have used this thing centuries ago. It would have saved us all from the Huan debacle. Perhaps I would still have Vivienne here and now, to help with the impending war. My thoughts stung deeper still when I realized that if Nandi hadn't pursued vengeance, Vivienne would still be alive, and so would Yanni is his original form. Alas, here we are, and the dead are gone, but by the strokes, my Yanni's soul has returned to me.

The globe also gave a glimpse of the truth. A brief image of the root of the lie would emerge, then dissolve in the glass. It was quite intriguing, and it confirmed what Viraclay claimed—he had no further knowledge of any of the Rittles.

The door swung open, and Aurora stepped in. She was irritable —her usual demeanor these days. Viraclay lifted his head for a moment to see who it was and then immediately resumed melancholic hopelessness. It was entertaining at the very least.

"What have you to tell me, Esther?"

I hoped I had discovered something that she would find valuable. "We have determined the capacity of all but two of the Rittles —the Gada and the conch."

"Have they abilities that will assist us in the upcoming battle?"

"Most do, yes."

Aurora looked over the lot on the floor. She reached for the globe. "What does this trinket do?"

"Deciphering deceit."

"That will be useful with our captives." She put it down and picked up the ankh necklace. "This one?"

"Reveals the relationships between souls."

"Seems useless." She threw it back down.

"It may help with later crusades." There would likely come a time where we would need to seek out Unconsu or Poginuli who sought asylum somewhere after the battle.

"Perhaps."

The Oracle turned toward the more obvious weapons. "These have discernible uses. Anything exceptional?"

"They all have several other endowments, thank the strokes." I quickly went through what we had discovered through experiments with limited casualties.

"They must possess more than what you discovered. Continue your investigation until all avenues have been exhausted." Aurora turned to leave.

A pang twitched in my stomach again, like I was being distracted by this pursuit. *But distracted from what?* "Have you asked Clive if he has any useful information?"

She glared at me. "No. He has not contacted me with any news, nor has he returned." *She is resisting this line of inquiry. Why?* I felt a familiar tearing at my soul. *Is it Yanni?* Panic surged through me. I felt paralyzed, but then the sensation dissolved. If Aurora noticed the shift in my demeanor, she said nothing as she exited the room, but a glow from the globe caught my attention. I almost missed it— a faint image of her and the hobgoblin conversing.

She lied to me. *Why would she lie to me about Clive's whereabouts and what he knew about the Rittles?*

OPHELIA

My consciousness shifted all of the sudden. Only moments ago I was talking to Apollo. Now my head was throbbing. It felt like I'd been hit with a two by four. I tried opening my eyes. They were swollen and crusty at the edges. *Where am I? They are keeping me captive, or Yanni rather?* I was back in my body. I could feel it.

The room was dark and smelled damp. I braced myself up on my elbow. The ground was cold and muddy on my skin. Déjà vu. I didn't want to open my eyes now. This had to be a dream, a very familiar nightmare. Something must've gone wrong when I stepped back into my body. As my senses came to, I knew exactly where I was. Where this had to be. I'd seen it before many times. The clanging of chains confirmed my fears.

Eleanor's weak voice met my ears before I found her face in the dimly lit dungeon.

"Olly, is that you?" She began to weep. "You're alive?" She started rambling. "Has he had you all this time? Have you been alive all this time? Oh no, Olly, they've caught you too. I'm so sorry I didn't tell you about your father sooner. Warned you that he was a monster."

Eleanor thinks this is her fault? She must be sure she is going crazy. I squinted in the dark, trying to make eye contact with my mother, to assure her she had nothing to do with this. But I was still discombobulated, and I couldn't tell who was who. Although, I knew all too well who the other woman was. It was Lilith, my grandmother.

"Mom." My voice came out hoarse, indistinguishable as my own. "This is not your fault. I'm so sorry you had to believe I was gone."

"I'm just so grateful you're alive. But Olly, it's your father. The monster that is holding us hostage, it's the man…" Her voice broke off. This must be so terrifying and painful for her. She was in shock. It was the only explanation for her ability to accept me being alive so easily.

"Ophelia." Lilith sounded a little more together than my mother, her daughter, but the curse Nestor put on her would make it very difficult for her to articulate anything that might be useful for our escape.

"Grandma, are you okay?" It was a ridiculous question. Of course, neither of them was okay. My eyes were beginning to adjust. Now I could see Eleanor to my right and Lilith in the far corner of the chamber, both naked and caked in mud, just as my nightmare had depicted it.

"Grandmother? Olly, your head is bleeding. I think you are hallucinating. This poor woman is just another victim…" Eleanor's voice trailed off. She was staring at Lilith in the corner, trying to see past the blood and bruises and mud. She was being tortured by her greatest villain, again. Her daughter, whom she believed to be dead, was now also facing the same monstrous fate. And I'd just told her that her mother was in fact alive and visibly younger than Eleanor is now. "Lilith? My mother Lilith? But you died."

Torrents of tears created mudslides down my mother's cheeks. This was all too much to bear, too much pain and confusion—too much torment. I needed to get us out of here and I had no idea how long I would be able to maintain control of my body.

A man's laugh echoed off the walls. "Don't you just love a family reunion?" I couldn't tell where it was coming from. It sounded like it was everywhere. "You never knew your mother, Eleanor. Too bad. Before she became a loon, she was rather articulate and warm."

I screamed. I expected it to come out as a piercing weapon, but it was muted—like a dull knife.

"Tsk, tsk, tsk, my child. Your tricks won't work down here. These walls can contain a dragon. They can certainly disarm you."

"You are an asshole. Don't call me your child. You are scum!"

"Harsh words coming from my captive. Don't make me discipline you, child." Suddenly he was at my back. I could feel his hot breath on my neck. I wanted to vomit. He whispered so low I barely heard him. "Quite the performance, Yanni." Nestor smiled, then took a fist of my hair in his hand, ripping my head back and talking loud enough for everyone to hear. "Your charms are dulled but mine are just fine. Don't make me torture your mother and grandmother for a show." He ripped off the scraps of clothes I had on.

This was a tactic, to try and get something from Eleanor and Lilith. *How could I tell them I was all right, stop them from bending to Nestor's will?*

"Get your hands off her," Eleanor growled.

"Or what?" Nestor traipsed over to my mother. She began to shake. Her real-life fiend was alive and inches from her naked body.

"I will kill you." She didn't back down.

I had to stop this.

Lilith began pulling at her chains, growling and hissing in the place of the words she couldn't speak.

Something flickered in his eyes when he flashed a glance back at me. A knowing that he was torturing them in every way possible. "Silence!" He backed away from Eleanor and I stopped holding my breath. I couldn't witness her defilement; it would be too much. "I'm not ready to expose the games I have in store for the three of you. Be patient." He was back at my side and purring in my ear while twisting his index finger around a tendril of my hair. "Soon enough."

I opened my mouth to say something, anything that might ease their suffering, but my soul began to tug at the edges with the familiar sensation I had as Yanni took possession of my body. I dug in with my will, but it did no good. I was spinning back into unconsciousness, back to the River Tins.

anni met me outside the room where we were keeping Viraclay. He was covered in mud and smelled like dungeon.

"What did she have you do?"

"It was Nestor who had me do his bidding. He is torturing the mother and grandmother. He thought my appearance would shake them up."

I laughed. "Well, did it?" We walked side by side toward our chamber. I would bath him when we got back. It would be a treat for both of us.

"Nestor felt it was a success."

I stopped and cupped Yanni's cheek with my hand. "Oh, my beloved, what a wicked little actor you are. Surely you deserve an Oscar."

He took my hand from his cheek and gripped it tightly, a worry line stretched across his brow. "There's more."

"Have you managed your gifts? That would please the Oracle. That would please me."

"No, there was a moment of loss."

"Of loss?" I was worried. *Was that what I felt moments ago, the familiar tearing at my soul?*

"It was nothing but a lapse in time. I still maintained all of my wits. Nestor said I performed brilliantly, but I don't remember."

My eyes searched his face for more, but it was clear that was all he could deliver. A thousand scenarios filled my mind. But I dismissed them all, because I had to in order to keep my sanity. *It was a simple surge of energy. He'd merely blacked out.* I took his face in both my hands, kissing his dirty forehead. "Tell no one of this."

OPHELIA

"Olly!" Zavier's voice was panicked.

I sat up and inhaled sharply, feeling as though the wind had been knocked out of me. It was bizarre to have such human faculties in the realm of the dead. Of course, just having returned from the land of the living, I was aware how much sharper my senses were in that reality.

"Miss Ophelia, what happened?" Rand looked down at me, concern furrowed in his brow.

I scrambled to my feet. "We have to go back to them! He's torturing them and he's using my body to play psychological warfare."

Zavier took my hand. "Who? Who is torturing whom?"

He was the last person I wanted to tell, but I had to. "My mother, your wife... Nestor has them as captives and he is doing atrocious things to them."

Zavier didn't disguise his defeat that quickly transmuted into rage as a warrior cry erupted from his chest with such passion, I thought the entire world might have felt it.

"Now, Zavier, that will get us nowhere," Apollo insisted.

"This is your fault! Your daughter had my mother abducted!" I

109

was terrified and furious, and I wanted someone to blame. *Why not the man who made her?*

"You're right, this is my fault. But not for the reasons you think, Ophelia."

"Then explain yourself! I don't have time for your vague, self-pitying stories!" But a part of me knew I might have all the time in the world. I couldn't entertain that thought right now. Right now, I was devastated by what I had just witnessed and desperate to get back to my family—to help them.

Rand grabbed my hand. "What's just happened? Maybe we can harness that episode, get you back to the other side."

Rand was so good to me. *How would I do life without him?* Another thought I had to squash for now. "I don't know. I am assuming it was a glitch… the very same kind that allowed Yanni to possess me."

"Good. Yeah, that's good. How can we leverage that?" Zavier was on board, while Apollo just stood back. Probably afraid I would bite his head off again.

"I don't know. What did it look like on your end?"

"Like you blinked in and out. It was terrifying. You were here one minute, gone the next, then back and in a state," Zavier explained.

His observation gave me nothing. The more I thought about it, the more it seemed likely that I needed to pass through that door to anchor back on the other side. *But do I know that for sure? How could I?* I stared at the ominous black threshold.

As though he was reading my thoughts, Rand said, "Before you do anything rash, let's recompose ourselves. Besides, I believe the villain in our midst would like to confess a thing or two more before our time together concludes."

The three of us looked to Apollo, who stood stoically unmoved.

LUCAS

"Stand back, everyone. Sometimes she doesn't watch where she's stepping when she comes through." Yessica giggled behind me as my entourage backed up. Ruit had asked me to call on Fetzle to transport us to Australia. It would save us precious time. I couldn't argue with that. We were the last ones to leave the Constantin Haven. The other two parties had left an hour ago. One toward The Cathedral and the other toward Russia.

I handed Vosega Virclay and Olly's bags as I pulled out the medallion. "Here, hold these."

I did my thing and Fetzle appeared quickly and much more composed than last time.

"FetzleisheresLucasandYessicas," she announced, and then looked inquisitively at the other faces we had with us.

"Sorry to bother you, Queen." I said it playfully, but truthfully, I was proud of her. She was claiming her place. "Could you get us to Australia? We're in a bit of a hurry and we think there will be answers there that can help us save Ophelia and Viraclay."

"FetzletrustsLucasyes, butwhosethesepeoplesbe?"

I introduced her to each of the Conduits and when I ended with

Ruit, I saw something shift in her demeanor. I wanted to ask more, but it wasn't the time, not with an audience.

"It is a pleasure to meet you, Queen Fetzle." Ruit and the others bowed. I was grateful to see them show her the respect she deserved. I even thought I saw her blush.

"FetzleneedstoknowswhereinAustralias."

I handed her the coordinates Ruit gave me.

"Fetzlethinksitwillsbefastesttrip,takeshands." With that, we were flying through Fetzle's shuttle and onto our destination. I could barely blink before it was done. We manifested on a suburban street. Thankfully, it was dark. Fetzle didn't bother to step out of the tree, but I heard her voice faint on the wind. "Fetzlesaysbecarefuls."

"I will," I called back. Then I turned to Ruit, who was standing very close to me. "What now?"

He pointed at a house across the street. It looked harmless enough in the shadows of night.

"Hey." I grabbed his arm. "Do you know Fetzle? She seemed to know you."

"I knew her mother," he said solemnly.

That made sense.

"She was a good queen, as was her mother. Fetzle will be the same, I can tell."

"Of course she will be," I agreed. "Is there something I should know?" His tone left me feeling like there was more.

"In due time. I believe the trolls play a larger part in this war than we may have first realized."

"Yeah, they are a great ally to have."

"More than that, I think they may have been one of the greater victims."

"What?"

But Oya interrupted us, "Come on, I'll show you the way. Make sure you watch your step." And just like that, Ruit was gone. But he better not think he was getting off that easily. We would be coming back to this. I followed everyone as they crossed the street, grabbing Yesi's hand on the way.

OPHELIA

"*I* know you have no reason to trust me, any of you," Apollo said.

Zavier shook his head and I was surprised. "I know what has transpired. I trust you."

That was oddly comforting, considering how little I knew of Zavier as well.

"Ophelia, it is your trust I desire most." Apollo turned to Rand. "I know she values your opinion."

"Like no other," I agreed as I hooked my arm into Rand's.

"Very well. Let me prove my integrity. I will enter the door to confirm what is on the other side."

Rand immediately objected. "We don't know your allegiances."

"This would be the quickest way to find out and may help us understand how we can return Ophelia to her body," Zavier argued.

"This is ludicrous, like giving a loaded gun to your enemy." Rand pointed out.

A woman's voice chimed in behind me. "I think it is the only way, my dear friend."

I turned around to see a familiar smile. It was Sorcey. I knew because it was unmistakable where Elias inherited that smile. Her long, wavy, black hair was swept to one side in a loose braid. Piercing blue eyes examined my face for recognition, or perhaps it was an evaluation. She stepped closer and took me in her arms.

"It is nice to meet you, Ophelia. You are more beautiful than I ever could have imagined." Her arms were stronger than I would have expected. Her embrace took my breath away slightly. I wrapped my hands around her back and pulled her into me, trying to let the gravity of the moment sink in. I was hugging Elias' mother, an opportunity he would never have again. I was meeting my mother-in-law, my deceased mother-in-law. Neither of us was quick to end the exchange. I let go when I felt Sorcey gently pull away. "You are stunning. You glow." She beamed at me as she took in the whole sight of me.

"Photographs don't do you justice, I'm afraid. You're quite the knockout yourself."

She laughed and modestly looked away. Now I knew where Elias got his humility from. "You honor me with your words, sweet Ophelia."

Rand cleared his throat. "May I receive one of those warm embraces, dear friend? It has been far too long."

Their bodies collided and it was clear that time had done nothing to diminish the bond they shared.

"How is my brother? How is Cane?" Rand asked.

"He misses you, but he is well met beyond the River Tins. All are well met."

Tears welled up in Rand's eyes at the implication that his Carissa was also there waiting and in good spirits. "Why, then, do we bother ourselves with this tapestry of life?" Rand wiped at his eyes as they met each other's gaze.

"Because the painter has the greatest love for his children, he desires our evolution back home," Sorcey surmised.

I interrupted, "Home is beyond the River Tins? Home is death?"

"No, Ophelia, home is not death or beyond our world. Home resides within us and through us, as well as between our merging souls. We have simply confined ourselves to our own mortal coil.

The illusion that home is a place separate from any other is the perfect demonstration of our delusion."

What she said resounded in my body, but I couldn't place where. I wanted to ask more questions. Surely she knew the answers to all of my questions, what has happened in the past and what I could do to end this war in the future.

"I know you must have many questions, more than a lifetime could answer. I hope to reconcile as many of them as I can, but in this moment, I am here to validate Apollo's pure motives. He desires to see you succeed, to see you made whole." Sorcey looked at Apollo while she spoke and I witnessed a distinct twinkle of admiration. That was telling.

"But the war? The thousands of lives lost... My Carissa." Rand shook his head in disbelief.

Sorcey took Rand's hand in hers. "There is more to this story than can be explained in our brief time in limbo. You will understand soon enough, my brother, and will be reunited with your Atoa. But for now, we need to break through our preconceived notions and help Ophelia become restored."

The love between them was beautiful. Sorcey turned to me. "Apollo will not betray you. Let him show you with this act of honor."

I looked at Sorcey and then to my two grandfathers, who stood patiently waiting for me to concede. I nodded, not sure I could form words without crying. I was feeling overwhelmed by all the love, support, and new knowledge.

"I will not fail you." With that, Apollo entered the threshold and slipped into the darkness.

The Oracle had not so politely requested we command all remaining Nebas join us at the compound. I, in turn, demanded Astrid and Claudia get the order out. "Astrid, how are our numbers?"

"They have nearly doubled since last night, Mistress."

That was excellent news. Viraclay could not have known that when he marked the hidden Nebas, he would push their allegiance to our side. It was in the favor of our strokes that they finally had to come out of the shadows.

"The Oracle will want to convene with the new arrivals this evening. Make certain they know to congregate in the courtyard after sunset."

"Mistress." She nodded and slipped out of my chamber. Having exhausted the exploration of the Rittles, I was now left to my own devices until Aurora could give me another errand. I had a moment to watch Yanni practice.

I draped myself in my long violet robe and took the back passage to the courtyard. My chamber had several secret passages that I found very useful. I could be almost anywhere in the compound in seconds and without detection. As I approached the courtyard, an uneasy and familiar wave of sensations flooded my chest, the same feelings I would get when Yanni would weave in and out of this plain of existence. I remembered the episode he had described earlier, and I began to panic. I sped up my pace, emerging on the balcony that overlooked the congregation area. Ophelia's body lay unmoved in the center of the floor. I dove off the balcony, landing beside him.

"Yanni!" I cradled his head in my lap, looking for any signs of injury or an explanation for his state. There was nothing. "Yanni!" I shook him gently.

Ophelia's body animated, and relief surged through me, but almost immediately I knew something was wrong. The eyes that peered up at me were not the coal black eyes of my beloved, they were different.

I dropped Ophelia's head from my lap in shock, trying to understand what was happening. "Who are you?" I spat the question as I got to my feet, only then realizing I should have taken control of the Sulu's body. *What if Ophelia has returned to her form?* So many questions and such deep sorrow, I couldn't think clearly through it.

"Este." Ophelia quickly got to her feet and back-pedaled out of my reach.

"Who are you?!" I demanded, rage replacing the sorrow. Which was good. I could think through the rage.

"There is much to tell you, Este."

The rage dissolved once more as confusion consumed me. Only one being on this earth ever called me Este. "Father?"

I stepped forward. Ophelia's body simultaneously collapsed in a heap on the floor. *What is this sorcery?*

The sensations in my chest confirmed he'd returned to me once more. I fell to my knees as he sat up. *By the strokes, what is happening?*

OPHELIA

I was holding my breath, not sure what to expect next. *Would Yanni appear among us? Would I just propel back into my body?* The faces of my companions shared the same distinct fear of the unknown.

Then, just as quickly as he had disappeared into the dark passage, Apollo manifested on the ground between us, gasping heavily and clearly disorientated. I knelt down. "What happened? Did you see Eleanor or Lilith?"

He reached up and grabbed my shoulder, locking his eyes with mine. "I did not. I was met by my daughter. We only had seconds, but I know she knew it was me."

"What did you tell her?"

"There wasn't the time. Yanni's soul is strong and it evicted me quickly. But I realized, when I looked up at Esther, she can be our ally. Este can help you win this war."

"Apollo!" I shook my head in disbelief. "How in the strokes do you think that your daughter will ever align with the Pai Ona?"

"The truth! The truth will change everything."

I looked up at Sorcey to see her nodding in peaceful agreement.

LUCAS

I looked around at my companions as we approached the dilapidated house. Ruit, Yesi, the in-laws, Helia and dear old Dad with his arm candy. I couldn't help but chuckle. This was probably one of my worst nightmares realized. Helia seemed all right enough, a woman of few words. *I liked that.*

"Borte, do you remember exactly where the entrance was?" Helia asked.

"Of course I do," the bitter woman snapped. She didn't want to be here either, but the Khan insisted he follow his daughter. I was surprised she caved and came. It wasn't like the empress to not get her way. "Why did you join this journey, Helia? Your debt for trying to kill Ophelia has been paid. The girl isn't even here."

"Excuse me, what the fuck is she talking about?" Now I liked one fewer of my companions.

"I didn't try and kill her."

Borte snorted.

"It was an accident during the trials. I really had a beef with Elias."

I couldn't blame her for that, and under different circumstances I may have aligned with her. I had a quick flashback to my own betrayal of Ophelia in San Francisco, with very similar motivations to Helia—the downfall of Elias. No matter my motivations, I still put Olly in very real danger. I wanted to shake off the shame, but the exchange with Yanni wouldn't let me. Instantly, I was back there on the night that Yanni attempted her abduction in our apartment.

❊

HE SMILED at me wickedly from across the street and gave me a playful wave. As I walked toward him, he spoke. "What brings you out of hiding, Lucas? It must be good if I am to exchange your life for it."

My skin crawled. I hated this monster before me. I hated Yanni. But who was I to judge as I stood here making a deal with the devil once more? It wouldn't be the first time, but it would sure as hell be the last. I was taking Olly and getting out of here. "I can give you Viraclay."

"Viraclay? Now?"

"Now."

"Why should I trust you?"

"I don't care for the kid, and I want to save my own neck." I scolded the voice inside that was screaming at me for betraying Cane's son. "Can you kill him? Tonight?"

"So soon? You know I like to toy with my prey."

"Tonight," I asserted. "Or no deal."

"Then I'll just kill you and hunt him down."

"Because you have been so successful at that."

Yanni growled and jetted out his hand. "I will find you."

"We will see." Then I handed him the piece of paper with Elias' address. I would've done anything to keep Olly for myself, to keep her safe. Turns out I would do the unthinkable.

❊

Helia's voice brought me back to the present. "Olly forgave me. That's all I need to be at peace."

Of course she did, I thought. Olly is probably forgiving Yanni as we speak for possessing her body. I could only hope I would get a chance to beg for her forgiveness. "If she forgave you, why are you here?" I asked.

Helia stopped in front of me, grinding the whole party to a halt. "Because Olly is my friend, the only friend I have left after the siege of The Cathedral. I will do anything to see her restored to her body." Helia stepped closer and squared her shoulders. "Make no mistake, Lucas, I know how you feel about her. I know you would do anything for her. You are not the only one here who would lay down their life for Ophelia." She gestured behind me. "I have seen your father do incredible things for Ophelia, as has Oya. Stop treating the rest of us like we don't have skin in this game, and stop being a dick to your dad. He's a cool guy, and he cares about you."

Yessica giggled. Helia put me in my place in a way that not many had before. I had to give her credit, maybe she would become an ally. I turned around and caught Vosega's longing eyes. I shook the look off. *We could get sappy later.* When I turned back around, Helia was already in the house. I quickly followed her lead.

The house was disgusting. Worse inside than it was on the outside.

"Borte, is it here?" Helia stood over a hole in the floor.

"Yes."

"Ruit, you'll have to enter first. You have the Loktpi."

Ruit pushed past me to where Helia stood. "I just jump in?"

She nodded. Then he was gone, having disappeared into the darkness. Helia jumped in after him.

I took Yesi's hand. "Ready, baby girl?"

"Ready as I'll ever be."

Then we both jumped and, before I could second-guess whether it was the entrance to the Haven, we were standing in a living room that was filled with small figurines. One by one, everyone else followed. Once we were all successfully in the house, Ruit calmly explained our agenda.

"We are looking for the Conduit Moira. She is a powerful channeler of the dead, among other things. It was her gift that left dear Ophelia prey to Yanni's seizure. She will have the answers we need in order to exorcise the villain from the Sulu. She is reclusive and, as of recently, she appears to have become deranged. I astrally projected here to make sure she was still in the Haven. I found her very indisposed. I am warning you to proceed with caution when you find her."

"Is she dangerous?" Yessica asked, squeezing my hand tighter.

"Dangerous? Not purposefully. But she is somewhere between realms, and when you are lost as she is, you don't know friend from foe."

"How will she help us if she's gone mad?" Oya brought up a good point.

"I have my means." Ruit then slipped out of the room and down the hall.

Helia moved through another threshold. I pulled Yesi with me. "Let's follow the straight shooter, shall we?"

Yesi pulled me in close. "I like her," she whispered, I could hear the smile in her voice.

"You would."

Helia moved through the kitchen and opened a small wooden door that appeared to lead down to some sort of cellar or basement. "She's here!"

As I suspected, Helia had an idea of where the crazy lady may be. Yesi let go of my hand so I could fly down the stairs. By the time I reached the basement floor, Helia was in a full-blown brawl with Moira, quickly and efficiently wrestling her down to the floor. I was impressed.

"Doesn't look like you need any help."

Helia looked up at me with a devilish grin. "I can handle myself."

Everyone else shuffled in behind me and I moved to get out of the way. The basement was large, the same size as the house, with lower ceilings. My eyes scanned the room for anything of value. It was a bare space with a crappy paint job. The walls were a faded grey, with sporadic dark and light patches.

"Great strokes, what have you been doing, Moira?" the Khan said, aghast, as he walked up to the wall closest to him.

"What?" I tried to see what he was looking at. "Has she been redecorating?"

"You could say that." Vosega came up beside me and put his hand on the wall in front of me. "Do you see the symbols?"

The moment he said it, my eyes adjusted to see that it wasn't a crappy paint job. It was layers and layers of markings on the wall in a grey chalk.

"Malarin speaks to me all day and all night. There is too much to write, too much to hear." Moira's face and hands were grey from the chalk. Her eyes were crazed.

"What do they mean?"

Ruit came on my other side. "If we knew that, Lucas, we would know all things."

"Where is the Oracle?" I demanded. Yanni was in our chamber, lying down after the episode he'd just had, and I was in a frenzy. I marched down the hall, shoving people out of my way, determined to find Aurora. "In the arsenal?"

"Yes." Claudia pointed behind her.

I ran the rest of the way until I was at the metal door that hid the coveted arsenal from the rest of the world that might otherwise get curious and attempt a glimpse at the Rittles. The entry was enchanted so that only I or the Oracle could enter. I placed my palm on the frame and the door swung open. She stood in the center of the room, looking at the trident.

"Esther." Her voice was flat. "I looked at your notes. This item must do more than what you claim."

"Yanni had an episode."

Her expression flickered a minor change, almost indiscernible. "Oh. What kind of episode? I hope it entailed him discovering more about his abilities. He is starting to aggravate me. We would be better off to have the Sulu in her body so that you could command control."

"It had nothing to do with his abilities." I stepped in front of her so she could look at me instead of the weapons that hung on the wall. Behind her was a shelf with the rest of the Rittles.

"What then?" Her eyebrows furrowed in annoyance.

"Did you see him having episodes?"

"Esther, you exhaust me with this inquiry. You have not even told me what the episode entailed."

I weighed my options swiftly. Either she knew and she was not telling me the truth, or her visions were even further distorted and learning this would agitate her even more. I quickly decided to not poke the bear. I needed answers about the birthmark, her lies about Clive, and now this…but I knew she would not be cooperative with demands. *And what will she do if I tell her I suspect Apollo has manifested in the Sulu's body? How will she react to that?* No, it was better for me to hold my questions tight to my chest. She either already knew I was growing antsy, or she was in the dark, which could mean a number of things.

"He passed out." The globe lit up behind her and I hoped she didn't notice my omission.

"From?"

"You tell me. Have you any idea what may have come over him?"

"Exhaustion from your pawing over him," she sneered. But the globe lit up behind her, indicating there was more to what she was saying. She was lying to me again.

"You haven't had a single vision about his state?"

"No. Are you being elusive on purpose? My patience is thinning." The globe lit up again.

"I know no more than it was an episode." Again, a blue haze filled the globe from my omission.

"Let him take care of himself then, and you shall leave my company, as I am tired of this exchange."

I moved to the side so she could resume her examination of the trident. But she had been dishonest again. I saw the globe expose it. *What is she hiding? She knew something about what's just happened, but she has not seen it. What, then, does she know, and how?*

"Is there more, Esther? Your presence irks me. I am trying to read something off the Rittles since your investigation was not thorough enough."

I turned to leave, then thought of something. "Have you heard anything from Clive?"

"No." she said plainly. But once more, the globe lit up with a foggy image I could not quite make out. She was lying and I knew in my heart that her deceit had something to do with what had just happened to Yanni.

"Ｗhat is your plan? How do we extract information from someone who has lost their fucking mind?"

"Patience."

I shoved my fingers through my unusually long hair. "You must have known how crazy she was because you witnessed her through your fucking astrology bullshit!"

"Astral projection."

"You know what I fucking meant."

"I saw her state, as I said."

"Lucas, calm down." Yesi was gently stroking my arm. "The Alchemist will not lead us astray."

"She will help us. Whether she is capable or not."

I took a couple of deep breaths. My temper was getting the best of me.

Oya entered the room with Helia on her tail. "Her chamber is filled with the symbols as well. It's like someone left the water running and she is being flooded with the Martian downloads continuously."

"Oh shit." I rubbed my forehead. "Are you telling me that she thinks these markings are from Martians? And this was her theory before she went crazy?" *This was a terrible plan.*

"It's just what she calls the markings for posterity's sake," Helia said.

"The woman thinks she talks to Martians." I turned to Borte. "Can you understand it?"

"No."

"So maybe she is talking to Martians." I threw my hands up in the air.

"It's not like the journal the girl kept. I can't hear the whispers that I could from those pages, but still, there is something familiar."

"You understand the language of the stones?" Ruit moved closer to the skilled Linguist.

"No, not entirely. But I get snippets. The language shares what it wishes, when it wishes."

"Have you any insights now?"

"It's the same message over and over again. It is the same symbols she wrote on the floor after our fated séance."

"That's what they told you?" I asked.

"No." Borte scowled at me. "I remember what it looked like. I am not one to forget a language that eludes me."

"So, we have nothing to go on here?" I felt so helpless. I didn't even know what had been going on with Olly for the last few months. So much had taken place since China. The Summit, the emergence of Dragons, and Olly's gifts betraying her. *How are we going to get her back?*

"I am the great Alchemist. I have a few things up my sleeve. All is not lost."

*Y*anni was still passed out when I entered our chamber. I paced as I looked at his limp body. *I can't lose him again,* was all I could think over and over. *I won't lose him again. What does Aurora know that she isn't telling me?*

I had to do something. "Viraclay." His name rolled out of my mouth, and no sooner was I bounding down the hall toward his prison cell.

Calypso was keeping watch at his door. "Leave us." She scurried away without a word.

I stepped inside the dark room. "Would you like some light?"

He said nothing as I lit a torch to my right. "You have been in the dark for some time. Surely a little light will be welcome." My seductive voice would do nothing to seduce him into cooperating, but perhaps hours of neglect, starvation and seclusion had softened him. *It appeared not.* Elias hung from the wall like a wet rag, dirty and disheveled, dried blood caked around his absent wounds. That was odd. I got closer to examine his body where I had inflicted pain only hours before while interrogating him. There should have been open sores. *Has someone healed him?*

"Who has been here?" I grabbed his hair and pulled his head up to see his face. The black eye I had given him was gone. "Someone has healed you." I threw his head against the wall behind him. "I can happily remedy that; we can start all over. Play with some of the Rittles again."

He said nothing. "Or, perhaps you can answer a few simple questions about the condition of your Atoa. Olly's life depends on it."

That got his attention. "You will not hurt her because she is not my Olly right now."

"True, but she is also not my Yanni." It was a risky move, to disclose the episode to Viraclay, but if it played out right, he may fall right into my web.

"What?"

I walked around him slowly, pausing to let my admission sink in. "She is of little use to me if my Yanni is not in possession of her body." Of course, that was not entirely true either.

"Who is in possession of her body now?"

"Tsk, tsk, tsk. Certainly you know better than to think I would share that information." I swept his hair from his face so he could get a better look at me. He didn't even flinch at my touch. Viraclay was strong, stronger than almost every Consu I knew to still be alive. *It was impressive. If half of the Nebas had his stamina, his endurance, we would be in a very different position right now.* "Yanni had an episode, and the soul that returned was not his. Nor was it your pet's."

Worry creased his forehead. I continued. "She may be lost forever, her body a vessel for souls to interchangeably circuit through."

"A single episode means nothing."

"So, she suffered from many and always returned?"

His lips tightened into a thin line. He would say no more. But he had already said enough to give me some comfort.

"Tell me, Viraclay, when will you let your torment end?" Without any reservation, I backhanded his cheek as hard as I could, and it felt good. It felt so good that I did it again. "There is no one to save you. Your parents' mission to unite the Pai Ona will die with you. The Oracle has seen it."

His mouth bled, his lips and teeth crimson as he spoke. "Then certainly the Oracle can answer any inquiry you have about my Ophelia. She must have told you she was the Sulu before the siege of The Cathedral, right? That is unless her vision is not as accurate as it once was."

I backed up and looked at him. She had not told me Ophelia was the Sulu before the siege. *Is he that perceptive?* Furthermore, how had he concluded the Oracle's sight had been spotty, something only she and I knew to be true. *Has Aurora told him? Why?* "You are a fool for thinking she is any less powerful."

"Am I?"

"The Oracle has singlehandedly destroyed everything you have ever held dear and yet you mock her?" I spat at him, and he turned his face just in time to make me miss my aim.

"The Oracle has played all sides like puppets. You are no different. If she is as powerful as she would like us all to believe, then she let your Yanni die. That is the very same as her slaying him herself. So, what is it? Did she betray your Atoa, betray you? Or is she suffering from gaps in her sight?" He chuckled to himself. "Who is the fool?"

My blood boiled. Because what he said rang with veracity. The Oracle had betrayed the Pai Ona, lied to them, murdered others, but if it were true that she was my ally, then she should have been able to prevent Yanni's death. Rage swelled up in me, a rage I had long since held back. It crawled up from the depths of my soul and erupted from my mouth and in my arms as I pummeled Viraclay with my fists until I felt someone pulling me off him—I couldn't say who, just that the next thing I knew I was covered in his blood and lying on my chamber floor.

esi stared at me as I paced. "Is that helping?"

"Is it bothering you?"

"No, not in the slightest. But it seems like a waste of your energy." She patted the bed next to where she lay. "Let me massage your shoulders."

"I…"

"Lucas Healey, it will do you no good to resist me."

Just then the door opened, a gesture that would have normally bothered me. I didn't like it when people entered my space unannounced. Ruit stood there with a piece of paper in his hand. "I think I have formulated a way for us to extract Yanni's soul from Ophelia."

I was beside him instantly. "What? What do you need?"

"The items on this list." He handed me the piece of paper.

"This is an obscure list," I said as I scanned it. "Where the fuck am I going to get this shit?"

"I have faith that you will find a way."

Then Ruit turned and shut the door.

Yessica was looking over my shoulder inquisitively, trying to read what I had in my hand. "What? It can't be that bad." I handed her the list. "Oh, well, maybe…"

We both just looked at each other skeptically. I opened the door and stepped into the hallway, looking for which direction he had gone.

"Ruit!" Suddenly he manifested in front of me. "What the fuck?"

"Yes."

"This list… What is it for, exactly?"

"Moira does not generally conjure specific souls. We need her to make an exception. I believe this concoction will give us the power to do that."

"Ophelia's soul?"

"Yes and no. We need the soul that is occupying her body. I want to pull him out and lock the door."

It was a good plan. "This will do that? A one-hundred-year-old succulent leaf of the Welwitschia plant? Where the hell am I going to find one of those?"

"I think a simple google search will assist you more than I can. Australia has many resources. I think you will find the task simpler than you're making it out to be. Do let me know as soon as you have finished your acquisitions." Then he was gone again.

❀

After several successful thefts, I was pretty proud of our bounty. Yessica and I made an incredible team. It was nice to be reminded of that. I tossed the bag at Ruit's feet when we entered the Haven. "Here you go. Everything you need to summon an asshole and lock him in the afterlife where he belongs."

"Much gratitude for your quick work." Ruit picked up the bag. "Now I need you to properly prepare yourself."

"For what?"

"This recantation will bring him to us, but it is you, Lucas Healey, who will fortify Miss Banner's body and prevent him from possessing her ever again."

"Me?"

He nodded. "Do what you must. It will be three days from now that we commence the banishment casting."

"Three days?" I went to follow him, and Yesi grabbed my arm. "We need to talk," I called after him.

He waved an arm in the air. "Soon. Rest."

"I can use some rest." Yessica's eyes validated what her words said.

"Of course. I'm sorry. Let's lie down." I took her arm and headed toward our room, looking over my shoulder at where Ruit had disappeared. I had such mixed feelings about his strategy, but I also had no better solutions.

"Mistress, the Oracle wishes to see you. The hobgoblin Clive has returned with news."

I turned to Astrid, too exhausted to say anything, and began walking in the direction of Aurora's chamber.

"Mistress?" The concern in her voice annoyed me.

"Your questions infuriate me. Do not infuriate me today," I demanded, and picked up my pace. Astrid stayed behind. Aurora didn't keep the company of anyone other than myself and Clive, so it meant that I was the middleman who had to bark orders at the rest of the Nebas on her behalf. Astrid was allowed to call for me when she heard three knocks at the Oracle's door. It was becoming intolerable, this new pecking order.

I made it to her chamber quickly enough that no one else had an opportunity to bother me. I waved my hand in front of her door to open it. After I assaulted Viraclay, she insisted on moving all of the Rittles into her chamber. Apparently my behavior was erratic. This now meant we now needed to employ the same magic we used on the arsenal here, at the entrance.

Clive was standing beside her. They both looked to be admiring the wall of Rittles. But I knew better. This was how they communicated. In silence. Both sharing a glimpse of the future. The Oracle was the only Conduit I ever knew who could communicate with hobgoblins. They were a different type of stroke. It made them unique. No other creature could converse with them, *perhaps the dragons?* And as far as I understood it, Clive's entire clan had been wiped out by a random meteor shower while he happened to be on the Island of Atlantis with Aurora and all the other living Conduits of the time. Come to think of it, I didn't know what could kill a hobgoblin. They were formidable. But apparently, not even the formidable could survive fiery rocks crashing down from the sky.

I shook my head at the thought of it. I didn't like to go back to that event at Atlantis. I'd lost my mother that day. She, along with countless others, were slain by accident after the dragon Gwenora killed Yilliana the Alchemist and her Atoa Jolena at the last Trials. It was hard to believe that I would be the instigator of so much death at the next Trials that would follow.

That was a different time, a different world from the one I lived in and actively corrupted now. The loss of Shatki changed my father's life forever. Changed my life forever.

"Are you just going to stand there? Dear God, child, you were put on this earth to vex me."

I stepped closer. "Sorry, I assumed you two were in an exchange." I bowed at Clive, and he reciprocated. He wore his black cloak. I had never seen him without it. "What news do you have? Are they coming? Should we prepare the army?"

"They are mobilizing. I have seen it. Clive confirmed it."

"All of them?"

"All of them."

I saw the blue hue of the globe behind her. She was lying, or Clive was lying, but someone was being dishonest.

I had to confirm. "Lucas and the Alchemist? The others that were in the basin? More?"

She nodded and the globe lit up. *Why in the strokes would she lie about something this important?* She would not rally our defenses in vain. That would never serve her.

"There may be more with them. I am certain they have been gathering those who would save Viraclay and the Sulu."

I looked between the two of them. *Could she sense my confusion, my knowing?* If she did, she did not divulge it. Perhaps I misunderstood what the globe did all along. This was baffling.

I shook off my misgivings. I could ask more questions later. If there was an army heading our way, I needed to prepare. "What would you have me do?"

She spouted off a flurry of orders. All the while my thoughts were muddled with the display of the globe.

"Are you listening to me, Esther?"

"Yes. Yes, of course. I will prepare all as you have asked. How long do we have?"

"Three days."

The globe exposed her lie once more. *What in the strokes is going on? Did she lie about everything?*

"Be gone! Prepare our troops and send Yanni to my chamber now."

But I did not want to. I was overwhelmed. Confused, worried about what was real and what Aurora truly had planned. I said nothing as I left the room. I needed answers. I needed them soon. There was no one to trust. Viraclay had proven he was useless. *Who else could give me another lead to follow?*

I listed my current questions. *What is the Oracle lying about? How can I keep Yanni safe and in the Sulu's body? What was the message my father was trying to impart on me? What was my connection to Ophelia, and what about our similar birthmarks?*

The last question inspired an action I had yet to consider. The mother!

esi kept me calm for the remainder of yesterday, but today I needed answers. I stormed down the hall, looking for the Alchemist. I had checked all the rooms when I heard a shuffling down the stairs into the basement. The flicker of candlelight danced along the walls leading down into the dark space.

Moira's voice was shaky but more coherent than it had been yesterday. "No, stand there… Yes, there."

What the fuck is she up to?

I hurried down the stairs to find Ruit, Moira, Helia and Oya taking their positions for some sort of ritual.

"Wait, what is going on here?" I demanded.

"Lucas, you are supposed to be resting." Ruit looked annoyed, a slight crack in his constant calm demeanor.

"I thought we weren't doing the dirty work for three days. What the fuck is this? Because it looks like a séance to me."

"It is. We need to call on Ophelia and give her a timeframe to work within. To let her know when the siege will take place to rescue her and Viraclay and instruct her as to where she may find him in the compound."

"Olly is going to be here?"

"Yes, for a moment."

"I need to be here. I need to tell her I am going to get her out of this mess." I need to tell her I'm sorry.

Ruit bit his lower lip. I suspected he was sizing up how hard I would fight to be present, and I needed him to know there would be no fight because I was not going anywhere.

"You cannot be in the circle. You will need your strength for the Gattilak seal."

"Whatever. Sure," I agreed. Then decided to ask. "What is a Gattilak seal?"

"I have been studying the Gattilak charm that binds you and Ophelia, I am going to harness the soul tie between you two and with your shield you will seal her Gate of Consciousness, so that Yanni can no longer enter her body. It is a similar incantation to the one I created when stealing the Siren's song in Merr. I used a dreidel to bind the Siren Molpe because she does not have a corporeal form the same as we do. The item was of no consequence, only out of convenience. "

I wondered if that was the same top I saw in Olly's bag. When Ruit realized I seemed satisfied with his explanation he continued.

He nodded at Moira and the others. Moira took her place in the center of the circle. She held onto some elixir in a glass bottle in her right hand. I had never seen a séance before. It was sort of exhilarating to not know what to expect. Moira began to sway and dance and gyrate while she chanted rhythmically. Suddenly she stopped and drained the bottle of its contents. Her body fell to the floor in an awkward heap. I stepped closer. She began to convulse violently, then she looked up and I could tell instantly that it was no longer Moira in the room.

"Olly?"

She looked up at me. "Lucas? You're okay?" She got to her feet and came to the edge of the séance circle, careful not to step beyond the energetic boundary that was being maintained by the others.

"I'm fucking amazing, thanks to you." I wanted to hug her, hold her, kiss her head and tell her everything that had happened.

Ruit's voice echoed off the wall, although he was not moving and his mouth was eerily unanimated. "Miss Banner, we have called on you to warn you that in two days the compound will be beleaguered and your body restored to you. We will summon you two more times to ensure you know where to find the captives and how we intend to collect you all."

"But— Can Yanni acquire this information from me?"

I stepped closer. "Do you think he's in your thoughts right now?"

She closed her eyes and did a mental inventory, then began shaking her head. "No, I can't feel him or my body."

Relief surged through me. "Good. That's fucking good."

"How will I know where to find everyone, to find Elias?" She was looking to me for the answers.

Ruit responded. "I will share a transmission with Elias and we will map the compound."

She put her head in her hands. "He's okay? You know he's okay?" Tears streamed down her face.

"He is alive, Miss Banner. That I can assure you."

Moira's body started to tremor.

"Lucas, you have to save him and my family," Olly pleaded. "Promise me."

Of course she would be worried about him above herself. "I will save you both. Eleanor and anyone else you need me to," I assured her just before Moira's body fell to the ground once more. When she came to, her eyes were her own.

"Did it work?" Moira asked as she got to her feet.

"Yeah, it worked." I let out the breath I had been holding.

Ruit met me as I made my way to the staircase. "For this to work, we have to all engage as a unit. There can be no wild cards here."

I tried to push past him, but he was stronger than he looked.

"It isn't simply Miss Ophelia's life on the line, although her well-being is in all of our best interest. For that reason, I assure you, I will do all that is in my power to see her rehabilitated and out of harm's way."

"Good. We're on the same page."

"We are, so let me be more blunt. If you choose to take matters into your own hands, I will be forced to disarm you myself, and make no mistake, Mr. Healey, I will disarm you swiftly and effortlessly to keep everyone safe." He stepped aside so I could slip past, and as I did, he whispered, "Now we are on the same page."

I didn't care for threats, but I had to hand it to the Alchemist, he demanded respect. And as long as he held up his end of the bargain, I would give it to him. But if I sensed for a moment that Olly could be collateral damage, whatever page we were on would burn into a thousand ashes. *He could disarm that.*

"Where did you go this time, child?" Apollo and Xavier were staring at me.

"I was back in Australia, at Moira's house. Ruit was there and he told me that the Pai Ona were storming the compound in two days, and I needed to be ready."

"That is excellent news." Rand gripped my shoulder.

"It is," Zavier agreed. But Apollo looked skeptical.

"What? You don't believe them?"

"No, I do. I am grieving my own loss. Two days is too little time with you." I felt endeared to the man already. Strange how bonding can happen so quickly. He shook away his sadness. "More importantly, we have much to share, and I must find a way to speak to my daughter. To warn her of what is coming. She can be reasoned with."

"We are talking about Esther, right?"

"There is more to her than you will ever know, or perhaps someday you will understand each other. But until then, she will better serve all if she is warned and gathers her own evidence against the Oracle."

I opened my mouth to protest but Sorcey stopped me then addressed Apollo.

"It is time you tell her about her father."

With all that was happening, I lost track of one of the most important questions... *How were Apollo and the Oracle my grandparents?*

My body was healing quickly from Esther's attack. I had almost wished the pain had endured. It was a welcome distraction to the continuous realizations. There was no way I could have known what the Oracle was doing, *but how has she so easily fooled my parents? And what could my mother have possibly known that led to her death after centuries of immunity to Aurora's vengeful wrath? Why does the Oracle continue to visit me every day?* Perhaps it had not been days but rather mere hours since our defeat in the basin. I could not truly say. Nothing but a parade of images and heart-shattering conclusions kept me company.

Until I felt the familiar tingle of the Rune. I stopped breathing, afraid anything or everything could disrupt the transmission. *Who would be on the other line?*

Ruit's voice came in loud and clear. "Make no cause for inquiry. Viraclay, she stirs. We have a plan to retrieve you both. My communications must be brief and vague. In two days' time, the strike will occur. Stay strong."

Then it was gone. Hope swelled in every cell of my being. *She stirs* could only mean one thing. Olly was coming back to me.

"Nestor, take me to the hostages," I demanded.

"As you wish, Mistress. They are where they have been this entire time, the dungeon."

"I know where they have been. Take me to them." I held back my inclination to hit the Incubus.

He turned around and headed toward the staircase that led to the lower chambers of the compound. We kept most captives on the second floor, but Nestor preferred his privacy for his tricks, so he had the entire fourth level down to himself. The only other room utilized at this floor was the poison room. I never went to that floor. We all have our personal preference for inflicting pain. I found Nestors disgusting to listen to.

We quickly traversed the spiral staircase.

"What state are they in?" I asked him, grateful I could only see the back of his head because I could hear the wicked grin in his smile.

"They can speak. And you will be happy to know I just took the hex off Lilith so that she may speak coherently. I found her mutterings bug-some. I wanted to understand how my torture was affecting her."

Well, that was in my favor. It hadn't even occurred to me to ask if they were that incapacitated. When we hit the fourth floor, Nestor sped up his pace. A wooden door at the end of the hall was the entrance into the dungeon. The smell of piss and feces got worse as we approached. "How do you stand it? That smell?"

"It is a fond, familiar one to me. It represents the hold I have over my victims, so I rather enjoy it."

I shook my head in disgust. "Unlock the door and leave us."

"Are you sure you don't need me here to help mine for information? I have tactics that work quite efficiently, especially with these two."

"No, your presence will be a hindrance. Be gone."

Nestor looked dejected as he unfastened the lock and skirted past me. I picked up my red velvet dress so that it wouldn't drag in whatever fluids were on the floor. I didn't want that decrepit smell following me around all day.

There was no light. I could hear breathing. Eleanor was Unconsu. She would need to see me to answer my questions. "Ladies, it is I, Esther. I am blessing you with my presence. I will expect your full corporation, or I will be forced to ask Nestor to increase his efforts."

A whimper in the darkness was the only acknowledgment I received. "Well, that is rather rude." I walked to the furthest wall and found the torch I knew to be there. I quickly lit it and turned to see two naked bloody heaps on the floor. Nestor had been making good work of his time with them. I knew by the dirty pale hair that Lilith was the one on my right. I turned to address Eleanor.

"Get up. I must ask you a question and you will give me answers."

The heap didn't move so I kicked her in her kidneys. She cried out in pain.

"Leave her be, witch!" Lilith was now standing in a pathetic attempt to defend her daughter.

"She will get up and answer a simple question or she will suffer. By all means, advise your daughter. Surely, she will listen to you."

Eleanor moved her head slightly to look at her mother. Her face was covered in mud and dried blood, with the distinct tracks of tears exposing patches of her cheeks.

"She is still mortal, Esther. Her body cannot withstand much more. She is no good to you dead."

"Is she that broken?" I knelt down to see her body better. "It still appears she has a few bones to break."

"Please, please don't hurt me anymore," Eleanor pleaded.

"Answer a few questions and I will not only leave you be, but I am feeling so inclined that I may send someone down here to give you a bath." I wanted this whole place scrubbed, including these pathetic masses.

Eleanor pulled herself up to face me. "What information could I possibly have that you would want?"

I exposed my inner thigh. She scurried back, alarmed by the quick movement. "This mark," I pointed to the birthmark. "Do you have it?"

She shook her head.

"Where did Ophelia get it?"

"She was born with it." Then Eleanor choked on her words. "What have you done with my daughter? Oh God. Oh God." The panic grew in her voice.

"Calm yourself, woman. She is right as rain."

"But,…why? How could you know about the birthmark on her inner thigh?"

"None of your business. She is fine. Now focus." I didn't need her falling apart. I needed answers. I turned to Lilith. "Do you have this mark?"

She shook her head.

"Damn it all!" I shouted as I stood up, kicking the chain that bound Eleanor to the floor. She cried out as it tugged at her swollen wrists.

"Olly was born with that mark. That is all I know. I swear. I assumed she inherited it from her father, because he has it the same as you. On the inner right thigh."

"Her father?"

"Yes, Nestor. Ophelia's father."

What in the strokes does that mean? Nestor has the mark? I felt dizzy. I needed to get out of here. Something was off. There was something I was missing, and I did not like being in the dark.

"**I** think you should sit down."

I wanted to object but thought the better of it. This was all unravelling so rapidly. *Who knew how I would handle this next revelation?*

Instantly, four more chairs appeared, and we all sat down. I gripped Rand's hand like it was life support. Apollo didn't take his eyes from mine. Sorcey was also staring at me intently.

"You are aware that we can procreate and birth full Consu children before we meet our Atoa?" I nodded and he continued. "I met Aurora when we were both very young. I was fifteen and she was seventeen. Times were very different then. I would not do it justice to describe it, as I have been out of your world for over a thousand years."

Wow, was all I could think… *Wow.*

"We fell in love, the kind of sweet, innocent love… at least it felt innocent to me. Of course, we also knew what we were as well, which meant that our love was a season until we met our other half. If you had asked me then how long I thought that would take, I would have said a few years. Aurora and I were traipsing around the globe with the agreed intention that when the day came, we would be ready to give each other a gracious goodbye. It felt true that it would be that simple. Of course, we did not account for two things. The first being that we would spend twelve glorious years together, building a life and making precious memories."

"You're telling me that you held the woman that you first loved captive? This is twisted."

Zavier put his hand on my other arm. "Please hear him out."

Apollo took my silence as an invitation to continue. "We were in the warm lands, east of the Central Sea."

Rand interjected. "Somewhere between Morocco and Liberia on the African continent."

"Shatki appeared like a goddess before me. I knew exactly who she was to me when our eyes met in that late afternoon. She was me, I was her—there would never again be another. The love I had for Aurora was still there, but it was as though that love was a distant star and Shatki was the whole sun. There was no comparison.

"Aurora did not handle the news the way we had agreed we would. Looking back, I cannot blame her. It would be difficult to be the last one to pair between us. But in that moment, I was taken aback by her rage, her disbelief. She threatened Shatki's life. So, we fled, leaving Aurora to fester, to grieve the love and companionship we shared. I regret that decision every day of my life, and every moment since my death."

"That must've been awful for her."

"I cannot imagine her pain then, especially since she was with child."

I gasped. "You didn't know?"

"I did not. I do not believe she knew when I left. She would have told me, anything to keep me close. She carried herself through term on her own, lonely and heartbroken, perhaps wandering from place to place looking for me, but I did not know. I swear it, I did not know. I would have come back. Shatki and I would have supported her together."

I was seeing the bigger picture. I knew what was coming. "She gave birth to Nestor."

"She did, but she also gave birth to Esther that very same night."

I cupped my hand over my mouth, afraid of what my expression would look like.

"Esther and Nestor are twins?"

Zavier and Apollo nodded, and Rand looked just as shocked as me.

"Do they know?"

"They know nothing of their true origins," Apollo said and hung his head in shame.

PART II

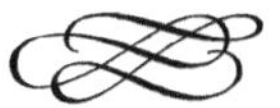

ESTHER

I was not in my right mind. I would bark orders, then run to observe Yanni and his practice in the courtyard. He had gained better control of a few gifts, but that didn't concern me. Nor did the impending attack the Oracle glimpsed. It was only he who mattered, and for the first time, long since this war began, I wished it was just him and I, and we could run away. Leave this whole domination thing behind, forge something different in our strokes.

I smiled. *Perhaps we could one day.* When the Oracle had things her way and we were no longer needed to defeat the enemy. And that time would most certainly come. There would be no way anyone could defeat her, the Rittles, a Pierses, and the Sulu. Not to mention the army that stood behind her, ruthless and now desperate to gain their freedoms back. She had been collecting the worlds most powerfully gifted Conduits per each faction. This not only weakened the enemy, but gave her the power to create a Sulu wheel as she called it. *Would she really need Yanni and I after that?*

"What are you smiling about?"

I was so distracted by my daydreaming that I didn't hear my beloved sneak up behind me. "Just you. You are impressive."

"Not impressive enough to appease the Oracle, I assure you. She is relentless."

"You do not need to tell me." I grimaced.

"Of course." He turned me around to face him. "I do wish to operate this heavy artillery in order to keep you safe."

"I know all about your heavy artillery and you manage it just fine." I nibbled on his ear. "I think it's time you took a break, don't you?"

He looked around sheepishly, as though anyone could stop us. *Well, I supposed there was one who would argue, but she was busy.* I had already made sure of that.

We sprinted down the hall giggling as Yanni pulled me along. He was certainly fast in the Sulu's body. He swung open the door and immediately fell to the floor. I knew what was happening, I could feel it in my chest. He was having another episode.

I fell to my knees and cradled his head in my lap. "Come back, wake up, please. Yanni, hear me and come back." Tears streamed down my face.

I heard the familiar footsteps of Aurora traipsing down the hall. I didn't want her to see him like this, but there was no making excuses for this scene.

"What is happening here?" she growled through bared teeth as she swung open the door. She was alone, thank the strokes. "I have to see these things in my sight? You would rather lie to me?"

"I don't know what's happening to him." *I asked her about the episodes*, I internally stewed.

"Do you not? Is that not why you beat Viraclay inches from his life?" She knelt down to look at his face then stood up, hovering over me, rocking her body in disgust. "He is unable to contain the power."

"It's more!" I spat back at her.

"Is that right? What, pray tell, is that?"

Then his eyes shot open, and I saw that they were once again my father's. He looked at me then up at Aurora, a flicker of fear in his gaze. I turned to see what he saw. It was her expression—shock, disdain, pain.

"What in the strokes…"

The next thing happened so quickly, I could hardly make heads from tails. "You must listen to me Este. She is—" His words were abruptly stopped by the Oracle's heel to the Sulu's face. Again. Again. I jumped over Ophelia's body, sheltering it from the battery.

"Aurora! Aurora, stop!"

She kicked me twice before stopping the onslaught.

"What is this, Esther? What are you conspiring?"

I looked up at her and all I could see was rage. I knew she hated my father, but this was deeper, darker than anything I had ever witnessed.

"This is the second time this condition has happened."

"And what of the first?" She drew back her hand to strike me and then decided not to for some reason. "You did not find it of consequence to share this with me?"

"I had hoped it was a mishap. I questioned Viraclay but to no avail. I asked you about the episodes."

"Your treacherous father has taken possession of the Sulu's body, and you only tell me now?" She began to pace. "I ought to have you killed for this type of treason. At the very least imprisoned with the rest of my tools in the cells below."

"I was not certain—"

She raised her hand and this time she came down hard. "Do not lie to me, you disgusting coward. You are lucky I need you. Because without you, I will never get the Sulu to cooperate."

I wanted to stand up and break her neck. *How dare she speak to me this way?* But I was afraid to leave Yanni unattended.

"You will clean him up and you will take care of yourself. Then I will be briefed on his first episode. Do I make myself clear?" She turned around and headed toward the door, before I could respond. With her back to me, she made a final statement. "If you lie to me again, I will kill you."

All I could think was that he was cooperating. *How could he be cooperating any more than he already is?*

OPHELIA

$\mathcal{A}$pollo had entered Yanni's door once more and we all patiently, or in my case impatiently, waited on the other side for his return. Sorcey scooped my hand up into hers.

"I am so grateful for you." Her eyes stared deeply into my soul. "Elias is so blessed to have you."

"I'm blessed to have him, I assure you."

She nodded in agreement.

"How long do you think it should take, for him to get his message to Esther?"

"I reason that it will depend on whether or not she is there to give the message to." Sorcey patted my hand encouragingly. "Time moves differently here because it doesn't actually exist. That is why we must act with urgency. Two days in the earthly realms has no relevance here."

"So, the time could have already passed?" Anxiety was swelling up in my chest.

"Or it could have been a matter of minutes. The strokes move in mysterious ways."

"But you trust Apollo?" My grandfather still had not explained everything to me. My companions seemed to agree with him that we needed to get through to Esther first and foremost, do all that we could to end this war.

"I do. His strokes were of the deepest misfortune. I have witnessed him do all he can to rectify anywhere he may have mis-stepped and do his best to protect his legacy."

"Protect his legacy? You mean protect Esther and Yanni?"

"No, child, I mean you." She sighed emphatically. "Apollo was not in his right mind when he influenced his daughter and her Atoa as he did. He was—"

Just then, he manifested in front of us on the ground.

I scrambled to his side and pulled him up. "Did you tell her? Were you able to reach her?"

"She was there, but so was Aurora."

Zavier growled under his breath.

"So, it was unsuccessful?"

"I am afraid it was. But I saw something in my daughter's eyes."

Sorcey stepped closer. "What did you see?"

"Fear. I have never seen Esther afraid, not once."

LUCAS

When I finished telling Yesi what had happened in the basement, she looked ghostly white. "Moira was able to stay coherent enough for that?"

"Apparently. Who knows, maybe Ruit drugged her up to keep her lucid."

"I did not have to. She is more intelligible than she appears." We both turned to see the Alchemist at the door. "May I speak with you both?"

"Of course." Yessica quickly invited him to sit on the bed beside her.

"Thank you. I will stand." He entered the room and shut the door. "We have two days to perfect Moira's ability to summon specific souls, determine if the markings she has been infiltrated with can help us, prepare a strategy, and create a map of the Chernobyl compound to assist the siege, while fortifying the seal that you will need to administer on Ophelia. Not to mention prepare and execute the mobilization of all the Pai Ona who are courageous enough to help our efforts."

Yessica released a heavy sigh. "Is that possible?"

"I believe it is."

"And we have to do it in two days because they are torturing Viraclay and Olly's mom and grandma." I wished we could do it today.

"Among other reasons, yes, time is of the essence."

"What other things?"

"There is more at play here than I can articulate. It is more a hunch. The Oracle grows impatient, which can make her act recklessly."

That I could understand. "Okay, so where do we start?"

"We start with a Bidding."

"What?" I looked at Yesi for recognition and she shrugged.

"Between you and me, Lucas. I meant what I said. I cannot tolerate anything impetuous. I desire a Bidding from you so that I can focus my energy on more important matters. Will you comply?"

"What the fuck? Really?"

He just nodded.

Yessica put her hand on my forearm, her silent plea for me to cooperate.

"What's the Bidding? I mean, I want to know the damn verbiage. I get the gist of what it actually is—a really tight contract."

"Indeed, impenetrable."

He handed me a sheet of paper. "You will read this exactly?" I scanned over the contract.

Ruit nodded.

"Fine." I looked at Yesi. "Does this make you happy?"

"It does."

"It is a blood Bidding."

Of course it is, I thought.

"Give me the knife."

Ruit pulled a knife from a sheath he had conveniently strapped to his belt.

I cut my palm and read the Bidding.

"I, Lucas Healey, honor the Bidding before me with my life and the life of the Bidder that I will not act outside of the good of the Pai Ona as a whole during the siege of Chernobyl. I will follow whatever procedures are put in place at all costs and only deter when all other options have failed. I will choose to collaborate with my fellow Pai Ona and save as many lives as I can while pursuing the safety of Ophelia Banner."

"Very well. Yessica, give me your hand."

"Wait… what? You're the Bidder."

"I did not say who the Bidding was with."

Yessica promptly gave her hand to the Alchemist. "Wait! Yesi, did you know about this?"

He cut her palm, and she held her hand up to me, waiting for me to seal the Bidding, binding her life to mine. They both knew this would keep me very cooperative. "It's what's best for everyone, my love."

I shook my head in disbelief, but I wouldn't deny her.

I clasped her hand in mine and held back the tears that were welling in my eyes. I was enraged. I hated being double-crossed, but the sting of the deceit coming from Yesi made me sad. I felt the promise take hold and I left the room at a sprint. I needed to run, scream, hit something…anything but being in that room.

ESTHER

I watched Yanni sleep, my mind riddled with questions. *What is happening and who can I trust? The Oracle has to know more than she is letting on about so many things. Could her sight be so faulty that she knows nothing about this birthmark I share with not just the Sulu, but also Nestor? The globe has indicated that she and Clive are being dishonest about something, perhaps many things. And the rage that she exposed upon my father's appearance was almost untamable for her. I have felt that rage before within myself, and for that reason the one thing I can be certain of is that she will kill me if I lie to her again.*

But if she would kill me because of the appearance of Apollo, what would she do to the vessel that held his soul? Before this moment, I would have trusted that Aurora would rather keep the Sulu's body to utilize its power to meet her ends, but now I was not certain. I replayed the moment in my head again and again. *What was my father trying to convey to me? Do I have to trade my father for my lover? Can I make that decision? What did Aurora mean by needing me to make the Sulu cooperate?* Usually when she demanded that, it was when I snatched a body, and I couldn't snatch Yanni's body like this.

Yanni stirred. I brushed the loose hairs that fell from his bun from his face. "Another episode?"

"It appears so."

He opened his eyes slowly. I was grateful to see they were his. I did my best to greet him with a stoic but present expression.

"What? What happened?"

I failed. I explained what had transpired.

"She's going to kill me."

"I will never let her." But even as I said the words, I wondered how I could stop her.

Since Ruit's transmission, it was all I could do to contain myself. I had to keep circulating my thoughts around a dozen other things, anything to keep them hidden from unwanted trespassers. I had no idea what abilities were on the other side of that door. The Ramalan herself was practically able to read minds when she was in full form.

Just then, Aurora entered my cell. I scattered my thoughts, then honed in on the one thing I knew would distract me, Lucas.

"How are you healing up?" She came and picked up my face, examining it. "Quite nicely. You inherited some of your mother's gift."

I looked up at her.

"Aw, that caught your attention. Did you think I didn't know?"

"You never said anything." I figured talking would keep my mind occupied.

"Delightful!" She clapped her hands together. "You're in a talkative mood. Thank the strokes."

I rolled my eyes. I could not be too eager to please her. She would suspect something.

"I wasn't being facetious. I have missed our conversations, Viraclay."

"Really? Is that so? Have you not toyed with me for long enough? What other manipulations do you wish to execute?"

"On the contrary, I want to share some truths."

I realized she was being honest, but not because she wanted me to know any crucial information. No, this was far more maleficent in intent. She wanted to gloat.

She pulled a chair up in front of me. The Oracle wore a beautiful gold gown today, her hair swept up in small braids intertwined with gold chains and pins. I wondered what the occasion was.

"I warned your mother that conceiving as she did would create a ripple effect in the strokes. Admittedly, at the time I did not know what it would be. My sight was not equipped to foresee the birth of the Sulu. It took years before the true impact of your birth became clear to me. But something in me knew that upon your miraculous conception, you would change the strokes." She shook her head in delightful reverie. "The unknown is scary, so initially I advised against her pregnancy. I was infuriated when your parents went ahead with the plan anyway. Imagine how excited I was when I realized the mutation was a powerful Sulu, the exact type of power I have been looking to harness once more. It was a beautiful service that your parents did me, by defying the odds—and me."

"All of this is so that you can act as a Sulu once more?" I thought about the conversation Nara and I had had in The Cathedral. Nara had exposed the deviousness of Aurora's captivity.

"It's magnificent, isn't it? I have been accumulating powerful Conduits in order to create the most powerful Sulu I can, and then I discover your Atoa."

"You have captives? They are here so that you can create a Sulu circle as you did in Delphi, then."

"Oh, dear boy, think much larger than Delphi. This Sulu will be all-powerful, the manifestation of all twelve factions, and I, their vessel. A Sulu Wheel." She smiled maniacally. "But this was all put into place before I saw Ophelia, before I felt her strength. The girl changes everything."

My head was spinning once more.

"Her conception sent me scrabbling to try and put other plots in motion. Some were successful, like the prophecy. While others, like killing Lucas and his family, failed miserably. But Malarin is always presenting me with better strokes. I thought that having Lucas around was going to be a hindrance to many things, but it has proven to deliver her straight to me. Thank Dalinkas!"

"You were the one who put the hit out on Lucas' family? That was centuries before we were born."

"Of course it was me. Your parents were considering your conception for hundreds of years. A thought put into their heads by crazy Kassandra and a High Priestess of the giants. I saw very clearly that Lucas was going to create rebellious waves—he has always been a loose cannon. I was also the one who ordered Yessica's capture. Lucas is such a wild card, he is constantly changing my visions, creating gaps. Between his shield and his recklessness, I cannot predict what he'll do from one moment to the next."

For the first time ever, I was grateful for Lucas' rashness. It likely gave us an advantage at times.

"When the assassination failed, I knew I had to have leverage. From the moment they consummated, Yessica was a target."

"How many captives do you have?"

"Tsk, tsk, tsk. Wouldn't you like to know?" She got up. "I think I have divulged enough of my tactics for a day. Mull them over, why don't you? Let me know how foolish you feel when you realize how many of you have been eating out of the palm of my hand for centuries and this is not even the half of it."

She brushed her hand through my hair. "You smell atrocious. I will have to clean you up before Yanni will consider consummating with the likes of you."

"I will never!"

"Do not worry about that dear child, Esther can possess your side of the exchange."

Then she glided out of the room, turning off the lights and leaving me with much to think about. My body was dry heaving with disgust at the very thought of consummating with a possessed Olly. I had to believe she was telling the truth, that she would take those measures and that this was the tip of the iceberg. Although she liked to boast, I was aware she would not share anything that she really kept close. My imagination was running wild. I was grateful for the distraction and terrified of the actualizations that may transpire.

"So how do we know when you should try again? Right now?"

"Were you able to recover right after your episodes?" Zavier asked.

I shook my head. "Sometimes it would take nearly a day for me to come to. But we don't have that type of time."

"How would Yanni be able to slip in so frequently, unless he just waited in the in-between?" Rand suggested.

"So, you want Apollo to enter the threshold and wait?" Sorcey clarified.

"I am willing to do what I must."

"Of course you are, but then how will you do that and also tell me all that I need to know in order to fix this when I recover my body?"

"She has a point, Apollo," Rand agreed.

"And it should be you who tells her." Zavier looked at me sympathetically. "In case she has questions that only you can answer."

I was about to demand answers when a female voice with an indistinct accent called out. "Rand, I believe your work here is done. It's time to come home to me."

"Carissa?" Rand's eyes lit up as he looked over my head, to the River Tins. I turned to see a stunning woman in a maroon sundress. She had short golden blonde hair and pale pink skin, nothing like I had pictured her. Rand stepped around me and ran to his wife, sweeping her up into his arms and kissing her all over her face, neck and then firmly on the lips. I looked away when the kiss got a lot more passionate.

I closed my eyes to hold back the tears, because I knew what was coming next and I wanted more than anything to be happy for Rand and his reunion. But I was also terribly sad, because I hoped it would be a long time before I would see him again.

"There is someone you must meet," Rand insisted.

I swallowed hard and wiped away the tears as they approached.

"Carissa, this is Miss Ophelia. Miss Ophelia, this is my Vixen, my Carissa."

She immediately pulled me in for a hug. "Ophelia, it is a pleasure to meet you." She kissed my cheek. "I feel as though we know one another already."

I wished I could say the same. It was kind of odd to realize these people all knew me, because of whatever wisdom that came from the River Tins and the finality of death, while I knew very little about them.

"Rand speaks so highly of you. He has missed you in the deepest way." That was a truth I could speak to. Carissa released me and stepped back to be beside her Atoa, admiring every inch of him. "Thank you for sharing him with me."

And with that, the tears began to fall. There was no holding them back. Rand mirrored my grief.

"I hate farewells," he mumbled as he stepped closer and took me in his arms. "You have been like a daughter to me."

I was sobbing. Rand was my ever-vigilant hero. He had saved my life on multiple occasions. He saw me, loved me, and held space for me in ways that no one has ever done before. I thought of our first meeting in Hafiza. He was so eccentric, so animated and bizarre, it was hard not to fall in love with him right away.

"I love you," I managed between sobs, with my head buried in his shoulder, squeezing him tighter than ever before.

"I love you." He put his hand on the back of my head and held it, while gently stroking my hair. My chest shook between gasps of air and the words I couldn't formulate. I don't know how long we stood there, but when the grief subsided, I slowly pulled away.

"We will meet again."

"I am certain of it." He leaned in and kissed my cheek. "But do me a favor. Make sure our next meeting is not in the near future. And do take care of my boy for me."

The tears started again. This time Sorcey pulled me in to console me and I watched with a mixture of joy, gratitude and heartbreak as Carissa and Rand stepped into the River Tins and washed away.

LUCAS

I'd been gone for an hour. I approached the Haven sweaty and feeling much more composed. I would shower and talk to Yesi, let her know I understood why she did it. Because the truth was, I did. She wanted me to stay alive and she knows me better than anyone else. When I get locked in on something, I can get lost in my impulses. But I'd never do anything to harm her or put her in potential danger. I entered the nasty building and suddenly realized I didn't know if the door would be open for me.

I stood looking at the rank hole I needed to jump into. "Here goes nothing." I stepped in and landed on a pile of shit. "Fuck!"

Suddenly Ruit appeared. "My apologies. Let me get the door for you." He pulled me up slightly and to the left, a minimal falling sensation, and I was in the living room. Ruit was standing across from me. "I did not know when you would return. It didn't seem safe to leave it open."

I brushed myself off as best I could. "Yeah, I get it." I moved past him.

"Lucas, are we...okay?"

I stopped. I wanted to be mad, but I respected the guy too much.

Shit, I had to admit I liked his style. He was cunning and ruthless—he reminded me of me. "Yeah, we're good."

Then I was down the hall, ready to face my next swindler. She was lying on the bed, still dealing with bouts of exhaustion. The sight of her so weak only softened me that much more.

"How mad are you?"

"The maddest," I teased.

She sat up as I approached. "No, really?"

I crawled in beside her and lay my head on her belly. "I'm already over it. I know why you did it. I'm not exactly easy to work with."

"I can't lose you," she whispered as a tear fell from her cheek onto my forehead.

I sat up and kissed her nose. "I know. I can't lose you." I held up my palm to show where the cut had almost healed. She did the same. "This is just a not-so-subtle reminder for me to keep my cool and choose calculated moves."

Her shoulders relaxed and she pulled me in for a long, hard kiss.

"You taste like sweat and you smell like garbage."

"Thanks." I laughed. "I didn't quite make it into the Haven on my first attempt."

"Can I wash you up?"

"You bet your sweet ass you can."

She giggled as she jumped off the bed and ran into the bathroom.

***

YESSICA and I'd made love, and she was back to needing rest. I was ready to finally have the conversation I'd been avoiding with dear old Dad. Vosega and Oya had a room on the opposite side of the Haven. I knocked and Vosega answered.

"Can I talk to you for a minute?"

He looked over his shoulder, then shut the door. "Do we need privacy?"

"Not really, but I thought you should know I traced the hit on our family to a hobgoblin named Clive." Vosega's eyes got big and welled with tears. "And yes, that is the name of the Oracle's creepy-looking sidekick."

Vosega grabbed me and pulled me in tight. "Thank you, son." His tears were getting all over my shoulder and shirt. I wanted to pull away but instead I hugged him back, which only made him cry more. "I love you. I have always loved you."

I let my shoulders soften slightly. *What am I resisting anyway?* I wasn't a child, and we were at war. More Conduits were going to die. *Will I be able to forgive myself if I don't just let this go?*

I wasn't ready to say I love you too, but I didn't pull away. "Thanks," was the best I could muster, but hey, it was something.

ESTHER

"**W**hy would she lie to me about Clive's mission?" I looked up into Yanni's eyes as I lay on his exposed belly. He'd been lucid for a few hours now and I was grateful for it.

"Fear not, goddess. The Oracle can be evasive at times."

I sat up. "You believe she lies often?"

"Would that be a great surprise?"

I looked at him. There was no honor among thieves. I was, after all, known for my double-handedness among the Nebas. I thrived on their fear of me. I have kept her secrets, built her empire on my back. That must warrant honesty.

Yanni brushed the hair from my face. "Beloved, the Oracle has her methods. You will come to understand them when she is ready to share."

I lay back down. "Perhaps you are right." But something wasn't settling well with me. Either Aurora chose secrecy often with me and this was nothing out of the ordinary, I was just simply becoming aware of her covertness, or she desired to keep something from me that I would object to. I looked up at the now familiar face of my beloved. And there was only one thing I would protest to—anything that would risk me losing him again.

"It will all come out in due time."

"Do you really believe that? What if she has been deceptive all along? She must know about the birthmarks. Could she be our villain, my love?" But as soon as I asked the question, it was as though the accusation dissolved, leaving a vague shadow of a thought that I could no longer grasp in its wake.

"What did you say?"

I shook my head. "I do not remember."

"I should get back to the courtyard and practicing. Will you escort me?"

"I can think of nothing better to do." I kissed his belly and stood up to get dressed. We walked in silence to the courtyard. Once I saw he was focused, I excused myself. I wanted to talk to Nestor, see if he had any insights into this shared trait. As far as I knew, that was the only thing we had in common. Certainly, we both enjoyed torturous tactics, but he took his work to a very different level. I preferred to keep sexual torment out of my toolbox. Nestor thrived on that energy. It was his nature, after all. He is an Incubus.

I assumed he was down in the dungeon. I walked down the hall attempting to exude all the confidence I could muster. I used to rule this compound, dominate these idiots that now belligerently ran into me. I wondered if it was on purpose. *Are they testing the pecking order, the chain of command? Or perhaps the Oracle spread some order in secret, urging them to antagonize me?* Maybe even bait me into battle so that they may try and kill me and she could choose someone she felt would be a better second-in-command. I sneered at everyone I made eye contact with and hissed at those who were brazen enough to bump into me.

"Mistress." Astrid's voice carried off the walls. "The Oracle calls."

"Please let the queen know I am in route."

Everyone immediately got out of my way. It was both pleasant and infuriating. Only when they knew I was being beckoned did they show me the proper respect. So many had arrived in just over a day, I wondered how many more we could expect. I'd be outlining our battle strategy for the upcoming attack in a little over an hour.

This was a Haven of my making. I knew her the best. Chernobyl honored me more than any other. Aurora's door loomed in the distance. My stomach twisted in knots. Of late, I was loathing every one of our interactions.

The door opened just before I reached it. "Come in quickly and shut the door."

I obeyed and found Clive and the Oracle standing beside one another on the other side of the room.

"How is our little sickling?"

"He is recovering and already back to harnessing his abilities." I had to force myself to not spit the words.

"Very good." Aurora moved so that she was sitting on her bed. A giant mirror leaned against the adjacent wall and I could see all of the Rittles in their secure places in the reflection. "We must clear the air between us, Esther. It is not good for us to be soured by bad blood. It could cause dissension."

"I agree." *But what can we do to clear the air?*

"I have been harsh, impatient with you and Yanni. For that I am sorry."

The globe lit up ever so slightly in the reflection, validating what I already knew—she wasn't sorry at all. *Why the games?*

"Yanni and I have been disappointing you. I understand your frustrations." I did. I might have already killed me if I were her.

"Clive and I have been discussing it. We think it is best if you work with Yanni exclusively. Help him manage his gifts. Perhaps your abilities can assist him in his progress. Have you tried snatching his body yet?"

"Yes. It was empty."

"You must try harder, don't you think?"

"It stands to reason that it's worth a shot." *Why hadn't I?* Because it was my beloved in there, and he hated when I did that.

"Perfect." She adjusted herself onto the bed, lying down and propping herself up with her elbow. "I will lead the strategy meeting. You will assist Yanni from this moment on. He is not to leave your sight."

I nodded. I should be pleased with this charge, but there was more insinuated in the statement. I sensed it. I wanted to leave the room before I found out. Still, something nudged me to ask the question. I needed to validate the suspicion that was nagging at me. "Before I go, do you know anything about a birthmark on Ophelia's inner thigh? It bears similarities to one I have on my body." I chose not to reveal that I knew Nestor also bore the mark.

"Why would I know anything about birthmarks?" The globe lit up a deep, dark blue. "Certainly, I have more on my plate than to catalogue freckles." Her agitation seethed through.

"Of course." I clenched my jaw. One more confirmation of her games, *but to what end?*

"You irritate me, and after we had such a pleasant exchange. Get out of my sight." She waved her hand in disgust.

I turned to leave, my fingers on the knob when she spoke up once more. My skin crawled, aware that this was the implied statement I wanted to avoid. "Esther, if your father or Ophelia returns to that body again, you will seize control and never—I mean never—release your charge. Or I will dismember the Sulu myself, it is of no use to me if we do not have the upper hand. Am I clear?"

I nodded, but did not turn around, afraid my rage would get the better of me. *This is how she expected me to make the Sulu cooperate.*

OPHELIA

I just stared at the banks of the River Tins, letting my mind get swept away by the rainbow current. It was a healthy distraction from the pain. I could hear the three of them whispering behind me, deciding what to do next, no doubt.

I needed the grief to pass for me to think straight, for me to actually contribute to any further strategy. As I sat there, I realized that I'd been flooded by grief, anxiety or fear for months now. My past life of being a psychologist played in the background, listing off all the reasons why constant emotional flooding was causing me to shut down. Reeking havoc on my nervous system. Logically, I understood why my brain was foggy and why it felt disconnected. It was chemically unbalanced and dysregulated.

Get it together, Olly! I scolded myself. I wasn't some woman who was combatting stress. *I was the fucking Sulu! Act like it!* I got to my feet, shook off all of the pain and anguish that trailed after deep loss, and decided to get my head back in the game. I had more loved ones to save and I was fortunate enough to get a true goodbye with Rand. That was more than anyone else got. I was blessed.

"Are you stepping into that black hole to wait for your next opportunity at communication with Esther or are you going to give me some answers before I am sucked back into my body to fight the good fight and save the world?"

"Right." Apollo looked at his cohorts. "I think it is best if I enter the threshold and wait for another opportunity. Sorcey and Zavier will fill you in on all that they know, and I will return with enough time to answer any further questions."

"You're sure you'll be back?"

"No, but I am certain that Sorcey and Zavier understand enough of what happened during Aurora's years in captivity to explain where it all went wrong." Apollo grabbed my shoulders. "There isn't enough time to explain how horrific I feel for the events that transpired. But they can help you accumulate the facts. The peculiar thing about the River Tins is, the whole story is not divulged until all participants have entered the River."

"So, what does that mean?"

Sorcey answered. "It means we can't see all of the Oracle's part, we cannot see her solitary strokes, but we can see enough of her collaborative strokes to help you understand what transpired."

"I needn't waste any more time." Apollo cupped my face with his hand and then quickly stepped into the dark door's abyss.

LUCAS

"*L*ucas, I need your help mapping out Chernobyl, and we will need to spend some time perfecting the seal that you will need to extend to Ophelia, securing her in her body. We are fortunate that you share the bond with the charm and you are a shield—the strokes were in our favor."

Borte sniggered. "Of course you need his help. He is the only one of us who has played both sides."

The Khan looked at his wife disapprovingly but said nothing. Yessica stepped forward as though she was going to defend my honor but before she could, dear old Dad took a shot.

"Listen here, you bitter woman, you will respect my son." He threw a fist down on the table that we all stood around.

"Hey, listen, I can take Borte's shit. Besides, she's right. I have played both sides and now I finally get to use it to our advantage." Which is why I got caught up in that mess to begin with. A part of me was grateful I would finally get to give Esther and her thugs the fucking finger.

Oya took her place by Vosega and surprised me when she said. "Mr. and Mrs. Khan, it was quite peculiar the way the two of you were able to stay in the public eye while the rest of us scurried through the shadows during the assassinations. Tell me, how did you manage that? Did you play both sides?"

Wow, thanks, Oya. I nodded and smiled at the woman. That was appreciated.

"Father, certainly you can explain this." Yesi looked at the Khan with such curiosity it made my heart melt.

"Borijin! We owe no one here an explanation. Our business was with the powries. The Nebas are not the only power on this planet."

"None of us is innocent here." Ruit stated matter-of-factly. "We all have blood on our hands. It will serve us all better if we stop pointing fingers and start locking arms."

The room got shamefully silent. *He is good, too good.*

"Helia, your mother was the greatest strategist I have ever known. I trust that you studied beneath her."

"I did. It was an honor."

"Then you will honor us and work with the Khan creating detailed tactical maneuvers, we need to evacuate the captives. We will have a better idea of our true numbers by this evening." They both nodded and moved to a corner of the table to discuss battle plans.

"Borte, you will work with Moira and see if the markings give you any further information."

The wicked woman opened her mouth to object but decided not to. Unbecoming of her, but welcome, nonetheless.

Ruit pulled out a list from a pocket inside his coat. "Vosega, Oya, I need all of the ingredients on this list as soon as possible." It was nice to have someone else on grocery shopping duty.

Oya took the list and the two of them were out the door before another word was spoken. I wondered as I watched them leave what the fine people of Australia would think of the two pelt-wearing neanderthal types perusing the aisles at the local market.

"What about me?" Yesi looked inquisitively at Ruit.

"You have a very special job, my dear. You see, you must rest because before we leave this Haven, I intend to experiment with a few concoctions that may or may not cure your condition. I need you as physically prepared for whatever happens as possible."

I looked at Ruit like he had gone crazy, because he clearly had. I would not let my wife be his little lab rat.

"Rest does sound good," she agreed. "I will be ready to try anything you need me to once I have taken a few moments."

"Take all the time you need."

She walked over and kissed me gently before heading toward our room.

"I won't let you poke holes in her like she's a little white mouse in a cage."

"I wouldn't dream of that," he said in hushed tones. "She needs her rest, and the minor tests I will perform later will only help rule a few things out and give her purpose here as well."

I just nodded. She needed purpose too.

I HAD DONE my best mapping the compound. It was by no means comprehensive, but it was better than nothing. Or at least that was what Ruit told me. Now we were in the basement, working on the seal.

"Do you feel the tether?"

"Not really." I was trying to find the hairsy charm in my shield, but it just wasn't there.

"It is there, I assure you. I can see it."

"Well, how the fuck can you see it but I can't fucking feel it?"

"Expand your shield out, encompass the Haven. Try and detect it from a greater perspective."

I pushed my shield out, first out of this room, then out of the kitchen, into the living room, up through the entrance...when I felt something. "Someone is coming."

"What do you mean? Vosega and Oya have already returned."

"I know. But it's a Soahcoit and they are entering the Haven grounds."

Ruit and I scrambled up the stairs and entered the living room just as two Conduits appeared before us. The female looked vaguely familiar, but I couldn't place her as friend or foe. The rest of our company were now also on guard and at our backs to greet our unannounced guests.

The man stepped forward, shielding the woman with his body. He was tall and well-built, with sandy-blonde hair and a thick but closely trimmed beard. "I am Garrett and this is Vita. We have come to return something that is yours, great Alchemist."

Vita peered around her partner, making eye contact with me before locking eyes with Ruit. Her name sounded familiar too.

Vita pulled a chain from around her neck that was previously hidden under her shirt. A copper coin dangled from the necklace. I recognized that piece. It was Huan's. Ruit stepped forward.

"That was my son's. Where on earth did you get it?"

"He gave it to me when he saved my life." The Alchemist walked toward Vita with slow, deliberate steps. My mind replayed scenario after scenario, trying to place the name and the face before me.

Then it hit me. "Vita, you were the one Huan saved before he was murdered, right? Saving you exposed his agenda."

She nodded solemnly as tears streamed down her cheeks. Ruit got close enough to take the necklace and instead, he took the woman up in his arms. "Vita," he repeated as he held her close while they both cried.

I counted the minutes, quite literally. It was all I could do to measure time.

They did not need me, for anything other than to consummate with Ophelia's body. A thought I found entirely repulsive right now, considering the circumstances. *Would I be able to prevent that from happening?*

Aurora quietly entered the room. "I am not sure you are still of any use to me alive, Viraclay. We have your Atoa, I do not know that we really need her to be consummated." As though she was answering my question.

"But you keep captives now."

She laughed. "I would like to think of it as more of my personal armory." She stroked the hair from my face. "I have never seen your hair so long. It suits you. It reminds me of your father when he was young."

I had to fight back the impulse to lunge at her. It would do no good. I was still chained. She continued. "I kept notes on which Conduits accelerated my gifts the most effectively. Or the ones who amplified and stirred new abilities. Imagine, if two Conduits could fuel Sulu strength, what will twelve Conduits do?"

"You have twelve captive Conduits?"

She laughed again and ignored my question. "The problem is I need Yanni to learn how to manage Ophelia's body, or I require that he vacate the premises so that Esther can wield her properly."

"Esther would never concede to that." I said it more to myself than for the all-knowing Oracle.

"Correct. So I suppose we will see who the strokes will favor."

"Why would you tell me this? What is your play?" I was tired of being her pawn and it had become abundantly clear I played into her hands all too easily over the years.

"This will be the determination of the value of your life, dead or alive. I need you to reach out to Ophelia in any way you can. With your Rune, perhaps when I parade Yanni through here. Surely you would rather her be a prisoner in my company than a hostage of Yanni in her own body?"

"Those are no options at all."

"Suit yourself. I will give you until the end of today to consider my proposal."

"Garrett and I answered the call to The Cathedral. I had hoped you were there, great Alchemist, so that I may return what was so graciously given to me." We all sat around the dining room table now, even Moira, listening to Vita explain why they had come and how they had found us. "When we met Aremis and explained our agenda, he sent us here."

"Certainly, I could have received Huan's Loktpi when we convened at The Cathedral. You did not need to come all this way. Or perhaps you could have given it to my wife for safekeeping. I am grateful. I only wish you had not left the sanctuary of The Cathedral for this."

"That is not all we bring." Garrett pulled a long tube of paper from behind his back. "I am a Codex."

"I give up. What's that?" Helia prompted. *I like this woman.*

"I collect and file data so that it can be organized in a logical way for further use."

What a mundane gift.

"As you know," Vita looked directly at me, "I was a captive of the Nebas for years. I am a Rumor Mill. I take the truth and distort it. They used me to keep the captives secret. I am one of the few who can confirm there are many prisoners in Chernobyl. They wanted everyone, including their own operatives, to believe that there were no survivors, that all those the Nebas hunted were killed. They did that so that there was no great uprising or storming of the compound. This meant I heard the truths from thousands of the Nebas for hundreds of years. This included information about the compound itself. The various chambers, secret tunnels, any special equipment, and even some of the wards and protections. I depicted all that I learned to Garrett, and together we recreated this."

Garrett rolled out the paper onto the table. A series of sighs, utterances and awes followed. It was a detailed blueprint of the Chernobyl Compound. This was better than any intel we could've dreamed of. This was a real chance at victory.

OPHELIA

"The story we can piece together for you is not an easy one to tell," Zavier admitted. "Where to begin?"

"At the beginning?"

"If only it were that easy." Sorcey shook her head. "I think we should start with her supposed captivity. It is the story that will serve Ophelia best when she is returned to her body. It will help you to understand the greatness of the Oracle's power."

"Very well, but it is more your story to tell, as I was not there."

I sat down while Zavier paced and Sorcey rocked gently back and forth. It was unnerving how much anxiety this brought them.

"I will start with the tale we were woven to believe, because you must understand this before you will be able to convince anyone of the truth. Cane and I were notified of Cadmael's demise at the hand of Apollo as we sat in our home in what is now considered Patagonia. News travelled differently then. There were few secrets; there was no need for them. And to hear of this atrocity was devastating. There had not been a death of a Conduit since the tragic Katuan Trials and the fall of Atlantis. I remember how we sat staring at each other in utter disbelief.

"'We must see to what has happened at once,' Cane insisted. But something in me did not sit right, even then. I had a secret; one I had not even shared with my husband. Still, I kept it to myself, afraid of how it would devastate Aurora if I were to expose a truth that was not my own. Besides, now she was suffering the loss of her Atoa, could there be anything more terrible to endure? Cane and I agreed to travel to what is now known as Eastern Europe to console Aurora and figure out what had happened. How did Aurora not foretell of his death? There must be justice for Cadmael.

"When we arrived, we were met by Aphrodite, who informed us that she and Walthrup determined that the Oracle had been taken.

"When Cane asked where and by whom, Walthrup explained that the whispers indicated she was Apollo's captive at Delphi.

"Di and Cane were prepared to act immediately and perhaps we should have. Maybe it would have stopped the bloodshed that would follow."

Zavier put his hand on Sorcey's shoulder. "You couldn't have known. No one could have."

"Knowing what I knew then and what I know now, I should have told my husband of my unease about the incident."

Zavier nodded. "We all have regrets." He looked at me apologetically.

"The four of us called a Paksyon together to consider what we should do about the Oracle and Apollo. A small group decided to visit Delphi to confirm that she was indeed there against her will. It was relayed to us after their meeting that Aurora appeared to be there of her own volition. They witnessed no bondage, no animosity, and she participated in a small Covening while they were at the temple. Di and Cane were not satisfied with this observation, but maleficence was so far removed from our nature that it was difficult for any of us to believe that Apollo was actually harming another Conduit. At the time, the group reported that Aurora excused Cadmael's death as an accident, describing a regrettable event where their home caught fire and she was fortunate enough to be saved by Apollo."

Sorcey began to pace now, as well.

"This is where the stories become increasingly convoluted and distorted. As years passed by and the human world began to pay more and more homage to the Oracle of Delphi, so did the Conduit world turn to her guidance. There were whispers once more, that Aurora was in fact a captive all along, being dictated by the daughter of Apollo, Esther—the powerful Body Snatcher. Surely, with Esther's gifts, she could possess the Oracle and make her appear cooperative and there of her own free will. Esther could perhaps even force Aurora to lie about what really happened to her Atoa. Nevertheless, the hoards still visited the temple, seeking the wisdom and the power of the Oracle. They desired the unique experience of engaging in a Sulu Covening—a novelty for Conduits who rarely experienced anything new anymore."

"It seems appropriate that Conduits would have their suspicions. Esther is very powerful. She can make anyone do anything," I agreed.

"Can she though?"

"She had Aremis kill his own wife, so yes, she can possess anyone do any horrible thing she would like," I argued. It wasn't that I believed the Oracle was innocent. I'd seen her kill Di with my own two eyes. But maybe it was this incident, this betrayal by her people, that led her to the dark side.

"Can she make them speak?"

I really considered the question. I'd never seen anyone that Esther commanded speak. "I don't know."

"The answer, though none of us would know it until we reached the River Tins, is no. She cannot. She seizes control of their body, their gifts…not their mind."

"But why would the Oracle run when Di freed her if she wasn't a captive?"

"Clive."

"She ran from Clive?"

"She ran to him."

"I'm admittedly lost."

"Bear with me, because this part takes some piecing together of facts. Just before Atlantis fell during the last Katuan Trials, Aurora, Cadmael and Clive had appeared on the island. This is where our strokes are limited because the Oracle has not been swept into the River Tins. Clive and Aurora share a special bond. As far as we know, she is the only Conduit to ever engage with a hobgoblin. They communicate through minor glimpses of the future. Their true story is unknown, but what has come to light is that hobgoblins are some of the most powerful creatures in the strokes. Clive is the last of his kind. His clan was wiped out just after he and Aurora met. They are creatures that syphon magic from other beings, even objects. Because of this, they accrue more power and greater gifts than anyone could have realized. It is now known that Cadmael was put under some spell to control his every move, as was Jolena."

"Jolena?"

"To tell you the whole story would take too much time, indeed. Jolena was Yilliana's, the great Alchemist of the times, Atoa. Jolena attempted to kill her Atoa when she was not in her right mind. We know from Cadmael's strokes that Aurora killed him, not Apollo."

I was trying to follow this train of thought. "So, you believe that Clive was controlling Aurora when she did this?"

"Perhaps, or…" Suddenly her words trailed off as I was being tugged into the ethereal in-between. I landed with a jarring but familiar sensation in the body of Moira.

LUCAS

Moira's body twitched and I could tell instantly that it was Ophelia. "Olly!"

Her eyes opened and she looked straight at me. "That is so disorientating."

"But you're okay?"

"Yeah. Yeah, I am okay. You're not going to believe what I'm learning."

Ruit interrupted her. "Sorry, Ophelia, but we don't have much time. Moira is still struggling to maintain her connection."

"Of course. Is Elias okay? My mom? Lilith?"

"As far as we know, nothing has changed," I assured her. Ruit gave me a warning glare.

"We called on you because we need you to burn this image into your memory. It is the detailed plans of the compound. It will ensure your survival and the survival of all those you love."

Way to put on the pressure. He didn't need to lay it on so thick. The drawing was already laid out in front of her, on the floor. She knelt down and examined it intently.

"I feel foggy in the in-between. What if I lose my memory when I get reinstated back into my body?"

She had a good point.

"We will have to hope for the best. I will do my best to relay it to you once more when you return to your body, and we may use our Runes again. That circle indicates where we believe Elias is being held."

"And my mother?"

"Leave them up to me." I hoped she could feel my dedication. "I won't let you down. You just do whatever Ruit tells you to do."

His body was catatonic, but he attempted to reassure her with his words. "We are going to get everyone out unharmed. The next time we call on you will be the moment you need to strike. There can be no hesitation. Get to Elias and get out. Anything else you need to know will be parlayed when we resurrect you. Do you understand?"

"Perfectly." She was still studying the blueprint. "I can feel the tug. Moira is coming back."

"Olly, I love you!" I shouted the words as Moira's body went limp.

ESTHER

I was doing exactly as Aurora had ordered. I hadn't left his side. Which meant I would have to question Nestor after the imminent threat was over. I heard unintelligible murmurs of the strategy meeting in the courtyard, and from the intermittent cheers I deduced she came up with a suitable action plan. *Although, what would those idiots know about military tactics?* Aurora may have been pulling strings in the shadows, but I was the strategist. I was the one who deployed the right weapon at the right time. The Oracle may find herself at a disadvantage when it comes to the art of war.

Did I really care about that? I looked at Yanni, who was doing everything he could to obey her orders, to do better. I considered all that we had already lost. *Am I willing to lose anything else? Do I have the choice?* I waved at him, and he waved back.

"My beloved, how are you faring in there?"

"I will master this body as I have mastered all powerful things." He leapt in front of me playfully and pulled me in for a kiss. Then his body stiffened and collapsed in that now-familiar way.

His eyes closed, then opened abruptly, but they were once again not his. They were my father's. Panic surged through me. *Where is the Oracle? Will she see this exchange once more?*

"Este, there—"

"Shhhh. You risk both of our lives."

"There is something you must know about the Oracle." He had hushed his tone, but that meant very little. Aurora could be seeing this exchange right now with her sight. *What should I do?*

"You must vacate this body and not return. She will kill us."

"The answers are in front of you. The birth—"

I heard the footsteps. I didn't care who it was. I seized control of the Sulu's body, cutting off Apollo's warning. When my energy entered the Sulu, I felt a wave of power surge through me. I had never encountered anything like it before. It was wild, like a storm. A strange echo vibrated through my consciousness. It sounded like my father. But the voice was fading too quickly. All I could make out was "...nothing is as it seems." Then I was back in the deep vacancy of the Sulu's form. There was nothing there, but everything all at once.

I was discombobulated, but grateful I had decided to act when Aurora turned the corner. I waited in silent anticipation, hoping she would disclose her business quickly.

Meanwhile, the power in the Sulu's body was making me dizzy. I couldn't harness it.

"He is incapacitated? What is happening? Did Apollo return?" She walked over to me slowly, sizing up my mood. Clive was right behind her.

"I tried to take control of his body as you requested, and this is what happened."

"What a waste. How long was he out after the last episode?"

"I-I..." I couldn't think and continue to command control. I released the hold and held my breath. Yanni's eyes stayed shut.

"Come out with it, Esther! You infuriate me. Are you trying to infuriate me now?"

By the way she was reacting, I could assume she had not detected the interaction with my father. "I was thinking. Hours. The last episode took him hours to recover from."

"We have two days before the compound is attacked by our

enemy. We haven't the time for this. When he comes to, bring him to me. I desire some information from your dearest."

"Certainly," I said through bared teeth.

They swiftly left the room, and I let my head fall on Ophelia's chest. "You occupied my body. You know I hate that," Yanni mumbled.

I laughed with relief. "It is a mess in there."

"Now you understand why I am not more adept." He tried to sit up and I pushed him back down.

"Please, my beloved, stay lying down. Recover your strength."

"Because I am incapacitated or because Aurora desires my company?"

"Both." He looked up at me with the eyes I loved but through a lens of exhaustion. I wanted to run away with him. "What if we ran away?"

"Then she would find us."

"There is something about this body. It creates holes in her vision. We could use it to our advantage."

"She would find us, or the Pai Ona would."

"My father came through again."

"What did he say?"

"Not to trust her, and I believe he was going to report something about our birthmark."

Yanni's eyes got wide, and I leaned in and hugged him, holding him as tight as I could. Realizing it was likely that these moments were numbered.

OPHELIA

*S*orcey and Zavier stood on either side of me and pulled me to my feet. "And this time, where were you off to?"

"I was back in Moira's basement. The next time they call on me, it will be the last. I don't know how much time that gives us. What about Apollo?"

I looked at the black door.

"He has yet to return," Zavier answered.

"Do you need to sit down, dear? It must be disorientating." Sorcey pulled up the chair.

It was, but I didn't feel like I had the time to recover. "Where were we?" I look up at her expectantly.

"Give yourself a moment, Ophelia. We have a moment."

"Do not be so sure of that," Apollo warned as he walked towards us from the row of doors.

"What did you discover?"

"Not much, and my warning was interrupted once more. But there is something stirring in my daughter's eyes. I don't know what she will do next."

"What does that mean?" Anxiety gripped me. *Is she going to dismantle my body?*

199

"She is getting desperate, and the Oracle is threatening her, so much so that she took over your body to keep me quiet—afraid Aurora would kill them both. Things are unraveling fast."

"And you did not get your message across?" Sorcey asked.

"I do not believe I did." He looked at me. "I have failed you. But I must at the very least explain what truly transpired at Delphi."

He had my full attention.

ELIAS

I mulled over Aurora's proposition for hours. A proposition that did not necessarily promise any outcome. There were multiple scenarios here and I did not care for any of them, except for the plan Ruit had in play. Considering that there were numerous things I did not know about how they intended to execute their siege or install Ophelia back into her body, I had to evaluate the options before me carefully.

Aurora desired Olly to resume control of her body so that Esther could anchor into her powers and utilize them against the Pai Ona and facilitate a massive Sulu that would be controlled by the Oracle. To help Aurora accomplish this felt like the greatest betrayal I could ever conduct against my people. But to allow Ophelia to live in some unknown abyss or limbo while Yanni occupied her body— how could I live with that, knowing I may have an opportunity to give her a fighting chance at resuming her life? I also had to believe that ultimately there would come a time when the Oracle would desire me and Olly to consummate to unleash the greatest amount of power the Sulu could offer. *Or perhaps she is afraid of what Olly is capable of if she reaches her fullest potential?*

Sensing that the Nebas' leadership was self-cannibalizing was useful. Aurora was already turning on Esther. *What would Esther do if she knew that the Oracle was trying to exorcise Yanni from Olly's body? Would it be enough for Esther to switch teams, align with the Pai Ona? Or would she run away with Ophelia's body so that I may never see her again?* Exposing this truth to Esther hung on her believing me, and I had no reason to think she would.

If I were to consider Aurora's proposition, *how can I break through to Ophelia? What do I know about her episodes, how to invoke them?* Because it was the episodes that weakened her, allowing Yanni to possess her. *But if Yanni could not manage the Sulu's power, then he could not be overwhelmed by them. Or was I missing something?*

The door flew open. It meant another day was through, which brought me one more day closer to Ruit's plan being realized. I shut down the thoughts and focused on the silhouettes in the threshold.

"Where do you stand?" Aurora placed a lit torch on the wall and approached, Clive behind her.

"I think what you are asking is impossible. But for Olly, I would do anything." The truth was I just wanted to see her once more. I did not think I could invoke her spirit to reclaim her body, but I could see her, see that she was okay.

Aurora flicked her wrist and Clive left the room, returning moments later with Esther and Yanni in tow.

"What is this about? Viraclay has nothing to give us. I tried everything I could." Esther held Olly's hand as they entered and she protested. The sight made me sick to my stomach.

"We must see how fortified Yanni's spirit is in the Sulu's body."

"What?!" Esther stepped in front of Ophelia. "What are you going to do?"

"She has been in front of Viraclay before and Yanni did not falter. Calm yourself, Esther!"

"This is unacceptable. He has already been…" Her words trailed off, but she had said enough for me to draw valuable conclusions. *Yanni has been having more episodes.*

"Just be ready for anything. You know what you have to do if he cannot maintain composure," Aurora hissed at Esther. The rage in

Esther's eyes was beyond anything I had witnessed before. She wanted to kill the Oracle. Perhaps I could reason with her. But we both wanted the same body. *How can we align with each other?*

"Well, Viraclay, all eyes are on you, dear boy."

My skin crawled. I loathed the way she said 'dear boy' to me. *What am I to do?* If I knew how to reach Olly, I would have already. *It was time to put on a show.*

"Ophelia. Olly, if you are in there, if you can hear me, please, please, I beg you, present yourself."

Yanni laughed.

"I know you are in there. You have to fight."

"This is it? This is what you dragged us down here for?" Esther sneered. But there was more in her expression. She was scared.

I continued. "Feel my Rune, feel our connection. Remember who you are."

"Give him to me." Aurora pulled on Yanni's arm, yanking him away from Esther. "Touch her."

I reached up with my shackled arms and caressed Olly's face. Yanni grimaced at me and snapped at my hand with his teeth. Aurora quickly smacked him in the back of the head, silently ordering him to comply.

Touching her face gave me no solace. Everything about her aura felt cold—unlike my Olly's.

"Kiss her."

Both Yanni and I looked at the Oracle in disgust.

"Kiss her now!"

Esther stepped closer, wanting to object but refraining.

I leaned in, while Yanni closed his eyes, stiffened his mouth and let me place my lips on his. Ophelia was not there. Her essence was completely absent. My heart ached with that deep loss. She was not of this world. She was not in this body. *How can she ever return?*

"Enough!" the Oracle demanded. "Get out of here!"

Esther and Yanni quickly exited without a word.

Aurora got very close to my face and whispered in my ear, "That was a pathetic attempt." She grasped my face with her nails, digging into my skin. "I know they are coming. I know she will resume control of her body." My eyes got wide. If she knew all of this, why would she not escape the compound? "I want the Sulu returned so that I may be her captor. Esther is my pawn and your Atoa will be forever indentured to me. Know this. Whatever they are planning, I will see it first and they will fail."

"What does Esther think of this plan?"

Aurora just laughed and began to walk toward the door. "Your hours are numbered, dear boy."

LUCAS

"I have to get this fucking right!" I scolded myself.

Ruit shook his head. "Be patient. You are doing great."

"Patient? I get one shot at this. And that one shot is in less than a day."

The Alchemist walked over to where I stood and put his hand on my shoulder. "Everything else is in place. We have plenty of time to perfect the seal. You are strong…" His words drifted off.

"Thanks." I looked at him. "Are you okay?"

"You were poisoned too, just the same as your wife?"

"Yeah, but only for a few months."

"But your vitality, your force is strong. There is no residual poison in your aura. As I examine you, I cannot see any energetic signs that you were ever drugged."

"They seemed to keep me more lucid. Maybe I received more of the antidote?"

Ruit circled me again, as he did when he was looking at the hairsy charm magic. "No, something has changed since you left the last Haven, since I last inspected your frequency with the charm. I was so distracted I hadn't noticed until now. What did you do? What have you done differently than Yessica?"

"Nothing." I retraced the last few days. Then it occurred to me. "There was a moment, with Fetzle."

"The troll queen? She is the missing link. I knew it!" Ruit was ecstatic, his usually stoic demeanor broken open by unbridled excitement. "What was the moment?"

"We met so I could ask for her help, like you requested. It was an intensely emotional reunion, since she thought both my wife and I were dead. We were hugging and crying, when I finally felt like myself again. The fog just seemed to lift completely."

"Just being in her aura cured you, but not Yessica?"

That didn't sound right to me either. Then I remembered. "Her gooey, nasty tear touched my shoulder."

"Troll tears." I was concerned his eyes might bug out of his head. "It all makes sense. The dragon slayings and the war on the trolls. It was all a long game for the domination of the world. Create the disease and control the cure."

"I am not sure I'm following you, man. Slow down."

"Can you call on her? I must speak to the queen immediately."

"Yeah. Find me a tree."

"As I said, those years at Delphi were a blur. I was lost in a fuzzy bog of what I now know was some sort of mind control."

"By Esther? Your daughter?" It was my first thought. Who else had that kind of gift?

"No, by Clive and Aurora."

"The Oracle can do mind control? Why would she hold herself captive?"

"She was never a captive. I was the captive. Esther was the captive. Even Yanni was a captive."

I looked at Zavier and Sorcey, who were nodding in agreement.

"Remember, I said hobgoblins are very mysterious strokes and extremely powerful. Clive can mark a Conduit with a hex that makes them do his bidding."

"How do we know that Aurora is not a victim, just the same as the rest of you? How do you know you were marked?"

Apollo turned around and lifted his shirt. There was a small welt, crescent moon-shaped. "This is the badge of the hex. Anyone who bears it can be manipulated by Clive at any time. When you wake from his influence, you vaguely remember what happened, as though you are waking from a dream. Then any recollection fades away, and you feel as though nothing occurred at all. If you press your memories, you will feel the onset of a terrible headache."

"So, the Oracle could be hexed?"

"It is true, until she enters the River Tins, we cannot see her strokes or determine exactly how everything transpired. She may be completely unaware of what has been taking place," Zavier conceded.

But the glance shared between Apollo and Sorcey told me there was much more to the story.

"There is more."

"There is." Apollo wrung his hands together nervously. "It is difficult to know what to share next."

"Finish explaining what happened at Delphi and shortly thereafter," Sorcey suggested.

"Aphrodite came to Aurora's rescue, having believed I was the fiend who held her captive for hundreds of years. My captors played their part perfectly. Aurora's Atoa was murdered, a Ramalan seemingly confined to a temple. Clive was in the shadows during those years, going completely unnoticed, and I was known to dislike the dilution of our powers into the human populace. I had on an occasion suggested we be more particular about how and who we fraternized our strokes with."

"You were the perfect scapegoat? Hungry for power, and you didn't like Swali or mortals?"

"Let me be clear, I had experienced the enormous tragedy that could occur when Conduits engaged in relationships with others before their Atoa. My daughter Esther never knew her true mother. I witnessed the pain Aurora went through when I met Shatki. It nearly destroyed her. Instead of being honest and hurting those who were involved in my own trespasses, I conjured up a story of power and disdain that would later be my demise."

"You didn't want to hurt Aurora anymore or tell Esther who her biological mother was. Therefore, you made up a bogus reason to discourage fraternizing with each other before meeting your Atoa."

He nodded solemnly. "I did not wish to hurt those I loved. I chose secrecy over truth, and it made me an easy villain."

I can empathize with that dilemma.

"The Oracle's rescue was a fate of the strokes for me and my daughter. We were free of the spell we had been under for centuries but were now hated by many and feared by others. What was worse was that we couldn't deny or explain our actual circumstances at Delphi. A part of me believed I was the villain. Rumors escalated our reputations. Meanwhile, the Oracle went into hiding. When Conduits began missing, I could have never imagined Esther and I would be blamed for it."

"But Esther and Yanni have killed many Conduits. I have seen it."

"They have and I know that what was once mind control turned into a poison of the worst kind, lies and deception—revenge." Apollo stopped moving, growing very still. "My execution by those my daughter had seen participate in the rituals at Delphi planted a seed of rage. I once coined the phrase Nebas as meaning, pure stroke. Esther formed the Nebas out of her grief for me and with the help of Aurora."

"How do you know that if neither Esther nor Aurora have entered the River Tins?"

"It's a knowing I have deep in my heart." He put his hands to his chest and closed his eyes. "A father knows. And my daughter has lost so much. She has been defiled by loss and pain. She is hardly recognizable." He shook his head in disbelief. "My execution was the perfect catalyst for the Oracle to unite with Esther and use her as a pawn for power and revenge."

"We will know more still once Yanni's soul enters the Tins," Zavier reasoned.

"None of what you have told me is definitive evidence that Aurora isn't being manipulated by Clive. Even killing Cadmael doesn't prove that."

"This is true. We cannot and will not know this truth until we are meant to," Sorcey agreed. "However, something shifted in Aurora when she gave birth to her children."

It occurred to me they only spoke of Esther's evolution. "Where was Nestor? Who raised Nestor?"

"That is part of my secret," Sorcey said shamefully.

"And mine." Apollo stepped beside her and took her hand. "We both sheltered the wrong truth."

"So many lives have had to pay the price for our missteps." Sorcey leaned into Apollo, and he hugged her.

"I want to be patient. I want to honor that this is hard for both of you. But I'm running out of time, and I have to convince the Pai Ona that Aurora is not as she has seemed. I need to understand."

"You are right," Apollo agreed, and Sorcey composed herself.

"As I said before, this story started with love."

Fetzle looked very uncomfortable as she stood surrounded by unfamiliar faces once more. "This may sound like a very strange request, dear queen, but may I confiscate some of your tears?"

"Fetzlewantstoknowswhatsconfiscatesmeans."

"Of course. May I have one?"

Fetzle scrunched her face in a way that indicated she thought Ruit lost his mind, but she would comply. "Fetzle'sfriendsLucas-thinksthishelpsYessica?"

"Yes, Fetzle, it may help."

"OhsKay." Then she promptly poked her eye, screamed "Ouch," and a giant gelatinous tear oozed down her cheek. Ruit was right there to catch it in a large glass pitcher. Fetzle kept her eye closed while she recovered. "Nowswhats?"

Ruit walked over to Yesi, who waited expectantly. He dipped his finger in the goo and then put a small amount on the back of her neck. Immediately, there was a visible difference in her demeanor. I couldn't even see her aura and I knew she was being restored. Relief surged through me.

"Thank Chitchakor, I feel like myself." She giggled. The Khan cheered and Vosega grunted in approval as well. I kissed her all over her face and neck and shoulders, I was so grateful.

"Thank you, Fetzle! Thank you again, my dear friend!" I walked over and hugged her giant stump of a leg.

"Fetzleishappiesttohelps. NowstimetogetstinkyOpheliasandElias?"

Fetzle was a troll on a mission. I had to give her that. "Not quite yet. Tonight, we will need you back here to transport us to the compound, while the rest of your fleet transports the others." I turned to Ruit, expecting him to explain more. He had spouted off some big assertions back there about the troll war.

"We will likely need more tears, once we have recovered the rest of the prisoners. Will you and yours be able to assist?"

"Fetzlethinksyes!" She nodded her head vigorously. "Maybeslesshardofpokes. Butyes. Fetzlereturnstonights." Then she was gone.

Yesi was speaking to her father, and I was grateful to see her instant turnaround. But I had questions for the Alchemist. "Are you going to explain what all of this has to do with the troll war? And why didn't you tell Fetzle? She deserves to know."

"All in due time, Lucas."

"Can you tell me?"

He looked at the pitcher of tear, still grinning. "I believe that Aurora discovered the effect dragons' blood had on magical beings. It is quite cunning of her. Dragons are the only creature in the strokes that can incapacitate all magic, from any being. How she discovered that the only antidote was troll tears, I cannot fathom. But she did, and I believe she orchestrated the powrie attacks in an attempt to wipe out the only thing that could restore her captives to full health."

"That is a big pill to swallow."

"It is indeed, but the Nebas mobilized with the powries two thousand years ago. Why?"

"Shit..." This was so much bigger than any of us realized.

I was still enraged from that stunt Aurora pulled with Viraclay. *What if Ophelia had returned to her body?* I would have had no warning, no goodbye, no choice.

"Stop worrying so much. I am in complete control," Yanni insisted.

"But you still have not been able to properly engage with this body's power. The Oracle is up to something." It had everything to do with the lies and Clive.

"Why don't you just snatch her body, my beloved?"

I turned and looked at Yanni. It was a brilliant idea. Yet never once had I ever considered seizing control of the Ramalan's body. *Why?* I considered how I could do it, but no sooner did I think the thought than it started to dissolve. I desperately tried to grasp hold of it, but it was fleeting and then gone.

"I am sorry, what were we talking about?"

Yanni explored the recess of his mind and came up empty. "I cannot remember. But I do believe I am up for some drills. I am determined to do something with this body before the enemy arrives tomorrow.

I wanted to tell him no, that we should spend the next few hours together in our chamber entangled in each other's arms. But I didn't. I agreed to help him with this impossible task.

214

"I have regretted abandoning her the way we did for the entirety of my existence. She was such a light, such a kind-hearted soul when we were unabashedly in love. When I broke her heart, I marred her essence. Darkness befell her compassionate spirit."

"Poor Aurora." I empathized.

"Yes, poor Aurora. But my solace at the time was that I knew she would one day feel the same wholeness I was experiencing. She would meet her Atoa and all would be well. The night before I fled with Shatki, I went to Aurora. I begged her to forgive me, I even pleaded with her to continue to travel with me and Shatki—to ensure her safety until she met her other half. She fiercely denied my requests and threatened to slit both of our throats in our sleep if I didn't choose her."

I gasped. "You both were still mortal. That would have killed you."

"That is why I fled with my beloved. There was no reasoning with her, or at least that is what I told myself. I wonder now if that was cowardice. I should have known there was more to her rage." A tear cascaded down his cheek and I felt the compulsion to comfort him, but I abstained.

Sorcey comforted him once more. They had a special bond, one that her son knew nothing about. It must have changed once they knew each other's truths. They were able to connect in a new way. I wondered how Elias would feel about this when I told him.

"I wrote to Aurora months later. I used an enchanted scroll. I told her where we were and invited her to join us if she felt compelled to make amends. My heart still wanted to know she was safe. I loved her."

I thought about Lucas and my love for him, his love for me. It paled in comparison to our love for our destined partners, but it was powerful, and I desperately desired for him to be safe and happy. After all, that was what got me here.

"She never replied, but two months later a baby lay on our doorstep, with a note. It read, *'Take care of our Esther for I cannot. Keep her origins a secret. That is the least you can give me.'* I knew who it was from. I knew that penmanship well. It was the only time Aurora ever acknowledged Esther as her own. I honored her choice to not be a mother. Shatki adopted Esther without hesitation and raised her as her own until the day she died at the Katuan Trials when Atlantis fell into the sea. I kept the Oracle's secret because I was ashamed of how I broke her heart."

I was flooded with emotion, sympathy, heartache and confusion. "But that doesn't explain how you are my grandfather. Where was Nestor?"

Sorcey took my hand in hers. "This secret is mine to share, or rather another of Aurora's. I felt compelled to keep it until it was too late. As you know, I am a Healer. One night, Aurora called on me through a tether we created. We were dear friends. When I heard the panic in her voice, I knew it must be an emergency. She pleaded with me to come alone. I called in a favor I had with the troll Queen Peozleo and got there almost immediately after her summons. When I arrived, I was startled to see she was covered in blood. We had not seen each other in months. She told me through anguished sobs that she had been pregnant and that something had gone wrong during the labor. The delivery maiden had to cut her belly to save the baby. Aurora held a baby boy in her arms with wild red hair, umbilical cord still attached. She said the maiden didn't know what to do. There was too much blood, and the woman had made off shortly after making the incision. Aurora would have died that night. She was bleeding out fast. But I saved her and helped her welcome a baby boy she named Nestor."

I inhaled sharply.

"I should have asked more questions, gotten more answers. I sensed how distraught she was. I knew that there were often two delivery maidens at a birth and that it was rare for them to cut the mother to save the child—it was too risky back then—but I didn't ask about any of it. I did not even ask about the father, although I suspected it was Apollo because it was known that they had been lovers. I was just grateful my friend was alive. When she asked me three days later to take the baby and give him up for adoption, only then did I realize something was very wrong. Aurora was flat. She was not bonding with the child. I had never been a mother at that point, but I felt her coldness toward the baby. I complied with her request, and when she had me agree to never tell anyone of this incident, I vowed to keep her secret safe."

"Esther and Nestor are twins. And they know nothing of how they came into this world?"

"No, they know nothing."

"Where did you take him? How did he end up so evil?"

"I took him to a dear woman I met in the Celtic lands. His fiery hair would fit in well there." Sorcey half-heartedly smiled. "She was a sweet widow who always wanted children but never got the chance. I would go back from time to time, guised as a dear friend of the family. I knew a day would come when I would share stories of our creation with him, waiting until he was old enough to tell him the truth. Nestor was always a peculiar child. At the time, I described him as distracted. Just before his eleventh birthday, the year his adopted mother and I decided we would tell him the truth of his Conduit nature, I arrived in their village to discover that their cottage had been burned to the ground. It was believed they both were dead."

"But he survived? Where did he go?"

"No one really knows. He and his Atoa emerged shortly after the fall of Atlantis."

"So, no one knows why he's such an asshole? Great." I shook my head in disbelief. I wanted to collapse. *How could I convince the good guys and the bad guys that this whole war was being manipulated by a scorned woman?*

"There is something," Apollo interrupted my hopeless moment. "Your birthmark." I looked down at my right thigh.

"The brown spot that looks like half a heart?"

"Yes." Apollo came over and put his hand on my shoulders. I wasn't sure it was to steady me or comfort me. "All of my kin have it. I saw it on you, just as I have seen it on Esther when she was babe."

"And I witnessed it on Nestor," Sorcey admitted.

"Wonderful. I just have to get the three of us in a room, take off our pants and have a civilized conversation." My head was spinning. Yep, he was definitely there to help keep me steady.

LUCAS

I had successfully accomplished the seal twice, which still didn't feel like enough practice for me to be confident, but we were out of time.

We all stood around the table for one final meeting.

Helia and Genghis had briefed us on the battle coordination efforts. We were bringing in three groups at the exact same time with Fetzle's fleet. The intel at The Cathedral confirmed over six hundred Pai Ona were waiting to execute the plan and destroy Chernobyl. Based on Vita's detailed blueprints, we were able to determine the likely whereabouts of the prisoners, including Eleanor and Lilith. Several small factions would descend into the lower levels to retrieve the hostages while the others attacked the Nebas on the surface, hopefully creating enough of a diversion for us to successfully execute our plan and save everyone we could. Yessica and I were going with Vosega and Oya to retrieve Olly's family.

Ruit turned to Borte. "What have you discovered about the language? Anything that can help us?"

She shook her head in disgust.

Moira interjected. "It is the painter. He has a message for the

Sulu Ophelia. She will know what it means when the time is right." Moira's eyes were crazed as she spoke. Her hair flitted around her head. I had to admit she was now more lucid than when we first arrived, but she was still bat-shit fucking crazy. Ruit just nodded then moved on to the last order of business, the lynchpin of the entire plan. Coaxing Yanni out of Olly's body, me sealing it, and Ophelia resuming control.

"We begin the séance in an hour. We will need everyone to participate. As soon as Moira has summoned Yanni's spirit, Lucas will seal the door into Miss Banner's consciousness. Moira will release Yanni back into his Gate of Consciousness and shut the door. Once Moira has resumed control of her body, we will call on Fetzle to shuttle us to the compound. Ophelia will burn the place from the inside out. It is up to us to give her the opportunity to escape."

"We may finish this war tonight," Oya crowed.

"I would not be so certain of that. We are at many disadvantages and we would be smart to remember that and stick to the agenda. Save the Sulu, Viraclay, and the other prisoners with as few casualties as possible."

Oya looked slightly dejected. "You are right. Of course you are right."

"What about the Rittles?" Vosega contested.

"We would be lucky indeed if we managed to recover any of the ancient weapons. However, they are not the priority. Be in the basement in one hour," Ruit reminded everyone and as they scattered out of the room, he grabbed my arm. "How do you feel? Are you ready?"

"I have to be."

"You are. I see it." He looked me up and down. I wasn't sure if it was real assurance or just positive reinforcement. Either way, I would take all I could get right now.

OPHELIA

"Is that everything?" The truth was I didn't think I could handle much more information.

"It is everything you need to know for now," Zavier concluded. "This is all so very much to take in."

I felt a tug at my consciousness. "Someone is pulling on me. Could it be time already?"

"As we said, time moves differently here." Sorcey's voice cracked with emotion. "You know the truth. That is what is important."

"How do I convince Esther or Nestor? How do I convince the Pai Ona? I can't do this alone."

"You are not alone. We can all assure you of that." Zavier grabbed my hand. "Give Lilith a kiss for me and tell her I love her."

The tug got stronger, like I was being pulled through a vacuum.

"Do I go through the door?" I looked at the ominous black threshold. *Did Ruit tell me to go through the door?* My mind was drawing a blank.

Sorcey kissed me on the cheek. "I am so grateful to have met you. Let my son know his father and I are so very proud of him."

Apollo took my hand and kissed the back of it. "You are the best of everyone you meet. Remember who you are, how incredibly powerful you are, and that you have many souls who love you on both banks of the River Tins."

The tug was violent this time, almost painful. "I think something is wrong."

Then I was spinning or falling…catapulting into an abyss.

"I almost moved that pile of earth. Did you see that?" Yanni laughed as he put his arms around my waist. "The Oracle will be indebted to my aptitudes now."

It was nice to see him playful. But the truth hung in the air like a dense fog. It wasn't enough, and we were running out of time. "You are making progress. We will return to the courtyard in an hour and practice through the night."

Yanni said nothing behind me. His arms went limp, and I turned to see he was suspended in midair, with his eyes rolled back into his head. *This was bad. This was very bad.*

"Yanni! My beloved! Come back!" I shook him violently, but his body did not reanimate. This wasn't like the other episodes. I tried to take charge of the Sulu, but there was nothing there. The vessel was soulless. I still felt Yanni's presence in this realm.

I was seized with fear and began searching for a solution to this madness. But nothing came. I fell to my knees and did the only thing I could imagine—I prayed.

LUCAS

I looked at Yesi as I took her hand in mine. "You ready for your first séance, baby girl?"

"Sounds like fun!" Her spirits were up now that she had been cured of the dragon blood. It was a blessing to see her fully healed. It took a weight off my shoulders going into this rescue mission. I was feeling really fond of the Alchemist these days—a rarity for someone to endear themselves to me so quickly, but the guy was brilliant and likable.

"Don't be so sure about the fun. The last time we were down here is why we're in this mess. The dead should stay dead." Helia shuffled her weight back and forth on her feet. Clearly the last séance had left an impression.

"Let us begin."

"I am just disappointed we didn't have to eat the eggs this time." Borte scowled.

"Shhhh," Moira scolded. "Let us begin," she repeated.

We had done a dress rehearsal beforehand, so we knew what to do. I took Helia's hand to my right. Moira began to sway and chant in the center of the circle like I had seen her do before when she was calling in Olly. Then, suddenly, she stiffened. Her body collapsed to the floor, then rose from the ground, limp.

I couldn't move, stuck in place during the ceremony. I looked at Ruit. He was alarmed. This didn't feel right to me.

Moira's arms splayed out and her legs came together as she hovered a few inches from the ground. Her eyes were rolled back into her head. I searched the eyes of the people who had witnessed her gifts before, looking for a knowing, an acknowledgment, but they cried out with the same fear that I felt bubbling up within me.

Moira's body shook and vibrated violently and when the irises of her eyes reappeared, they were not hers, they were Olly's. This wasn't right. Olly was supposed to be in her body, not here. The shaking got more violent, and Moira closed her eyes once more, or Olly, whoever was in possession of her body. When they snapped open, it was the coal black irises of the man I had killed.

Yanni cackled. "What is this? You better try harder than this to evict me. I am going for your girl now, Lucas, and there is nothing you can do to stop me." Once more, the suspended body shook, vibrated, and then there was nothing.

What is happening? Where is Olly? Where is Yanni? What will he do to her?

I couldn't make heads or tails of where I was or what was happening for what felt like an eternity. The haziness was heavier than it had been before. I was feeling torn in two at points. There was no pain, just a sensation, like when you're awake during surgery and you feel the stitches being sewn in, tugging at your flesh.

Suddenly I was in Moira's basement. But this wasn't right. I was supposed to be in the compound, saving Elias. Panic surged through me. *Something is wrong!* A second later I was in-between again, not even in the basement long enough to express my fears. I was now back at the River Tins, but all of the other doors but Yanni's were gone.

What is happening? Everyone else must have returned to wherever they had come from. I was gripped with fear. *I'm alone, completely alone.*

"What is this madness?!" Yanni's venomous voice demanded. I turned around to see him in the threshold of his door. "What have you done, pet?"

If he was here and I was here, *who is in my body?* I was in shock, stuck in place. Then Yanni propelled himself at me. I found the capacity to shift out of his way just before we would've collided. I was no match for him without my powers.

"I will kill you here. That will end this dispute over your body once and for all." He came at me again, and this time I wasn't fast enough. Yanni took me down.

We rolled around on the banks of the River Tins for a moment before he planted himself firmly on my torso, his hands around my throat. I wiggled and writhed to get out from under his grip, but he was strong. For a moment I broke free from his hands, but I couldn't get him off me, so he quickly locked them around my neck, this time tighter. *This was how I was going to die...*

LUCAS

oira's body fell to the floor, limp, lifeless. The power of the séance dissolved and we were able to move from our positions. I ran to kneel by her side, but it was clear she was dead. I didn't think that was possible. *This was bad, really bad.*

"What the fuck! What do we do?" Ruit was examining Moira's body beside me along with Vosega.

Vosega put his hand on my shoulder. "It's okay, son. We will save her." I shrugged him off, pointing all of my fury at the Alchemist.

"What do we fucking do?"

"The seal. We do the seal. Now." He stood and took his place in front of me.

"But we don't know where Olly is right now. Couldn't we seal her out of her own body?"

He didn't answer me, which was the answer.

"Ruit, what if we seal her out of her own body?"

"We have no choice but to follow through with the plan."

"We do have a choice!"

His expression got firm. "We do not."

I wanted to object, but I also knew time was of the essence. I did something I hadn't done in years, I prayed to Malarin. *Please spare her, please save her. She is everything that is good in this world. Everything that is right. I would do anything.*

I looked at Yesi as I finished my prayer and she just nodded, a single tear streaming down her cheek. I mouthed the words *I love you* and refocused my attention on Ruit.

"I'm ready."

He just nodded and began chanting his part of the seal.

I was frantically putting my hands all over his body, wherever I could reach as he floated in midair.

"Yanni! Yanni!"

I tugged on his legs, trying to pull him out of whatever trance he was in. There was nothing I could do. I couldn't take control of his faculties. I couldn't reach him.

At the same time, I became acutely aware that something was stirring in the compound. The Nebas were mobilizing. *But it was a day too soon? Aurora had said we had more time. Why would she say we had more time if she knew otherwise?* I brought my attention back to my beloved. The Sulu's body was unmoved. *What kind of sorcery is taking place here?*

I heard the Oracle's voice echoing through the hall as she called the Nebas to arms.

"It is the moment we were waiting for. They are striking just as I said they would. Give no mercy. Spare no one. Protect the dungeons and the Rittles with your lives. I am going to safeguard the Sulu."

She's coming? What will she make of this? Why didn't she warn me that her vision was faulty or that it had changed, that the Pai Ona were attacking early?

"Yanni!" I pulled at his legs. "Please come back to me!" I wailed.

My vision was going dark around the edges. I clawed at his grip with my hands, but I was getting nowhere. Then suddenly, there was a loud scream and someone collided with Yanni, shoving him off me. I could barely see, but a hand took my wrist and got me to my feet.

"Hurry, Ophelia. You must run through his threshold. Take your body back while it is vacant!" Moira was pulling me toward the black door. Yanni was back on his feet as well, and my vision was almost restored. "Hurry. The painter has much in store for you!"

Her words were interrupted as Yanni came barreling into both of us, kicking Moira to my left and shoving me back onto the ground. Once I was down, he grabbed hold of my left foot and swung my body back around so that I was inches away from the River Tins. I could feel the rush of the rainbow water cooling the air as it came bubbling up. It was an oddly simple sensation in an instant of terror. I was quickly torn out of the moment as Yanni launched himself on top of me while I tried to crawl away from the water's edge.

There was a cracking in my right calf. *Can I break bones in limbo?*

I supposed I could. If I could die here, then I could most certainly be injured.

"You are pathetic. The hag here fights better than you," Yanni jeered as he walked toward me, slowly, intentionally.

I was able to scramble to my feet. I looked for Moira on either side of me and didn't see her. I was no match for someone versed in battle. I'd become reliant on my powers. I tried to remember my lessons with Ying. *Make eye contact and show no fear.*

I rolled my shoulders back and stared deep into Yanni's eyes. There was a twinge of something just below the surface. *He was afraid.*

"Aw, how cute, pet. You are finally going to give it a go." He cocked his head curiously to the left. I saw Moira approaching him from behind. I took two steps back and could feel the river was directly behind me. I had to move. I had to attack.

"I am nobody's pet. And you need to vacate the premises!"

He laughed, and as he did, Moria leapt on him, latching onto his back and jarring him forward. He stumbled, and I took the opportunity to trip him with my left foot. He jolted forward again, falling on his face, Moira still holding onto him. She was now mauling and punching Yanni, anything to cause damage. I kicked him twice in the ribs. He was growling and hissing. I wondered if we were only going to make his wrath that much worse when he was able to break free.

"Get him in the River Tins!"

Of course, that was how we could pass his spirit along. I kicked him again. We were nearly to the banks. It wouldn't take much more to get him in. *But how could I keep Moira from being swept away too?* She had to get off him. I darted left and got out from between Yanni and the river. Now I just needed the right opportunity to shove him in.

"Moira, let go." I saw my chance. She jumped off his back, and Yanni growled ferociously.

"That was not smart, pet." He came at me with lightning speed. I stepped to my right while simultaneously swinging a roundhouse kick up high and to the left of his head. He dropped to his knees. I stepped back and gained momentum to plant a high kick in the center of his chest. *It was perfect.* Yanni fell, his black hair grazing the stream. He quickly pushed himself up onto his knees. I planted another kick in the middle of his chest, this time with everything I had. Yanni flew back, but he was able to grab my ankle. I went down hard. Half his body was now in the current of the River Tins, and he was fighting with everything he had, clawing at my calf. Pulling me in. I was going to be swept away with him. I rolled onto my belly, digging my fingernails into the bank, but it was doing nothing to stop him. Yanni was yelling and hissing. I couldn't understand what he was saying, but I felt the grief in his words. He was mourning, grieving, pleading for another chance to see Esther.

Still, he sank deeper into the water. I was resigning myself to the fate that was coming when Moira propelled above my head, landing on Yanni's arms just as he was almost entirely submerged and as my right foot entered the stream. He released his grip on my calf, locking arms onto Moira's body instead.

"Moira, give me your hand!" I shouted. She was sinking into the water. Yanni was completely submerged. A wild shock shot up my right leg. A download of images and sensations surged through my entire being. I couldn't make any sense of it. It was overwhelming and yet comforting all at once.

"It's my time, Ophelia. I am ready to reunite with my Henrique." Moira was smiling as she drifted down the River Tins, slowly sinking into the rainbow current. "The painter has much in store for you. Listen to the symbols before you. All you need to know is there." Then she was gone.

I dragged myself to my feet. There was no time to process what had just happened. Moira had saved my life. Yanni was gone. My right leg was still pulsating with an unfamiliar energy. I looked up to see that the black door was fading before my very eyes.

A voice tickled my ears. "Hurry, you must hurry."

I shook off the confusion and remembered what was coming next. We still had a compound to siege. I needed to save Elias. I pushed myself with everything I had left and hurtled my body through the door just as the last wisps of the threshold dissolved into thin air.

ESTHER

hat is happening? It was all moving too quickly. The Oracle was on her way. I could hear the echo of battle above me.

"Yanni!" His body fell and he was limp in my arms. I was losing him, I knew I was losing him. I could feel it. He was ripped from this world, ripped from my arms. Grief was consuming me. Then his eyes shot open, but they were not his. I was so discombobulated I dropped him. *Who is in his stead this time?*

I was in shock. It had to be shock because I could not move. I could only sink into the knowing that I had lost him again—for good. Ophelia's body scrambled to its feet.

Aurora's voice reverberated off the walls of the courtyard, diverting my attention. "Seize her! Seize her body now!"

I got to my feet. I could tell by the way she held herself that Ophelia had resumed control. She raised one hand toward me and one toward the Oracle. A huge gust of wind knocked me down, while a massive fireball flew toward Aurora and her entourage. They scrambled to get out of the way. I was at a much closer range. Surely, she would kill me. I closed my eyes, welcoming the relief. I heard Ophelia's voice on the wind, dancing into my ear.

"You have to believe me. The Oracle has betrayed everyone, including you. The answer is in the birthmark."

My eyes shot open, and I made eye contact with the Sulu. She nodded and threw Yanni's ring to me. I caught it. Bewildered, I stared at the token of my love, then again back at the girl. She quickly commanded a pile of stones to fall all around her, shielding her from any more questions or further attack.

OPHELIA

I was in the familiar cocoon of my own skin.

"Don't open your eyes," a melodic voice resounded in my head, the same as the one on the banks of the River Tins. "The Alchemist calls."

Then that voice was gone and Ruit's familiar voice channeled through the Rune. "Ophelia, we have sealed your body. Elias is directly above you. Lucas and Yessica will save your mother and grandmother. The others are beginning their attack. The time to strike is now!"

"Now!" was all I needed to say, then I opened my eyes to see Esther bewildered and in shock. My heart twanged with her pain. Maybe it was Apollo's inherited gift or the knowing that she must be devastated to know she would never see her Atoa again. Even though I only knew Yanni and Esther for the atrocities they'd committed, now I understood they were pawns, just like the rest of us. Except worse, because Esther has been greatly betrayed by her own mother.

No sooner did I think the thought than Aurora's voice echoed down the hall, diverting Esther's attention long enough for me to get to my feet. "Seize her! Seize her body now!"

But I needed to say something. I owed Apollo that much. I owed us all that much. "You have to believe me. The Oracle has betrayed everyone, including you. The answer is in the birthmark." I did my best to sound as sincere as I could, hoping she could hear the truth her father desperately tried to share with her. I felt the ring on my finger and quickly assessed it must be Yanni's. I pulled it off. I nodded in reassurance when our eyes met and threw the ring, hoping it was a gesture that would be considered an olive branch. And I prayed to Malarin that it was enough to stir her curiosity.

Then I commanded a wall of stones to fall all around me, exposing the chamber above and creating an obstacle for the enemy. All I needed was a sliver of time to get myself and Elias out of here, to help the rest of the Pai Ona.

LUCAS

"She has returned." Ruit's words were like music to my ears. The entire room exhaled with relief. Helia let out a triumphant cheer. "We must be off."

Vita and Garrett were first up the stairs. Each of us grabbed our bags and headed toward the door. I took Yesi's hand in mine. She was withdrawn slightly. I could feel it in her touch.

"What is it?"

"We're just going to leave Moira's body there, after all she's done?"

"We can't bring her with us."

Vosega and Ruit came up just behind us. "We will be back for her. Right now, we need to be present with the task at hand," Ruit asserted.

"We will come back for her, I promise." Vosega was sincere and I appreciated him reassuring my wife. Her tender heart would get the best of her, if we let it.

She nodded and wiped away her tears.

Then we were exiting the Haven and heading for a giant eucalyptus across the street. Fetzle was waiting there, not so patiently.

ELIAS

I felt the walls shake before I could process what was happening. Halfway between dreaming and waking, I was disorientated at first. Confusion turned into elation as I realized this must be what Ruit warned me about—the siege had begun. The stones crumbled around my chains, and I pulled my arms from the wall. They ached with fatigue and stiffness.

"Elias!" Olly's voice pierced the darkness. "We have no time. Minutes."

She took my hand and simultaneously dissolved the shackles around my wrists and legs. I couldn't speak. My mouth was dry from astonishment and relief. "Are you okay?" I just leaned in and kissed her, pulled her body as close to me as I could manage. The walls were continuing to morph into something else around us.

"Almus has just informed me Mikkel has the perimeter in a time warp, but it will not last long."

"What about your mother? Lilith?"

"Lucas and Yessica are going to find them." She hooked her arm under mine and grasped my right side. "Hold on."

I listened and felt the rush of movement all around us. We were flying up through the walls, out of the compound.

"How did you let the Sulu get away?" Aurora growled.

"You said they would storm the compound tomorrow," I spat back. "Your sight has become useless."

The walls shook around us as we ran down the south corridor.

"You will not speak to me that way again." She nearly whispered the command, but I felt it throughout my entire being.

"We are just abandoning the Rittles? The Pierses? The captives and our army?"

"I took measures. We have the Rittles and the Pierses." She gestured to Clive, who gracefully moved behind us with a bag over his shoulder. "The Nebas are mobilizing through the escape tunnels. I ordered they collect the captives in their retreat."

"But the tunnels have been closed for decades. When did you excavate them?"

"I haven't the patience for your incessant questions right now, Esther. We would have the true advantage if it weren't for your soft heart and incompetence."

Her words struck me like the back of her hand. *My soft heart... my beloved was ripped away from me once more.*

"Clive! Get to the poison chamber, then meet us with the powrie king."

"We are meeting King OAD? Where?"

We were nearly at the end of the south wing tunnel. The passage would turn upward and spit us out along the woodlands of Pripyat.

"More inquiries?"

"You dispatched Clive with all of our weapons on his person. You have been conspiring secret strategies for battle without my knowledge... I deserve some answers, Aurora!"

She laughed me off.

"You haven't collected the poison yet? Do you have the vats of antidote?"

"All will be revealed."

Just then, Nestor appeared in front of us, his silhouette outlined in the door leading to the surface. "They have taken the dungeon."

We swept past him, and he followed in pursuit as we climbed the stairs. Aurora paused for only a moment. "Did you see Clive?"

"No."

"Was the poison room compromised? Did they find the dragon?"

"As I said, they have taken the dungeon."

Dragon?

The Oracle wavered for a moment longer before resolving something in her mind.

My head was spinning with questions, grief, shock and rage...

"Esther, give me your hand. You don't appear well..." the Oracle commanded, and I obeyed, too tired to fight and too lost to make decisions.

ELIAS

Chaos ensued around us as Olly propelled herself up through the walls of Chernobyl. I could hear it, but I was also completely immune to all distraction—all I could see was her. I stared at her face and the rest of the world distorted into a blur. She was intent on our escape, focused and fierce as she moved effortlessly through the debris.

We erupted into the sky. The air was cool, fresh, and welcome in my lungs after days of being in the depths. I inhaled sharply and felt the sting of the cold. Ophelia's face shone in the moonlight as we hovered there in midair for an endless moment. *She was back. She was here.* My heart had never felt so full…so relieved. Her eyes met mine and she kissed me, slipping her tongue in gently and caressing my parched lips.

"I'm so happy you're alive," she whispered in my ear as we held each other. "But we must save this reunion for later. They need us."

Ophelia looked down, as did I. From this vantage point I could see hundreds of Pai Ona surrounding the compound. Staggered between our allies were the huge, menacing forms of she-trolls. *It was impressive.*

Ruit's voice interrupted my thoughts. "The Oracle must have

known we were coming. The Nebas are moving beneath us. The trolls are going to lead a party into the tunnels, but our greatest feat has been realized. You two are safe."

Olly added her own transmission. "The captives. Where can we recover the captives?"

I looked at her and nodded. There was still much to be done.

LUCAS

*Y*essica and I had just reached the lowest level of the compound according to Vita's map. "Lilith and Eleanor should be down here. We recover them first, then we see who else we can find."

"Of course."

After all, I had to act in accordance with the bidding I'd made with my clever little wife. I took her hand in mine. She wouldn't be out of arm's reach. I didn't know what we'd encounter down here. We turned a corner and at the end of the hall was a wooden door. My gut said this was not a good place. Evil emanated off the walls. And I had a vague memory of it.

"They are in there, Lucas. I know it."

I nodded and we sprinted toward the door. It was locked. "Step back."

Yessica stepped behind me as I threw myself against the door. It splintered on my first attempt. Screams inside validated that there were women in the room. I threw my body against the door with more force, and it ripped from the hinges. The chamber was pitch black. I could see two crumpled forms on the floor. "Light, Yesi."

She lit up the room and Eleanor and Lilith shielded their eyes. "A little less, baby girl."

I knelt beside Eleanor's muddy, bloody, naked body. She was still shackled to the wall. "Help Lilith." Yessica was already doing her best to finagle with the chains.

"Eleanor, it's Lucas. You're safe. I won't let anyone else hurt you." I cupped her face to my chest. She shook all over. Waves of shivers vibrated her whole body.

"Olly, they have Olly. She isn't dead, Lucas. She is here. You must find her." Eleanor's voice was hoarse and desperate.

"Olly is safe. We already have her." It was the least I could give the poor woman, and I believed it was true. *I had to.* "Now scoot to the side and let me deal with this little chain problem." Just then, the walls trembled violently. For all we knew, this place was going to collapse. We needed to move. I took the chain in one hand and got to my feet. I stomped on the slack between the wall and the fistful I had. It quickly crumbled. I would take the shackles off when we got to safety.

"Sit here. Let me help Lilith."

Eleanor cradled her legs to her chest, trying to cover her bruised body. I wanted to reassure her, but there was no time. Yessica was still trying to break the chain-links. "There is something different with this one."

"Of course, because she is a Conduit. Normal irons wouldn't hold her." Lilith still had not made eye contact with me. The walls shook again. Part of the ceiling crumbled and fell on Yessica's head.

"I'm okay," she immediately reassured me.

"Lilith, do you know what these shackles are enchanted with?"

"It's no use," Lilith mumbled. "He'll never let us go. He will find us again."

This poor woman's soul was broken. She was barely holding on. Another issue to be dealt with at a later time. "Okay. Yesi, I'm going to encapsulate the chains, hopefully warding off the magic that is assisting them, while you break them the good, old-fashioned way."

She nodded and I focused my shield around the individual links, pushing the spell that I could detect just enough off the surface to create a gap. "Now!"

Yesi promptly took a rock and broke the irons with one fierce blow. "Yes, that's my baby girl!"

She giggled slightly before turning her attention to Lilith. "Can you walk?"

Lilith nodded and got to her feet while Yesi assisted. I walked over to Eleanor. "I'm going to carry you."

"But I'm naked," she protested.

"Now isn't the time. I just want to get you somewhere safe. I promise not to look."

Eleanor nodded sheepishly. My heart broke for her. This was too much for anyone to handle. I swept her up into my arms. Yesi and Lilith were already at the door. We stepped into the hall, and I froze in my tracks. It was Clive. He stood in the shadows, staring at us with those dark, calculating eyes. My blood boiled. This was the very monster who ordered the hit on my mother. Now he threatened my wife and Olly's family. Rage, pure rage consumed my body. *It was time to end this.*

I landed beside Ruit and Winston just outside of the compound walls. "They are all getting away?"

Elias took my hand as we approached the Alchemist. I wanted him just as close as he wanted me. "Aurora knew we were coming, that is clear. The queen has already taken three of her best and a small band of Pai Ona to scour the tunnels Vita mapped out for us."

The name struck a chord. I looked to my left to see a uniquely chiseled face, almost like stone.

"You're Vita?"

She nodded. I wanted to say more, but the time would come.

"What can we do?" Elias interrupted the exchange.

"Thank the strokes we have had no casualties. The Nebas' retreat into the tunnels has eliminated bloodshed. But they appear to be transporting many of the captives."

I felt like the wind had been knocked out of me. "Eleanor, Lilith?"

"Lucas is still in pursuit," Winston assured me.

"Show me where."

"We cannot risk losing you," Ruit protested.

"I will not let them suffer anymore."

Susuda came up from behind in his gidim form, grunting and snarling. My eyes welled with tears. Even in this demonic body, I could feel his love and support.

"Very well. The three of us will join you." Ruit looked at Susuda and Winston, who both nodded in agreement.

"Miss Ophelia, after you." Winston smiled. It was enough to make the tears fall. I quickly wiped them away. Elias turned and I was right behind him when I heard the familiar voice of the journal.

"Ruit, do you hear that?"

He shook his head.

"Do you have the journal, the Sorcerer's Stone on you?"

He pulled it from the inside of his jacket and handed it to me. I flipped through the pages, the whispers growing louder. I stopped when a single word seemed to jump off the pages. *"Feworbusalee."*

It was the same incantation Ruit had used to steal the Molpe's siren song in Merr.

"What does it mean, Ruit?"

"I haven't the faintest idea. I created something similar to seal your soul to this realm just now. Perhaps it pertains to that?"

I shook my head. "No, this is something different. I know you used this to steal the Siren song." I accused.

"The Sorcerer's Stone gave me that spell hundreds of years ago. I did not know what it would do or how it would harm."

I heard the Sorcerer's Stone whisper again. *Feworbusalee.* "Maybe it will make sense later. We have to go."

All three men nodded and we headed toward the tunnels.

We entered an eerily empty compound through an east entrance, the closest to the dungeon where it was suspected Lilith and Eleanor were being held. Susuda moved in and out of the walls until we hit a certain depth, and then he took his human form.

"Oh, Su!" Olly quickly threw her arms around him, as did I, in a brief reunion. "I'm so happy to see you."

"As am I you, Miss Olly." He held her tight before receiving me just as warmly. "I have missed you too, Mr. Elias."

"And I you."

"There will be more time for reunions later," Ruit insisted, moving past us. "I am afraid Chernobyl will not be standing for long, and with her fall, so too will perish anyone left in the rubble."

"Indeed."

We all moved swiftly into the deeper levels of the Haven.

"Lucas is below us," Ophelia suddenly asserted. "I can feel him."

The hairsy charm must still be intact.

"I can break through this floor easily enough." She moved to make some space where she might dismantle the stones.

"I do not know if that is a wise decision, Miss Ophelia. The integrity of the building is weak." Winston said.

"What should we do then? That's even more reason to get to them quickly."

Ruit turned to Su. "Can you retrieve them? This Haven is not The Cathedral and she will not be kind. But can you do it?"

Susuda nodded, then he was gone.

LUCAS

"Take her and, whatever happens, you get them out of here." I handed Eleanor to Yesi.

"But the bidding. Lucas, you promised."

"I met the bidding." We both knew that was true.

Suddenly, a familiar blade appeared in Clive's hand. The Dirk of Inverness. On one hand, at least I knew what this Rittle was capable of. On the other hand, I didn't really care to die as a frozen statue.

"I have a bone to pick with you." The hobgoblin's mouth opened into a wide and sinister grin, exposing his long needle-point teeth. "Creepy effect."

He dropped the bag he was carrying. The walls rumbled again, and I took the opportunity to throw myself at Clive while simultaneously pulling the two knives I was armed with from their sheath behind my back. He saw me coming and darted to the left, slipping against the wall and barely missing the swipe of my blade. I quickly circled back around, kicking my left leg up, planting it across his jaw. There was a subtle cracking noise, but the satisfaction of the blow was short-lived as he swept my right leg out from under me, landing me on my back. I rolled to my right and got to my feet before he could pounce on top of me. Clive moved fast. He sliced the blade through the air, and I felt the coolness of it as it almost cut my face. I backed up and hit a door. The knob turned in my palm, but it didn't open. I moved against the wall again before pushing off, using the leverage to propel forward and catch the hobgoblin off guard. My left blade went into his shoulder.

"What, not even an ouch?" I mocked.

His eyes narrowed on me. He examined the damage with his free hand before once again diving at me. We collided in the hall, and he pushed me through the door I'd fallen against a second ago.

"Lucas!" Yesi shouted as I disappeared into the room. Immediately, I wanted out of this space. It felt cursed. The energy was dense and hopeless. Something stirred in the corner. Before I could get a better look, Clive was on top of me, the Dirk of Inverness at my throat.

Susuda reappeared with my mother, Lilith, and Yessica. Relief surged through me while at the same time panic gripped my chest. "Where is Lucas?"

My voice got my mother's attention. "Olly!" She jumped from Yessica's arms and fell into mine.

"I'm so grateful you are okay. These men are going to get you out of here." I handed her off to Winston. "But I need to help Lucas."

She nodded and compliantly fell into Winston's arms. "Take care of them."

"With my life."

"Susuda, take me to him, now."

"Take us to him," Elias corrected me.

Su looked beyond me to Ruit before silently adhering to my request. We dissolved into the floor and manifested into a dark room. The hobgoblin was on top of Lucas, a blade at his throat. I raised my hand toward the creature, commanding a gust of wind toss his body to the side, but it did nothing. *What the fuck?*

The walls shook more violently than ever before.

Susuda attacked the hobgoblin just before he could pierce Lucas' skin. Pushing the creature off of him, but Clive was faster than he looked. Su pursued him down the hall as I ran to Lucas and kelt beside him. "Are you okay?"

Lucas pulled himself into a seated position. "Yeah, I think so."

The floor beneath us quaked.

"We need to go!" Elias put his hand on my shoulder. He was right.

"Su!" I called. "We need you to get us out of here." We got to our feet, Susuda was instantly there. The next thing happened so fast I couldn't make heads or tails of where everyone was. Clive appeared out of nowhere, still brandishing the blade and now something else in his hand. He dove out of the shadows as the walls began to crumble all around us. I went to step back and move both Elias and Lucas out of the way of the attack when Susuda jumped in front of me, taking the blade to the gut, then crumpling to the floor.

Elias fell on top of him, while I pointed all of my fury and shock at the treacherous hobgoblin. I commanded Shiva's gift with all of my strength but it did nothing. I screamed in outrage. Large stones began to fall from the ceiling.

"We have to go, Olly!" Lucas shouted, pulling me from my rage. Elias looked up from the heap that was now Susuda's impaled body, his eyes pleading for me to do something.

I captured one more look at the hobgoblin, who smiled back at me in a maniacally smitten way before grabbing a bag that lay in the hall and darting out an adjacent door. I knelt down, putting my hands on all of my men, not sure what to do next.

Then Ruit sent a transmission through our Runes. One word. "Feworbusalee."

I repeated it aloud. Elias and Lucas looked at me like I lost my mind. I screamed the word into the ethers. "Feworbusalee!"

A fierce voice filled the space in between the sounds of ruin raining down on us.

"I am free!" Followed by an animal roar like no other.

ELIAS

*E*verything was unfolding so rapidly. Susuda could not transport us out of the deteriorating chamber, the Dirk of Inverness still plunged in his stomach. I thought he was invincible. *What is happening?*

"We are in the dungeon. How do we get out of here?" I turned to Lucas, the only person with any real experience in the compound.

"I don't think we can." His eyes were fixed on something behind me. Ophelia was examining Susuda, trying to contain the blood loss. I stood up to see the sight that captivated him. A purple dragon was expanding, or growing rather, in enormity by the second. The walls, everything around the creature was crumbling. Wings stretched in either direction and the ceiling caved, causing a fissure that ran the length of the hall and above our heads. We would be buried under the rubble in a moment.

"Olly!" Lucas shouted.

It was enough to snap her out of her panic over Susuda's wound. She raised her hand above her head and a narrow tunnel manifested. The dragon roared again, the wings flapped, and a wave of debris propelled itself directly for us.

"Grab him," Ophelia ordered.

I took hold of Su while she stood up and commanded a tornado of wind to eject us through the tunnel, narrowly missing the onslaught of shrapnel. We quickly reached the surface, just in time to see the purple dragon take flight, gloriously spreading its enormous wings and rocketing into the air. I had never seen anything like it. Olly left us hovering for a moment and I realized she must be communicating with Ruit.

Chernobyl was falling in upon itself. Blue and purple flames consumed the rubble. Several small explosions and mini-eruptions spread across the canyon of ruins. My heart fluttered, because the fall of the compound represented a level of victory against the Nebas that my father only dreamed of, and here I was to see it. To see the stronghold of our enemy fall to ruin. A tear ran down my cheek, from pride, relief and grief—for all that was lost to get here.

"Your family is safe," I whispered in Olly's ear. I had a flash of concern for the other captives. I knew there were many more. *How many have we saved? How many did we just lose?*

"Yes. We need to get Su to Ruit, now." With that, we were catapulting through the air.

e were moving along the woodland when a sound like I had never heard before erupted from the wreckage of the compound. We all turned around to see Chernobyl exploding into the air, but it wasn't flame that caused the shrapnel of metal and stone to project in every direction. A huge purple dragon soared upward into the sky.

"What in the strokes?" I couldn't believe my eyes.

I knew that dragon. That was the very same one who had caused the fall of Atlantis and the death of my mother Shatki. Confusion, astonishment and sheer terror stabbed my heart. "The dragons have taken their side."

Aurora screamed as we watched the shadow of the dragon dwarf the illumination of the moon. Suddenly, Clive manifested at our feet. I had never seen him in a state before. Aurora fell to her knees, cradling his head in her lap. I couldn't tell if he was wounded or not.

The Oracle's eyes looked around before fixating on me. "We need shelter. Now!"

"Where can we hide from a dragon?"

"Collect the Rittles. In the bag." She pointed at the sack on

Clive's back. "Be quick with it! There is a trinket for travel. Take us to the Orb Forest. Help her Nestor!"

"Is that where we are meeting King OAD?"

Aurora growled, "Do as I say!"

I searched the bag. I suspected there was something of this nature in the Rittles and that Clive had used it to get us back to Chernobyl quicker than was possible after the battle of the basin, but Aurora had evaded my questions. "It is the compass! Find the compass!" The Oracle was hysterical. "Help her, Nestor!"

"Are they safe to touch?" Nestor asked.

"Do not be stupid. Of course you can touch them. Clive disarmed the curse that kept them dangerous days ago."

We were both sifting through the bag. My hand gripped something smooth and round.

"I have the compass. Now what?"

"Whisper our destination."

I did as I was told. Suddenly we were in a flurry of wind and color before we landed in Death Valley and the Orb Forest. I looked around. Nestor, the Oracle, Clive and I were in a long dirt shaft beneath the earth. "Where are the others?"

"They will make their own way." Aurora kept her attention on the hobgoblin in her arms.

LUCAS

Olly had successfully evacuated us out of the collapsing compound. I watched as the enormous dragon that we had somehow released soared through the sky. It was majestic. I'd never seen anything like it. Only Yessica's sweet voice could distract me from the astonishing sight.

"Lucas!" I turned to see her running toward me with Ruit at her side. Lilith, Eleanor and Winston were trailing behind. Mikkel and Sparkle were rushing to meet them with some blankets to cover their broken bodies. Eleanor was limp in Winston's arms, over-whelmed, exhausted but alive. Yessica threw herself into my chest when she was close enough to make contact.

"Thank the strokes you're okay."

"Of course. I told you, baby girl, it's you and me." I squeezed her and kissed her face, at the same time hearing the anxiety in Olly's voice behind me.

"What's wrong with him? I thought he was immortal."

Ruit was seeing to the shadow monster-man Susuda. "I am afraid I do not know."

"I need to see if I can help, Yesi," I whispered in her ear, and released her from my arms. I quickly turned around to see that

Susuda had not returned to his shadow form. He was still the young man, and he still had the Dirk in his stomach.

I knelt beside Olly, Elias on her left, Ruit directly across from her examining the wound. Susuda was writhing in pain.

"My son, I thought you were impervious to harm. What has happened? May I pull out the knife?"

"No! There is something different about this blade," He sputtered, and blood came out of his mouth. "It is as though it is part of me. If you remove it…I am afraid you will take me with it."

"This makes no sense." Olly was in tears. "It's a Rittle. Is that why? We have to help him."

Ruit took her shaking, bloody hands in his. "We will." Then he turned to me. "Find Fetzle. She can transport us to The Cathedral. I must convene with Cataphet at once."

I nodded and got to my feet, heading toward the last place I had seen a troll. Yessica grabbed my hand and kept my pace. "Do you think the gatekeeper will be okay?"

"I hope so."

As we walked looking for Fetzle, I took in the sight of what had truly transpired here. Chernobyl was still crumbling into itself. The entire perimeter of the compound had been surrounded by an army of Pai Ona and she-trolls. From what I could tell, we suffered no casualties. Mikkel's time warp had given us just the right window we needed to execute the rescue mission effectively. I saw pockets of recovered captives being tended to by other Conduits. Some of the small groups were already administering the cure. It was obvious which ones by the wails of joy and confusion that were humming around us. I wondered how many we had saved and if we would find any others in the rubble.

"There she is."

Fetzle's frame was large even compared to her fellow she-trolls. She towered over them. Her face lit up when she saw us approaching.

"FetzlesissoshappystoseesherfriendsLucasandYessicas. DidswerescuesstinkyOpheliasandViraclays?"

"Yes, we did."

She squealed with delight.

"We need your help though. Someone's been hurt and we need to get him back to The Cathedral right away."

"Fetzlescanhelpswithhersshuttles. Fetzlesknowsthatsplace."

I gestured for her to follow me, and she did without hesitation.

"Fetzlesgrandmothersknowslotsofdragons."

"What?"

"QueensPeozleoFetzlesgrandmothersbroughtstheRittlestoCataphets."

I didn't know anything about how we had gotten a hold of the Rittles. I wondered if Ruit knew how they had gotten to The Cathedral.

"StinkyOpheliasknowsdragonstoos!" Fetzle pointed ahead, and there was Olly standing face to face with the winged dragon. Fear surged through me. *Is she safe? She must be, right?* I remembered that Olly and only a handful of others had collected four dragons. She could handle herself. Old habits die hard. I still wanted to protect her.

As we approached, I heard Ophelia translating something to Ruit.

"Her name is Gwenora and, as you suspected, she has been a captive for many years."

But when she saw us approaching, Olly stopped what she was doing, apologized to the dragon and quickly took stride with us. "Can you take us now, Fetzle? He is hurt really bad."

"Fetzleisgladsyourssafes."

"Oh, of course, I am so sorry. Thank you so much for being a part of this massive rescue effort. I owe you so much."

I thought I saw Fetzle blush. "Fetzlesaysnoproblems. Letshelpsthegatekeepers.   Fetzledoesn'tevenneedshishelpopeningsthegates. Fetzlesgrandmothersisgoodfriendswithdragonstoos."

Olly looked at me for some explanation and I just shrugged.

Susuda spoke up through gasps of pain. "That explains how you were able to enter and exit my gate without my detection. The

Cathedral has some explaining to do." He tried to laugh, but it came out as more of a gargle. "Well met, Fetzle."

Olly quickly positioned herself to have Su's head in her lap. "No jokes right now. Let's just get you better." He nodded and closed his eyes.

Ruit approached with Jezebel. Olly looked over her shoulder, hearing a voice none of us could hear. "Gwenora will meet us at The Cathedral. We must go now."

Fetzle nodded and with that, Elias, Olly and Susuda, Ruit and Jezebel and Yesi and I were in the shuttle and on our way.

OPHELIA

I sat beside Su on his bed. *Is this his chamber? Or one that Ruit had dreamed up? Does it matter?* His hand was clammy in mine. Elias had left me alone with him to check on Eleanor and Lilith. Everyone was slowly trickling into The Cathedral, and they had just arrived. Aremis had settled them in and was now helping others find quarters, while familiarizing himself with the captives we had recovered.

Maybe I was avoiding seeing my mother's face, the brokenness in her eyes, but I also couldn't bring myself to leave Susuda's side. He had saved me, saved them. He was my friend and one of the sweetest souls I'd ever met and now he was suffering. Sweat pooled on his forehead. His long black hair was wet and matted to his neck. I dabbed at his face with a wet cloth. The door opened and I turned to see Elias with a halfhearted smile.

"How is she? How is Lilith?"

"They are both resting. I healed all of Eleanor's physical wounds. Lilith is also recovering."

"Did you introduce yourself?"

"Are you asking if I explained that I am her daughter's other half? No, I did not. I thought that conversation would be best had with your presence." He came up behind me and squeezed my shoulders gently. "She has had enough revelations for one terrible day. Enough for a lifetime, truly."

"Did she ask about me?"

"Of everyone she encounters. Her caretakers are Sparkle and Lucia. They are calming her nerves as only Sparkle can."

Relief washed over me. I couldn't ask for two more compassionate people to help my mother during this time.

"Thank you."

"How is he?"

"No change. Ruit is convening with Cataphet in the caves. But I can't help but feel this has something to do with the story Susuda told me about his… conception, for lack of a better word. There was a blade involved. Reshi stabbed him. It was part of the magic that created him into the gidim anomaly he is. Could this be the same blade?"

Elias stopped massaging my shoulders. "I do not know where my mother collected this Rittle."

"I do." Ruit's voice made me jump. I hadn't heard him come in. "Your intuition is very close to the truth, according to Cataphet. The dragon believes this is the missing blade of the Staff of Banishment. The same blade used to spear Susuda during the War of the Sisters 5,000 years ago. The very feud Su became a casualty of, and the very battle that occurred just before the last annihilation."

"What? Annihilation?"

Elias' voice was almost inaudible. "Ganesha's story of the last Sulu."

"Precisely."

My face got cold. I looked down at Su. *What does any of this have to do with my friend?*

ELIAS

J pulled up a chair beside Olly and took her shaking hand in mine. Ruit took a seat on the other side of the bed, alongside Susuda. The gatekeeper was coming in and out of consciousness and was asleep at the moment.

"I am only able to piece together the stories I know to be truth from various witnesses. I know from Su that he was born of a magical blade. His immortality and abilities came from a melding of magics not unlike the creation of a Haven. The will of Reshi and Innana, the powers of the blade and the intention of his father Neti coagulated into his being—creating the gatekeeper. When Susuda woke up in his father's Haven, the blade was gone. If you recall, his father left on an errand, to never return. When Su emerged from the Haven, he was not met by another Conduit for centuries. The sisters too seemed to have disappeared," Ruit explained.

Susuda's eyes flitted open for a moment. Perhaps he was more coherent than we realized.

"Su, did you hear that? Your biological father didn't abandon you. He loved you." Olly pulled her hand from mine and gently massaged the back of Su's hand as she held it.

Su did not respond, so I responded with my own observations.

"The timing aligns with Ganesha's account of the vanishing of an entire world of Conduits," I quickly concluded.

Ruit continued. "Indeed, and further evidence implies that this was just after one of the blades of the Staff of Banishment went missing from King OAD's custody. This was the event that later led to the instigation of the war between the trolls and the powries."

"How did my mother get it?" I asked.

"Queen Peozleo of the trolls charged it to your mother's keeping when the Staff of Banishment was dismantled in order to stop the end of the world."

"And you are certain this is the same blade?"

He nodded.

Ophelia continued to be silent. *What could she be thinking?*

"The best I can speculate is that because the blade was part of his inception, it is the only weapon that can lead to his demise," Ruit concluded.

"Stop! Just stop! You are talking about him like he's some experiment, some statistic! He's so much more than that, he's…" Ophelia's voice cracked.

Susuda took hold of both Olly's hands. "Hush now, Miss Olly. Do not be so disheartened. My father meant nothing by it." He turned to Ruit and smiled. "He considers all scenarios first. It is his strength."

Ophelia put her head on the back of Su's hand and silently sobbed.

"It feels like the blade that you speak of, Father. I could never forget that sensation, that moment I was certain I was meant to meet my maker." Susuda cupped Ophelia's face with his other hand as she lifted it to make eye contact with him once more. "But it was not my time then. The painter has given me over five thousand more years and more love than I ever could have expected."

"You can't just give up," Olly pleaded as she wiped at her face. "We have to try and do something."

Ruit looked at me before he choked out the next words. "I will honor my son Susuda's wishes and he has requested that we remove the blade and leave his fate in the hands of the strokes."

Tears welled up in my eyes. I needed to stay strong for Ophelia right now, but my heart was breaking too. Olly no longer muffled her sobs. She wept loudly but did not protest, only held and kissed Su's hand in hers.

Elias held my hand as we aimlessly walked down the hall of The Cathedral. I was in shock, numbed and on fire all at once. *So much loss.* Rand and now Susuda… Di and so many others. I wasn't sure how much more I could take.

There hadn't been time to process or tell Elias about my time at the River Tins. All I desired to do was be with Su. I'd still be there now, but I wanted to honor the privacy that the Tallus family deserved with him. After all, he was theirs before he was mine.

"What can I do to help you?"

"Nothing. I understand that these are his wishes. But if he hadn't been there to save me, we wouldn't even be in this predicament. I can't help but feel like his blood is on my hands."

Elias stopped walking and pulled me in for a hug. "No one's blood is on your hands. No one's. You need to purge that thought from your mind."

I want to, I really do. The guilt and the grief were almost killing me.

"When was the last time you ate?"

I just shook my head. I had no idea if Yanni had even bothered to eat.

"Let us feed you."

"I'm not hungry," I began to protest, but then I thought about Su and how much he loved us describing our food experiences with him. "Okay, I'll eat. On one condition."

"Anything."

"We make something extra delicious and share the experience with Susuda."

Elias smiled and the tears streamed down his face. "Indeed, that would be a brilliant farewell."

Moments later we were in the galley. We were limited by what was available in the kitchen, so we decided to make something simple that we knew Susuda had appreciated before, tomato soup and grilled cheese sandwiches. Together we poured love into the recipe as we reminisced about some of our favorite moments with the gatekeeper. When it was ready, I had second thoughts. I wanted to march up to Ruit and demand he do more for the man he called his son. But my heart stopped me.

Elias and I manifested outside Susuda's door and knocked gently.

"Come in," Inca's sweet voice trilled.

The Tallus family stood around his bedside, all tear-stained cheeks and red eyes. It was enough to make me want to lose it once more, but I swallowed hard and held back the tears.

Susuda sat up when we entered, sniffing the air playfully. "Have you come to treat me to the experience? What a wonderful gift." He adjusted himself again, wincing in pain.

"One of yours and my favorites, tomato soup."

Jezebel laughed and stepped back by her husband's side, making room for Elias and me at the bedside. Elias placed the tray on the nightstand as Ruit pulled up two chairs. Together, the seven of us enjoyed the meal. Even the Consus took turns taking a bite and trying to describe the flavors. Susuda delighted in each person's interpretation of the dish. The last bite came around to me. I hesitated, knowing what this meant.

I navigated the spoon of soup into my mouth slowly, closing my eyes. Savoring every spice, tang and zest. I would always enjoy my food a little more because of Su. In all actuality, I would savor more of every moment of life because of Su. When I opened my eyes, I saw everyone was watching me mournfully, aware of what was coming next—the unknown, loss, and the certain pain. Susuda took his time making eye contact with everyone, one at a time.

"I love you, each of you. I am forever grateful for all of the moments we have shared. And I am so blessed that my final strokes in this life will be spent with my family. I am ready to see my Urnina once more, so fret not for me or my spirit. It is in joyous celebration as it anticipates the reunion with others who have long since left this world. And when each of your time comes, I will be waiting to hug you once more." Then he nodded at Ruit. "Father, send me home."

I bit at my lip. I didn't want to break down yet. I wanted to smile and reassure my friend that he was loved and would always be remembered, honored in my heart. Elias held my hand and pulled me in closer with his other arm. I leaned into him and put my head on his chest, grateful for his presence and compassion.

Ruit leaned over the other side of the bed, kissed Susuda's forehead and then quickly pulled the blade from his son's belly. Su didn't make a noise. He just smiled and looked beyond Ruit's face as though he was seeing an amazing sunset or an old friend in the distance, and maybe he was.

Then I heard a voice. It sounded like it was carried on the wind. "Come home." I glanced around but no one else seemed concerned, so I turned my attention back to Su.

His grin got wider before his body began to disintegrate into fine ash. The fine ash seemed to transform into a million beautiful rainbows of glitter, wafting into the air and showering us all with a cloud of vibrant shimmering color before disappearing completely.

I nestled in deeper to Elias' shoulder and let the tears wash over me. I held nothing back, and neither did anyone else. Together, we mourned one of the most courageous and devoted souls the world would ever know.

PART III

"How many did we salvage?" Aurora demanded. Clive was still recovering from whatever he had encountered, lying on top of one of the giant Orbs that were dispersed about Death Valley in Russia. I had never been to the Haven. It was deep underground and large enough to entertain a few hundred Conduits. I wondered if Aurora was expecting all of the Nebas to reconvene here or if her plan was more involved—I suspected the later was true.

Astrid had just arrived and was visibly shaking. That type of response meant weakness, pure weakness. I looked down at my own hands that were still trembling from shock. I hadn't given myself a moment to really digest what had happened, to feel the loss that was penetrating every cell in my body once more. I needed a distraction.

"How did you come to know of this place?" I examined the dirt walls with exposed beams and the primitive furnishings. The majority of the space was open, with low ceilings. The Orbs were strewn about, in what appeared to be random placement. I counted five chambers that fed directly into the main hall. We were currently in one of the rooms with an Orb. A few wooden chairs occupied the large, barren space. It felt more like a tomb than a Haven. *Maybe it was.*

"I do not have the patience to entertain your queries, Esther!" She spat.

Astrid cleared her throat. I narrowed my attention on her. "I have counted fifteen captives still in our custody, my queen."

"Have you heard from the other two Havens? Fifteen? Of seventy-two, we have fifteen?" With every question, Aurora's voice grew in hostility.

"We followed the protocol you set in place. We were ready for the attack, and it arrived just when you said it would. But they knew. It was as though they knew every nook and cranny of Chernobyl. The Pai Ona went directly for the captives."

The Oracle screamed ferociously, gripping the closest wall with her nails and tearing a huge chunk of wood from the exposed beam. Her chest heaved with rage. I watched her disappointment spiral into the fury that takes over when you feel surrounded by incompetence. Ophelia's warning popped into my mind. *"You have to believe me. The Oracle has betrayed everyone, including you. The answer is in the birthmark."*

Astrid's assessment of the attack on Chernobyl, more evidence of Aurora's deceit. She knew when the Pai Ona would arrive. She had prepared the tunnels to transport the comatose captives. Clive had the Rittles and Pierses on his person. She intentionally misled me to believe they were arriving a day later—*to what end?* The image of the enormous purple dragon soaring through the sky flashed across my mind. The day my mother Shatki died, the first loss that devastated my heart. Seeing the dragon tonight was a painful reminder of her death. *Does this mean the dragons have taken up arms with the Pai Ona?* My father's sudden appearance in Ophelia's body. I hadn't had even a moment to myself to process his unexpected and all-too-brief emergence. I winced, the deep ache of the loss of Yanni again washing over me. The emotions bubbling to the surface were about to become too much, and the last thing I desired to do was cry in front of these three.

I started toward the door.

"Where are you going?!"

"I have something to tend to." I didn't turn around. The tears were already coming.

"I need you here, Esther! You must confirm how many captives were recovered. I don't trust this one's abilities. And I must learn how the Pai Ona knew where to find them."

I wiped at my face as discreetly as possible before turning around and facing her.

"Of course. I will gladly discover who is responsible for this blunder. But first I must tend to something personal."

Her expression didn't exactly soften when she realized I was emotionally flooded, but it did convey a knowing. "I will give you a few moments to mourn your infatuation. But don't think your failure went unnoticed either."

Infatuation? I didn't bother to protest or legitimize the anguish I was feeling. A monster like Aurora could not be reasoned with right now. I knew this because I was a monster. I left the room quickly but could still hear the Oracle's rant well into the hall as I sprinted for the exit.

I needed to drown out the noise and feel what was coming—the pain, the deep, familiar loss of part of my soul. I stepped out of the tomb and into the brisk Siberian air. It froze my tears to my face. It tingled and burned. I inhaled sharply and let out the greatest scream I could muster before falling to my knees in the snow and letting the cold take over my body.

LUCAS

*Y*essica was feeling much better since Fetzle's cure. We had enjoyed several hours of lost time together while the rest of the Pai Ona settled into The Cathedral and Olly and the Tallus family took care of the monster guy Susuda. *I liked him. I hoped he pulled through.*

I felt like one of the lucky ones these days. It was strange, and I liked it. The Pai Ona had recovered many captives from Chernobyl, and that gave me a deep sense of pride. I'd been a part of the recovery effort. Despite all my shitty decisions, wrong turns and fucked-up assumptions, I felt like I'd done something right and it almost made me feel like all of Huan's hard work and ultimately his sacrifice were realized. Tears welled up in my eyes as I thought about my friend. I hoped he was with Nandi and that they were raising a toast to the victory tonight.

Yessica's long hair was draped all around us in our bed. We manifested the little cabin we had in Monte Patria. It was the perfect place to tuck away and reconnect. It was almost like I'd come full circle, since this was the very site I went to mourn her when Viraclay contacted me to keep Olly safe.

"I could get used to this," she said as she curled up under my arm.

"Me too, baby girl."

There was a knock on the door, and I could tell from the cadence of it that it was Olly. I kissed Yesi's forehead.

"It's Ophelia, isn't it?"

I nodded.

"Take all the time you need. We owe her our lives. Please tell her I'm so grateful for her."

"I will," I assured her as I put my pants on and pulled a white T-shirt over my head. I took a deep breath before opening the door, a mixture of emotions swirling up inside me. This whole opening back up thing was fucking shitty. I was always feeling something.

I opened the door and there stood Olly in a pair of purple yoga pants, a teal tank top and her hair pulled up into a messy bun. If I wasn't incredibly aware of all the pain that was on her face, I could've convinced myself we were back in our apartment in San Francisco, getting ready to go for a bike ride in the park. It was one of those surreal moments when all the lives you've ever lived in and through collide and you feel baffled by it all. She threw herself into my chest and hugged me hard.

"Oh Lucas!" I wrapped my arms around her, feeling her tears soak my shirt. "I'm so glad you're okay. Everything is impossibly hard, but I'm so glad you're okay."

"Thanks to you." I squeezed her a little tighter. "Can we go talk? I have some things I really want to say."

She nodded. "I know a place." Olly put her hand on the threshold, and we were suddenly in a garden. She pulled her head from my chest and walked over to a bench. I followed and took my seat beside her.

I dove into my confessions, the shameful moments I hadn't forgiven myself for but hoped against hope that she would have the heart to forgive me. "I killed Huan, yes, but it was in agreement to the pact we had made, and it nearly killed all the humanity that was left in me." I didn't even breathe between words. I had to get it all out. "I worked for the Nebas in search of Yesi and I did terrible, terrible things. But none as bad as the night I put your life in danger when I arranged for Yanni to get Viraclay out of the way of our relationship. I wanted you to myself, to keep you safe my way, to take away your freewill and your forever, and by doing so I also put your life at risk." The tears were unstoppable and the shame unbearable. "But I didn't kill Cane and Sorcey. I was just caught off guard when you asked that question and I've been flooded with guilt because of the last conversation I'd had with Cane. I failed him as a friend."

She took my hand in hers. "I know, I know, and I forgive you for it all. I don't have room in my heart for hate or judgement, it's too full of grief." Olly rubbed her eyes with her free hand and the moment she pulled her hand away her tears started once more. "Susuda is gone. Rand is gone. Di is gone, and so many others, I've lost count." She looked up at me with such pain; I wanted to wash it all away. She didn't deserve this. She had already been through so much. "I can't even bring myself to go see Eleanor. I know what he did to her. I saw it." Olly put her head on our hands, let out two loud sobs before wiping at her face again. I tried to console her. I rubbed her shoulders. "I have so much to be grateful for."

I almost viscerally shook my head in disbelief. I didn't see that one coming.

She continued. "You're alive, Elias is alive, my mother and grandmother are alive. Aremis is here and I'm surrounded by so many friends." She threw her hands in the air. "I'm back in my body for the strokes' sake. Never thought I would have to say that one." She laughed at the ridiculousness of it all. I smiled sheepishly, understanding the absurdness that can only be felt when you say something like that aloud. "But I'm in this constant paradox of emotion, feeling simultaneously blessed and devastated.

"Lucas?" I knew this introduction well. There was a loaded question on the backside of this pause.

"Olly?"

"What are we doing this for? What's the purpose of all this conflict, of all this pain?"

I sat there for a moment as she looked at me expectantly. I wasn't usually a contemplator, but this question had been ebbing at me since I discovered Yesi was alive. I considered all I did to try and avoid the pain I felt at her loss, only to discover the walls I built had to be torn back down again so I can open back up and receive her and the love we shared.

I took Olly's hand in mine and cupped it between both my palms. "I don't know why there is so much pain, why this life is filled with conflict and loss." Her shoulders slumped in defeat, as though she thought I might really have the answer. "But I know this. I've been deeply loved by two women in my life—far more than I deserve. I've felt and watched your love transmute hate into compassion. I've seen Yesi choose the courageous act of love and defy fear and oftentimes the odds. I've been saved by love, first my wife's and then yours. Unlike you both, I chose fear, defensiveness, rage, hatred, solitude and revenge when the pain and loss fell at my feet. Instead of feeling it, I bottled it up and used it as a reason, weapon, and wall to keep others out while I festered in it. I did atrocious things, things I'm so ashamed of, things I'll spend the rest of my life begging forgiveness for. Fuck, I almost let the pain destroy me and everything I ever cared about with it. Your love, Yesi's love, they gave me grace, and on the other side of the anguish, I see how if I hadn't lived through the pain, I couldn't be cracked open wide enough to start to truly love again. There's something to this shit about accepting the light and the dark. We have to accept it all as part of this life. Our evolution comes from the dance between the good and the bad, right?"

Her tears had stopped. Her jaw was almost on the floor, and her eyes were examining me like she wasn't sure if I'd been possessed by some sort of demon.

When the silence went on for too long, I started to get uncomfortable. "Too much?"

She shook her head. "No, just right—it just wasn't your mouth I thought I'd get that insight from. But because it was, it's that much more powerful." She pulled me in for a hug. "Thank you. I've missed you so much. Losing you was unbearable, but hearing the way you're transforming...well, it almost makes it all worth it."

I held her as tightly as I could. "I'm so sorry, Olly. I never meant to hurt you."

"Shhh, I know." She kissed my cheek. "I already forgave you."

We sat there holding each other for a long time. This time in comfortable silence. It felt like home.

"I wanted to tell you, out of respect for you and our relationship. I know Yesi is here, and I'm so grateful to discover she is alive. I see what she does for you, and it makes my heart happy. Still, I want you to know, Elias and I are consummating in two days."

I didn't deserve this from her. "Mazel tov!" I lifted my hand for a high five and she punched me in the ribs.

"Alright, smartass, but seriously, will you be my best man?"

"Nuptials first? Count me in." I pulled her in once more for a hug. "Do I have to wear a dress?"

Ophelia was finally ready to face Eleanor and Lilith. I had asked her if she desired my support, but she insisted she could do this by herself. I escorted her to the shared chamber that Lilith and Eleanor occupied. I hoped they were getting along well and somehow making up for lost time. I was anxious to hear how Olly and Eleanor's reunion would go. In the meantime, I was tasked with getting up to speed on the success of the siege, discovering how the search for the final battle has progressed, and I wanted to discuss some personal concerns with Ruit.

We were in the conference room, the same one that we convened in just before departing to collect the dragons. Many familiar faces looked back at me, while three very crucial ones were missing— Rand, Susuda and Di.

Vosega and Oya entered the room and nodded at Ruit. "Indeed, now that we are all present, let us begin."

"What about the Sulu?" a wiry man I did not recognize inquired.

"Ophelia has been through a lot these past few days. We have decided to give her respite with her family that were recovered in Chernobyl. She will be with us in her full capacity tomorrow."

I wondered if Ruit suspected what Ophelia and I intended to do, concerning our consummation. After Susuda's passing, we spent several hours recapitulating our experiences. She told me all about her time on the banks of the River Tins. How she learned of Aurora's treachery in far more depth than any of us could have imagined. The unbelievable truth that Esther and Nestor are twins and are Aurora and Apollo's children. She relayed my mother's secret and her message to me. Olly now believed there was a chance that Esther could be swayed to our cause. It was a long shot, but I felt the dissension among the Nebas too. If Esther learned the truth, it could be the lynchpin of their undoing. I told Olly about the catalogue of Rittles and the admissions from Aurora herself. We decided that it was not the appropriate time to tell the entire Pai Ona congregation the alarming news. We needed to apprise our closest comrades and determine a strategy for delivering the information. But perhaps the most important matter to be determined was that we decided we would not wait any longer to consummate. We were ready to fortify our union.

My minor hesitance was what little we knew about the annihilation that occurred five thousand years ago. But even still, we had no reason to believe the incident had been provoked by consummation. On the contrary, the source implied otherwise. Admittedly, the risk we were taking was still great. Anytime one stepped into the unknown, there were always consequences that followed. There was one thing I knew with absolute certainty; I would not lose Ophelia to her powers again. She deserved the advantage of being a Consu. She, more than anyone, had earned the right to reinforce her body, to see her full potential, and I was honored to be able to walk beside her during her transformation.

I considered the prophecy that had held me back from following my heart the moment I saw Olly... Aurora had said she'd enchanted it, but she never said it was not true. Nevertheless, Ophelia and I were writing our own fate, once and for all.

"Viraclay, did you hear me?" Aremis asked.

"I am so sorry, Aremis, I was lost in thought. Please forgive me. What did I miss?"

"I wanted to inform everyone that I spoke with Napitae upon my arrival back to The Cathedral. He and I have unfinished business to attend to. I will be journeying with him to China the day after tomorrow for an undisclosed amount of time. But what's more, is that the dragons are infuriated to discover that Gwenora was being imprisoned all of this time. They are in the process of deciding how they may intervene on her behalf, how they may bring those who violated her to justice."

Ruit spoke next, "Cataphet relayed as much to me. The Sovereign of the Dragons had no intention of participating in the violence of the Conduit world, but the fact that it has spilled over once more and led to the captivity of an Original has changed everything. She also reminded me, as Napitae did Aremis, that for the final battle to be in favor of the Pai Ona, we must determine the point where the world ends."

Where the world ends? That sounded familiar... I had forgotten Cataphet's message to me. So much had transpired since Olly had given it to me. "Indeed, Cataphet conveyed the same instructions to me."

"That is promising news. So the dragons may stand beside us in this war?" Winston asked.

"It appears that is a strong possibility. Further fueled by the loss of the gatekeeper," Ruit replied.

"That will give us a great advantage," cheered Vosega as he clashed forearms with Stalt.

Ruit continued. "As previously strategized, we cannot delay. We have flushed them out of their stronghold and now is the time to funnel them to where we will have the tactical advantage. Almus, before the battle at the basin, you and your party had narrowed down a few advantageous locations, correct?"

Almus stood to address the room beside his father. "We had narrowed it down to two locations."

"Death Valley in Russia and the Solomon Islands south of Australia."

"Curious. I thought the Giants were not interested in choosing sides in this war?" I noted.

"The Giants are still considering our proposal and—"

Aruna hurried into the room and whispered something in Ying's ear. "It appears Death Valley is no longer a viable option. We have intelligence that confirms many of the Nebas have fled to the Orb Forest Haven."

"That is not favorable for our strokes. Perhaps the devilish Clive can use the Orbs for something terrible," Winston reasoned. More buzz filled the room.

Genghis retorted, "Or perhaps it gives us an advantage to know that the enemy intends to use the Orbs."

A shock wave of murmurs moved through the room.

Almus continued. "Now that we have recovered the captives and Ophelia is returned to her body, we can put more energy into discovering the most advantageous location for battle and discovering 'where the world ends.'" Almus looked around at the familiar faces. "Ying as well as many others have joined me in the research as well as on-site surveillance of the final battle location. If you feel the call, please meet us after the burial rites tonight. We will be convening in the library."

"As my son alluded to, we will be honoring the dead later this evening. We suffered only one casualty. The gatekeeper passed just hours ago." He did not make eye contact with anyone, for the same reason I did not with him—I was afraid I would cry. "And thanks to Vita and Garrett, we successfully rescued fifty-nine captives who are recovering in the south wing of The Cathedral. Queen Fetzle has graciously donated several pitchers of troll tears for their recovery."

Fetzle was in attendance. She just giggled when Ruit said her name. I had not heard how many captives had been recovered until now. That was many more than I had suspected. No wonder the Oracle had scoffed at my minimal vision. That was six times the amount I had guessed she had imprisoned.

"There was one other casualty," Yessica's sweet voice interjected.

She held onto Fetzle's arm in the corner. I had not noticed her there. "Moira. She gave her life to evict Yanni from Ophelia's body, saving the Sulu."

Ophelia had told me of Moira's courage and sacrifice. It touched me deeply.

"Vos and I collected her body. That was why we were late." Oya nodded at Yessica in assurance. "We will honor her tonight, alongside the gatekeeper."

It was hard to believe Moira would be the vital key for all of our survival. But that was the way of the strokes. We never truly knew what or who would be the tipping point in this war.

"Who are the survivors? When can we find out if they are our loved ones?" Mikkel sat beside Helia, wringing his hands nervously. He had already lost his brother in the fall of The Cathedral, but I supposed he had other family and friends he hoped had survived.

"We will have names for those we do not know already by the end of the hour. But I ask that you remain patient. Those who come to will be anxious for a reunion as well. From what we witnessed with Yessica, the recovery can be swift. That being said, some of them have been asleep for hundreds of years." That sent another wave of whispers through the room. "I want to thank each of you who heeded our call to stand at the siege of Chernobyl. You did not have to come. The next call will be the bidding and the final battle. We were lucky. The Oracle was apparently caught off guard this time. We may not be so fortunate the next. Furthermore, Vita gave us integral information that allowed us to orchestrate a plan with minimal violence. The Nebas were prepared to flee Chernobyl, and with that they still have more captives, the Rittles, the Pierses, and their captain is the Oracle."

"How do we know she is not a captive?" Friedrick asked.

I stood. "I can speak to that. First, let me start by saying thank you, to all of you. Your courage is why I stand here today. On behalf of both Ophelia and myself, I want to say we are eternally grateful for your bravery and swift response to the call to action." I made eye contact with as many faces as I could. "I can confirm that the Oracle is acting on her own volition and with her own motivations." Gasps and objections alike circled the room. "She personally tortured me and admitted that she was Alistair's accomplice—rather he was her minion. Aurora has been playing us all for fools for many, many years. Her treachery is deeper than any one of us may ever truly know. But I ask that we keep this revelation discreet for the time being."

The voices grew louder as people tried to reason with what they were hearing. I could not blame them. I still grappled with the disbelief myself. "I understand your doubt. I would be of the same mind had I not witnessed her wickedness myself. She is hungry for power. Ophelia was in limbo on the banks of the River Tins while Yanni had possession of her body. During her time there, many truths were revealed to her by those who have long since passed."

I could not explain in detail what Olly had experienced. First, we needed to convince them that Aurora was a traitor, before we could explain that Apollo was a victim, as was Esther. It was too much for me to take in and process. It was too soon for the truth to be delivered to the masses.

"Who did she speak to? What did they say?" Friedrick asked.

"Couldn't this be some trickery of the body snatcher Esther?" a voice called out.

I ignored Frederick's pointed questions and addressed the other. "Esther was not present during most of my interrogations. Aurora acted of her own accord, I assure you. And it has come to light that Esther cannot make her captives speak under her spell. Furthermore, the Oracle told me of her plans to create a giant Sulu with the captives she held. It is she who would benefit from imprisoning our loved ones and seeing them be a cog in a mechanism of power."

More murmurs.

"What about the hobgoblin?" A man maneuvered through the crowd of Conduits.

"Do you know much about hobgoblins, Mr...?" I did not recognize him. It made me uneasy since we were trying to keep this information restricted for now.

"You can call me Ramy, just Ramy." I studied the man. He was tall, fit, with wise and fiery eyes. His dark curly hair was pulled back into a low bun. He had a short beard and two distinct freckles on either cheek. The right side of his mouth curled up into a cunning smile as he watched me evaluate him. "We weren't able to meet at the Trials, Viraclay, but you can find many who will vouch for my integrity among us." Ramy had a noticeable Mexican accent. It added to his charm as he bowed slightly. There was something about the man. *I liked him.*

"I am sorry we were unable to make introductions sooner."

"That is of no consequence." He waved it off. "Hobgoblins, however, are of great consequence. I was born near Teotihuacan in Mexico, where the only clan of hobgoblins migrated to, in the mountains to the east of the valley. They are mysterious creatures of great power. Somehow, our histories have forgotten their capacity. Or perhaps it was intended that they slink into the shadows of the strokes, dismissed, and nearly obliterated without a thought." The way he said it, I understood that Ramy had an intuition for why or who would want to wipe out these apparently gifted and unassuming creatures. "Whatever the case, they are not to be trifled with. My parents spoke of mind control and the ability to siphon a being's life force directly from their strokes. Masters of disguise, hunting, and with an aptitude for thievery... Truthfully, no one really knows their full potential. Except for the Oracle, that is."

"Because of Clive?"

"The last hobgoblin alive."

Whispers raced through the room.

"How can you be certain of this?"

"I witnessed his clan's extinction as a boy. It appeared to be a random meteor shower. Fire rained down from the sky, wiping out each one, almost as though there were targets on their backs. Clive was with the Oracle on the Island of Atlantis, just before it sank into the sea." Ramy raised his hand to silence the crowd. "Destruction does appear to travel in Clive's wake, and so, one must pose the question, could the Oracle be being manipulated by her companion?"

Now the room erupted. I looked over the table at Ramy and bowed slightly, appreciative of his information on one hand, while painfully aware this stirred more questions among the Pai Ona on the other. Questions we would not soon get answers to. This was exactly why I wanted this information to stay in the hands of the few. I tapped into my Rune. "Ruit, do I tell them that I know she killed Cadmael?"

"No. It will do nothing to eliminate suspicious of Clive's mind control for now." Ruit stood and I sat down. "Thank you, Ramy. You have given us much more to consider. I assure all of you that this will be investigated at great length. If Aurora is being manipulated, we will discover the origins and bring all responsible to justice."

My stomach twisted, because I knew that the Oracle was responsible for all of this. I'd seen the look in her eyes. I felt the satisfaction she got from recounting her betrayal. I was grateful I kept the truth vague. And I wondered, *could mind control portray nefariousness?*

"Either way, we are faced with the next order of business. Elias and Ophelia will be calling on the bidding in a matter of days. The remaining Pai Ona will be pouring into The Cathedral before we take our final stand," Ruit shared some words of encouragement. "There is much to attend to. Our enemy is sharp and has many advantages, but we are united by much more than hate, revenge or greed—we lock arms with love and the intention of freedom and peace for all of the strokes. Take with you the certainty of victory."

The room began to empty. Everyone was in mostly optimistic spirits. As though they could read my mind, our core community simply stood around waiting, patiently watching me.

"Well?" Lucas nudged my shoulder.

"Ophelia and I are getting married tomorrow, and we would love it if you could join us."

There was a boisterous round of applause. I was sad that Olly did not see the excitement our family had for our union.

A big hand patted me on the shoulder. "Tete thinks it's about damn time."

"What he means is congratulations are in order." Medusa shoved her friend playfully. "We wouldn't miss it for the world. I'll even make this guy wear a shirt."

A few more hugs and salutations were exchanged, and as the room began to disband entirely, I approached Ruit, first contacting him through our Rune. "Can I speak to you in private? There is a matter I wish to discuss."

"Congratulations. Two people have never been more deserving, or patient. Is it safe to assume that you intend to consummate your union?"

I nodded.

I could not decipher the look on his face. "That may change our timeline and approach slightly, but never worry, we all support you."

"The timeline? I have some concerns—"

He took the conversation back to our minds. "Would you consider an audience later this evening, after the rites? I made an appointment with Cataphet that I must attend to now."

"Oh yes, of course. Will you also extend an invitation to the wedding?"

He raised an eyebrow, smiled, and put his hand on the wall. As he dissolved away, I heard him say. "I will contact you shortly. I do wish to hear what you have to say."

"*D*id I miss anything important?"

"Is it not all important these days?" Elias said as he kissed my forehead. "You missed a gentleman named Ramy. He has a history with the hobgoblins. I very much look forward to hearing his account."

"Interesting." I sat up in bed. "Does he know Clive?"

"It would seem so. At the very least he knew his clan and suspects Clive had something to do with the annihilation of his people."

Dark. Clive was turning out to be scarier and scarier. "How did they take the news about the Oracle?"

"With skepticism, so I kept it brief. We need proof that she isn't being manipulated before we divulge the depth of her deception."

I suspected as much. There was no doubt this was going to be a difficult task. We were basically trying to convince the Conduit world their superhero was the villain and then we would take it a step further and explain that the villain was a victim. It wasn't going to be easy, and it required a lot of tact and some lucky strokes. I could only hope my gesture with Esther was stirring her own suspicions of Aurora. If we could get Esther on our side for the final battle, just as the Oracle exposed her true colors, we just might have a chance. How any of this would unfold was beyond my guess. But on a personal level, I knew this was very difficult for Elias. I situated myself to rub his shoulders. "How did that make you feel?"

After all, now Elias knew for certain that Aurora had killed his parents, it couldn't feel good to not demand justice.

"I feel impatient, but somehow at peace. The message you relayed from my mother gave me incredible comfort." He pulled my hand up to kiss it. "And knowing now the secret that she kept for the Oracle for all of those years, well into the Nebas assassinations… It must have weighed heavily on her and would explain why Aurora suddenly found her too much of a liability to have around."

"Yeah. How would it look to be the Pai Ona's sweetheart while your daughter is the Nebas leader and your son is a monster? It's not good for publicity." I said it sarcastically, but it made my skin crawl. I needed to use humor to deflect the magnitude of the situation we were facing. Even if we captured her, it would be nearly impossible to convince the Pai Ona she was as evil as she was. She could fall back into being a martyr and hide with Clive for another millennium, and start this chaos again. "I don't think she's running a democracy though."

"Indeed, she is not." He grabbed my arm and pulled me around to straddle him. "Are you ready to become Mrs. Kraus?"

"More than I've ever wanted anything in the world." I put my mouth on his and traced every nook and cranny with my tongue, until I had to come up for air. "How about you?"

"I would prefer to be Mr. Kraus, if you do not mind."

"Ha-ha-ha."

"Would you mind grabbing us a glass of that Chardonnay you found?"

"It's like you read my mind." I popped off his lap and scuttled into the kitchen, quickly poured two glasses of wine, and when I turned around Elias was on one knee with a little box in his hand. My hands started to shake. I all but dropped the glasses. It was silly. We'd already decided to get married, *so why am I a nervous wreck?*

I set the glasses down on the side table and walked over to him slowly. It occurred to me I'd thought I'd miss this part. I just assumed I wouldn't get to be a fiancée. We were just jumping right into the nuptials. But something in me wanted every step, every commitment from him that I could possibly receive or give. That's why I was nervous. I was experiencing another one of my dreams coming true.

"I know we are doing this in an unconventional way. A wedding in the middle of a war. Even for the Conduit world, we have chosen the road less traveled. But I did not want you to miss a single stage of this commitment we are making to each other. If that means we are engaged for a day, then so be it." He smiled that grin that drove me crazy.

"From the moment I ran into you in Chicago, all I have ever wanted was to be yours and for you to be mine. The strokes would have it another way, but never did I doubt that they would lead us here. You are the strongest, bravest, and most vulnerable person I know. I will never understand why I have been blessed with you as my Atoa. The painter must have known that I would see how precious you are. I am certain he trusted that I would honor you, respect you, adore you, and protect you for all eternity. And when our strokes have run their course, many, many years from now, I will follow your magic into the next life, where we will choose our unique story once more." Elias opened the box, exposing a beautiful vintage rose gold ring with an emerald-cut pink stone in the center surrounded by tiny diamonds. It was exactly what I would've picked out if I'd ever known I'd get the chance. He placed the ring on my finger and tears of joy welled up in my eyes. "Ophelia Alicea Banner, will you marry me?"

"Yes! A million times yes! In a million lifetimes, I choose you always and forever!" I practically tackled him to the floor. He picked me up in his arms and cradled me on the couch. I kissed every inch of his face.

"You are too good for me." He always knew exactly what I needed, even when I didn't know myself. "You surprised me."

"I did?" Elias looked aghast. "I did not think that was possible these days. You are, after all, the great Sulu."

"You did good, mister." I rubbed our noses together.

The familiar sensation of my Rune pulled me from the moment, and by the look on Elias' face, I knew they were contacting him as well. It was Almus. "Tonight, we remember the dead. Please be prepared to share a few words about both the deceased. Susuda and Moira deserve the highest honor, and your presence and testament will give them both." Then, in true Almus fashion, he was gone.

And the gravity of the situation was no longer able to be denied. The feelings of regret and grief encompassed me once more and I pulled myself off Elias' lap. He looked at me with the same withdrawn expression. It was a paradox of emotion—intense sorrow beside climactic joy. We'd been living in this medley for months, but it still left me in shock.

The tears began to fall again, and my sweet fiancé silently pulled me in and held me as close as he could.

here were hundreds, maybe even a thousand beings in attendance of the rites. Trolls, dragons and Conduits had all filed in together. I leaned over and whispered to Yesi, "Do you think all these Conduits knew either of them?"

"You don't have to know someone to understand that their sacrifice impacted you."

I kissed her temple. *She was right. Of course she was right.*

"You are wiser than most, baby girl."

"And you have a bigger heart than you realize." She took my hand to her mouth and kissed it.

"Don't go starting rumors."

I looked around the large hall, or maybe it was better described as an amphitheater. We were all sitting slightly elevated from the center, in stadium-style accommodations, yet it felt more formal. The seats surrounded a large stage with an entrance that came in from beneath where we sat. Suddenly, an orchestra began playing a familiar song, but I couldn't place it, and all eyes were drawn to the procession of the Tallus family entering through the central entrance. Ruit held a dark brown cloak, Jezebel's arm hooked into his. His son and Inca were just behind them. The whole family wore grey, a symbol of the strokes being melded back to their origination. I'd only recently been informed of the formality, that it was considered respectful to the dead. I wondered who made up these rules. A beautiful casket rolled in behind them, open and revealing the serene body of Moira. This was a rarity, maybe even a first. Since Conduits generally died by fire, I'd never heard of an account of a funeral with a body.

Immediately following the casket walked Olly and Viraclay. I adjusted in my seat to see if I could get a better view of her face to assess how she was holding up, but all I could see was the back of her head. She and Elias also wore grey; *I guess they got the memo.*

The procession stopped in the center. The casket was in the middle, and beside that, Ruit had placed the brown cloak on a small table. The six of them took their places in a half circle around the remains. These burial rites were going to be different than those for Di and Rand, for obvious reasons. One of the deceased was a shadow monster who'd apparently turned into sparkly ash, and the other was still intact. The previous ceremony wouldn't be appropriate. Now that I could see Olly's face, it was clear she was a wreck. *Poor thing.* Funeral today and a wedding tomorrow. She couldn't catch a break. Guilt washed over me. She had been torn between extremes for too long.

Ruit stepped forward and his voice projected into the auditorium. "Thank you all for coming here to pay your respects to my son Susuda and the courageous Moira. None of us would be here today if it were not for these brave souls. Their sacrifice altered the strokes in order to save many lives. They believed that where we are going is better than where we have been. Their love…" Ruit choked on the words. "My son's love was the purest thing I and my family have known."

All of the sudden The Cathedral shook, and I realized she was mourning too.

Ruit continued. "Susuda was perhaps the most loyal and innocent being I have ever come across. It seems appropriate that his remains evaporated into a million tiny rainbows, because it is a reminder of the mark he left on all those around him. A season of making the world a little brighter, a little more playful, and a lot more colorful. There could never be enough time with him. We could never have had enough time with him." Ruit looked back at his family.

"The truth is I did not know Moira well, but Moira chose to protect Ophelia with her life. She had become a recluse in recent years, not one who had many friends, which is why her choice is that much more sacrificial. She gave her essence for the lives of strangers. For that, she will always be remembered." Then he stepped back and Olly and Elias stepped forward. She looked like she was holding onto him for dear life.

Elias spoke first. Good man, I thought. He could see she needed the space to breathe. "We loved Susuda like a brother. He was the best in all of us. Strong, compassionate, virtuous, and as Ruit said— loyal. He was always eager to help, to encourage, and to fix the problem. I have never met a more enthusiastic soul who endured so many terrible misfortunes."

Olly interrupted him. "He was pure, as pure as a sunrise. Su always saw the best in every situation, and all he ever wanted was to enjoy the simplest pleasures in life. He taught me to appreciate the fundamental joy in life. Fierce and fragile, all at the same time. Hearts like his are rare and I cannot imagine this world without him." She paused and Elias took the cue to step in while she openly wept. Her loss broke my heart, tears welled up and over in my eyes.

"Su fell on the sword, literally. He gave his life for friendship and for what he believed was a cause worth fighting for—to protect this world, our world. Moira did the same. She chose to give the only thing she had left, her life, in the hopes that all of us could create a better future."

Olly spoke up again. "No one person deserves that much sacrifice." She clutched her hand to her chest. "I don't feel worthy of that much faith. But I realize as I stand up here, pouring my heart out to each of you, that we all have a choice. We can all choose faith in something. Today, I choose to have faith in the world these two imagined would be created from their choices. For Susuda, it was a world of freedom and simple but delicious delights. For Moira, it was the reality of liberation, where life's mysteries could persist and our gifts could be rejoiced. We can give them that. I know I will fight for that." Then she hung her head low as she shook with sobs. And it felt as though the entire room shook with her.

A pyre appeared and the casket of Moira elevated to the top, along with Susuda's cloak. Once in place, a flicker of flame was conjured in the belly of the construct of wood. The flames grew hotter and higher, and Yesi squeezed my arm. Music erupted from the orchestra, a celebratory note that felt somehow fitting and yet out of place. The fire reached Moira's body and, as it was enveloped by the flames, Ruit flicked his wrist and the cloak exploded, sending millions of dancing rainbows reflecting and bounding off the walls. It was like nothing I'd ever seen before. It was glorious. It was a true celebration of life.

"The powrie king is here," Claudia announced while I knelt over three of the captives we had with us here in the Orb Forest. They were still comatose, but for how long I did not know. It was brought to my attention that the poison room had been destroyed when the dragon escaped. There were many disconcerting elements to this latest development. The first was that I was unaware that we were holding a dragon in captivity, and not just any dragon, but the very dragon that had destroyed Atlantis and ultimately killed my mother. *That would have been nice to know.* I was even more alarmed to learn that Nestor knew of this secret because he assisted in building the room that helped conceal the dragon with the same enchantments he concealed his own Consu victims with. As the leader of the Nebas, it felt like treason to not know what was happening in the underbelly of my own compound. I fumed inside. I did not know why the dragon was being held captive or what relation it had to the poison we used to sedate the captives, but Clive was unable to secure the sedative when the dragon escaped.

I ignored Claudia and repeated my question to Astrid, "Do we have any of the antidote still?"

"Why would that matter?"

I growled at her insolence. "Because there will come a time when the Oracle, your queen, desires to wake up these slumbering instruments to effectuate her plan. If we cannot rouse them, they are practically of no use to her." I actually did not know if that was correct. Perhaps she could reach the Sulu capacity with them in this catatonic state. Nevertheless, I desired answers because it seemed the questions were continuing to mount.

"Queen Oracle moved the antidote viles into her chamber just before the Pai Ona attacked."

The hair on the back of my neck stood on end. Another precaution, since she knew the enemy was coming sooner than she had told me. *Why did she not do the same with the poison? Did the poison need to stay in the secured lower chambers until the last minute, was it volatile in the open? Did the dragon guard the poison room?*

"Esther, the Oracle demands you greet the king," Claudia insisted. I flipped around so quickly I caught Astrid by surprise as well. My hand was at Claudia's throat, my nails piercing her skin. Blood began to trickle down and stain her pink cardigan.

"The Oracle has also charged me with identifying the remaining captives and their condition. How am I to be in two places at once? Perhaps you can let your queen know, that currently I am preoccupied with her first orders."

Claudia choked out the words as I squeezed her throat a little tighter. "I'm not telling her a thing. You can just explain your absence." She swept up her right arm and pushed me back, just enough to loosen my grip and slip away. "I'm not getting in the middle of your pissing contest." Then she left.

I had a little more respect for the woman. She was not just a lackey, like this one. I looked at Astrid, who was still in shock from the exchange. I wiped my bloody fingers on her coat.

"Is that what you think this is? A pissing contest?"

She shook her head. "No, Mistress."

"Good. I am glad you have some sense about you." Although that was the furthest thing from the truth. She was a tool. "I just want answers. Answers that not even the great Oracle has." I could've continued on with my rant, but I knew this wasn't the audience. She would fold to make the *Queen* happy. I had no allegiances here, Yanni was gone, and now I was sure more than ever that Aurora knew more than she let on about the Pai Ona's attack. She wanted me with him but did nothing to prevent him from entering the River Tins. I disappointed her, that was clear, but she left me in the lurch, so I didn't know all the moving parts. She took several precautions to insure the Nebas could escape with the Rittles, her Pierses, the captives, and the antidote, *but forgot about the poison? Or perhaps the poison couldn't be held in her room?* She allowed a dragon to escape and didn't give me the correct information. None of it made sense, but one thing was for certain. With Yanni gone, I had nothing to do but discover the truth.

*R*uit was in the hall, waiting patiently. We looked at each other for a moment before he suggested we take the conversation to his room. A moment later, he was pouring me a glass of red wine. "Would you like me to ask Jezebel to leave? She is in our chamber."

"No, that won't be necessary." Ruit sat across from me in the living room. His apartment was nice, large from what I could gather. The room we currently sat in had a sizable fireplace, and tall, vaulted ceilings with an ornate golden chandelier in the center. We convened just below it on two love-seats that faced one another.

"I missed this place. It was home for me and my family for many years." He raised his glass.

"I imagine it would be nostalgic to be back."

"And heartbreaking."

"To Susuda." We both raised our glasses. I held back tears because I wanted to stay present with what I was about to discuss with him. "Olly and I will be wed tomorrow and then consummate."

Ruit took a sip of his wine and nodded pensively. "Congratulations."

"Thank you."

"I suppose you did not seek my company in order to receive the well wishes I already gave. What matter needs discussing? You seem intent on the next steps, and I for one believe it is the best course of action."

Relief surged through me. I valued the wisdom of others in moments of mystery. Aremis had already long since given us his blessing. I respected Ruit and, without my father or Rand here, I guess I needed someone to tell me we were not being rash, that this was about more than love.

"So, you do not think it is reckless, to consummate even though we know from accounts that a previous Sulu caused the extinction of an entire planet of Conduits? It is also a consideration that there are no recollections of Sulus being anything remotely similar to the likes of Olly and her abilities. Not to mention we've just lost a dear friend and are in the middle of this war. Still, the prophecy may or may not have been true, and it alludes to a near impossible fate—"

"Viraclay, by the strokes, have you been carrying this with you the whole time? Take a breath. Would you like my honest opinion?"

"Indeed." I took a big sip of my wine. *That is all I want.*

"Matters of the heart are always a little bit reckless." He smiled coyly. "The accounts of the extinction are vague at best. We know there was a Sulu in existence, not that the Sulu caused the occurrence." I exhaled deeply. He was right. "Ophelia is exceptional in more ways than any of us can fathom. But as I see it, we are all safer if she is in her truest form, and that is a Consu. We almost lost her because this body is no match for the power she is accumulating. She deserves a fighting chance." My shoulders fell even further from around my neck. "Susuda and any others that we have recently lost will be honored to know you two are blessing your union. That I say with the upmost certainty. The war we wage will wait a few days, especially to fortify its leaders."

I stopped shaking my leg and realized for the first time in perhaps weeks that I was feeling some semblance of relaxation.

"As far as the prophecy," he continued, "it may be true, or it may never have held merit, except to serve as a form of control. Only time will determine its validity, but I am of the mind that we determine our own strokes. I consider the fable of Fih and his determination to create the first lines. That moment, his actions altered all of our fates forever. If it was not his choice to separate that which he coveted from everything else, where else would this world be? Why has so much chaos befallen in its wake? The painter could intervene, could he not? Rather, it would seem we are all dictators of our own fate, only one decision away at any given time from a completely different stroke."

"Olly sees it as you do."

"She is wise." He chuckled.

"She is, but then what am I? To have followed in blind faith, out of the fear that was incited from words on a piece of paper?"

"Selfless. You have lived your life from the day you were born choosing the betterment of all over your own desires. I would choose to follow a leader with that type of integrity to the end of the world."

A single tear streamed down my cheek. I wished I was having this conversation with my father the night before my wedding. But in his absence, this was a favorable substitution.

"You and my father were friends?"

"Yes, for many, many centuries. I know he must be very proud of you."

"Thank you. That means a lot." I took a sip of my wine. "Did you give him the old channels?"

"As a matter of fact, I did."

"They are extraordinary. I have been curious though. The communications room here is vast and you have that incredible press to enforce enchantments and secrecy—why?"

"I wondered when you would ask about that." He bowed his head in what I thought was admiration. "You are a sharp man. Much of what I have created and done in my life has been steered by this book." Suddenly, Nandi's journal appeared in his hand. "It's the greatest magical resource I have ever known. Many of the Alchemists who came before me concluded it must be a direct line to the painter. I dare not say if that were true or not, but I can attest to its power and I trust its guidance more than any other artifact in this world." I had no idea he held it in such high regard. Although admittedly, I had seen its value when it gave us the incantation that moved the giant dragon Zeffina. "Seven hundred years ago, the Sorcerer's Stone sent me on a series of what seemed like random errands. It is only in recent years that the meaning of these assignments and acquisitions has become clear."

"Seven hundred years ago? That is when you warned Susuda he could be expecting me and Olly?"

Ruit nodded and continued. "It is also when I built all of the old channels and the press in the communication room, called upon the Star Seed to supply me with the Pierses paper required to deliver that many messages, and I was directed to steal the siren song."

"Pardon me, Star Seed? Pierses paper? And why in the strokes did you steal that poor siren's song?"

"My dear Viraclay, your parents did not have the time to share all there was to know."

The observation triggered me. I tried to shake it off, but in recent years I had felt like they had left me in the dark completely.

He sensed my angst. "I do not feel they meant to be vague or misleading. I truly feel they felt as all parents do. That they would have more time with their children."

He was right. I knew he was right.

"I can shed a little light on a few things I know. The Pierses paper is a creation of the Seven Sisters, the Pleiades—surely you have heard of the constellation?"

I nodded.

"They are Seven Sisters, all connected by the Star Seed celestial being that took part in each of their inceptions. The Star Seed can be called upon with the truest of intention. If your heart is pure, she may hear your request."

Olly would be thrilled to hear about this. That could only validate Apollo and his will toward her. "Where are the Sisters now and how did you know of the Star Seed?"

"So many questions and so little time. The Sisters are a mystery to me. I only know that they created the Pierses because of our origin myths. When I consider the construction of the magical anthologies it makes sense that the Seven Sisters would create sister volumes, right? Your mother told me to contact the Star Seed for the Pierses paper, I would have never considered that an option. But Sorcey was wise beyond words."

"Indeed."

"As far as the siren's song is concerned, I was only honoring the request of the Stone. Still, I suspect that it may have something to do with creating allies for our dear Ophelia." That was an interesting theory. "And that reminds me, I was also charged with acquiring troll tears during the slough of errands." He tapped at his right temple. "Come to think of it, I kept that vile with me at all times. I thought it was the death of my son that broke my long sleep, but it seems more likely that some of the troll tears may have leeched onto my skin. Brilliant. Simply brilliant, the way this magic works." He kissed the journal.

"What is brilliant, husband?" Jezebel came out of her room.

"Many things. I am always delighted by the twist of the strokes." She kissed his forehead lovingly and I felt it was time to take my leave. After all, it was the night before my wedding. I had a stag evening to attend.

"Thank you for sharing your husband with me." I stood up and hugged Jezebel.

"Anytime. You are always welcome in the Tallus home, Viraclay." She kissed my cheek.

"That is an honor I will take you up on. It has been a pleasure, Ruit. As always, I appreciate your wisdom." He stood and gave me a hug.

"I will say it again. Your father is proud. Exceptionally so. You will be the first Conduit in thousands of years with dragons in attendance at your wedding."

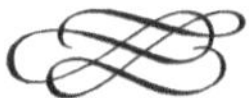

"How are you feeling?" Sparkle chirped. "Excited? Nervous? Sexy?"

"By Malarin, stop it!" I was blushing so much my face was on fire.

"I was so excited the night before my wedding, I threw up all night long." Even the way she said that, she sounded happy.

"Not me. I was terrified," Medusa said as she took her second shot of tequila. "I had to get tits up to get a wink a sleep."

"You ladies are not helping." I turned to Inca, who was sipping on a glass of champagne. "Help me out here. Give me calm wise words of wisdom."

"You will be fine, dear Ophelia. Most of us in this room were not only getting married but virgins. It adds an element of anxiety."

I looked around at the familiar faces, my wedding party of sorts. Helia nodded in agreement, Sparkle giggled, Medusa took another shot, Jezebel just smiled coyly at her daughter-in-law, and Lucia sheepishly hid behind her glass of merlot.

"Wait! Lucia, you weren't a virgin. You're like the youngest one here!" I said in disbelief.

"Winston knows..." She turned the same color of her wine.

"Times were different then. I was already a woman. It was only once."

We all laughed. I shook my head in disbelief because there was no way these virtuous ladies wanted to know how many men I'd been with up until now. A knock at the door, and in came Aruna. Beautiful, elegant, and holding my wedding dress. I stood up in shock and excitement. She'd only asked me for a picture of a gown less than an hour ago. "I hope it is to your liking. The tailor who made it is very proud." Aruna came toward me and only then did I notice Yessica behind her. She shuffled her feet uncomfortably.

"I know we don't know each other, and I will not be offended if you'd rather I left, but I wanted to see if I could celebrate with you. If it doesn't make you uncomfortable."

I took her in my arms. "Of course. I wouldn't have it any other way." I meant it. I desired a relationship with Yessica just as much as I did with Lucas. "Come in. Grab whatever you would like to drink, and sit over here." I gestured to the seat beside mine. "I have to try this thing on."

I scuttled into the bedroom and Sparkle came in after me. "I get to help!"

We shut the door and I quickly tore off my pajama dress as Sparkle held the gown up to put over my head. I'd asked for something simple, lacy, long, and bohemian in style. I had never put much thought into my wedding dress. Since the moment I met Elias, there hadn't been much time to think of more than how to survive. Sparkle gasped once the bottom trim hit the floor.

"Oh, Olly. You are breathtaking." Her hands were cupped over her mouth. "No peeking. Let me fasten these buttons before you turn around." She quickly finagled the buttons and the clasp and gently circled me around to the full-length mirror.

I couldn't believe my eyes. It was perfect. Champagne colored lace dripped down to the floor. A deep V-neckline lined with intricate flowers. The skirt bustled at the perfect spot on my midline, giving me a waist and smooth curves. I turned around to see that the straps over my shoulders became delicately thin until they disappeared into the waistline, making it virtually backless.

A knock came at the bedroom door. "Can we come in?" Eleanor's meek voice asked.

I had stopped to see my mother again before the ladies collected me and demand I spend the night away from Elias because it was tradition. She looked better than I'd expected. Lilith hadn't left her side since they were rescued from the compound. I expected to see a broken woman when I went to her bedside, but there was a new strength in her and a fierce compassion that I'd never experienced from my mother before. I explained that Elias and I would be getting married and if she was up for it, I wanted her to walk me down the aisle with Aremis. I was surprised how happy she was for me. I'd shamefully expected her to be lost in her pain and too consumed by it to want to celebrate with me.

"Please." The door opened and there stood Lilith and Eleanor. Both of their jaws dropped, and tears streamed down my mother's face.

"Olly, you look ravishing." She skipped over to me and pulled me in close. Lilith came in behind and held us both. Together, the three of us cried. I cried tears of joy, grief, gratitude and surprise. Never could I have imagined sharing a moment like this with my mother, and even less my grandmother. After a long, beautiful hug, Eleanor gently pulled away. "Don't let us old ladies ruin your big night. I just wanted to come tell you how proud I was of you and how excited I am to celebrate you tomorrow."

"Mom." I was speechless. My whole life I had waited for those words to come out of my mother's mouth. When Lucas faked my death months ago, as we fled San Francisco from Yanni, I thought I'd never see her again, let alone experience something like this. "I love you."

"I love you too." Eleanor kissed my forehead, then turned back to her mother.

Lilith cupped my cheek in her hand. "I love you and I am so very grateful to be here to celebrate you. I know your grandfather would tell you that you look like a dream."

More tears, a lot more tears. I was fortunate enough to have gotten the opportunity to tell my grandmother about my experience with Zavier on the River Tins yesterday. So she knew how much those words would mean to me.

Eleanor wiped at her eyes and rubbed her forehead. "I'm just getting used to all this madness, in a good way." She winked. Then the two of them left me with Sparkle. I was in shock.

"I think I need another drink."

❁

"Where are we?" I murmured.

Lucas looked my way and motioned for me to be quiet. I could hardly see a thing. Was this my wedding day? "Where's Elias?"

"Ophelia, be quiet or they'll hear us," he demanded.

Who were *they*? The wedding guests? I wondered. We were in a muddy tunnel. I was in my beautiful wedding gown and it was getting caked in dirt.

I lost control of my footing and slipped, then slid down a long shaft. The familiarity of the scene was coming back to me. I was terrified, but I couldn't scream. I landed alone in a huge cave. "Lucas?" I whispered, but he said nothing. There was a small flame opposite where I stood—in the largest part of the cave. "Aremis?" I called. It had to be Aremis. Suddenly, I knew exactly what this was. It was the recurring dream I'd had for months. But it had been a long time since I last had it. *Why now? Why on my wedding night?* The reality of my last recurring dream came flooding back to me. Eleanor, Lilith and I captives in a dungeon. *Did that mean this was real?*

I wanted to turn around, go the other way, but I couldn't. I walked toward the flame and it danced away. I started to run toward the tiny light, but as soon as I would get close enough to be able to see anything around me, it would jump aside. It finally stopped at a large rock. I knew instinctively to push the boulder aside. Just like I'd done before, I thought.

Behind the rock, the passage opened up into a vast cavern with huge stalactites everywhere. The small flame flew up. I looked after it, and when it reached the cavity's ceiling it grew into a massive fireball.

Suddenly, the whole place was illuminated, and I saw that I was no longer in a cave, but a large room, the ballroom where we were holding our wedding reception. The stalactites weren't pillars anymore, but people—Conduits I knew.

Elias stood in front of a beautiful altar, Ruit behind him. Lucas was walking directly in front of me. He turned around and smiled at me when he got to his place beside the altar.

"Are you ready, Miss Ophelia?" Aremis asked me, an enthusiastic smile on his face as he hooked my arm in his. My mother appeared on my other side.

"You are ravishing." Eleanor dabbed at the tears in her eyes, trying not to mess up her makeup. The room was full of all the Conduits I loved. Even Rand and Elias' parents were seated in the front row of chairs.

I looked up as we walked down the aisle. The fireball grew larger above us. Then I felt a cold hand touch my shoulder, and a familiar soft, sultry voice whispered in my ear. "Kill them. Kill them all," the voice said. It was Esther, and she had control of my body. I had no choice but to kill everyone.

I stood there in my wedding dress, staring at the terrified faces of every soul I'd ever loved pleading with me. Their mouths didn't move. Still, I could hear a cacophony of their voices begging me to spare their lives.

The fireball began to dive toward my friends and family, and a horrific dread gripped me. Then a voice echoed through the room. The same melodic voice I'd heard when Susuda died and when I regained control of my body, the same voice that directed me by the River Tins.

"Wake up, sweet child. It is only a dream. Some fates dissolve when other fates are chosen. Wake up. You always have a choice. You already know the way. It is time to embrace all that you are. Wake up."

I sat up in bed, sweaty, gasping for breath, shaking with fear. The voice trailed off in the distance. "You already know the way. Embrace all that I am?"

I paced nervously outside his room. For the first time ever, I was trying to be considerate. I didn't want to shit on his day, or rather, her day. But things needed to be said and I was ready to say them.

I knocked. "Come in." I opened the door to see Viraclay standing beside Winston, Ying, Aremis and my dad preparing to toast. *This is a little awkward.*

"Sorry to interrupt." I wrung my hands nervously. "Can I talk to you for a second?"

Elias kept his composure so well. *I definitely still hated that about him.* "Indeed. I will be only a moment, gentlemen." I looked him up and down. He looked sharp. A classic black suit, thin tie and brown leather loafers. He kept his hair a little long these days, so he had it tucked behind his ears and he was sporting a short, groomed beard. His father's watch caught my eye and I looked away, unusually swept up with emotions as I thought about Cane and how much he would want to be here, how lucky I was to be here with Yesi. I shrugged off the feelings and hoped no one noticed.

We stepped into the hall and as soon as the door shut, I got straight to the point. "I'm sorry I've been such an asshole... your whole life. And I'm really sorry I tried to have you killed by Yanni so I could take Ophelia from you." He said nothing so I continued. "I loved your parents and they would be ashamed of my behavior. I'm ashamed of my behavior. Losing Yesi made me… well, it made me a monster." Still, he said nothing. "I know you'll treat her right, and turns out you're a way better man than me."

He looked at me without giving a thing away. I shuffled my feet in place.

"I get it, you owe me nothing. But I'm sorry."

"I owe you everything."

I couldn't hide the shock.

"You saved her more than on one occasion, therefore I owe you everything." He leaned in for a hug and although it was exactly what I was hoping for, I felt uncomfortable as fuck. "Thank you."

"Yeah, well, thank you. And…"

"Have a drink with us?"

"Really?"

"Yes, really. I am no saint. This is hard for me too. Liquor will help, would you not agree?"

I nodded. We stepped back into the room, where the rest of his guests stood patiently waiting. Elias walked over to the bar and poured us two shots. We raised our glasses.

"Here's to not being an asshole," I said.

"Stranger things have happened," Elias poked, and I smiled at him before happily concluding this conversation with a stiff drink.

The others clapped vigorously. It was great to make amends, but I had no desire to stay. So I waved them on and left. I wanted to catch Olly before she was walking down the aisle, so the next stop was her room. I could hear the ladies clamoring about before I even got close. It made me smile. *Ophelia must be hating all this attention.* Aruna came darting out the door just before I was going to knock.

"Good timing." She winked at me and flitted off. The door was left ajar. I peeked in. Squeals and giggles coming from every corner.

"Hey, ladies, can I have a moment with the bride?" They all parted and exposed Olly in the center. I had to catch my breath. She was stunning. Her hair was in classic finger waves and her lips were painted red. She blushed at my expression.

"Can I have a minute with my best man?"

Instantly, the bridal party scattered, and we had the room to ourselves. "Champagne?"

"Already on it." I handed her a glass and took a big swig of my own. "You are stunning."

She blushed again and looked down at her feet. "I actually really love it."

"You should."

"Cheers." We clinked glasses. "Can you believe it? It feels surreal."

"It does."

"But so right, more right than anything I've ever felt before."

"I know that feeling and you deserve it. I'm sorry I ever tried to stand in the way of this."

She put her finger up to silence me. "Now, none of that. I wasn't ready to accept this either. When I met Elias and learned about my… fate, I resisted it just as much as you. I really didn't like the idea of some great being up there calling the shots and telling me who I would love. Besides, I already loved someone." She gently nudged me with her elbow. "But once I surrendered, I knew there could be no one else for me."

I just nodded. There was nothing for me to say.

"I'm glad you came by a little early because I have an important question."

I raised my eyebrows.

"Why didn't you and Yessica have a baby?"

Oh, that caught me off guard. "I mean, from what I understand, it's a conscious conception. During consummation, you and your Atoa choose to invite a soul to enter this world through your union. Why didn't you guys decide to have a baby?"

"I don't know exactly. We both had difficult childhoods. Yesi's stepmom, well, you know Borte, and losing my mom so young, I guess I was afraid of becoming my dad."

She looked down at her hands. They were shaking.

"That's kind of what I'm afraid of too." Ying had politely gotten me up to speed on all that I'd missed, so I knew that Olly's father had turned out to be that creep, Nestor.

"Oh, Olly." I cupped her face with my free hand. "You'll never be like that monster. You could never be like that monster, even if you tried."

"I don't know. I mean, the prophecy said—"

I cut her off. "Fuck that shit! You have defied all odds. There are no rules for you. The world has never seen anything like you. Don't let someone else's story determine who you are." Tears were welling up in her eyes. "Don't mess up that makeup or the brute squad that just left will kill me." She laughed a little and held back the tears. "Be that stubborn young woman who wouldn't let fate tell her who to love. You chose who you would love, you chose to surrender. That's my Olly, that's who you are."

She took a sip of her champagne, and a smile spread across her face. "I kinda like this new, vulnerable Lucas. You could be a life coach or something."

"Oh, shut the fuck up."

"No, really, the next big motivational speaker," she teased. "The world needs your soft heart and wisdom."

"That's it. I take it all back." Her smile was so big, so genuine, and the truth was I wouldn't take this moment back for anything in the world.

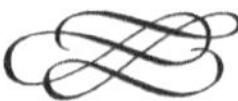

We kept it small, considering that there were thousands of Conduits in The Cathedral now and more arriving every hour. I looked around at the faces of all those I cared for. These were men and women I had fought beside, been raised with, trusted with my life... These Conduits were my family. I turned to Ruit, who stood in the center of the space we deemed an altar. We chose the garden to have the ceremony, and the ballroom to have the reception. It was a beautiful day on the grounds. A perfect day for a wedding.

Suddenly, Fetzle manifested behind the congregation of Conduits. She giggled when she saw me and my heart filled with even more gratitude. A few moments later, several Ancients appeared beside her. Many I had not yet met. This act of solidarity brought a sense of pride and accomplishment, a gesture of commitment to the Pai Ona. I had to believe that my father would have been very proud of this turnout, just as Ruit had said. And as though on cue, Franky, Gwenora, Cataphet and Zeffina surfaced, right on time, as the harp began to strum and everyone turned to see Lucas opposite the aisle from me. He wore a green suit. It looked nice on him. Lucas was a handsome man, a worthy opponent for Ophelia's affections. I considered the irony that his face was the first I saw walking towards me on my wedding day. I can only imagine the thoughts flying through his head, and by his coy smile, there were many. When he reached the altar, he leaned in for a hug.

"I'm grateful it's you who has her heart."

I cleared my throat reflexively out of shock. I was speechless. Lucas pulled back and looked at my face. "Yeah, I know. New me." Then he turned and winked at Yesi, who smiled enthusiastically at us from her seat.

The tempo of the music changed and everyone got to their feet. My heart began to beat so rapidly I thought I might lose consciousness. I made sure my knees were not locked as I fixed my eyes on the end of the aisle. Audible gasps came from spectators as they got their first glimpse of my bride. It felt like the longest moment ever as I waited for her to come into view. She turned the corner, and before me stood the most miraculous sight I have ever beheld. The emotion immediately overflowed from my eyes. The tears were unstoppable, *and why would I ever wish to stop this moment and these waves of bliss?*

Her eyes widened when she saw me, and a smile that could challenge the sun lit her face and my heart. This was it, this was our moment. The moment we had both been patiently waiting for. With every step she took, getting closer and closer to fortifying our union, my stomach danced around in my belly. I was elated I'd had no idea what elation was until this very second.

I dragged my eyes away from her to see the warmest smile on Eleanor's face. True happiness for her daughter. It was an event that Olly could have never imagined occurring—her mother at our wedding. On her other arm was Aremis. He wore a dapper plum suit and the widest grin. I was grateful for his presence in our lives every day.

When they reached the altar, I leaned in and gave Eleanor a kiss on the cheek and a hug. "Thank you for bringing this beautiful soul into the world."

"Thank you for cherishing her the way she deserves." Eleanor wiped at her eyes as she moved to her seat.

Aremis gave me Olly's hand as he unhooked it from his arm. "I have a million words I would say to the two of you because I adore you both so much. But I will simply say this. Honor each other, choose love every day, and don't ever forget how precious this union is."

I squeezed Ophelia's hand tighter as Aremis' wisdom sank in and he took his place as my best man. My eyes were fixated on my bride's, and all I could think was, there could never be a more perfect person for me, thank the strokes.

We positioned ourselves front and center at the altar and Ruit began officiating. "Today we are here to witness the divine union of Ophelia Alicea Banner and Elias Kraus. Never in the expanse of an eternity have there been two more deserving souls. Their sacrifice, their generosity, their selflessness is unparalleled. The world would be a better place if more people, more Conduits, more creatures chose love the way these two have. Love is bigger than all of us. It's bigger than any one stroke or a single lifetime or union. It is the thread that binds us all and keeps us anchored. Love is how we choose to show up in the world, how we choose to show up for ourselves. It is infallible and yet unbelievably fragile when mistreated. Love is and always will be the greatest gift ever received because it signifies true surrender to the mercy of another. And we are as flawed as a chip in a glass. So, for any other being to choose another soul to hand their heart to, is truly a miracle. But these two handed their hearts to the survival of our entire existence, sacrificed their hearts for our freedom to love and live the fullest life. For that, for them, that makes this blessed blending of the strokes more transformative than any who came before and for every soul thereafter.

"Ophelia, do you take Elias to be your other half? To live in oneness and in devoted unity, to blend your strokes, meld your souls and love with one heart?"

"I do." Her eyes welled up with tears. "Always and forever."

"Elias, do you take Ophelia to be your other half? To live in oneness and in devoted unity, to blend your strokes, meld your souls and love with one heart?"

"I do, for always and forever."

"Ophelia, you prepared your own vows for Elias. I invite you to share them now."

She let go of my hand and discreetly pulled a small piece of paper from the inseam of her dress. As she unfolded it, she cleared her throat. It was adorable to see her so nervous. "Elias, you captivated me from our very first collision. Your eyes were the realest thing I'd ever seen. If I'd known then how much my world would change, I would've been terrified, and I probably wouldn't have believed that a love like ours existed. I couldn't have dreamt up a more patient, considerate, intelligent partner. How you show up for me, for us, for all those you love is courageous and divine. I'm honored to call you my forever, to merge every cell of my being with you, because I know I'll be a better person for it."

Her words melted my heart. It was the truest thing I had ever felt. Love, deep and passionate. Her truth felt like mine. A single tear escaped, and I hoped she understood what her vow meant to me.

"Elias, you prepared your own vows for Ophelia. I invite you to share them now."

I did not write mine down. I desired to simply speak from my heart. It was not in my nature to come unprepared, but nothing could prepare me for this. "Olly, I choose to commit to you, to us, and ultimately to the journey we will share. I know with every cell of my being that you make me a better person. The challenges, the laughter, the terrifying moments that we have overcome and that lie ahead will be manageable with you by my side. I choose to commit to the struggles, to the growth, I commit to the pleasure and the imminent frustrations that can follow. I commit to the highs and the lows. I commit to showing you the worst and the best versions of me, and I welcome the beautiful and messy versions of you.

Because I know that is where love and deep surrender flourish, it is where the magic abounds, and you are the most magical creature I have ever encountered. For that reason, I am intensely committed to nurturing the most thriving environment for you and me, for us —forever and always."

LUCAS

The celebration was in full swing. Dancing, wine flowing, and incredible food. It was impressive, even more so since this thing came together in a couple days, alongside a funeral and in the middle of a war. All the more reason to enjoy the present and not to waste a minute of it. Yesi and I were dancing to one of my favorite songs by Bon Jovi. I'd forgotten how much I liked to move my hips but, more importantly, how much I liked it when she moved hers. Aremis' voice vibrated off the walls, announcing that it was time for speeches.

"Shit, I forgot about this part." I pulled Yesi in for a kiss.

"Did you plan something?" she asked when I reluctantly released her.

"No, of course not."

"Lucas Healey!" she scolded and tried to swat at me.

"What? I'll just be my charming self. Everyone loves that."

The music started to quiet. I'd never been a best man before. *Maybe I should be more nervous*, I thought.

Yesi was staring at me with her hands on her hips, but laughing, because we both knew it was no use. And I also knew Olly would feel the same. She knew who I was and what to expect.

323

"Too late now," I admitted as I walked toward the front of the room and took my place beside Aremis.

"You are up first." He looked at me with a demure smile.

I was happier with that order, because I didn't want to follow whatever sappy shit Aremis had to say. I might get booed off the stage. Olly and Elias took their place at the sweetheart table in front of us. I waved at her and she beamed back, raising her glass. A quiet and discreet Conduit walked past me and grazed my shoulder. I didn't recognize him but the look on his face let me know he was probably the sound system and I was all hooked up.

I cleared my throat and confirmed my volume was at a ten. "For those of you who don't know me, my name is Lucas and I'm blessed to call Olly my best friend. And I owe it all to this guy, Viraclay, the lucky man who can call her his own. Elias and I aren't exactly friends, and most of his life I've treated him with a blatant disregard. Truthfully, most of the time I was a complete asshole." Murmurs and muffled laughs echoed through the room. "I know, no big surprise there. I think I was always jealous of you, Viraclay. I loved your parents, and you were born with a cool nickname like Viraclay. What's not to be jealous of? I was angry at the world and angry that while the strokes seem to favor some, they abandon others. That's just an excuse, really. I didn't know that then but I'm sure of it now. Because the day your parents conceived you was one miracle, the day you called me to guard Olly was another, and the day you two saved my Yesi..." I choked on the tears coming up... "saved me. That was yet another miracle. But perhaps the biggest one of all is that I'm speaking here at your wedding. Didn't see that coming, did you, miracle boy?" I teased and he wholeheartedly laughed.

"Indeed, no one saw that one coming."

The entire room laughed, and a strange sense of community came over me.

"So, thank you, Viraclay, for being my miracle too." I raised my glass and then turned my attention to Olly. "Where do I begin with you, Miss Banner? From the moment you clumsily stumbled into my life, I was taken. Your heart is pure gold, you are loyal to a fault, and righteously stubborn. That fiery hair is just a glimmer of the fierce fire within, and every day we spent together as roommates will be burned into my memory as glorious. Elias is my miracle, but you are my savior. I was lost, enraged, and full of shame, but you saw the good in me even when I turned out to be the monster. You never gave up on me."

Helia interrupted. "She never gives up on anyone!"

The room applauded and cheered.

"Exactly! You are the best of this world and simultaneously headstrong and impulsive—a hundred percent authentically you. Your friendship means more to me than almost anything else in this world. I never thought I'd be so happy to give you away, especially to this guy, but you deserve this and so much more for all the ways you show up in every moment. And I couldn't be happier because I know the guy sitting next to you will spend every second of the rest of your life reminding you just how special you are." I raised my glass. "I love you! Congratulations!"

Several people stood, including my lovely wife and the bride and groom, which was more than I could've asked for. I waved them on and touched Aremis' shoulder, passing the mic off to him.

"Wow, it will be hard to follow that. Thank you for your vulnerability, Lucas." He leaned in for a hug and his assessment made me a little uncomfortable. "I have been blessed to love Elias since the day he was born. Aye, he was a miracle, and there were never two Conduits more deserving than his parents Cane and Sorcey. I have also been honored to love and admire this courageous lass since the moment we met in Hafiza. I believe we can all agree that these two were painted with the finest of strokes. Elias, your persistence and self-sacrifice goes unmatched. From the time you were a little lad, you had tenacity and stamina. You have always been able to see the big picture, and it turns out you are very good at establishing deep relationships, just like your father, and nurturing true allegiances, just like your mother. Miss Ophelia, you are a force, and I am grateful it is for love because it makes me believe that all things are possible because *you* make all things possible. You have overcome such adversity with brilliant grace. I cherish you like a daughter."

I turned to see Olly dabbing at her eyes. I knew that would move her to tears. She thought of him as a father.

"I could go on and on, but there is plenty more wine, and they haven't played my favorite song yet. Alas, I will leave you with this Irish blessing, "May love and laughter light your days and warm your heart and home. May good and faithful friends be yours, wherever you may roam. May peace and plenty bless your world with joy that long endures. May all life's passing seasons bring the best to you and yours!"

With that, the music started back up and Yesi met me and Aremis at the sweetheart table.

"Good job, gentlemen. Not a dry eye in the house." Yesi kissed Aremis on the cheek. Both Elias and Olly got up and made their way around for some hugs.

"This new you is turning out to be my favorite so far," she teased as I swept her up in my arms, lifting her feet off the ground.

"Don't get used to it, and stop spreading rumors."

"That's what he keeps telling me as well," Yesi teased as I let Olly down, and the two women I love gave each other a long, meaningful hug.

"I for one am still in shock." Viraclay took my arm and pulled me in for a hug. I reciprocated with very little resistance. What on earth was happening to me?

Aremis patted me on the back. "It was a tough act to follow."

Olly jumped into his arms. "You both had me bawling, and now my makeup must be a mess."

Aremis took her chin in his hands and examined her face. "You still look like an angel."

"Wait until we get her on the dance floor!" Medusa, Helia, Sparkle and Eleanor came charging through the exchange and grabbed Olly's hand, dragging her onto the dance floor just as "Brick House" came on.

Eleanor was cheering her daughter on and it was so great to see the two of them laughing and enjoying this unbelievable moment.

"Did you ever imagine this?" Elias asked as he nudged me.

"Never." Then Yesi grabbed both our arms and pulled us out into the center.

"Time to let your hair down, Viraclay!" my luminous wife cheered. Looking around, I catalogued that moment as one that I'd never forget.

The celebration was winding down and I was getting more anxious and excited about the bridal suite. I looked at Elias across the room. He was speaking to Aremis. He caught my stare and gave me that smile I adored, the one that lit up my body with all the right sensations. My lower belly swelled with heat and moisture flooded between my legs. This was a long time coming, the most intense game of foreplay I'd ever experienced, maybe the most anyone in the entire world had experienced.

I'd purposefully kept my shield down all night. I knew all the Conduits here. I'd already absorbed all of their gifts, so I could just bask in the glory and intimacy of our connection. I'd never gone this long without some energetic severance between us. Now that I was experiencing the intensity of our bond, the way it consumed me and washed over my body, I was grateful that I hadn't had to endure this level of foreplay for the last several months. There was no way I could've abstained. It was too powerful, too intoxicating.

In less than an hour we would consummate, and my story would be forever altered. I would be forever altered. The world would be forever altered. My head started to spin. I sat down before I passed out, took a sip of my wine, and blinked my eyes several times to clear the stars I saw.

"Are you okay?" Sparkle's comforting voice chimed. She touched my back and I felt a swell of joy wash over my heart.

I looked up at my dear friend. She was special, and I was grateful for her. "Yes, I'm wonderful, really."

"Okay, that is excellent news." She pulled up a seat beside me. "I see things are winding down here. How are you feeling about your wedding night? About consummating?"

"Funny you should ask. I'm excited. A little nervous about how our first time together will be. A lot nervous about the unknown, being that I'm a Sulu and all and the fate of the world is intertwined with my destiny. And Elias and I haven't decided if we want to conceive." I shrugged, trying to play it casual and failing miserably.

"Those are heavy burdens to bear, alright." She nodded in agreement and took my hand. "The lovemaking will be beautiful. The unknowns are the only constant in this world. But what is absolute is that you are dearly loved and supported, and we all know and trust that what is coming next is divinely painted into the strokes."

"Thank you for those words. I needed that reminder."

"Always."

We hugged.

"There is something else. We all discussed it and decided it was best to wait until after the celebration to bring it up. We didn't want to add to your anxiety."

I looked up and made eye contact with Elias. There was a worrisome expression on his face. He was getting the same talk. I used our Rune to ask him what was up.

"What am I going to be blindsided by now? Did you know about this?"

"I assure you I did not. My parents left out many pertinent details."

"Details about what?"

"Consummation."

Sparkle interrupted our internal exchange. "Don't worry, I will explain everything as best I can. Can I tell you a story?"

I took my eyes away from Elias and gave my attention to Sparkle. If we were both in the dark, then I better get as much information as possible. I took a big sip of my wine. "By all means."

She giggled and clapped. "It's my love story."

My heart melted. I didn't know what had happened to Sparkle's Atoa. Whatever was the moral of the story, it would be sweetened by learning more about my dear friend.

"I met Ajax in New Zealand. Of course, it wasn't New Zealand way back then, but those details don't matter. He was tall, with huge broad shoulders and thighs the size of tree trunks. His hair was chocolate brown, the same color as his eyes. Ajax was a warrior, and he had a thick long braid to attest to his strength and honor." Sparkle's face was a glow as she reminisced about her partner. "He was sexy."

"It sounds like it."

"Our courtship was brief. You don't need long when you find the one." She quickly corrected herself. "I mean, most of us don't need to wait."

I waved her on. We all knew that Elias and I were the exception.

"Three days, and that was only because I wanted my parents there. We had a beautiful wedding. We wed on the banks of a thermal pool. Gorgeous teal water with bright orange fringes framed the shores. Steam billowed up from the pool and danced in the air like a magical blanket encompassing us all. Ajax wore a beaded skirt, traditional for the natives on the island." She leaned in and whispered, "And I wore the same, but without a top. It was appropriate, I promise you."

"I trust you."

"We had a feast of fish and seaweed. I can still taste it. Ajax looked at me like I was the only star in the sky. He said I sparkled. That's why I changed my name."

"What was your given name?"

"Elspeth."

I scrunched my nose without thinking, a visceral reaction, as I tried to make that name fit the woman I loved.

"I know, Sparkle suits me best. When the feast was over, Ajax carried me to our tent. It was far from the others so that we wouldn't be disturbed or disturb anyone else." She winked. "My mother had tried to prepare me for the act of consummation, but there are not many words to describe it."

This must be the big reveal. I clenched my jaw, and my leg began to shake with anxiety.

"I'm telling you because you have to surrender to it, otherwise it's worse than it needs to be."

"What? What's worse? Is it painful?"

"Painful doesn't quite describe the sensation. It's an unraveling. You're exposing everything about your being so that when you are broken open and most vulnerable you can be restored with all of your power and infused with your Atoa's essence, soul and spirit. It's a rebirth, so something must die first and then be integrated into the whole—you and Elias will then be the whole."

Death. Broken. Unraveling. Exposed.

I exhaled through clenched teeth. "I'm scared. It sounds like I should be scared."

"There is nothing to be afraid of. We all die and are reborn multiple times in our lives. I just didn't want you to think there was something wrong with you. You are perfect. This is the process we all engage in when we consummate. A swarm of pleasure, beauty and pain. The deeper the darkness, the brighter the light. We must experience it all in order to step into our truest self, in order to obtain the most authentic intimacy. If you choose to surrender to the journey, it unravels quicker, and the destruction swiftly transforms into renewal." Sparkle squeezed my hand tighter. "Ajax was a warrior. He had been the iron hand that killed many men. It was his shadow, his greatest fear that this truth would stir an alarm in me, that I would become afraid of him. He resisted showing me, he resisted me witnessing his shame, and so our consummation went on for several days as he fought to dismantle the stories he had built to keep me safe from the truth. When he finally surrendered, we were able to see each other in all of our glorious colors and strokes. The anguish melted away and gave way to immeasurable pleasure and connection."

My leg stopped twitching. "You're talking about complete disclosure, of being truly bare in front of another person and hoping he won't reject me."

She nodded. "It's not just that he won't reject you, it's that he won't reject himself."

I looked up at Elias. He was hugging Aremis. I tapped into our Rune. "I love you."

"I love you."

ELIAS

"I should say farewell tonight, seeing as how I will be gone tomorrow and you two may take some time to emerge from your chamber." Aremis smiled at me impishly.

He started to walk away and I grabbed his arm. I had one more question. "The conscious conception—we must also make that decision in the midst of all the dismantling?" Olly and I had barely discussed children. We had not had the time.

"Ah, I see. You can call in a soul after the integration. There will be a moment." He put his hand on my shoulder, sensing my unease. *A moment...there will be a moment to decide if we want to have a child in the middle of a war.* Aremis continued. "Fret not, this moment will feel like an eternity, vast and knowing. Remember, you will have shared all with each other. It will be clear where you both stand, and I would wager that understanding will come without words. The summoning of the soul is automatic when the two of you are in alignment."

"Automatic?" My head was spinning.

"Just trust me, all will be exactly as it should be." He pulled me in for another hug. "Now I must say goodbye to your blushing bride." With that, he walked away.

I meandered to the bar to grab another drink before we escaped to our room. The reception was winding down, but there was still plenty of debauchery happening. Lucas, Vosega and Fetzle were stationed on some barstools, preparing to take shots.

"Can I have one of those?"

"Fetzlethinkssos!" The queen of the trolls may have been slurring her words. It made me smile. "Fetzlefeelsitsbestestweddingsalloverstime.

"I will drink to that, Fetzle." I raised the shot glass Vosega had handed me.

"To the best wedding!" Lucas and Vosega cheered, and we all threw the shots back. It was some sort of whiskey and it burned in the best way as it went down. I looked over at Olly, who was holding Aremis and crying. More emotions, more of the unknown. *What was to come of our dear friend?*

"Another."

"Can I join you, gentlemen?" Eleanor asked from over my shoulder.

"Of course," Vosega said. I was surprised she was still up. She was the only other mortal here and she looked like she could be the last one standing. A glass appeared in her hand and ours were instantly replenished.

"Wait, wait, wait. Tete wants in on this."

"So do we." Behind Tete stood Helia and Medusa.

Thracian peeked out from the other side of Fetzle. "I'd like one."

Yessica appeared with her dad by her side. "We are in."

Shiva, Borte and Ganesha approached with arms raised, and when I thought it could not get any grander, Franky the dragon padded up beside Ruit and his family. Apparently, dragons could drink as well.

The crowd that had assembled was filled with faces I loved and respected. When it parted to make way for my beloved wife, Aremis, and Sparkle, I thought my heart might burst.

"You weren't going to toast to us without me, now, were you?"

Olly kissed me on the cheek as a glass manifested in her hand. "What shall we toast to?"

I went with one we had all heard before. "To the strokes. May they favor your passage!"

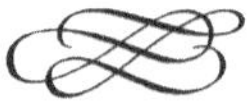

"Look who decided to join us."

I ignored her snide remark and addressed our guest. "King OAD, what a pleasure to see you. It has been too long."

The powrie king, with his red beady eyes and long stringy hair, smiled a wicked grin.

"Too long indeed, Esther. I am so sorry to have disturbed you."

"I do apologize. I was attending to another errand when you arrived. I finished it as swiftly as possible, I assure you."

"I am certain she did." Aurora was seething, *again.*

"No matter. You are here now, just in time for us to discuss the important matters at hand. This war... How do we emerge victorious?"

Why is the powrie king invested in the outcome of the Conduit war?

"I didn't know you had a stake in this war, fierce king."

"You did not?" He looked to Aurora as though she owed me the answer. "I only assumed."

"Some things are best kept concealed until the appropriate time. And that time is now." The Oracle stood. Her long, ivory dress was made of layers of sheer fabric. A golden chain swept around her waist to give her shape, and her hair was stacked on her head elegantly. "King OAD and I have had an alliance for many centuries now. It began when the king called on me after a blade of his staff was stolen. I could not see the perpetrator in my sight. It was the first blind spot I had ever encountered."

"You can imagine how dismal I felt when the great Ramalan could not identify the thief."

I tried to look empathetic.

"Then, fifteen hundred years later, he was betrayed by Queen Peozleo and the giants. They dismantled the rest of his staff, dispersing and concealing its parts."

"My power should have been gone with it, but thanks to the Ramalan and her dear friend Clive, the powries are thriving. Do you know how that is?"

"Obviously not." My patience was growing thin. *Why was I not informed of this alliance sooner?*

"Powries need two elements to survive. Blood and strife. There was a time I thought we simply needed blood. That would prove to be wrong, since when bestowed the opportunity for limitless blood, it did not translate into limitless power. The Oracle informed me of a glorious prospect that would present itself when I was at my darkest hour, when I thought all was lost. She saw Princess Chaness, the answer to my unfortunate strokes."

"Princess Chaness?"

"Yes!" His eyes lit with crazed excitement. "A half-giant, half-troll offspring with infinite regeneration energy. A virtual battery of blood, with a bleeding heart consequently, who naively fell straight into the trap Aurora laid out for me to plant. My staff may have been gone, but the Oracle saw another way for us to thrive off our enemies' compassion. Chaness offered up her life at the battle of the giants."

I turned to Aurora. "What investment do you have against the trolls and the giants?"

"The giants were wielding too much power at the time. The High Priestess was weaving the Golden Spool of Thread—her sight was too far-reaching. The trolls have access to the only antidote to the poison we need to keep our captives cooperative. Aligning with the king served both of our agendas."

"What's more is that we also had a mutual need for violence. Since blood isn't enough, we need depraved violence to flourish. The war between the Pai Ona and the Nebas has created much of that. And when we nearly annihilated the trolls with the help of the defector Pladzal, we charged our batteries for centuries."

"Batteries?"

The king walked over to the Orb in the room. Oh, of course, this made sense. "The Orbs are our batteries, created by Clive. You clever hobgoblin, you." OAD nodded in Clive's direction while the creature stood unmoved. "Below us is the detained Princess, bleeding away. Her blood circulates through the Orbs and blends with the remnants of the atrocities Clive has harnessed, giving us an endless supply of life force."

"But why?" I still wasn't understanding what the Oracle was getting out of this, and clearly OAD wasn't smart enough to see it either. There was more happening here.

Aurora stepped in front of me; she was infuriated by my line of questioning. "Because we needed the trolls out of the way to control the distribution of the antidote." Her eyes told me to stop this query or else.

"I see." But my mind was pulsating with scenarios and questions. Hobgoblins fed off energies of magical creatures and objects; that's why Clive needed to be here to recover. Aurora was trying to build a super-Sulu Wheel, to generate enough power to conquer the world. "How many Orbs are there?"

"Seventy-five," OAD said with pride.

We had seventy-two captives. Those numbers were curiously close.

I slowly slipped out of my dress. I looked at the assortment of lingerie that my considerate bridal squad had picked out for this special night. It was a thoughtful gesture, and the truth was I liked lingerie. I browsed through the pile, every color and fabric readily available. A burgundy red caught my eye. I pulled it up to my body and looked in the bathroom mirror. It was soft between my fingertips. The ribbon grazed my nipples, and the moment suddenly felt overwhelming. My stomach twisted and I thought I might vomit. I dropped the garment and put my head in the sink, turning on the cold water at the same time and splashing my face vigorously.

"Shit!"

Elias was immediately at the door. "What is it? Are you okay?"

"Yeah, I'm fine. I'll be right out." I looked up in the mirror to see that my makeup was completely ruined. I'd forgotten all about the meticulous work Lucia had done. It was all for naught, because now I looked like a drowned raccoon. As I washed the rest of the makeup off, I wondered if Elias was as nervous as I was. Did he know about the details, the untethering, as Sparkle had so gently coined it. My nerves were a bundle of fear and anticipation. We had certainly worked ourselves up into a lather, waiting until we got married, until one crisis after another was averted, not to mention that an exorcism had to take place for me to resume control of my body, and now here we were. I wanted him. I wanted him badly. I wanted to take charge of our destiny. I wanted to step into my power. I wanted to feel the completion of the oneness I'd only tasted with Elias, but I was also terrified. There were so many unknowns, and now there was some magical unraveling that was going to tear us apart and build us back together. Something so ethereal that it couldn't be put into words, yet required a warning.

"Olly, should I be worried?" He leaned against the door. "We do not have to do anything."

He was unbelievably patient and understanding with me. Elias deserved to know I wanted him. I desired this more than anything in the world. "No, I'm sorry. I'm coming." I patted my face off with the towel, examined my naked face and body. This felt right, giving myself to him in this way. Surrendering to our union with as few masks, pretenses or expectations as possible. I took a deep breath and put my hand on the doorknob. I was ready.

She stood before me, and I had to catch my breath. My heart was pounding out of my chest. Her pale skin glowed in the candlelight. The shadows seemed to accentuate every curve of her body, the slope of her breasts, the outline of her hips and the soft convert of her belly just above her delicate trail of hair. I quickly lifted my eyes to her face, searching for validation that she was ready, that we were doing this for the right reasons—for us.

Her eyes confirmed her desire for me, for our union, just as much as my own heart yearned to be inside of her. The shield was gone. It was just her and me. I felt every tingle, every burn, every throb.

I was acutely aware that there was more to come than a climax, but it did not deter how aroused I was by her naked body. Aremis had said to just follow my instincts. The consummation process was like breathing—you cannot resist it, and it takes on a life of its own once initiated.

She stepped closer, as did I.

"Are you ready for this?" Her voice was shaky.

"Indeed, more than anything I have ever encountered before."

I stepped closer again and pulled her body against mine. I put my mouth on hers and kissed her softly at first, then gently parted her lips with my tongue. Skin to skin, lips to lips, I wanted to consume her. I was hard against her thigh and, for the first time ever, I was not ashamed or concerned about pushing things too far. We could surrender to this passion between us. She wrapped her arms around my neck, and I lifted her buttocks with my hands so she could wrap her legs around my waist. Her breath was heavy and hot. She kissed and nibbled my ear. I walked toward the bed while kissing every inch of her face, softly, tasting her ambrosial sweat and smelling her exquisite scent. I lay her down on the bed and ogled her body once more.

"You have the rest of our lives to look at me. I need you in me," she demanded, and who was I to keep a girl waiting? I crawled on top of her and gently pulled her hair from her face, and kissed her once more before sliding my other hand between her thighs. I spread her precious pink lips and slipped two fingers inside. She moaned and I had to catch my breath once more. My index finger traced the entrance of her vagina and danced around her engorged clit. With each gentle roll of my finger, her moans became more intense.

"I need to feel you inside me," she whispered in my ear.

I brought my fingers up to my mouth and tasted her for the first time. It was perfect, salty nectar, fragrant, like warm honey. I could not wait a moment longer.

"Will you receive me?"

"Yes," she uttered through breathy moans, and I entered her without hesitation. Instantly, the room went black, and I felt like I was floating in a primordial womb.

One moment I was feeling the pure magic of Elias' penis gliding inside me with intense anticipation, the next it was pitch black and I was floating in a warm body of water.

"Elias?"

"I am here."

"Oh, thank the strokes." I felt around for his hand and found it a foot away. "This must be part of the unfolding."

"Indeed, I believe it is."

We both fell silent, waiting for what was to come next. Elias pulled me closer and spooned me in his arms, in this weightless tank of nothingness. It reminded me of a deprivation tank.

"Should we do something?"

"Aremis said it was like breathing… Do not resist it." We both completed the last four words. I don't know how long we floated there—it could have been hours or minutes—when suddenly there was a warm, golden light surrounding us. Several images, feelings and thoughts were bubbling up from the light. I squeezed Elias harder. The golden light began to permeate my skin as though it would burn right through it. The sensation became more intense, and the pain seared every cell of my being. I wanted to scream but all I could do was attempt to stay conscious. Was Elias feeling this too?

The voice from the River Tins entered my head. "First, we must dissolve all your boundaries, then we will expose your truths. To become one with another, you must courageously choose vulnerability in every way."

I trusted it, I had to, so I simply surrendered and let my body relax. My muscles unclenched. It didn't stop the pain, but it wrapped me in peace. Now the light was inside my being, no corner left unturned, no cell left unaffected, I could feel the illumination and restructuring transpiring inside my soul. I turned to see Elias was still clenching, still fighting the process. I wanted to call out to him, but instinctively I knew that this was his battle and his choice.

Images flooded my mind, every fear I ever had of true intimacy with another. I saw seven-year-old me in Sandra's house, the night her mother confessed her affair with Harvey and Sandra never spoke to me again. I learned then that I was too much and that something was fundamentally wrong with me. I was too broken. I would always be too broken.

Then, when I was sixteen, at a party in high school, there was a boy named Josh who asked me to join him for a beer out by his truck in the orchard. He wanted to get to know me somewhere where it was a little quieter. We sat on the tailgate of his truck until sunrise. It was one of the best nights I'd ever had. Someone was actually interested in getting to know me, the real me, not the me I showed everyone to look normal. We shared all kinds of stories about our childhood. He told me about his dad dying and his uncle coming to live with them. Josh told me how he caught his uncle sneaking into his room one night without pants on. I told him about my mom's third husband Kennedy. He would crawl into my bed and touch me, when I was ten. When the night was over and as he drove me home, I realized there was something stirring in him, I just didn't know what. I was too distracted by my elation from young infatuation. His last words when we pulled into my driveway were, "I've never told anyone those things before. I don't know why I would do that. Don't tell a soul." Then he peeled off in his truck, and the next day I arrived at school to find my name spray-painted all along the lockers with the words slut, whore and witch. That was the day I learned my truth is dangerous and it turns people away from me.

The next memory was of me in college. I knew this one well and I had to fight back my urge to resist. I didn't want to see this one. I didn't want Elias to see this one. I was so weak, so broken and insecure. Professor Horken sat at his desk while I explained my theory on why dissociative disorders could manifest and be misdiagnosed as postpartum. "Very clever, Miss Banner. I would like to discuss this further, outside of my office hours. Do you have time this evening?" I had a crush on Mr. Horken, so I was all too eager to comply. He took me to dinner at a very nice restaurant off campus. He talked most of the night and was very generous with the wine. When I did get a chance to speak, I divulged way too much information about my family history. I told him that I suspected my mother suffered from borderline and that my grandmother was a schizophrenic who'd died in an institution. I was so desperate for validation and acceptance, even if it was a diagnosis of my own family. The end of the night got blurry, and I didn't remember leaving the restaurant. The next morning, I woke up in my car, parked outside my apartment, naked besides my bra, and bruised from my knees to my navel. When I went to class, he wouldn't even look at me. I waited for Mr. Horken outside his office. When he finally arrived, the disgust on his face made me feel queasy. His next words still made me want to vomit. "What do you need, Miss Banner?"

"I just wanted to ask you some questions about last night."

He scoffed. "No one will believe a lonely little schizo with family illness. You'll just seem like another pathetic schoolgirl with a crush." Then he slammed the door in my face.

On that day, I learned that I was weak and unlovable, that I needed to hide parts of myself to be accepted or respected. If I took off the mask, I risked being seen for how broken I really was.

Bombarded with my greatest fears and shadows, I collapsed into the pain, and darkness once again consumed me. Motionless in the abyss of rebirth, I witnessed as Elias still resisted his process.

ELIAS

It was involuntary. The pain that was trying to permeate me was too much. This was all too much. I had worked so hard to keep it together, to repress all of these emotions. For years, I ignored these hurts to survive, and now I had to acknowledge them on my wedding night. Anger swelled in me. No! No! No!

Perfect. I have to be perfect, controlled and calm. Anything else is unacceptable, maybe even unsafe. I turned to look at Olly. Her demeanor was relaxed. She was not tensed at all. Perhaps I was shielding her from this pain, from the burning. But something in me knew that was not true, that I was fighting the process. The memories were trying to drown me. It was getting hard to breath. Ophelia deserved better than this scared little boy. She needed a strong man who was consistent and always kept it together. This behavior was not good enough for her love. I tried to squirm out from under the torrent of emotion. It was no use.

The memory leached in. I was back in that house. Five years old, attempting to eavesdrop on my parents and their friends. I should have been sleeping but the music was keeping me up. I sat at the top of the stairs listening intently. Rand was talking to my father and another man named Wes. "He will change the world," Wes insisted.

"He is the messiah if you will, a miracle spawn from the two most perfectly matched souls I have ever met."

"That is kind of you, Wes. We know he is very special and meant to do incredible things."

"The boy is exceptional. What's not to love about him? Handsome, well behaved, and fit for leadership, I tell you."

Rand agreed. "The apple does not fall far from the tree."

My mother interrupted the exchange. "You two need to stop carrying on this way. He is just a boy."

I heard footsteps shuffle away, but Wes started a conversation with another man. "Viraclay had better be as perfect as his parents if he ever intends to lead people the way his father has in this war."

I shook off the deep pressure that was building in my gut. The seed of perfection was planted that day, and I have known every day since that if I did not live up to my legacy, I was not worthy.

The next onslaught came in so swiftly I could not recompose myself. Ironic that this memory was validation that if I could not stay composed, I was not good enough. Fourteen, playing basketball with Winston, Caleb and Rand. Caleb was handsome and fit. I envied his stature as a young boy. I hoped that when I consummated, I would be just as attractive and constructive. He always had the ear of his father and mine. Suddenly, he came in hot with the ball. I was ready to show him what I could do, command some respect from these men I admired. Caleb approached on my left, then suddenly spun right and knocked me on my back. I hit hard. Both of my elbows burned from the impact. My face got red with embarrassment as I realized that my mother and father, with two other women I had not met yet, had just arrived to the court. Caleb laughed as he reached down to help me up. "Sorry about that, mate. I got a little carried away."

I swatted at his hand and got to my feet. He gently gripped my shoulder once I was upright. "Are you alright?"

But I was not all right. I was embarrassed and mad. "No! You fouled me," I hissed, then spat on his shirt. I did not see my father until he was on top of me.

"You will apologize immediately."

I stuttered out an apology and then was instantly flying through the air. My father was carrying me to my room like a toddler to be spanked. The embarrassment coursed through my veins. When he put me down, I wanted to rage at him. I lifted my hand and threw my fist hard to the wall, creating a dent. When I turned to face my dad, I was mortified by his expression—disappointment.

"Your behavior just now was unacceptable. I am ashamed to say I raised a young man who would act in such a way. You are held to the highest standard as my son. If you cannot uphold that standard, Viraclay… I don't know what will become of us." Then he left the room, and I wept and swore I would never lose my composure again.

My nostrils could smell the burning flesh before I was present visually in the next memory. That smell was the sense that haunted me the most the night my parents died, and I learned that everyone abandons you, sometimes without warning, and that no one could be trusted. I was flying down the stairs when Rand demanded I flee the house that was already up in flames. So I ran. I ran as fast and as hard as I could. While I ran, all I could think about was that one moment they were there, and now they were gone. I did not get to say goodbye. I could not even remember our last exchange, it was so mundane. And now I would never see my parents again. What was worse was that I knew someone they trusted had to have betrayed them for us to be found here. If my parents could not trust their alliances, then how was I to do so? Loneliness, a profound loneliness consumed me. I would forever be alone. There was no use in letting anyone in, only to either be betrayed or lose them. My heart ached with loss, and I felt the walls being constructed around my heart to keep me safely fortified.

That last memory broke me, and I could not resist anymore. I let go, and darkness shrouded me once more.

*P*eace, a level of peace I'd never encountered before. It was like every wall I'd built, every defense I'd constructed, the shields I carried to stay safe were gone and I was free.

"Now there is the room within you to embrace all of each other. Only when you face your own shadow can you face and love another's," the voice echoed in my ears.

A beautiful violet-purple light appeared above my head. I turned to see peace in Elias' eyes, and it made my heart smile. We had released. We'd both faced the parts of ourselves we were ashamed of, and now we could truly share this journey.

The violet light entered my crown and I saw Elias for the first time in all his glory. I saw his fears as he faced them, I saw his deep desire to love and be loved and accepted. I felt how our stories were so alike, yet different, and I empathized with his shame and the masks he wore to survive. I witnessed all of him.

The violet light moved through me, infusing love and admiration where there was once judgement and separation. My whole body trembled with intense pleasure, an orgasmic flow from my toes to the tips of my hair follicles. Waves of pulsating sensation and giddy playfulness washed over my skin and into my vagina, through my belly and out my navel. I moaned and gyrated with vibrations beyond reality, beyond this world. I somehow knew Elias was doing the same, but I didn't need to see him. I could feel him in my DNA, in my blood and bones—he was me and I was him. In an instant, I saw every moment that ever played out in this life, for both of us. His memories were mine. His knowledge was mine. He was mine.

The black, primordial fluid that we'd been floating in was slowly draining away, and as it did, we took a seat. I was straddling his lap. We faced each other. We were present in this all-but-nothing space that we'd been reborn into. When our eyes met, I knew what needed to happen next. Our bodies continued to express and move rhythmically with pleasure. Although we were still not having sex, it felt like he was penetrating every inch of me. We never took our gaze from one another, and together we called in our baby, the soul that was destined to walk this journey with us. Then he entered me once more, and as I received him, the entire space exploded with light.

ESTHER

I stood beside the Oracle as she addressed the small group of Nebas in front of her. My whole body fumed with rage and grief. Waves of both emotions repeatedly consumed my entire being. There was a mirror behind the small assembly. I looked at myself with disgust. Disheveled and withdrawn, I looked like a corpse. A shell of the woman I once was. I wanted to spit on my own reflection. My eyes were crimson red around the rim, my long black hair was matted in places, and my figure looked gaunt, sallow with nothingness. The purple gown I wore hung limply on my shoulders. I pulled up one strap and tried to round out my shoulders, pull presence back into my posture.

"Esther! What do you have to report?!" Aurora demanded, pulling me from my inspection.

"All fifteen remaining captives will be arriving here soon. Other than that, I have nothing of consequence to report..." She opened her mouth to scold me, no doubt, when I added, "Yet. I will have further information for you shortly."

That was a half-truth, and by the narrowing of the Oracle's eyes, I suspected she knew. Once again, she opened her mouth, but before her tongue began the lashing, the whole world shook.

352

Aurora's eyes got huge with fear. She hadn't seen this coming. The ground beneath our feet vibrated in a deep, guttural way, like it came from the core of the earth. A sound echoed in the air, as though a fierce wind would gust while moving through a canyon, but the air was still. I looked at my reflection once more and saw how my entire image appeared to expand and retract instantaneously, as though the tremor also shook through the core of my soul. A sharp pain pierced my right side, just beneath my arm. I reached to feel if something had stabbed me, but there was nothing.

In the mirror, I saw that Aurora's eyes were locked on Clive's. They were having an exchange. Then it all stopped, and the room blew up with shock and wonder—*What in the strokes has just happened?*

LUCAS

"What the fuck was that?"

Yesi's eyes were wide with terror. The unknown left all of us shaken. It wasn't normal for us to experience anything out of our scope of knowledge. On one hand, that made life pretty predictable and monotonous at times. On the other, it was scary-ass shit when something new manifested. I took her hand and pulled her into the hallway. Everyone else was piling out of their quarters and heading toward the banquet room.

"Let's go." I transported the two of us into the big hall.

"Calm down, everyone." Ruit was already standing on a small pedestal trying to quell the storm of anxiety and bewilderment from the Pai Ona who were frantically assembling.

"Is it the Nebas? Are we under attack?" a man called from the other side of the room.

"Should we arm ourselves?" another man asked.

My back tensed. *Am I ready for an attack?* I squeezed Yesi's hand tighter in mine.

She whispered in my ear, "My heart tells me we are safe. Lay down your arms, my love."

I trusted her heart more than anything in this world. That was all I needed to relax.

Ruit's voice stayed tranquil as he replied to the concerned mob that was forming. "There is nothing to fear. There is no imminent attack. The perimeter has been well enforced, and the dragons assure me there is nothing to be afraid of."

"Was that dragon magic then?" Medusa's voice echoed above the rest, and the crowd hushed, anxiously waiting for an answer.

"No," Aremis stepped in. "I was just taking my leave with Napitae when the quake occurred. He assured me it was not of dragon origins. But it worried him enough that we are postponing our voyage temporarily."

"Does he know what it was?" Sparkle chirped.

"He did not say."

A thought tickled the back of my mind, and I wanted nothing but to shake it off, but I wasn't the only one.

"Was it the Sulu?" a quiet, unfamiliar voice shed light on the very thing I was afraid to put energy into.

"I do not know." Ruit put his head down, as though he was ashamed that he didn't have all the answers all of the time. Jezebel comforted her husband with a hand on his shoulder. "But what I can assure you is that we are not under attack. You are safe. Please return to what you were doing, and we will call an assembly when we know more."

Slowly, the crowd dissolved, leaving only a handful of us standing around looking at each other with the same subtle fear. We convened in the center of the room once everyone else was gone.

"It's her, it's the consummation, isn't it?" I expected Ruit to admit the truth now that we were with the trusted few.

Oya agreed. "It's obviously them. Could this have something to do with the extinction?"

Ruit put his hand up. "We are getting far too ahead of ourselves, my friends. I do not believe this was necessarily the direct conse-quence of their union, although it will be considered."

"Aye. What was it then?" Aremis appeared on the left of the Alchemist.

"I believe it was a Paradigm Tremor."

"A what?" Sparkle was leaning on Aremis now.

"There are rumors, whispers of a timeline shift so powerful it shakes the whole world. The entire paradigm is left open to be transformed into something completely unknown."

"What is a paradigm exactly?" Vosega asked.

"It's an epicenter of all of the existing timelines."

"Tete thinks that sounds a lot like an extinction plan!"

Medusa was nodding in agreement, and I had to admit it sounded pretty fucking ominous.

"This has everything to do with the Sulu—that girl," Borte accused.

"Yes, Borte, it seems reasonable to assume that part of this shift has something to do with the Sulu and her consummation that is occurring as we speak. However, this isn't solely about her. This occurrence takes the alignment of multiple events to create such an energy that the loop of time is spliced open."

"Oh, sweet Chitchakor, what in the strokes." Yesi's hand was over her mouth as she whispered what we were all thinking. "This must be our doom."

ELIAS

We lay there in pure rapturous entanglement. The world had stopped for a moment, and it was just her and I. No war, no death, no fear—just love. My body was tingling with new sensations, as though I had just created an utterly new web of neurons to feel from. Perhaps we did just that, or maybe the pathways were always there, just waiting to be ignited. Either way, it was magnificent. I squeezed Olly a little closer to my body. Her head was on my chest. Her breath was soft, relaxed.

A deep, melodic voice echoed in my head. "What was that, Sulu? Explain yourself." I sat up abruptly.

"What? What?" Olly stammered in shock. "Is everything okay?"

"Did you hear that?"

She shook her head. "What did you hear?"

"A deep voice in my head. Not the Talluses. Not my Rune. It was feminine, yet not Conduit." I was babbling, looking for the right description, and it was evading me.

"That sounds like Cataphet." Olly's eyes got big. "How did you hear the dragons? I didn't hear a thing. What did she say?"

"'What was that, Sulu? Explain yourself.'"

Panic surged through Ophelia. I could feel it.

"Elias! I don't have any gifts! They are gone!"

I reached up to put my hand on her cheek, to comfort her. "We will get to the bottom of this." When my index finger grazed her lips, I watched in horror as her face turned to stone.

We were in a Haven further outside Death Valley and the Orb Forest. I needed a hot bath and some luxuries that the Orb compound did not afford. Aurora and Clive excused everyone abruptly after the earthquake. It made no difference to me. I was starting to feel like I was completely in the dark about their true comings and goings. That made participation feel futile. *I did not like being toyed with.* There were so many unknowns circulating around the Oracle and her plans, too many lies and half-truths, and whenever I tried to probe further into my loyalties for the cause I noticed I got foggy and quickly lost my train of thought. Without Yanni, everything was meaningless, but this was something different. I couldn't put my finger on it.

I was naturally paranoid, but I was starting to seriously consider that I was hexed. An incantation meant to keep me confused and compliant. Of course, this was only one of many things I was pondering. I looked down at my birthmark. There was a mystery within its origin that needed to be solved. My father had returned from the River Tins to warn me. The Sulu cautioned me about Aurora, and now everywhere I turn, I caught her lying. The secrets she keeps spans centuries, which leads me to believe her agenda is more sinister and extensively more complicated than I can even imagine it to be. When Aurora approached me and Yanni after my father's execution, I thought it was about revenge against the Pai Ona who condoned her imprisonment by their participation at Delphi.

I thought back to the time in the temple, but immediately my memories got murky. *Why is it that I can remember the day Atlantis sank into the ocean like it was yesterday, but I cannot picture the rituals performed with my father on the mountain, nearly two thousand years later?* I pressed my memory for more and my head started to throb. *This is ludicrous!* I'd spent my whole life paying for or running from the events that occurred at Delphi. My father was executed for those crimes, for the deaths of so many… but as I tried to cling to the thought, it evaded me, and the pain became excruciating.

There was a knock on my door. "Mistress?"

"What is it?!"

"Nestor has arrived. I am notifying you as you requested."

The pain subsided at the intrusion, and I was grateful for it. "Send him to me."

"Very well." Then Astrid was gone. I got out of the bath, toweled off and wrapped myself in a robe just as there was another knock.

"Come in."

Nestor appeared in the threshold. He quickly entered my room and took a seat on the bed. I resisted the urge to demand he stand and not soil my sheets. I needed him cooperative. "Can I get you something to drink?"

"Do you have bourbon?"

"Will a scotch suffice?"

"No, I'm particular about my poison."

"I can have one brought up."

"Will I be here long? Did I do something to upset you or the queen?" There was sarcasm to his tone. He hated authority as much as I did. Nestor had only sided with the Nebas because we allowed him to entertain his depravity.

"Nothing to dissatisfy me. I cannot speak for the Oracle." I poured myself a glass of red wine and pulled up a chair to sit across from him. As I sat, I decided to rip the band aid off, so to speak. I spread my leg, exposing my thigh, and showed him the birthmark. "I have come to learn that you have the same birthmark. Is that correct?"

"I do." He smiled maniacally.

"Does it mean something to you?"

"Only that all of my offspring share it as well."

"All of your offspring have this mark?"

"Yes, every single one."

"How can you be certain of this?"

He rolled his shoulders back and stretched his arms out in front of himself, as one would after a good day's work. "Surely you know of my reputation, Esther? I don't just visit my victims once, I like to pay their lineage a visit or two as well."

"You mean you like to molest your children." I spat the words because they disgusted me. He disgusted me. There were many monsters in this world. I was one of them, but his sort… I didn't care for those strokes.

"If they measure up to my standard, then yes, I enjoy leaving my legacy."

Legacy. I almost vomited at the thought of his legacy.

"So, the Sulu is yours? You knew this and you said nothing?"

"I did not know it until you sent me for her mother."

"Still, you said nothing?"

"It makes no difference. I never got to honor that offspring with a visit. Her mother was very clever. I couldn't find her after Oya and Realto freed her."

I was trying to piece together the puzzle. *What do I know about Nestor?*

"Who were your parents?"

He laughed sourly. "I am afraid, dear mistress, I am not as lucky as you. Being that you were so close to Mommy and Daddy. My parents abandoned me on the doorstep of some Celtic crone."

"You never met your parents?"

He shook his head.

"How did you discover what you were?"

"Funny you ask. No one has ever really inquired about my childhood, except for my late Atoa Mila." I realized I had never met his Atoa either. "I had a regular visitor as a lad, the virtuous Sorcey Kraus. She would come a few times a year and bring us trinkets and food. By the time I was eleven, I suspected there was something different about me, different than the crone. I was wicked. I demanded she give me answers, tied her up, raped her, and by doing so, I got her to divulge her vague understanding of what a Conduit was. I burned the house down, with the crone in it, and set out on my own. You can imagine the trail of trauma I left in my wake, until the day I found Mila. She was a sweet soul. We consummated, and although she said she accepted my shadow, deep down I knew that wasn't true. No one could accept a monster like me."

"But if you consummated, she accepted you."

"Because she had to, in order to gain immortality and access to her gifts. It was obvious to me that she never really loved me. After a century together, exhausted from maintaining my composure and keeping the monster locked in its cage, I killed her. I couldn't handle her dishonesty."

"You murdered your Atoa because you didn't believe she actually accepted and loved you?" I was aghast. After all, I was still in the deep pool of grief from the loss of Yanni. I couldn't fathom being the hand that killed him.

"What, mistress?" He hissed my title with disdain. "Some monsters are worse than others. Of all people, you should know that."

A chill crept down my spine. He was right, and I was afraid I was now in the snake pit with the worst monsters of them all.

"Are we done here?"

I nodded and he left the room, chuckling to himself all the way down the hall.

hat in the strokes is going on?! One minute I'm talking to Elias, the next it's lights out again and I can't feel my face. My lips wouldn't move, my eyes wouldn't blink. *Am I being possessed again? This is all wrong. All of it is wrong.*

The voice from the River Tins interrupted my panic attack.

"Trust, Ophelia. It is time to trust that things are transpiring exactly as they should be."

"Trust?! I can't see." I was about to protest some more when Elias reached out with his Rune.

"Give me a moment. I seem to have mistakenly turned your face to stone."

"You what? What is happening, Elias?"

"I do not know, but we will find out. I promise." Then, just like that, my face was back to normal and I could see the concern all over Elias'.

"How did you do that?" I looked around, halfway expecting to see Medusa in the room, giving him instructions.

"It felt natural. I just stopped the spread of Medusa's gift and used my mother's healing to repair the damage."

"And you just accessed all of those abilities?" I snapped my fingers. "Like that?"

"Indeed, it would seem so."

"Grrrr! Not only do you have all the gifts I've accumulated, but you make it look easy. This is almost unbearable. What did I do to deserve this?" I was acting like a child, I was well aware, pouting and throwing a tantrum, but I was peeved. I'd hoped consummation would fortify me, not eradicate my progress.

Elias pulled me in closely to his chest. "I know this feels dismal right now, but there must be an answer. Perhaps the Sulu engages in a different form of transformation."

"Perhaps." I internally huffed, then pulled it together. This was, after all, a very special day. Our consummation day, our union, and I wanted to remember it as such.

"Me too."

"Were you just in my thoughts?"

"Ooops."

I grimaced up at him but then couldn't help but laugh.

"Are you sure this is a good idea, Lucas? Ruit isn't interrupting them. Should we?"

"Ruit is a little old-fashioned, baby girl. I like the guy, but he just described doomsday and then dismissed us for recess. I'm going to get to the bottom of this shit."

"But what if they are still in process?"

I took her by the shoulders and looked her in the eyes. "We will knock quietly then. You and I both know that an atomic bomb can't interrupt consummation."

"What if…" I kissed her.

When I pulled away, I just laid it out there. "I know you're scared. I know you're polite. I know you want to stay on good terms with Olly. That's why I'm the one who has to be the rude, intrusive best man. Olly gets me, and I get her, and I know she'd want to know about this development as soon as possible."

I took Yesi's hand in mine and knocked on the door. It didn't take long for Elias to answer.

"Look, I know it's your honeymoon and all, but you guys need to know about something."

"Is that Lucas?" I heard Olly in the background.

"Give us a moment to get dressed." Viraclay shut the door, and I looked at my wife.

"See? All good."

She rolled her eyes. Elias returned quickly with shorts on, and as we entered, I saw Olly was in a robe.

"Sorry to intrude," Yesi said as she stepped inside. My ever-vigilant wife, always using proper etiquette.

"What's up? Everything okay?" Olly asked as she sat down on the couch in front of us.

"First off, you guys look great. Healthy and like you're adapting well. Congratulations on the transformation. It was a quick one. You guys are always the overachievers," I teased. I was more nervous than I realized.

"Indeed. What is this about, Lucas?" Elias took a seat beside his wife.

"Well, while you guys were consummating, you seem to have created some kind of splice in the time continuum called a Paradigm Tremor." No use in sugarcoating it.

Neither of them could hide their alarm. "Like the extinction?" Olly asked.

"Ruit doesn't think so. More like an anomaly that no one knows anything about. The whole world shook, and even the dragons are a little spooked."

"That explains why you heard Cataphet's voice in your head. This is bad, Elias." Ophelia fell back against the couch as Elias got to his feet.

Viraclay maintained eye contact with his wife. "We must meet with Ruit and the rest of our closest allies."

"Okay, I can arrange that. I'll go get them now." I turned to go. "I guess I should ask, did anything weird happen on your end?"

"That is an odd question, since neither of us have anything to compare consummation to. It felt miraculous and was singlehandedly the most terrifying experience of my life. Does that sum it up?"

"That sounds about right," I agreed with Elias.

"There is one thing." Olly got to her feet. "My gifts are gone." Her eyes welled with tears, and I instinctively stepped closer to comfort her but stopped myself.

"What do mean?"

"They all transferred to this hunk." She stuck her thumb toward Viraclay, trying to make light of it. "I'm just an empty husk of a Sulu."

"Olly..." I didn't know what to say. But my wife knew what to do.

Yesi walked directly to Ophelia, took her in her arms, and let her cry.

OPHELIA

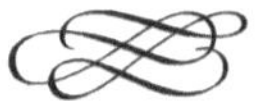

e sat patiently waiting for our guests to arrive. I was anxious and trying not to show it. Consummation was hard enough, but now this. A paradigm glitch, or whatever Lucas called it. It sounded bad. I wanted to get my head in the game, to focus on the bigger picture, like not instigating mass extinction, but the truth was I needed some answers about my gifts, and I could only hope that Ruit would be the one who could give them to me.

"He has to," I absently said it aloud.

Elias was holding my hand before I realized I was not having an internal conversation.

"He will."

Elias had become more handsome, more irresistible, more intertwined within my being. It was as though our cells shared DNA. The Atoa connection was beyond any true description. It was being reborn, but this time, whole. I looked deeply into his eyes, searching for some reason why this was happening to me. There was nothing there. Neither of us understood what was unfolding between us. After all, I was a Sulu and he was Viraclay. Only the painter could know what was in our strokes.

Then I heard that voice again in the recesses of my mind. "The Originals."

"Did you hear that?"

Elias' brow furrowed with worry. "What? Did I hear what?"

I threw my hands up in the air. "Really? This must be some kind of joke, right? We consummate, you absorb all of my powers, and I'm left with nothing, except the strange ability to hear ethereal voices from the River Tins." I got to my feet and began to pace. The others couldn't get here fast enough.

"What did the voice say?"

"'The Originals.' It said, 'The Originals.'"

"Well, that must mean something."

I just shook my head in disappointment. I looked down at my hands. The hands that held limitless abilities only days ago were barren of gifts now. Sure, I was stronger, faster, nearly indestructible, and whole with my Atoa… but as far as either of us could tell, when we consummated, something went boom and Elias integrated all of my gifts, leaving me devoid. Not to mention, because his body was fortified and all consummated, he also appeared glitch-free, as though the training manual had been downloaded with the equipment. He just naturally could access and control each of the gifts I'd encountered. Which seemed completely unfair.

"I agree."

"Hey, I thought we decided you would try and keep a cap on the mind-reading thing."

He gave me a sheepish smile. "I slipped."

I pulled him in for a kiss. It was impossible to resist him or be mad at him. It would be like denying or being mad at myself. Which, come to think of it, I had done a lot of in my mortal life. But something had shifted when we bonded. Through our shadows, amidst the darkness of ourselves, true self-acceptance and love blossomed into an entity beyond words.

"I was hoping, peeking into your thoughts, that I might hear the voice."

"It's gone, but if it comes back, you'll be the first to know." I kissed his nose.

There was a rap at the door.

"Come in," we called simultaneously. I was happy to see Sparkle and Aremis' smiling faces. Sparkle ran up and practically threw herself into my arms.

"I was so worried about you two. But of course, you don't have to tell me a thing." She squeezed me tighter. "And wow, only a day of consummation! That is amazingly swift for a pair."

"Of course they amalgamated in record time. They are, after all, our two merry miracles." Aremis leaned over and kissed me on the cheek. "You look even more stunning, my dear Miss Ophelia."

"I thought you were leaving with Napitae."

"I am, but when the earthquake happened, Napitae decided to convene with his kin. We will be leaving shortly."

"How is my mom?"

"She is splendid," Sparkle chirped.

My eyebrows shot up. That was a description I would not have been likely to use in reference to my mother. But she went through her own transformation, and the thought of Eleanor being splendid suited her.

"Delightful, really," Aremis added.

"Okay, you two are too much."

We all laughed. Sparkle insisted, "She is great, and I love being around her."

Of course, Sparkle would love my mother.

Behind them trickled in Medusa, Tete, the Tallus family, Winston and Lucia.

One by one, we hugged, kissed, and greeted our dearest friends on the other side of our transformation.

Helia, Aruna and Ying arrived after Vosega and Oya.

We were just waiting on Lucas and Yesi.

"I don't think we should be expecting Borte or the Khan," Medusa stated the obvious.

"Or Thracian for that matter," Tete added.

We were all taken aback when Thracian, Stalt and the Khan entered the room next. I looked at Elias quizzically, and he just shrugged with a smile.

"The party can start." Lucas walked in holding the hand of his charming wife. Yessica nodded at everyone as she took a seat in the nearest chair to the door.

"You'd be late to your own funeral," I joked.

"We are always right on time." Lucas winked at me as he took a seat on the arm of Yessica's chair. Everyone else quickly found a comfortable position in the room. I looked around at our closest allies. They were brave, loyal, and I felt blessed to call them my friends.

Elias spoke first. "Thank you all for attending our nuptials. It was the perfect ceremony."

"Yeah, yeah. Tete wants to know what your power is, Viraclay. C'mon, what did the Sulu end up transforming into? It must be something amazing, because you caused a paradigm earthquake or something. I mean, we didn't explode, so that's cool."

Medusa elbowed him. "Tete, shut the fuck up."

This was the part I was dreading. Elias looked at me as though he was asking my permission, but he already knew I wanted him to tell them.

"Indeed." Elias quickly manifested a ball of fire in his hand, a shower of rain from the ceiling, a gust of wind around the perimeter of the room, and then just as quickly snapped his fingers and it was all gone. He made it look easy. I had to physically stop myself from rolling my eyes.

Winston got to his feet. "Now you are both Sulu?"

I shook my head. "No, not both." I snapped my fingers. "I got nothing."

Gasps went around the room.

"What does it mean?" Aruna asked, her eyes filled with pity. That look made me feel shame, like I'd done something wrong. And the truth was I had. I'd misused my gifts many times during my rise as a Sulu. Perhaps this was exactly what I deserved.

"I was hoping Ruit could tell me."

"*We* were hoping." Elias took my hand in solidarity.

Ruit took his time getting to his feet. The silence was deafening. "I am afraid I do not know. I haven't answers to anything that is taking place here."

More tears. I couldn't hold them back.

"What about the Ancients?" Elias asked.

"Perhaps."

Then I heard a faint but familiar voice, *Nandi's journal?* Before I could catch what it was saying, Borte stormed in and her shrill voice cut through the room. "The book! The damn book has something to say."

"That is what that voice is?" Elias turned to me. "How did you keep it all straight?"

I smiled through the tears as he wiped them away. *I could still hear the Stone.*

Ruit pulled out Nandi's journal, or the Sorcerer's Stone, rather. "What does it say?" Jezebel asked her husband.

But just before he answered, I heard the faraway voice again and knew... I said it aloud. "The Originals."

<h1 style="text-align:center">ELIAS</h1>

I opened a conversation with Ophelia in our heads. "It would seem you can still hear the stone?"

She shrugged. "Maybe. But there is also a different voice."

"Are you certain?"

She shook her head. "I don't know, at first I thought I heard Sorcerer and then I heard the voice from the River Tins. They sound really similar."

Borte was still standing in the doorway, waiting for something. Validation perhaps.

Ruit scanned the pages and found the passage the stone was readily sharing.

"Well, what does it say?" Borte demanded.

Ruit was very good at ignoring her. He read the inscription aloud. "The Originals know the truth, the dance between dark and light, day and night, a Sulu and an Ulus."

"Ulus? I have heard that before." Olly walked over to Ruit. "May I?" He handed her the journal. "The holy man I met in China, Wailee —he was the man I met in the Tartar village—he called me an Ulus. I didn't know what it meant, so I just ignored it. I thought it was a reference from his native tongue."

"Wailee called you an Ulus? That is very curios, because the Tartar people were the last to maintain a relationship with the Originals. Their bond to the dragons far surpassed any other strokes or human populations for many thousands of years. Some say a dragon still lives in the lands below the village in China."

"Well, that can't be a coincidence," Helia stated what we were all concluding. "Let's go see one or two of the dragons that are residing in The Cathedral. At the very least, that last one must owe us a favor for saving it from captivity."

"I don't speak dragon anymore." Olly's tears streamed down her face once more. "I didn't hear Cataphet."

"You do not know that for certain. And either way, I can translate." I offered.

"Viraclay is right. We don't know where you absorbed the ability to understand dragons. That gift may have stayed with you." Ruit reasoned.

"I don't need you guys to hover around me and make me feel better for being a dud of a consummated Conduit."

"Don't say that, Olly," Lucas contested. "We'll figure it out. You're not a dud."

"Honestly, I'm okay. I promise." She brushed everyone off. "How should we proceed with contacting the dragons?"

"I will ask Cataphet for an audience." Ruit insisted.

"I believe she will be eager for a meeting, she has already made contact with me this morning."

"Rub it in." Olly's expression was so downtrodden.

"Can we ask one of the other dragons, like Franky?" Sparkle chirped.

"I am afraid we are at the mercy of Cataphet. I would not offend her by making requests of others. And, to be clear, there will only be three of us attending this meeting," Ruit said. That caused some disgruntled moans and sighs to erupt throughout the room. "You all must understand, the fewer the better. Cataphet can be—"

Vosega interrupted him. "Yeah, we all know her disposition well.

You can summon us all back here when you have something further to report."

"Has someone contacted the Ancients?" Lucia asked. "On behalf of Di. Do those who weren't at the wedding know about her death? They have rites they perform when they lose an ambassador."

"Shiva is returning to the arctic as we speak. He will tell anyone who has not heard the news yet." Stalt put his hand on Lucia's shoulder. "She will be missed by many."

"With your permission, may I contact Shiva and ask him to relay the new circumstances with the Sulu, to see if they have any information? And I would like to volunteer as ambassador," Winston said stoically.

I thought that was an excellent idea and said as much. "They would be so lucky as to have you serve them."

"I will escort you down to the channels room. You can send him a message." Ruit turned to Olly. "We will get to the bottom of this. After I assist Winston, we will wait for Cataphet's summons together."

Cataphet's voice echoed in my head. "Tell the Alchemist we are ready for your audience. Meet him in the galley as soon as he helps the Ancients' ambassador."

"Ruit, there is no need for a summons. Cataphet is ready for our audience. After you assist Winston, please meet us in the galley." I had to wonder, *was she always listening?*

"I will not be long." With that, he left the room, along with everyone else.

Olly collapsed into my arms on the couch, nestling into my chest. "I need a quick hug. This wouldn't be so bad if I didn't know what it was like to manifest all of those gifts."

"Indeed, that must make losing them dreadfully hard."

"I can't even feel others' emotions. My curse is gone too." She sat up and looked at me intently. "I never would have thought I'd be sad to see that go."

"The painter has a pointed sense of humor."

For the first time in thousands of years, I longed for sleep. I wanted the respite from these vicious thoughts that were circulating in my head. I wanted the suspicions and the questions to cease. Every second was haunted by a nagging in my gut, my father's warning, Yanni's final breaths, the Oracle's dishonesty—the weight of failure. There were only fifteen captives still asleep and in our custody. *What does this mean for Aurora's Sulu agenda? Can she still proceed as planned? Do I care?*

I paused. *What was the plan? Do I even know anymore? The plan has always been to recreate the Sulu power that Aurora experienced in Delphi on a greater scale, but to what end?* I looked down at the ring I had given Yanni, the ring Ophelia Banner returned to me before fleeing in my beloved's body. *Kindness? Or perhaps weakness?* Once again, I was plagued by the vision of my father's spirit in the Sulu's body.

The Sulu's body… The Oracle wanted to create a giant Sulu Wheel. That's what the captives were always about. *Perhaps she could bring my Yanni back?*

Just then, the door opened. It was Aurora and Clive.

"We need to get back to the Orb Forest. King OAD has something he wants to show us." I looked despondently at Aurora. Of course she wouldn't return Yanni to this realm. That would be kindness, and she was not kind. "I am not asking. I am commanding."

I put the ring in my small purse and threw it over my shoulder. "After you." I waved her on.

"You must get out of this melancholy, Esther. It is weak and intolerable for a leader."

"I am no longer a leader. I am just another one of your minions."

Her face flashed red with rage. "You are worse than one of my minions, because you're insubordinate." She stepped closer. "We need to show a united front to win this war."

"United would imply we have the same agenda, but I am not certain we do anymore. I feel I do not know in the slightest what your intentions are, only what you have led me to believe."

A crazed look glinted in her eyes. "After all these years, after all our conquests, and when we are so close to achieving domination—now you choose to distrust me?"

She stepped closer again and a thought flitted through my brain so quickly that it was almost gone before I caught it. *Touch her. Snatch her body. It's the only way you will get answers.*

The thought tried to vanish but not before I took action. I reached out and snatched the Oracle's body. A flurry of images flooded my being. They came in at such a pace, I was discombobulated. A blade handed to her by Clive. A pregnant Aurora cutting her belly. Aurora taking a syringe of blood from a small purple dragon. Cadmael looking terrified as his wife sliced him in two, then tied him to a stake to be burned alive. Aurora witnessing my father's execution. Clive telling Aurora in images that the Pai Ona would attack Chernobyl in two days' time and they needed me to snatch the Sulu. I saw the moment of the earthquake and the exchange between the hobgoblin and the Ramalan. Their sight was nebulous and growing vaguer. A spell was broken. There were more glimpses flooding in, an endless stream of sight and memories.

Suddenly, Clive was between us, and I felt the severance of my gift from my host. The Oracle stared at me, mortified. "How did you... Why did you do that? What did you see, Esther?!"

"I d-don't know…" I stammered.

She looked at Clive for answers. "Do something! Seize her!"

I was in shock, but that order brought me back to my body. There was no way in the strokes I was going to become a prisoner of this monster.

e entered the dark hall off the galley and, moments later, we were in a beautiful meadow. I couldn't tell you where within The Cathedral this majestic meadow resided, but that's the thing about aberrations like The Cathedral. The strokes here are so powerful, there is no way to know their true capabilities.

"This is beautiful, but where are the dragons?" I looked at Elias and Ruit.

"She manifested us here, so there must be a reason," Ruit assumed.

Then they came from behind a mountain, and there was no missing them. With one single step, the gargantuan Zeffina was in front of us. I suddenly felt her presence in my head, my eyes welled with tears. I wasn't completely broken. "I get to be here on land, just like you said. I get to roll in the mud with the pigs and the dogs. I am so happy and I owe it all to you. You saved me from an existence of solitude and grief."

My heart welled up with so much joy that I couldn't contain the tears, but they were truly symptoms of a full heart. Zeffina was happy. She was more deserving than most people I've ever met.

"I'm so delighted to hear that you have found the home you deserve."

The gentle giant nodded her enormous head. "I am free here," I turned to see my husband also in tears. Then Zeffina took another step over our heads and she was well on her way in another direction. "You must also know, that your wedding was perfect, and I was so grateful to get to be in attendance."

Ruit picked up the conversation in our heads. "You will have to tell me how in the strokes you got her here unnoticed."

I chuckled. "It's a suspenseful thriller."

He raised his eyebrows.

A gust of wind came up from the west, blowing my hair in my face, and when I was able to see again, we were no longer in the meadow. Instead, we were in the dark cavern with gold flakes strewn across the floor, the cave where I first met Cataphet. Her gold-green eyes were the only source of light in the black abyss.

I heard a faint voice, similar to the River Tins voice but quieter. "You can still hear me too Ophelia."

Ruit and I both looked at each other.

"Was that Sorcerer?"

Ruit nodded.

"What am I missing?" Elias asked with our Rune.

"I can still hear the Stone."

"So that is why you could understand dragon just now?" He asked.

"I don't understand, because I know I didn't hear Cataphet in our room."

"That is because I was not reaching out to you. I was contacting the Sulu." Cataphet's deep voice echoed.

Before I could ask another question, I was interrupted by a familiar voice tickling my ears, and joy filled my heart. "Blimey, turn on the lights, Cat. It's bloody dark down here," Franky complained. I searched for him in the room. "You're a true blue to have around Alchemist. That book is mighty handy. I reckon I knew a bloke or two of your caliber once or twice, because one of you did something similar in my den. Always appreciated that." A shadow moved, and then the entire lair was aglow by wall sconces and hundreds of candles.

"Franky!" I dropped to my knees as he traipsed over.

"Ophelia, mate! I couldn't miss a chance to see my favorite Conduit again. And bloody hell, you've changed! You're consummated." I squeezed him so hard, I would have hurt any other creature. "You didn't waste any time after that swell wedding, now, did you?"

"It's so good to see you. Even better to hear you!"

"You have a grip on you, now, don't you?" He chuffed. "Set me straight. I gotta look at ya when I say this thing."

Just then, a huge purple dragon flew down from a crevice in the ceiling. Cataphet just looked on at the exchange, still saying nothing.

"This is my Gwenora." Franky looked up at her adoringly. "She was a captive in the Nebas compound. You and your mates set her free. And I am grateful beyond any strokes you could imagine. I thought she'd died during the fall of Atlantis." Franky nuzzled her large leg, and she swept a long wing across the top of his back. It was a gentle and sweet caress.

The dragon bowed toward me. "Pleased to meet you, Ophelia. Franky speaks very highly of you. Thank you for relieving me from my prison."

"I wish I could take the credit for that, but I was a captive myself. I think your appreciation belongs to this man." I pointed to Ruit. "The Great Alchemist Ruit."

"The Alchemist?" Gwenora bowed. "Thank you. I knew of another Alchemist."

"Yilliana, the creator of the Sorcerer stone that we hold in our hands now."

"Sorcerer!" Gwenora's face lit up in a way that you couldn't imagine on a dragon. She dipped her head low and got as close as she could to examine the journal. "Oh, it is you! We have so much to discuss."

I chuckled to myself. *A dragon and her stone.* I would love to be present for that reunion.

"Of course, we will leave the stone with you for as long as you require it, dear Original."

"That would be a blessing that I will happily receive."

I turned to Elias. "This is my Atoa, Elias Kraus."

"Are you related to Sorcey Kraus?"

"She was my mother."

"Was?"

"She died, along with my father."

"I am so sorry for your loss. She showed me a great deal of kindness, and Sorcerer. It is she that Sorcerer derived the namesake from."

Elias was aghast. He put his hand to his chest and pride washed over his face into a wide grin. "That brings joy to my heart, indeed."

Cataphet's deep voice reverberated off the walls. "Perhaps stories and sentiments can be extrapolated on at a later time."

"Right, so then we should be going?" Franky looked up at Cataphet and then back to me. "I cannot repay you for bringing her back to me."

"Not so fast, Franky. There is more business here to attend to than the Ulus. An Original was held captive for thousands of years. The Alchemist has suspicions that only Gwenora can satisfy."

"I have reason to believe that dragon's blood is what has been sedating the Nebas captives."

"Do you have supporting evidence of this, Gwenora?"

"I do. During my captivity, they took much of my blood. The hobgoblin administered many experiments on my flesh, my blood, my energy." Franky nuzzled her as she recalled what must have been awful to endure.

"What else have you discovered, Alchemist?"

"We have woken up all of the Nebas captives by administering troll tears. I theorize that the war against the trolls was also orchestrated by the Nebas to wipe out the only antidote to the poisonous dragon's blood."

"Can anyone speak to this?" Cataphet asked.

"It would make sense to me that the tears of the trolls would counteract the blood of the Originals. While we can absorb all gifts, rendering a creature senseless, the trolls can manifest the gifts of all creatures. Duality often harmonizes, therefore counteracting any imbalance," Gwenora explained.

"Very astute, sister," Cataphet said. "Has anyone shared this with the Queen?"

"She offered her tears, but I have not elucidated any further about my perceived origins of the war and attempted genocide of her people."

"The Queen must know."

"I will tell her as soon as we surface," Elias volunteered.

"Thank you for your time, Gwenora and Franky. I will have the Alchemist pass along the Sorcerer Stone after our exchange the Ulus and Ruit need it to participate in the conversation and Ruit can only understand whilst holding the book." Cataphet nodded and they were gone. I was left once more hoping I'd get a chance to see my friend Franky again. "Do not worry, Ulus, you will see him again. The Originals are now fully invested in the outcome of your strokes. The whole world is invested, now that there has been a Paradigm Tremor."

"You are confirming that was a Paradigm Tremor? What does that mean? Will this lead to our extinction once more?"

"You ask the wrong questions, Alchemist, but I will answer them nonetheless. Yes, their union created a Paradigm Tremor. No, it does not confirm that your generation of Conduits will live or die. It is a chasm in the time loop lines. While it is open, all fates are malleable—even for us dragons." Cataphet narrowed her eyes on me. "As for you, girl, I told you when we first met that Elias was the Sulu. You thought I was a simpleton?"

"I thought you were mistaken." Elias' voice in my head pleaded with me to tread lightly. "I was a simpleton, and very mistaken. I didn't mean to insult you."

"You are young, foolish and ignorant. I will not hold it against you—this time." She continued, "Elias is and always has been the Sulu. You are an Ulus."

"So, I was feeding off his power before we consummated? Why can I hear you, but all my other gifts are gone?"

"No, of course not. He is the container. That's what a Sulu is. The imposer, the enforcer of boundaries that keep the power safe and manageable. That's why you were struggling to control the gifts you absorbed. You were never meant to contain that type of energy. You haven't the strength."

It was like she was taking some of my deepest insecurities of not being worthy and stapling them to my forehead for everyone to see. I couldn't help but wince with every word, with every blow.

"The Ulus is the syphon, the master of absorbing and receiving. Nothing is ever really theirs, but everything is always theirs all at once. You cannot hold onto power that way. Its purpose is to flow through you and into him. Yet you still maintain all the power, because you two are one. Some of your gifts are anchored into you more securely, like the power you absorbed from Sorcerer that allows you to understand dragon."

"So, I am just a mechanism to funnel the energy and gifts to Elias? That's all I will ever be? With the occasional special parlor trick?"

"You are an Ulus and you speak of it as though you were sentenced to mediocrity. Speaking to dragons is a parlor trick? Have you ever heard of an Ulus?"

"No."

"Any of you?"

"No," Ruit and Elias agreed in unison.

"That is because they are rare, so rare that I have only met one other. They are the counterpart of the Sulu so that a vacuum is not formed, so that the power doesn't consume the world. Many Sulus have destroyed much of the world without their counterparts to balance them."

"Are Sulus always paired with an Ulus?" Elias asked what I was thinking.

"Did you hear me? Are you listening to anything I am saying? Honestly, Alchemist, how do you tolerate this?"

Ruit didn't respond to that, which I for one appreciated.

"This is the first Ulus I have seen since Lorif."

"Of the three sisters?" Ruit asked, his mouth agape.

Cataphet nodded, then continued. "As for your mission to discover where the world ends… I had initially intended to let you and the strokes decide if the Pai Ona could determine the divine whereabouts of the final battle. I had felt that directing you to the congregation of energy was enough. However, the Paradigm Tremor has made me reconsider many things. All is at risk of destruction now, therefore I have decided to return The Cathedral to where the world ends. She will begin relocation at dawn. You must all vacate the grounds for the effort to transition seamlessly. Is that understood?"

"Yes," we all agreed. But the questions were mounting. *The Cathedral can move. And where is this place?*

"Yes, The Cathedral transplants as it wishes, Ulus. How else would we stay hidden for so many centuries at a time?" I guess reading my thoughts had its benefits. "You may present yourselves in three days' time at her gates. Without the Gatekeeper and with there being one last missing Loktpi, we will be taking extra measures. I will not have one of my kin violated ever again." She hissed, and rage flashed across her face. Then Cataphet softened her expression in a very subtle way. "I speak for both The Cathedral and I when I say we miss him very much."

Ruit nodded, and I could see the tears welling in his eyes.

"Where are we going?"

Cataphet smiled a toothy smile. "The most powerful epicenter of the strokes in the world besides The Cathedral herself…"

Before Cataphet could finish, I heard the River Tins voice in my head. "New Orleans."

"New Orleans," Cataphet confirmed. Then I heard the dragon's voice in my head alone. "You heard him? You would be wise to listen to that voice above all others, Ulus."

"What? I don't understand!" I blurted out, but it was no use. Before I could ask more questions, we were standing in the hallway near the galley. My mind was racing. *Who does the voice belong to? Who is so powerful, even a dragon respects them?*

We were all waiting around for news of what transpired with the dragons, when Olly came storming in first. "Where is Aremis?" I pointed toward the back of the hall and walked toward Elias and Ruit.

"What's going on?"

"There isn't much to tell. The dragons confirmed that Ophelia is not a Sulu. She is, in fact, an Ulus. An even more rare creature with even less information available."

"More rare than a Sulu? What the fuck is more rare than a Sulu? Who is the goddamn Sulu then?"

Elias sheepishly raised his hand. *You have got to be kidding me*, I internally huffed at the ridiculous turn of events. *Of course! The golden boy was the Sulu. Of course.*

"Cataphet spoke of only one other Ulus ever known to exist. It was Lorif, of the three sisters." The look on my face must've accurately depicted my bewilderment because the Alchemist quickly explained, "Lorif, the sister whom Fih loved and coerced into abandoning her kin, while in fact he had murdered the other two, creating the first lines."

I had a vague recollection of the fable, enough to know it didn't end well for Lorif.

"Okay, so how do we get more information? Does Aremis know more? Is that why she is hugging him like they are going down on the Titanic?"

"No, she is trying to fill him in before he gets swept away by the disgruntled dragon named Napitae again. Olly is particularly disenchanted with this dragon," Elias admitted. "And she's just had another abrupt goodbye with Franky, so she is feeling sensitive."

My head was spinning. I'd missed out on so much in my captivity. It was like trying to get the CliffsNotes of "The Iliad." *Impossible.*

"I assured her once more that I will be okay." The three of us turned around to see Aremis cooly standing there. "I do not believe those tears are for me and my impending departure. I believe she is just in desperate need of expression."

"Indeed." Viraclay gave him a hug.

"I will find you once my promise is fulfilled. I will be at the last battle where the world ends."

"I know you will." Elias agreed. "We will see you in New Orleans."

"Wait, New Orleans?"

"We will fill you in, in a moment," Elias assured me.

"Take this token." Ruit put something in the palm of Aremis' hand. I couldn't see what it was. "It will serve you when the time is right."

Could you be any more vague?

"Thank you, my friend." Aremis gave Ruit a hug as well and turned to me. He bowed slightly in my direction. "Lucas, I trust you will assist Viraclay in keeping Miss Ophelia safe."

"You bet your ass I will." I pulled him in for a hug, and although he might've been surprised, he leaned into my arms and returned the gesture. "Thank you, for everything." I was very aware that Olly had had an entire team helping her out, keeping her safe, and ultimately saving me and Yesi.

"Aremis!" Olly shouted as she ran toward him. "You'll be in China, right?" She was in front of him now.

"That is how I understand it."

"While there, if you get a chance to connect with my friend Wailee of the Tartar tribe, mention Lis and tell him you're a friend of the Ulus. See what information he might have."

Ruit chimed in. "Remind him of his oath to the Loktpi. Here are the coordinates." Ruit pressed his hand to the back of Aremis' neck, and you could see in his eyes that something registered internally. *Man, this Alchemist had all kinds of tricks.*

Aremis addressed us all. "I won't fail." Then he literally vanished.

"Another classic dragon sendoff!" Olly threw her hands up in the air. Sparkle rushed over to console her.

"We're going to fill in the others," Elias said as he rubbed Ophelia's back and let her complain about how rude dragons were to Sparkle, who was enthusiastically agreeing.

I chuckled, but not loud enough for her to hear. Ruit started to walk away. I grabbed his arm. "Can I ask you something?"

"Yeah, anything."

"Ruit, I need to know one thing."

He nodded to go ahead.

"This paradigm thing—are we going to survive it?" Because the truth was, if we only had moments left and he knew it, I wanted to use them as wisely as possible.

"To be honest, not even the dragon Cataphet could assure our fates, but she said something that gave me great hope."

"What was that?"

"That she could not assure our fates."

I cocked my head at him. *Is he going a little crazy too?*

"That means it is up to us to establish our own."

I liked this guy.

Clive raised his left arm. I did not know what to expect next, so I grabbed the first thing I could reach—the small baton that I'd recovered from the fight between Nandi and Vivienne. I swung it in the air, attempting to combat whatever sorcery would come from Clive's gesture, and when I raised it to hit him, it unfolded, expanded from itself, and took its original form—a long metal staff.

When the metal struck his forearm, I heard a deep, bone-crushing crash. Bewilderment flashed across his face, he clearly anticipated another outcome. I immediately swung it around the other way, this time hitting him in the head. Clive's knees buckled, and it gave me a moment to flee out of the glass window. While Aurora screamed for reinforcements, I ran barefoot and bleeding in the snow. I needed the bleeding to stop so I wouldn't be as trackable. While I prayed I would heal faster than usual, I ran as hard as I could until I found a stream. At minimum, this would mask my scent. I stepped into the icy water and welcomed the pain. It would fuel my efforts.

There were voices behind me, surrounding me. The Haven was harboring about fifty Nebas, and now every one of them was hunting me. All of them would love an opportunity to make me feel pain after the ways I led with fear and torment. I turned when I heard someone enter the water behind me. It was Astrid.

"Come easily, Esther, and this will be as painless as possible."

I chuckled to myself at the irony of it all.

"You know me better than that." I swung the staff around and tripped her. She fell hard on her back in the water. I leapt into the air and landed on top of her, taking control of her body. Someone stepped out of the shadows to my left. It was Claudia. *She has to be loving this.*

I mentally prepared myself for the onslaught of nightmares that would ensue now that we had made eye contact. More voices were trailing behind her. They would be on me in seconds. Claudia surprised me by putting her hands up. "Hey, I don't want any part of this, Esther. I just want to get out of this shit hole alive. I wasn't meant to be a lackey. My time here is through."

"What?" The footsteps drew nearer. I didn't have time for this. "You hate me."

"Yeah, and everyone else. There's more to my story, but for now, all you need to know is that I want out of this hierarchy. Let me go with you, stop bossing me around, and I'll help you get out of this mess."

There wasn't time to think it through. "Yes!"

Then Claudia moved into the shadows. I maintained control of Astrid's body as she was positioned, crouched in the center of the stream. I had distanced myself from her by about twenty feet and stood on a large boulder in the middle of the water.

Two Nebas emerged from the trees. The first one was Calypso, a formidable opponent, and the second was Elizabeth the Luress. Elizabeth would be an easy out.

"Come, little ladies. Please, by all means, come and get me."

I took a warrior's stance with the staff firm in my hand. The rock shook beneath my feet. Calypso could easily throw me off it with her gifts. They were almost in reach. I leapt from the boulder onto the shore and shoved Calypso into the water while simultaneously commanding Astrid to send high voltage from her hands into the stream. Calypso screamed in pain while massive currents of electricity coursed through her body.

Elizabeth was faster than I expected. Apparently, I'd underestimated her. She had a knife to my throat in seconds. I tried to spin out of her grip but misjudged her strength and she slid the blade across my neck. Blood spewed from the wound, and I immediately grew lightheaded. I could not give up this easily. I forced myself to push on. Elizabeth was standing there, assuming she had just defeated me. Poor misguided Luress. I swung the staff and planted her in the stream of electricity, where she, too, began to wail.

My knees buckled from the loss of blood. The wound was too shallow to take me out completely. I just had to control the bleeding. I ripped a strip of material from the bottom of my burgundy dress and wrapped it tightly around my neck in an attempt to slow the flow. When I got back to my feet, I saw twenty-five to thirty Nebas emerging from the woods. *This would be the end of me.*

"Esther, surge the electricity on the count of three," Claudia directed from the distance. I couldn't see her. My vision was getting foggy.

I blinked my eyes into focus and realized Claudia was behind me with Jillian in her arms. Jillian would amplify Claudia's gift. It was brilliant. The Nebas who were descending on me suddenly got distracted as their vision was replaced with their worst nightmare. They began to stumble forward. I stopped the electrical current so that they would absently walk into the water. Claudia smiled when she realized what I was doing. Most of them were now groveling on their knees in the stream. I stepped back into the cover of the trees.

"1, 2, 3!"

I lit the stream up with torrents of electricity. Then Claudia, with Jillian in her arms and me on their tail, ran.

OPHELIA

"So, let me get this straight. Even if they aren't here now, but they were here and took the bidding, they will get the call?" I asked Ruit.

"Yes. That is how a bidding works. There are no boundaries or distances."

"But we are calling an assembly because there are Conduits here now?"

"We are calling an assembly because in addition to activating the bidding, we need to inform them that we will need to vacate the grounds and reconvene in New Orleans for the final battle."

"How do we tell the people who aren't here where to go? And how do we know that the communications are secure?"

"Once a bidding is enacted, a communication tether is created. Therefore, all who are bidded can act as a unit."

"Got it. Aren't you worried about New Orleans? I mean, it's a highly populated city. Is that really the best place for open battle?"

Elias answered, "I may be wrong, but I suspect that, just as the last open battle took place in multiple planes and in a variety of times, this will be the same."

"I am assuming that is correct, Elias."

"I don't get it."

"You will. Trust me, you will."

We turned the corner to a full room patiently waiting to be steered towards their next course. Elias took my hand in his. "We got this," I said it to him, but it was more for my benefit. For the first time, maybe ever, I wished I could access my curse to get a read on the room, or maybe I wanted a better read on him—or I just wanted a distraction.

"This is the easy part." He kissed the back of my hand, and we stepped into the amphitheater.

Ruit waved at his family in the first row of seating. Almus and the party searching for the final battle returned only hours ago, once we informed them that we knew where the world ends. They each conservatively nodded back. I spoke in Elias' head, "Maybe you should take the lead in this meeting since you are the Sulu?"

"Our people have chosen their leader, and it is you. No matter your extraordinary title."

We'd already discussed this. It made no sense to disclose our current status. We still had a Sulu, and now we had an Ulus, too, but to try and explain the significance of this anomaly when we understood so little ourselves would only create anxiety, an insecurity we didn't need just before the final battle.

"Showtime." We both turned to face the assembly. They cheered thunderously. It was amazing how many Conduits we had rooting for us. There were at least three thousand here, and over four thousand had taken the bidding when called.

Elias amplified my voice. "Thank you. We appreciate all of your support and show of solidarity. Thank you for coming to the call. To those of you who were there for the sack of Chernobyl—I owe you my life."

Elias added, "We owe you our lives, and that will not be soon forgotten."

A voice called out from the third row. It was unfamiliar to me, but it commanded presence. "You restored our loved ones to us. For that, I owe you my life." He stood. "My name is Finnegan, and my strokes will forever be at your service." He bowed slightly.

"As will mine." Thracian stood behind him.

A man got to his feet beside Thracian. "You gave me back my life. There will be no greater honor than to serve in this war." The man looked at Thracian, and I realized they must be related.

One by one, the survivors and their family members stood and proclaimed their allegiance to the cause. It moved me to tears. In truth, it moved half the room to tears.

Then Lucas got up. "I am ready to take the bidding and give you my life." Yesi took her husband's hand in solidarity. It was hard to imagine the transformation my best friend had made. From being a rogue renegade who relied on no one, to a team player who was ready to commit his life to a cause greater than himself.

I nodded at Elias to respond. "The bidding will be yours to take."

The two men I loved the most nodded at each other in a way I never believed would be possible, with respect.

When the room grew silent once more, Elias addressed the crowd again.

"Today we employ the bidding. If you are prepared to bid, please stand." The rest of the Conduits got to their feet in unison, and my heart swelled with pride. "We have the dragons, the trolls, the Ancients, and all of you by our side. Victory feels near. The end of the bloodshed, once and for all. We must trust one another and lock arms with our allies. The rest is in the strokes. I can feel it in my bones."

A shout from the crowd, "And we have the Sulu!"

I squeezed Elias' hand. "Yes! We do!" I shouted back, and the entire room erupted again.

"Elias and I will summon the bidding now."

Together, we repeated the oath that each bidder made. "I will come when called, to fight the final battle, prepared to give my life for the salvation of our people. I will align with my allies and offer my sword, gifts, and any other assets that may aid in victory, without exception and with all the honor I possess."

When we first implemented the bidding, it all sounded very intense to me, but Elias explained that this bidding was a respected allegiance given before the last open battle. By using the same verbiage, we invoked the same respect. And although many lives were lost during the last battle, there was still a high regard for the price paid by all of those who fell.

As we finished the oath, a mist seemed to expand from our bodies, enveloping the crowd and moving outward. I could only assume it broadened to encompass all the corners of the globe and every bidder, so they could answer the call and receive the communication tether.

The room grew still and stayed that way for a few long moments. It felt like there was some sort of silent exchange happening within each Conduit. *For all I knew, there was.* When the heaviness of the moment subsided, Ruit spoke.

"On behalf of myself and my family, the dragons, and The Cathedral, I want to thank you for answering the call and committing to the salvation of our people. The other day, an anomaly occurred that even the dragons know little about, it is referred to as a Paradigm Tremor. This event is a mystery, but it is one of the catalysts that have enlisted the Originals to stand beside us in battle. When convening with Cataphet this morning, we were told that the Originals have decided to relocate The Cathedral to a new destination, where we will take arms for the final battle. The place known as New Orleans." That sent a buzz through the hall. "In order to do the transport effectively, we must vacate the grounds by dawn. Upon three days' time, we will be admitted back into The Cathedral, at her new locality. Any further instruction will be communicated through our bidding tether."

"Are there any questions?" Elias asked.

A single Conduit raised their hand, a slight woman in the fifth row. "Where are the Rittles?"

I wondered when this question would come up. I stepped forward. "I miscalculated a strategic move when we were attempting to recover some captives from the Nebas. In doing so, I enabled our enemy to steal the Rittles. I cannot properly describe how sorry I am for this terrible mistake. I'm so sorry."

Ruit intervened, "We still have the upper hand, especially now that we have the allegiance of the Originals and we have a volume of the Pierses."

A man stood up at the top of the amphitheater. "Are there more captives?"

"Yes, we believe there are."

"Who? Do you know who?" a woman's desperate voice called from somewhere in the crowd.

"We don't know the names of the remaining captives, but we suspect there are quite a few more," I admitted.

"How can we destroy the Oracle? She sees all!" a Conduit in the shadows of the hall yelled.

"The Sulu has absorbed some of her sight and we have reason to believe there are holes in her vision," Ruit explained. "We know this is scary, and we know that there are more questions than answers right now. But we hope to have more information by the time we reconvene in New Orleans. Please trust us."

A buzz went through the room. I couldn't read what they were feeling. But Elias could, so he answered in my head. "They are restless and afraid but still committed."

That was a relief. *Commitment was all we needed.* And I hoped Ruit was right and that we could give them more answers soon. I asked Elias through our Rune, "Did you really absorb some sight? I mean, besides crazy Kassandra's?"

"I did, but they both feel murky right now. Perhaps it is because I am new to this, or perhaps it is because this paradigm shift has tilted the strokes in our favor."

The crowd started to trickle out of the amphitheater. They may not have gotten the answers they wanted, but they'd completed the bidding, and that was the agenda for today. In addition to a mass exodus of the Haven.

Almost everyone was gone when I looked up and saw a vaguely

familiar face, but I couldn't place it because I was aware it was not from my memories.

"Caleb Garrith!" Elias greeted him, and now I understood the familiarity. "It has been too long." The man approached us with his unique-looking Atoa, a cocoa-skinned beauty. "I am so sorry about your father," Elias said as he pulled him in for a hug.

My eyes instantly welled with tears. *Rand. My dear protector, Rand.* Caleb immediately turned to me. "My father said we would be fast friends. I am Caleb, and this is my wife, Sofie."

"He told me the same." I hugged him tightly and noticed he smelled similar to his father.

"We will be off shortly but are prepared for the final battle. My family deserves to be avenged."

I couldn't agree more.

"So many deserve to be avenged, but your parents are held in the highest regard," Elias agreed.

"I have something for you, from my dad. He gave it to me before he left for Hafiza. It is a key to a secret storage space in our cottage in Austria. Do you know of it?"

"Of the cottage? Indeed."

"He kept something of your father's there for safe keeping. That is all I know. And he gave me clear instruction that, should something happen to him, I give you this key and directions to find the safe."

"Have you opened it?" Elias asked.

"Never. It was clear it was your legacy, not mine."

"Thank you."

I wanted to say more, but I was just stupefied by the resemblance and air about Caleb. It was like seeing Rand's ghost.

"Perhaps we can sit down for a pint after this is all through?"

I finally found words. "I would like that very much!" It came out fast and over-enthusiastic.

He smiled at me. "As would I."

LUCAS

Yesi and I had our bags packed. We were ready to go. I just needed to say bye to Olly and Viraclay. We'd decided we were going to spend the next couple of days with Fetzle. We wanted to reconnect with her and see if there was anything we could do to help prepare her militia for the war to come.

"Are you afraid?" Yesi asked as she put her backpack on.

"Of the dark?" I teased. "I mean, it's only for a few days. Listy must have some torches or something, and I've got you, my little beacon of hope." I pulled her in and tucked her head under my chin.

"You know what I'm asking about."

"The war, combat? No. I've survived my worst nightmare—losing you. Nothing scares me now." Except for, of course, losing her again, but that was not going to happen. I would not let that happen. "Are you afraid?"

"Yes. Of course I'm afraid."

"You know you don't have to fight."

"I'm not afraid of fighting. I will be by your side, and there is nothing you can do to stop that. I'm afraid of losing people I love. I'm afraid of losing myself in the bloodshed."

"I will not let you lose yourself. I'll always be there to find you and remind you who you are."

She was quiet, and I sensed there was more lingering in the pause, but we were interrupted by a knock.

"Coming," I said as I kissed her forehead and went to the door.

On the other side stood Thracian and Dari. "We heard you're going to Listy. We want to join you."

I wasn't looking for company. I was about to say as much when Yessica opened the door further. "That will be lovely. The more the merrier."

Genghis came around from the left. "We will join you too."

"What?"

Borte appeared at his side, grimacing.

"That will be wonderful, Father."

When I heard Vosega's voice, I thought I was going to be sick. "Oya and I will join you as well." The burly red-headed man towered over the other four as he came up from behind. Everything in me wanted to protest, run, or just plain ignore them, anything to prevent this entourage from joining us in Listy.

Dari picked up on my discomfort. "Look, man, I can't speak for all of these guys, but I have been asleep for six hundred years. Troll tears woke me up and gave me a second chance. I want to be on the frontline with the trolls. I owe them that."

Thracian followed up with, "They gave me my brother back." He put his arm around Dari.

"And you four?"

Yesi pinched my butt. "You know why they are coming."

"Alright, well, we are leaving now. If you aren't ready, then we're going without you."

There was a chorus of readys and I looked in the hall to see their bags were there and packed. *Shit!* I was hoping that would weed out a couple.

"Nice try." Yesi giggled as she pushed past me and into the hall to give her dad a hug.

I internally huffed and grabbed our bags from beside the door and shut it behind me.

"Where is Fetzle fetching us?" Dari asked.

"You should probably call her Queen."

"Lucas!" Yessica scolded. "You know she doesn't care about formalities. You call her whatever you like, Dari."

"She will meet us in the garden. Why don't you take these guys there, Yesi, while I say goodbye to the newlyweds."

"I'll take your bags, son."

I reluctantly handed Vosega my bags. This was going to be quite the family vacation. Since there was nothing I could do, I just transported myself to Olly and Viraclay's. I stood there for a moment, still agitated with the turn of events. It was long enough that Olly came to the door.

"I thought I heard someone out here. Do you want to come in or you'd rather just be creepy?"

"Sorry. I'm just a little annoyed with some uninvited guests."

"You look to be alone to me. Should I be worried I'm losing my vision too? Or are you seeing things? Are the uninvited guests here now?" She looked around dramatically.

"Shut the fuck up." I playfully punched her arm. "No, they aren't here now. They are packed and going with us to Listy."

"Oooooh. Let me guess. Your dad and Oya." Ophelia took a seat on the couch as Elias walked in from the other room.

"Would you like a beer?"

"A shot would be better."

"I bet that can be arranged. What do you say, baby, got a shot for our poor defeated friend here?"

"Will whiskey do?"

I nodded, and in a moment, we were all raising a toast. "To a family vacation with dear old dad, the in-laws, and Thracian and Dari."

"Ouch. I can understand your need now," Olly teased before we all threw them back.

"I'm just here to say goodbye. We'll meet you in New Orleans in three days."

Elias took a seat beside Ophelia, and I admired the couple that previously made me want to hurl. They were happy. She was happy, and that was good.

"Hey, can you relay to Fetzle a message that I've been meaning to share?"

"Yeah, of course."

"The giants have her crown, and they'll only give it to the true Queen. Shiva and the others tried to get the giants to help our cause. We don't need the islands for the last battle anymore, but their help would still be appreciated. Maybe she could check in with them while also grabbing her crown?"

"It seems worth a try. Anything else?"

"We will be in Austria before heading stateside. Rand has left me something of importance from my father," said Elias. I wished I could be a fly on the wall for that discovery. "You can communicate with us via the bidding tether. But I can also detect you with this."

"With what?"

"The hairsy charm," Olly said, forlorn.

"But it was between me and you."

"I don't understand it, but it's no longer accessible to me to feel. Still this guy can see it."

"But…"

"I can see the connection between you two. We are not connected, do not worry."

"But I can't feel it anymore." Olly explained. "Can you feel it?"

I searched around my energetic body, there was something, but it definitely felt different. I assumed that it was because we used it for the sealing ceremony. "I don't know why, but that makes me feel duped. A good, old-fashioned bait-and-switch."

"Hey, bring it up with the Queen. It was her fancy magic."

"You bet your ass I'm taking this one to the source. Now come here and give me a hug."

Olly got up and I pulled her in tight.

"Be safe."

"You too."

Sparkle had come to retrieve Olly a few moments ago, to say goodbye to her mother. I sensed that Sparkle was feeling forlorn since Aremis' absence. She and Aremis had become quite close over the last few months. I knew Aremis found Sparkle attractive. I wondered if she felt the same about him.

Eleanor was leaving with Sparkle, Lilith, Tete and Medusa. We all felt it was safer if she stayed with us until this war was over. It was beautiful to see how Eleanor and Olly's relationship was transforming into something new. Vulnerability was giving them a second chance.

We had only a few more hours until we would need to vacate The Cathedral. I decided to make my way down to the library. I wanted to see what I could find on Lorif and the three sisters. It had been many years since I had heard the tale. Now I desired nothing more than to remember the story that I'd dismissed as fiction. I was disappointed to see I was not the only avid reader in The Cathedral. Ramy turned to face me as I entered the room.

"Pray tell, Viraclay, what keeps you from your newly betrothed at this hour?"

I liked Ramy enough, but I was not in a sharing mood. I was

anxious and confused. Honestly, I was scared.

"She is occupied, and I was looking for some light reading."

"This library is a treasure. Anything you could possibly want to read, at our very fingertips. Can I help you find something? I have become quite familiar."

I sighed. I wanted to resist his help, I wanted to be alone, I wanted to sulk, but it was not in my strokes.

"The three sisters?"

Ramy raised an eyebrow but said nothing. "I only read this one the other day. I hadn't indulged in the fables since I was a child. Yet, a few days ago, I was moved to read them all." He paused in front of a shelf, where he searched the titles. "There was much wisdom in the pages, far more than I could have grasped as a boy."

"How so?"

"Well, we are all simple creatures. We really just want love and to feel part of something bigger than ourselves—to feel complete."

"That is why we come in pairs."

"Perhaps, or perhaps that's why the painter created us in one grand stroke." He handed me the book. "They are all in there, every creation myth."

It was a large book.

"The order is peculiar though."

"In what way?"

"I don't know, it felt like it went in a circle." He waved his hand in the air, as though to brush off the thought. "It may just be me. My head is either in the books or in the clouds, as my Mae always said."

"She is gone?"

"She is. Mae entered the River Tins during the last battle, by the hand of Esther herself."

"I am so sorry for your loss."

"She is still here. I feel her strokes all around me. In the steps I take, the words I speak. Her strokes are mine and mine hers. No transformation can change that. And that is all death is, another transformation." Ramy turned to leave. "Enjoy that book."

Then he was gone and I was left alone with my thoughts.

OPHELIA

"What are you reading?" I asked as I took my seat between his legs in front of the fire. I picked up the large novel. The pages were stiff and the book smelled musty.

"It is a compilation of the creation myths."

"Lorif's story is in here." I fanned the pages. The script was hand-written in Asagi, a language I now understood fluently. One of the perks of being consummated—a complete download of the Conduit language. It just popped into my vocabulary like it had always been there. "What did you find?"

"Shall I read it to you? You can make your own assessment."

"Should I be worried?"

He kissed the back of my neck. "Never. We will traverse this, just as we have traversed all the obstacles before it—together."

I melted a little more into his chest. "Okay, I'm ready."

Elias opened the book toward the end. I was surprised it was one of the last stories.

AND SO, it was Lorif resided with Fih in the Ekkle Forest. But her sadness did not wane. She wept and she yearned for the companionship of her sisters. When Fih would leave to see his brothers at dawn, she would watch on. Often, Fih invited her to join them, but she could not bear to leave the forest. When she saw Fih with his brothers Tindle and Priloc, it made her miss her sisters even more. Lorif's sobs were so loud they could be heard in all directions of the wind. She wondered why she could not hear the sobs of her sisters. They did not miss her as she missed them, and this only made her more melancholic.

Priloc spoke to Fih about Lorif's grief one day. "Brother, surely we must do something to soothe her pain. Her anguish is felt by the ocean."

Tindle added, "By the caverns of Cataphet as well."

"What would you have us do? I would do anything to ease her pain. To see her smile at me once more."

"Shall we call on her sisters? Or escort her for a sojourn?"

Fih became immediately enraged. "No! Absolutely not! Her sisters let her leave. They will never see one another again. Their strokes are no longer welcome."

Tindle and Priloc looked on at their brother wearily. He spoke so harshly, with such conviction, it worried them both. The brothers spent the rest of the day with very few words between them. When the sun began to set and they went their separate ways, Priloc and Tindle discretely signaled one another and they meet in Cataphet's deepest chamber.

"We must do something." Priloc demanded. "She is heartbroken, she cries endlessly, and Fih is not to be reasoned with. He fears he may lose her to her sisters."

"Brother, it hurts my heart the same as you, but what is there to be done? Fih forbids our involvement in the matter."

The brothers sat in silence for a long moment.

"Go to the sisters. Let them hear of Lorif's broken heart. Surely, they will feel the same and come here to live among us all," Priloc insisted.

"But they did not choose their sister before. Why would their choice change?"

"Absence does wicked things to the heart."

There was truth in that, and they agreed it was worth it, for the harmony of all, to try. The brothers Priloc and Tindle hatched a plan. First they would go to Lorif and ask for a token or a letter that she may share with her sisters her grief and desire for reconciliation. Then they would tell Fih that Tindle was tending to business with Cataphet, as he sometimes did, but instead, he would make the journey to the Valley and return with the sisters.

"Will Fih believe my errand? Or do you think he will grow suspicious?"

"I will keep him busy, and surely, with Lorif's support, he may not suspect a thing. She will most certainly engage, knowing the errand you run is to reunite her with her kin. I believe we can occupy his thoughts and reduce his suspicions."

The intentions were set and the plan in motion. Tindle would go to Lorif tomorrow in the Ekkel Forest.

What the brothers did not know was that while Fih slept and the brothers masterminded, Lorif made a wish to the stars. Lorif gazed up at the Seven Sister Stars and pleaded with all she had. "Dear Seven Sisters, surely you can hear my heart. I miss Goyta and Orail with all of my being. I miss their laughter and their curiosities. I miss their hugs and their joy... Surely you can give me some token to share with them. A token that will let me feel their presence even though we are so far away. I beg you for such a gift that my heart may stop breaking and I may find peace and happiness once more in the arms of Fih."

Just then, a bright golden star descended from the sky. Unbeknownst to Lorif, the Seven Sisters had been watching her for some time. They could hear the cries that only a sister with a broken heart can hear. Before Lorif appeared a luminous being made of light, and a rainbow of color. The creature was breathtaking, not in how she appeared but in the abundance that emanated off her essence.

"I am the Star Seed, dear Lorif, mother of the Seven Sisters, and I am here to grant your wish. Two of my daughters have mourned with you and had already set in motion a creation that they believe will give you the presence you seek." The Star Seed pulled out two large books bound in leather and metal strappings. "These are the Pierses, great volumes of magic. Where one goes the other will know. They are sisters just as you are with your kin. Their magics are shared and their wisdom plentiful. While you possess one volume and your sisters another, you will be able to speak through the subtle language of castings."

Lorif exaltedly took the Pierses into her arms, thanking the Star Seed and looking to the heavens and thanking her daughters. Although she did not know then how she would get a Pierses to her sisters, she was basking in hope. The strokes have a divine way of setting things in motion that change the course of everything that ever was or ever could be. This night would mark one of the most impactful twists of fate the world will ever know.

The next day, Lorif woke up overjoyed. She had hidden the Pierses in the root of a Tonglin tree many yards away, certain Fih would not find them. Fih was ecstatic to see that Lorif had finally seemed to be done mourning her sisters and was ready to create a life with him. The relief Fih felt was immense. He would finally be able to share with Lorif all the dreams he hoped they would see met together. It was nearly impossible for Fih to leave her that morning to meet his brothers, but he kept his word, and on this day, he was excited to share the news—Lorif was cured of her grief.

Fih was surprised and slightly disappointed when he only saw Priloc.

"Where is our great brother Tindle? What keeps him this day?" Fih asked as he gave Priloc a hug.

"I went to Cataphet when he did not arrive and she said he is assisting her with an addition to her deepest chamber. She did not tell me how many spans it will take, but I am sure he will be with us as soon as he is free."

"Oh brother, do you think he is cross with me for my outburst yesterday? Perhaps I should go to him, to set things straight?"

Priloc put his arm on Fih's shoulder. "You know our brother better than that. He only wants you to be happy." Priloc put his hand to his ear. "It sounds as though today may be a better day?"

"Yes, brother! I have the best news. It seems Lorif's grief has reached its end."

Priloc did not hide his surprise. He wondered if that meant Tindle could abandon their plan. He trusted his brother would know what to do.

Lorif was singing softly and tending to a small patch of earth where she wanted to plant flowers and fruits. She was startled when Tindle spoke.

"Dear Lorif, today seems to have found you in good spirits. This overcomes us all with joy."

"Oh my!" She clutched her chest. "You scared me, Tindle, and yes, I am feeling hope today."

"Hope is a favored state. What brings you such optimism?"

Lorif considered what she would say, when it occurred to her that perhaps Tindle was the very person she needed to deliver the volume to her sisters. It had to be divined by the strokes. "Can I share a secret with you? One you swear you will never share with your brothers?"

Tindle shuffled his feet nervously. This made him very uncomfortable. He never kept secrets from his brothers. Then he considered what his agenda had been for the day. Surely, he could make an exception if it made Lorif happy. He nodded.

"Come with me." She took his hand in hers, and Tindle felt a spark of something he had never experienced before. A flutter in his stomach. It was lovely. "It is over here." They reached the roots of a very large tree, and Lorif released his hand. He felt slightly dismayed, and it made him curious. Lorif dug around for a moment and pulled up two large books.

"The Star Seed visited me last night, and she gave me these. They are the Pierses, sister volumes of magic. They are connected. The Star Seed said that if my sisters were to possess one volume while I possess the other, we would be able to sense the presence of each other. It would be a gentle connection that I could carry with me so I may feel them close always."

"That is amazing. May I?" Tindle reached out to take one of the books. Lorif gladly handed it to him. "This is powerful, Lorif. What an incredible gift."

"Would you be willing to deliver it to my sisters? I know it is too much to ask, but Fih will never support me leaving. He feels that they made their intentions known, but something in me feels they were just hurt, that given the chance they would want this too." Lorif put her hand on Tindle's heart. It skipped several beats. "Please."

Of course he would do it. It was nearly what he had intended to do to begin with. "It would be an honor." He wrapped one of the Pierses in a Tonglin leaf and strapped it to his back. "I will return." Lorif kissed him on the cheek and his face got red like fire.

"Thank you. I am so grateful for your kindness. Please tell my sisters how much I love and miss them."

Then Tindle was off. He traveled for fourteen days over the Eld Mountains, into the Yollik Valley, and while he did, he thought of Lorif. He thought of how his skin got hot, his heartbeat quickened, and his stomach tickled with her touch. What did it mean, he wondered?

He arrived in the Yollik Valley just before dawn on the four-teenth day. He was surprised to see that it looked exactly as they had left it moons ago. He went to Goyta's shelter and knocked on the door. She did not come. He tried the knob. It was open. He walked into the small room. There was nothing out of place, yet no sign that she was there either. Curiously, he noticed a pool of vibrant colors on the floor. It caught his attention because it looked like the purest of all of the strokes, a medley of liquid color. Tindle stared at it for a long time, wondering what it could be. The birds chirping outside brought him back to the present.

He walked over to Orail's small dwelling by the river. After knocking and again without an answer, he entered and looked around. The scene was the same. No sign of Orail, and a large pool of rainbow liquid on the floor. Exasperated, Tindle took a seat in a chair. What was he to do? This news would devastate Lorif, that her sisters abandoned their home and did not leave even a note to convey their new settlement. This realization would surely set Lorif back into a cloud of grief, and something inside him could not see that happen. He pulled the Pierses off his back and unwrapped it from the Tonglin leaf.

"What do I do, great painter?" he said as he flipped through the pages. Just then, he felt the gentle connection between the two books. Subtle in nature, it was as though he knew the other book was also being read. Tindle skimmed through and landed on an incantation that could allow another to visit one's dreams. As his finger brushed the page, he somehow felt that the other reader was also touching the page. Of course, he knew the other reader was Lorif, and it gave him a sense of peace. This was the connection she was seeking with her sisters.

"I can give her this. She needn't know that her sisters have abandoned her. All she needs is the sense that someone is on the other side of these pages." He kissed the words and closed the Pierses. "I will keep her heart from breaking once more."

Tindle looked around the room one last time. A thought occurred to him that perhaps he should burn the dwelling so that Lorif would never have to endure the pain of the truth. Without another thought, he lit the wood planks on fire and watched it go up in flames. Tindle did the same to Goyta's home, and then moved to Lorif's cottage in the trees. "What should I do with this place?"

He stepped in and looked around. Lorif did not have many things, but a simple ivory comb caught his attention. It had five teeth to brush her long blonde hair with. There were several strands woven through the teeth of the comb. Tindle brought the item up to his nostrils. He could smell Lorif's sweet floral scent. He loved her scent. Tindle put the comb in his pocket and decided he would leave her cottage as it was. He did not have the heart to burn it.

Then he took off back toward the pass that would lead him home to the Amawin Meadow. Every few days, he would stop and read an incantation in the Pierses, just so Lorif felt she was present with her sisters. Every time, he felt himself grow closer and closer to the lovely Lorif. These feelings were so foreign to him, but he could not deny them either. Was this what Fih felt for Lorif, he wondered?

He arrived in the meadow after the moon rose in the night sky. His brothers had long since retired to their respective corners of the world. Tindle wondered how he would be greeted at dawn. Would Priloc be relieved? Would Fih be suspicious of his extended absence, and would Lorif be there now that she was feeling better?

Cataphet greeted Tindle with a boisterous welcome. "You are home. I have missed you. Please come to the depths and see me."

"A moment, dear friend. I have something to tend to."

While Tindle had been playing the part as Goyta and Orail, he had begun to absorb some of the incredible information available in the Pierses' pages. One spell caught his attention. It was a token called a Gattilak charm. It was a braid made of two creatures' hair. When the knots and braids were completed, the two souls were forever bonded. They could sense each other anywhere in the strokes. The connection could literally move anything and everything out of the way to ensure their bond was not severed. It kept both of them safe, warded off ill intentions of any kind, and eliminated the magics of foreshadow in the charm's presence.

Tindle pulled out the comb with Lorif's hair and plucked a strand from his own head. He admired how similar they were in color, unlike his brother Fih's, who was so much darker in his characteristics. Much like their natures, Tindle felt their appearances hinted at their differences. Tindle began to weave the hair together.

"What are you doing, Tindle?" Cataphet's voice demanded in a tone he had never heard her use before.

"Nothing that matters to you."

"I am afraid what you choose now will affect us all, sweet Tindle. Some bonds have consequences that reach far and wide."

Tindle ignored the warning and continued with the enchantment.

"If you do this thing, you will lose me. I see the strokes bending with every knot you tie. Our paths with be ruptured forever. But if you stop now, if you choose to value my warning, my friendship, my love…" Cataphet paused, hoping her words were making an impact. "You and I will have an eternity and the circles will stay intact as they were always meant to."

Tindle weighed the words of his closest and truest friend. "Cataphet, I will never let anything come between us. You must know that."

"If you ignore me now, there is no way of stopping what will be put in motion. We will no longer be together."

Tindle loved Cataphet, but the new feelings that were stirring within him were demanding to be felt and he desired nothing more than to surrender to them no matter the cost. So, without another word, he completed the Gattilak charm.

✾

ELIAS CLOSED THE BOOK. "What happens next?"

"The collection was never completed by the mysterious author. There are several blank pages at the end."

That is the worst cliffhanger ever!"

"Indeed."

"They don't even talk about Lorif being an Ulus. And what is up with the order of these stories? Which one comes first? The fable about The Cathedral, or the sisters, or Fih creating the Rittles and stabbing his brother?"

"It is curious, but they do all overlap. It is as though they are all happening at the same time, but not as we interpret time."

"You're losing me," I admitted. But there was a nagging question, now, lingering in my mind. "Elias, you don't think that the Gattilak charm could be the hairsy charm, do you?"

He stayed quiet, and it made me more uneasy. "I feel it seems highly likely."

I let out the breath I'd been holding. "That is a little terrifying."

LUCAS

"Fetzle takes magics, so Fetzle be's just like yous."

"Just like us. Thank you, Fetzle," Yesi agreed. "We could not have a more gracious hostess."

"Fetzle likes having her friends in her city. Fetzle thinks it's the best."

"We are honored Fetzle," Dari said as he looked at the dimly lit remnants of Listy. I remembered when Listy was thriving, shuttles heading in every direction of the globe. The buzz of the trolliage was evident in the earth. Now, as I examined what was left in this deep cavern with millions of tunnels and a small population, I was sad.

"How many of the trolliage remain?"

"Fetzle counts four hundred and twelve. Fetzle knows there be's three hundred and thirty one male trolls and eighty one she-trolls, the strongest trolls." Her voice got a little lower. "Fetzle knows something even more specials, because there are two Sholl-guard stills alives and is trainings Fetzle's new guard."

Oya responded first. "Wow, that is amazing, Queen Fetzle."

"Fetzle just be Fetzle to her friends." She patted Oya on the head.

I was in shock. From a population of over a hundred thousand at its peak to less than five hundred, and so few of them were female.

"Fetzle, are there any new trollings?"

Her head hung low. "No, Fetzle doesn't count any new trollings since the war."

Thracian spoke up. "What happened to the defector, Pladzle?"

Fetzle visibly stiffened at the mention of his name. It hurt my heart. "When Fetzle tooks back her city, she comes to Listy and sees fat ugly Pladzle being bossy and telling all the male trolls whats to do and keepings the she-trolls alls chained. Fetzle says no, she's not standing for anymores bossy Pladzle. Fetzle used rare Dalaketnon magics and makes hundreds of Fetzles to fight the Pladzle and his stupid male troll armies. Because she-trolls are strongest and fastest, Fetzle takes captives army and imprisons Pladzle. Fetzle will never lets him go. He will turn to stone in the garden."

"What did you do with the army?" Vosega asked.

"Fetzle talks to them and it seems that they don'ts really like Pladzle and they misses their she-trolls."

"Why did they follow him in the first place then?"

"Fetzle thinks this is most peculiars of all." She tapped the side of her head with her big finger. "The smaller, silly male trolls don't remember why, and theirs auras smelled very suspicious."

"What kind of magic could do that? To an entire army of male trolls." Genghis was asking the question more to himself than to the queen. But she just threw her hands in the air, as if she just couldn't imagine what could do that. A thought was percolating in my head.

"Do you have more of that Dalaketnon magic, Fetzle?" That would save the lives of the few she-trolls she had, the last living members of her trolliage, and the only chance to carry on her legacy.

"Fetzle doesn't haves any more, but maybes some in Fetzle's mom's shuttle. Yep, Fetzle thinks you can looks there, because that is where you will be staying." Her mouth spread with pride. *Man, I love this troll.*

ESTHER

$\mathcal{W}$e fled in virtual silence, only sharing the occasional word to decide on the next direction. We made it to the junction portal where Russia meets Kazakhstan. It was bustling with an assortment of creatures, none of which paid any attention to us or our half-sedated companion. Jillian had popped in and out of consciousness for the entirety of the travel.

"Can you hold her for a while? My arms are killing me." Claudia practically tossed Jillian at me as she pulled off her backpack. "I grabbed a few other things on my way out."

I was rather speechless. Never in the wildest of strokes would I have considered Claudia to have this much sense, especially in an un-orchestrated escape. Jillian stirred in my arms and nuzzled in closer. She mumbled something that I couldn't make out.

"How did you retrieve her?"

"She was in Aurora's room when I went in there to grab these." To my astonishment, she pulled out the compass and the crystal ball. "I would've grabbed more, but I decided this gem was more important." She nodded towards Jillian.

"I am impressed." Three words I rarely said. They weren't the most lethal of the Rittles, but helpful, nonetheless. "The compass could have been useful a few hundred miles back."

Claudia just shrugged. "I didn't know what any of them did. I just thought they might help at some point."

"You are correct. These will be helpful." A brutish centaur shoved me against the wall, and I almost dropped Jillian. "Let's get out of here. This isn't the place to talk about such magical tokens." We could use the compass and go anywhere in the world, but I was not entirely sure that its magic didn't leave some trace. It was best to utilize where we were to get where we needed to go.

"Where do you want to go?"

I had nowhere to go. I was now an enemy of all sides. I thought of a few places that Yanni and I had shared together, before any of this began. But a voice inside me demanded attention and it was suggesting a place I really had no desire to visit.

"Esther, where do you want to go?" Claudia repeated.

I wanted to react, lash out, but that would be of no use to my only ally. Everything inside me wanted to reject this destination, but still something was insisting I lean into the discomfort. I'd never been afraid of challenges before. *What was unravelling within me now, to make me so weak? Weakness was not an option. Not now, not ever.*

"We will go to Delphi."

We travelled from India to Austria via troll shuttle, since there was very little time before we needed to be in the Americas. Fetzle arranged our shuttle with a very kind she-troll named Itzlee. She did not talk much, but that was all right by us. We were still overwhelmed with infatuation, and I was really excited to have the time alone with my wife. She delivered us just outside of Innsbruck, in a town called Neustift, nestled in the Austrian Alps. The land was covered in snow, quite the contrast to our last accommodations in India. Stunning views were in every direction.

"This is incredible," Olly observed, then looked at our clothes. "We will stick out like sore thumbs in our shorts and t-shirts."

"Indeed. Fortunately, we are only going just there." I pointed to the cottage not twenty feet from where we stood. The next closest inhabitants were miles away.

"It looks like the drawing I saw in Rand's room in Hafiza. He said he'd stored all his art here."

"That and much more, or so it would seem."

"Have you been here before?"

"Twice, in passing, with my parents. The Garriths had not lived here for a long time by the time I was born. I think it was too much for Rand after Carissa died." I took Olly's hand in mine as we quickly made our way to the door.

"Is it a Haven?"

"No, just a home that they raised Caleb in." Caleb had told me where to find the key. But we entered with my Loktpi easily enough. I turned the knob and exposed the contents of a slightly dilapidated structure. The furniture was covered with sheets, and there were obvious spots where the roof leaked.

"Does this feel intrusive to you? I suddenly feel like I'm stepping into someone else's time capsule."

I pulled her in for a hug and kissed her neck. "I understand, but remember, Rand was always very calculated. Therefore, he must have been comfortable with us coming here."

"What do you think Caleb will do with all of this stuff?" she asked as she peeked under the sheets.

"I do not know. But I say we pull off the sheets, patch the roof, and get a little cozy before we open the storage and learn what my father had to say. The truth is, I feel I need to ground myself before I tackle this concealed information."

Olly stopped peeking under the sheets and walked over and gave me a hug. "Of course. You must be so nervous. How insensitive of me. I hadn't even considered how strange this must be, knowing your father has left you some secret intel. Is there something I can do to support you right now?"

I kissed her. "Just help me make this space comfortable for the big reveal."

"Done!" She kissed me on my nose and we got to work.

I started on the roof. There was a shed behind the house that had a good supply of tools and a few extra roof tiles. I was by no means a tradesman. My knowledge and experience with a hammer and nail was minimal, but I simply hoped to decelerate any damage to the cottage while Caleb was away. Olly was busy on the inside removing the sheets, hanging up some art, shuffling other pieces to give ambiance, and dusting the furniture. There was a quaint fireplace, and I found some dry wood in the shed. My next order of business would be to build a small fire.

"Hey! Guess what I found?" she shouted from the kitchen.

"I do not have the faintest."

She stuck her arm out the window so I could see it from the eaves. "A few bottles of home brew. They smell just right. Do you think Caleb would mind?"

"Not at all."

She squealed with delight. "I'll have a glass ready for you when you come in from your manual labor."

The work was quick, and it felt good. When I stepped back inside, Olly was done cleaning up and it looked lovely. I took a seat beside her on the couch. There were two glasses on the table in front of us with a burgundy vintage in them. "Rand would be proud."

She nestled in next to me. "I think so too." Olly looked around. "He and Carissa had beautiful taste in art."

"I agree." I grabbed our glasses, handed her hers. "Shall we toast?"

She hesitated. "I was thinking, am I pregnant? Should I be indulging?"

I put my hands on her belly. "Our sweet soul is in here, safe and sound. I have been told by several Conduits that the way we carry our progeny is different. You are a vessel, a safe Haven that gives the spirit a quiet and secure place to sprout and thrive. We can pour in beautiful intentions, just as we did the moment our soul chose us. But there is nothing that can be done to touch this baby in a way that would harm their development."

Her shoulders relaxed. "Thank the strokes, because I kept having visuals of someone kicking my stomach in battle and killing our precious little one." Tears welled in her eyes.

"My love, that must have been so scary. I am so sorry. Why did you not tell me?"

"I didn't want to worry you. In case the thought didn't cross your mind."

"We will confirm with Ruit, but I feel we have nothing to worry about. The best we can do is shower our baby with joy and love, and right now that is enjoying each other, the art we are surrounded by, and the delicious wine made by a dear friend."

"I will toast to that."

We clinked our glasses and tasted the wine.

"Oh, it's good."

"Indeed." I put my glass down. "Time to start a fire." I made quick work of it, and in a matter of moments we had a crackling hearth.

"Are you feeling better?"

"Yes, much."

"Do you know where the secret storage is?"

"In the bedroom, behind the wardrobe."

"I think it's time, don't you?"

I looked at the fire. *What am I so afraid of?* I could not explain how I was feeling, but it had something to do with the vast amount of information my parents had kept from me. *Can I handle more secrets?* But I had to, and I was not alone. I squeezed her hand and got to my feet. "Shall we?"

We walked in silence. When the wardrobe was in sight, my stomach turned. I placed my hand on the side of the furniture and pulled. It opened easily. Caleb had given me a special ritual, but the Loktpi circumvented all of that. Behind the wardrobe was a small alcove. In it was a single item. The box was no larger than a shoe box. I reached in and grabbed it. "Let us take this to the living room."

We turned around and solemnly walked into the room we had only just left.

"Let me grab the bottle," she insisted while I sat down. When Olly sat beside me, I lifted the lid. Inside was an envelope with my name on it, and several other folded sheets of paper. They looked like many of the other fragments of maps that my father collected.

I gently opened the seal and pulled out the letter.

"Are you comfortable reading it aloud?"

"Of course."

December 19th 2005

My son, Elias... *I am so sorry that it has come to this.*

If you are reading this, I am gone, as are your mother and my dearest friend Rand. I know that many things have probably transpired for this letter to be in your possession. I hope you know that your mother and I are so proud of you. We have always been proud of you. I don't think we told you that enough. You have always been our greatest joy. There are so many things that we could not actualize in our vast lifetimes, and that is such a bizarre realization. The legacy has then passed to you.

As you know, it is of the upmost priority to unite the Pai Ona. I intended to do that with a grand summit. I was very vague with you. I gave you very few details about my agenda or my means to do so. I can only hope you have acquired many of the clues I left along the way. I have suspected for some time that the summit must be held at The Cathedral, although I haven't the faintest idea how to detect where it may be. The Haven moves like no other, and the great dragon Cataphet resides in her depths. You must find The Cathedral and call the Pai Ona together for the Katuan trials. The stones were transported there by the troll Queen Peozleo. Her progeny will be able to direct you to their whereabouts. The Rittles are in The Cathedral's caves as well. They were stored there after the Niffler died trying to help the troll queen and repay the giants for what he stole.

I know this must be generating more questions than answers. Why did your mother and I not tell you about this while we were still alive? Frankly, right now you are just a boy, and I do not know what information you will possess by the time you are a man. Just know that our intent was to keep our oaths to others, and most importantly, limit your exposure to ensure your safety. But after Yessica was abducted, I am uncertain we can keep anyone safe anymore.

Your mother has a very special weapon, given to her by Queen Peozleo. The High Priestess of the giants sacrificed herself to fragment the Staff of Banishment that once belonged to King OAD of the powries. The priestess foretold of the ending of the world if the king remained in control of the staff. But there was more. When the staff was dismantled into three parts, your mother was charged with the Dirk of Inverness. The priestess gave your mother an enchantment to make the Dirk invisible, but she also whispered this divination: "When the final battle ensues where the world ends, the Staff of Banishment must make the final blow."

The giants and the trolls hid the other pieces somewhere safe. But when the time comes, the staff must be reassembled. It is up to you, my son, to locate and reconstruct the Staff of Banishment, ready for the final battle. I know it must seem like an impossible task, but the very same priestess saw your birth, and that once felt impossible too.

You can do anything. We believe in you. No matter what prophecies stand before you, trust yourself to create your own fate. The painter gave us free will to defy the odds and bend the rules. If he wanted us to simply concede to prognostication, then he would have kept us all compliant. Instead, he gave us passion and fear, but most importantly, love.

We love you, now and forever.

Your Father & Mother

I FOLDED the paper back up and looked at Olly. Part of me was immensely proud that I was able to get so far without this level of assistance from my father. Certainly, it would have been more convenient to have the information about the summit before everything unfolded as it had. But we did it. We found a way. And it warmed my heart to know that the way had been paved by my parents.

"What are you thinking? I can't imagine what is going through that head of yours." Olly put her hand in my hair and scratched my scalp gently. I loved when she did that.

"I am thinking that we know our next impossible task." I reached to the side of the sofa and grabbed my bag that held the Dirk. It was enchanted and invisible now. I pulled it out and removed the charm, exposing the blade and hilt. I had not wanted to look at it since Susuda's death, but now it required our full attention.

LUCAS

etzle escorted us to her mother's shuttle. It was nice. Cleaner than Fetzle's. Tazzle seemed to have a better sense of organization. There was a large fire pit, the same as Fetzle's, and Vosega was already well on his way to creating a fire.

"How are you doing?" Yesi said as she wrapped her arms around my waist from behind.

"I'm doing alright."

"So, it isn't as bad as you thought?"

I pulled her around to face me. "No. I'm surviving the family vacation."

Borte interrupted our exchange, "My husband desires a word." I looked to see that the Khan was brooding in the corner.

"With me?"

"With both of you."

Why do I suddenly feel like I am in trouble?

He turned as soon as we were in earshot. "I should be with the Sholl-guard. I see that now. That is my place in this war."

Well, that was unexpected.

"I am a great strategist, and they need help. Their numbers are too few. I have won many battles with few men. They need my wisdom."

"Father, that is so generous of you. I couldn't agree more." Yessica threw her hands around her father's neck.

"Something is unfolding here that we do not know. I can sense it. There is an enemy in the dark. Pladzle did not conquer this kingdom on his own. He had the help of the powries. Which means they are likely to strike while the trolls are still weak."

The thought had crossed my mind as well.

"I must meet with the Queen immediately. Can that be arranged?"

I'd never seen the Khan so earnest. It was inspiring. No wonder he was so politically powerful. I wanted to rally beside him, too, and it had nothing to do with his persuasion tactics.

"Yeah. I'll ring her up." I pulled my medallion out of my pocket and placed it on the entrance of the shuttle. Within seconds, Fetzle was opening up the shuttle hatch. Underground troll shuttles were more like large RVs in nature. When they came to the surface, the vehicle disappeared, and the troll—which is actually the portal—did the manifesting, kind of like teleportation.

"Fetzle is here! Did yous find Dalaketnon magics already?"

"No, sorry, Fetzle. The Khan here would like to assist in your battle strategy. He is very well versed in the art of war and feels he can be helpful. What do you say? Can you humor the guy?"

She looked at the Khan quizzically, probably smelling his aura. "Fetzle thinks yes, thats will be just whats the Sholl-guards needs."

With that, my enormous friend was escorting the Khan and his wife out of the shuttle. When the door was shut, Dari approached. "Do you really think the Khan can help?"

"I hope so, because I don't want to see an entire stroke eliminated from this planet, especially not one as kind as hers."

"Yeah, me neither."

It occurred to me I didn't know what Dari's gift was. "What is it that you do?"

"I'm a Tahwils. Some call me a skin walker."

"You're a shapeshifter?" Oya asked excitedly. "Can you turn into anything, or is there something specific you manifest as?"

"I'm rare. I can be anything, any creature or inanimate object alike."

"Ohhhhh! Be me. Please be me!"

He rolled his eyes, and in an instant, he looked just like Oya, and I had to hold back my urge to vomit.

"That is so cool!"

"You're rare? That's why they held you captive."

He nodded mournfully. "Seems so." And he returned to his own skin.

I shook my head. "Sorry, man."

"Hey, I am here now. Thanks to the trolls and you guys, so I'm going to do whatever I can to help win this war and shut this shit down for good. I lost my Atoa while I was asleep in captivity. I have nothing else to live for but to make sure this is finally over."

"You have me, brother," Thracian said as he put his hand on Dari's shoulder. Dari put his hand on Thracian's, but didn't say anything. I understood his loss. There was nothing that could compare to the loss of your Atoa. Thracian knew that too.

"Let's find this Dalaketnon magic then."

Vosega was done with the fire, so he and Oya were ready to help. There were three long rows of categorized magic tolls. I didn't understand the system, but it wouldn't take us that long to go through all of it. There must be something that would be helpful on the battlefield. "You two take that row. Vosega and Oya, you have the last one. Yesi and I will make our way down this line."

It was tedious. We looked at every token, paper and dust mite to see what it might hold. The tags were vague, and we didn't want to actually employ the magic, wasting it, or worse—killing one of us by accident.

"Son, I think you need to see this."

I brushed off my annoyance. *Why can't he just call me Lucas?*

"What is it?" I asked as I walked over.

He was holding a book. "It has a lock on it. It says it's the troll histories, and it has a lock. Why would that be?"

Dari pushed past me. "An actual lock? I can fix that." He took my hand, and a moment later, I was holding a key. Dari was gone—or was in my hand, rather.

"Here goes nothing." I stuck the key in. It didn't quite fit at first, but I could feel him modifying his shape to mold to the hardware. I twisted and it opened easily.

Thracian said, "Put him down, unless you want to be holding Dari."

I set the key on the ground, and immediately, Dari reappeared. "What's in it?"

It was a very slim compartment, no thicker than a dense book cover, which is why it was not easily detectable. There was a single piece of paper inside, a letter addressed to Tazzle.

"Read it out loud, Lucas," Yesi suggested.

"Do you think Fetzle is going to mind?" I didn't want to step on my friend's toes.

"If she cared about what we would find, she wouldn't have let us dig around," Dari reasoned, and I had to agree. "Maybe she doesn't even know about it."

I shrugged and read the letter aloud.

DEAR TAZZLE,

I hope that someday you can forgive me for what I am about to tell you. Truth be told, I have never forgiven myself.

You will always remember the day that Princess Chaness saved us all from certain demise at the hand of King OAD on the shores of the Solomon Islands. That day was one that forever united the giants and the trolls in both our grief and in bloodshed. Even Empress Dafnee wept for the Princess and kissed the hands of your mother, humbled by her own misjudgments. Adanc and Ratatoskr wailed with all the survivors, lamenting the greatest hero we all have ever known. None were more heartbroken than me or your mother. I still weep.

The prophecies of the High Priestess and Pythoness were repainted in the strokes. The end of the whole world was averted by the sacrifice of those the world had not entirely accepted. Both the Niffler and Chaness had never been fully embraced. The queen was forever haunted by the High Priestess' words to the Princess the day before the battle. She told her that her part was always fated to save the strokes.

What you may not know is that after we picked up the pieces and collected our wounded and dead, your mother was dispatched to another duty she promised to fulfill. She spoke of it on the shore where you saved me.

How she had the strength to meet every challenge ever presented to her is beyond me. Nevertheless, bloody and brokenhearted, she fulfilled yet another promise to a friend on that day. Cane and Sorcey Kraus called on her to bring the Katuan Stones to the caves of The Cathedral.

The Trials had ended in destruction, just as the Conduit Kassandra had predicted. As Malarin would have it, Cane and Sorcey were deceived by the notion that they may never conceive. Time will tell how this plays out in our world, but one thing was for sure—all the other visions were realized. It seems likely that their strokes are still in the process of creation. How their fates will paint the destiny to follow will astound us all.

The day of the battle, the queen arduously collected as many Stones as she could from the ocean floor. At the same time, she saved as many Conduits as she could from the wreckage of the Trials' destruction. I could not be there for any of it. It took several weeks for us to find the magic that could unbind me from my chains and gag. It was an excruciating time for a million reasons, but none more than the secret I am about to tell you.

As I stand here, certain the day has come for me to take to stone, I have only one real regret, one true betrayal. When Princess Chaness and I needed to find a way to communicate, we shared in a nymph ribbon bond. We could read each other's thoughts. On the day she saved us, I could hear all that went on in her head.

She was certain she would never belong anywhere, that she would always be the beast that no one desired around. As she witnessed the love your mother had for you, for the trolliage, it overwhelmed her and she decided that she would do anything to preserve it.

Here is my treason, as plain as day...

As the Princess fell to the floor of the ocean, I heard her process. She did not die that day; instead, she made a deal with the devil. Her blood, her life, her essence for ours. She chose to be captive, she chose to be his life force for all of eternity. I could not tell your mother on that day, and by the time I had the capacity to use my words, I didn't want to watch your mother's heart rip back open. Worse yet, I knew she would spend the rest of her life chasing the Princess, at the expense of another war. Princess Chaness deserved all of this and so much more. But I couldn't do it. I didn't do it.

Now she lives her days in a prison, feeding her blood for our peace. I cannot bear dying without telling you the truth. You must tell the creature Adanc what I write here on these pages. She loves the Princess and will seek her release. She has more soul than I will ever possess.

Forgive me. The cost of peace was the price of a beautiful creature. I conceded to her last request of me to never tell your mother, but I cannot die not telling you.

ALWAYS YOURS,
   Goutel

WHAT DOES THIS MEAN? *Who is Goutel?* And did this have something to do with the Queen's crown, *Fetzle's crown being with the giants?* I'd totally forgotten about what Olly said. Now the message seemed urgent. Everyone was just looking at the letter in my hands, as though it was some ticking time bomb.

"Fetzle needs to know about this," Yesi whispered, and the nodding faces agreed.

We sat there in silence for a long moment, both of us staring at the Dirk. Another paradox to be added to the growing list, a blessing and a cursed item that destroyed one of our closest friends but may save the world.

Something came over me. Maybe it was the thought of the end of the world and the very real truth that our moments together may be numbered. Whatever it was, I became nearly crazed with lust for my husband. I pulled the blade from his hand and lay it on the table in front of us, then I mounted him. At first, bewilderment flashed across his face, then understanding. I felt his body surrender under me. All except for the most important member was prepared to surrender to making love.

I ripped off my shirt, literally, down the middle, exposing my hard nipples. He promptly took my left breast into his palm, then wrapped his mouth around my titillated nipple. Sensation tickled every cell in my body, and the lust revved up to yet again another level. I growled with pleasure and Elias returned the gesture with a full body shudder. I realized we were in tune with each other's sexual vibration, and he now knew as well as I did that this was going to be a different type of union altogether.

My mouth found his ear. I wanted him to know in every way that I was prepared for a new level of connection. "I'm ready to devour you." I bit his lobe, and he moaned, grabbing my ass with both his hands. My hips seemed to throb under his touch. I howled and gyrated rhythmically on his lap. With every thrust of my hips, the energy between us amplified. I could feel an animalistic frenzy snaking its way up my spine. I was being consumed by it. Elias was feeling the same frenzy. I could see the fire in his eyes as he gently stroked every inch of my body, but the tenderness had a yearning that was somehow insatiable and complete all at once.

My body surrendered more, and animal noises erupted from my belly. Elias put his hand on my clitoris, and immediately I felt my entire core explode with rhythmic waves of bliss. My husband was riding it with me. We were entirely intertwined with one another. My heart rode on the same waves of bliss. The snake continued to lace up my spine, and the primal piece of my soul that aligned with pleasure, with union, and with all that is, expanded into everything around me.

The deepest penetration was between me and my Atoa. This was nothing like consummation. This was transformation through unhinged pleasure.

Elias roared. He picked me up and pulled me to the floor, somehow removing my pants and his at the same time. Maybe they'd just dissolved from the heat between us. He entered me, and the world stopped. We were floating in a pool of pure sensational orgasm. He thrusted and I clawed at his back. The pain only amplified the pleasure. Pain and pleasure were the same, it was all sensation, all part of the divine experience. I rolled him over, once more riding my beloved with more excitement than I ever believed was possible.

My heart cracked open. I met Elias' gaze. He was receiving my essence. We were suspended in the space between, and all there was, was love. My hands began to shake. I lifted them above my head. We both watched on as a foreign energy was permeating the membranes of my fingertips. A knowing swept between us as we watched the energy move through me and into Elias.

In unison, we both said, "Carissa's gift." It was profound and that simple.

I collapsed into a heap on top of my husband, and he enveloped me in his arms. We were not communicating through the Rune, but I knew we were sharing each other's thoughts.

Whatever that was was incredible. It was so unique that we somehow conjured up the remnants of energy of a Conduit who had long since passed. Carissa was a Vixen. Her home was filled with the imprint of her energy, and our union somehow magnetized and integrated her gifts from this place through me and into Elias.

Elias pulled my hair from my face, kissed my forehead, and whispered in my ear, "You are something spectacular, Ulus Ophelia. Wait until I tell Ruit about this one."

I sat up and pretended to be aghast. "You mean you're going to kiss and tell?"

"Is that what we are going to call that one? Kissing?"

I nibbled playfully on his chest while we both chuckled. "Kissing might be an understatement."

ESTHER

The Haven of Delphi was exactly how I remembered it. To the human eye, it had dilapidated immensely, but to the Conduit world, it was a beautiful temple. I recalled the first time I entered its walls. Yanni and I had been summoned here by my father.

APOLLO MET us with open arms at the gate. "My daughter!" It was the first time I had seen him smile since my mother had died in Atlantis. "Yanni, my dear son." He hugged us both. "Come, come. See what Aurora and I have built."

We entered through the stone arches and walked among the white pillars. He continued to gloat, "We had the great architects Trophonius and Agamedes design the temple. Is it not glorious?"

"Yes, it is." I looked at Yanni skeptically, not because my father was wrong, but because he was acting so peculiar. I wanted to see him happy. I had missed seeing his smile and feeling his warmth. But it was a strange and sudden shift in mood. "I am pleased to see you so elated, Father."

"I feel so present, so free from the grief that has been shackling me since Shatki's passing."

The words stung. In a weird way, our grief kept her alive. Yanni took my hand, sensing my discomfort. We climbed a steep staircase.

"The Oracle is here, just at the top of the stairs."

I grabbed my father's arm, bringing him to a stop. "Father, are you alright?" I had heard the rumors that Apollo had killed Cadmael, Aurora's Atoa. But the way he was acting, the fact that the Oracle was here, although my father was under suspicion of murdering her partner—it didn't make any sense. "Did you kill Cadmael?" The words just came out.

Aurora was at the top of the staircase now. "No, Esther. Of course, your father would never do such a thing. Those are vicious rumors, stirred from your father and I choosing to elope to the Temple of Delphi. Cadmael died in an accident. May the strokes rest his soul." She put her hand to her heart, and I noted she did not appear to be in any distress.

❦

THE MEMORY suddenly got hard to hold, fuzzy and distorted. My head began to throb. I stopped in my tracks.

"What's wrong, Esther?" Claudia asked from behind, and I was completely back in the present.

I released the memory and the pain subsided. "Nothing." But there was something, and I was starting to see a pattern. One that I had missed before because I was so distracted with vengeance. Every time I put energy into my time here at Delphi, I was assaulted with pains, the same pains that struck me when I decided to snatch Aurora's body. There was something I had been missing for all these years, something that was hidden within the recesses of my mind. A story had been planted, and now I was not sure if it was mine or of an entirely different nature. What I did know for certain was that I would find the answers to what happened here.

"Alright," Claudia said skeptically. "Where do you want me to put Jillian?"

"Let us head to the Oracle's chamber. It is at the top of that staircase."

We entered the room, and I looked around the familiar space.

"Put her there." I pointed to a long bench with a satin cushion on top.

"Do you know how we're going to wake her?"

I'd been considering that myself. "Not yet."

"But there is a cure?"

"Yes."

"And you have no idea what it is?"

Her question poked the wound I was nursing, the realization that I'd been kept in the dark about much of the comings and goings among the Nebas. "I don't know—yet. But I will. Trust me, I will."

The Haven was beautiful. It still looked the same as the day it was built, including the purple drapes and wood furniture with vibrant colored pillows and specs of gold embroidery. There were several gold vases and metal sconces in the main hall. It gave a warmth to the room. To the left was a staircase that descended into the Oracle's channel chamber. It was dark in the depths of the temple. A hole was in the center of the room, where the Conduits and other spectators would sit while she conjured the visions of the future. I hated that room. *Why do I hate that room?*

I remembered the vapors rising from the abyss of the hole. *Where did that hole go? What were the vapors from?*

"You seem really out of it, and I don't usually pry, but since it's you and me against the world right now... I kind of need you on point. So, let me just lay it all out there for you. I don't have a side. Do you know why that is?"

I was annoyed, but welcomed the distraction from my own maze of thoughts, so I engaged.

"Because you lost your Atoa in this war and it has left you homeless." That is how it felt—homeless, rootless, lost.

"No. You should really get to know who you surround yourself with better, Esther. My Atoa is still alive and well. In fact, he was at the summit, participating as a champion, no less."

"What?" I got to my feet. "Are you here to kill me?"

"Sit down. I would've done that already."

I sat, mostly because I had no fight left in me. My intuition had led me here, to a cavern of dusty memories. There was nothing left for me.

"My Atoa is Stalt. Have you heard of him?"

"Yes, of course I have heard of the Vulcan." We had tried to add him to Aurora's collection several times, but failed. "Why are you fighting on the opposite side of your Atoa?"

"Infiltrating is not the same as fighting. The Nebas have our daughter, Aurelia."

I recognized the name.

"Aw, you remember her?"

"Not particularly."

"It doesn't matter. What matters is that Aurelia skirted the Nebas world with a group of delinquent fairies. When she went missing, the fairies told me and Stalt that she was abducted, not killed. They followed her captors all the way to Chernobyl."

"Aurelia is a powerful Varon. She can call on any creature—not just animals, but also the fae. You guys took her to use her for the grand plan that the Oracle is masterminding. You don't even know the extent of this plan, and now that Yanni is gone, you feel untethered." She knelt down at my eye level. "You didn't bear children, Esther, but let me assure you, that bond is nearly as fierce. I want my daughter back, alive."

"What do I have to do with this? You were better off staying in the coterie of the Nebas. That is where you will find her. Unless she got away?"

"No, she didn't get away. I can feel her." Claudia rubbed her heart. "They weren't naming the remaining captives, probably because the Oracle understands that there are those in her company who would revolt if they knew the truth."

"What is the truth?"

"That this is bigger than we know, and that she has been duplicitous for a very long time. And the truth is all you have left to live for. When we know the truth of Aurora's deception, only then can anyone truly choose a side. Until that moment, we are all willing pawns. So, I ask you, are you here to die a pawn, or live for the truth?"

I considered Claudia's compelling call to action. *She is good.* "You would've been a great leader."

"I know. That is exactly why the other part of this arrangement is that you stop barking orders at me like I'm your minion. I meant what I said when I helped you back in Russia. I'm tired of being a lackey. Now dust yourself off and do something about this tyrant, because the truth is, if Aurora saw Yanni's death and didn't inform you so you could try to stop it, she is just as culpable as the hand that killed him."

The rage swelled in me. Because I knew Claudia was right.

"Fetzle cants believe this."

"Do you know this Goutel? Do you know anything about this Princess Chaness?"

"Fetzle does. All trolls knows of Princess Chaness and hers sacrifices. Goutel was likes Fetzle grandmother. She was the closest of friends to Fetzle's grandmother, Queens Peozleo."

"Did your mother and father know about this confession?"

"Fetzle thinks nots. My mothers never woulds haves not searched fors the Princess."

"There is more, Fetzle. The giants have your crown and they said they wish to speak to the queen."

"Fetzle doesn't knows any giants."

"But they know you, or your mother or grandmother—one of them had an arrangement with the giants."

"Giants and trolls be friends after the wars of the Solomon Islands. That's all Fetzle knows."

Yesi stepped closer to the Queen and put her hand on the troll's leg. "This must be so confusing and scary, Fetzle, but it stands to reason these two matters are connected. They both involve the giants, and at the very least they, too, deserve to know that the Princess is a captive of King OAD."

"Fetzle agrees, they deserves to knows." She looked around. "But Fetzle is worried abouts preparings her trolliage fors battle."

Vosega stepped forward. "We will help prepare them, Queen Fetzle. It would be an honor."

"As will we," Dari agreed. "Together, we can prepare them. I'm certain of it!"

Dari's enthusiasm was just what she needed to feel at ease. "Fetzle trusts Lucas' friends..." She paused and corrected herself. "Fetzle trusts her friends."

There were heartwarming smiles all around, and I realized that I couldn't be doing this without the help of my dad, Oya, the in-laws, and these two random guys. The strokes were working in our favor. There was no other way to explain this stroke of luck.

I walked over to Vosega and gave him a hug. "Thank you for being here." When I pulled away, I saw he was crying, a moment that would usually make me feel really uncomfortable, but instead, I was just grateful. "Let's go."

"Tell my father I'll be back, please, Oya."

"Sure thing."

Then we were off on our way to the Solomon Islands in Fetzle's shuttle. This was going to be the first time I'd encountered the giants, and honestly, I was kind of excited. Cane had told me many stories about his time with them, and it intrigued me, plus, they apparently had excellent wine.

"Fetzle stops her shuttle. We're heres to see the giants." She promptly walked over to her hatch and opened it.

"The giants live underground?"

"No, silly Lucas, but the palace entrance is unders the islands. Yep, Fetzle knows from hers mother. Fetzle's mother was at the battle of the islands too. She told Fetzle alls about it, when I was olds enough, of course." She giggled.

"How old is old enough?" I asked as I stepped out of the shuttle and in front of a grand entrance with a colossal staircase and an enormous gate. It would take me and Yesi all day to scale these steps.

"Ohs, like five hundred years, Fetzle thinks."

"Why five hundred years?"

"Fetzle could haves nightmares. It's a very scary battles."

Troll maturity was vastly different than Conduit maturity. I needed to remember that. I shook my head and decided to ask the next important question. "Do you think you can carry me and Yesi, to hurry this visit along?"

"That won't be necessary," a booming male voice said in Asagi. A silhouette of a massive man appeared at the gate as it rose. As he stepped into the light, I saw he wore a brown animal pelt over his groin, and that was it. He was brimming with muscles, and had long golden blonde curly hair that had beads and braids in it. "I am so grateful that you have come, Queen Fetzle. We have been anxious to meet you." The giant practically skipped down the steps. He was at the shuttle in less than a minute. He crouched down and got on eye-level with Fetzle. From this angle, we could see directly under his loin cloth. I turned Yesi sideways to help her avoid the view. I averted my own eyes, but not before I caught a glimpse of a bit of excitement happening below that cloth. "I am Emperor Calt." The emperor seemed to like what he saw in Fetzle. I looked at my friend and noticed a glimmer of something in her eye as well.

"Fetzle is happy to meet you. These are Fetzle's friends Lucas and Yessica, good Conduits." Even her voice was a little softer, *flirtatious maybe?* Yessica caught it as well, and we looked at each other sideways.

"Friends of the Queen are friends of the giants. Come, let us get inside. I would be honored to get a banquet in order to bless your arrival."

"Fetzle doesn't thinks thats necessary."

"Oh, but it is, dear Queen. We have been waiting for you for many centuries now. There is much to discuss, and that is always better done over food and drink." He smiled at her coyly and put his hand on the ground. "May I?"

I didn't know if I was disgusted or entertained by what I was seeing unfolding between the Emperor and the Queen. Yessica and I obligingly stepped into his palm. *This was going to be interesting.*

OPHELIA

e'd decided to spend the night at the cottage. It gave us time to formulate our next move. Elias was all business after reading Cane's letter. I don't know if it was the shock of it all or that he wanted a distraction, but he was in full planning mode.

I put my hand on my belly. We'd made love multiple times since consummation, and although I didn't feel pregnant, I assumed I was. When we called in our little soul, it was as though a tremor radiated from the epicenter of my womb. *They were in there, and I knew it.*

I took another small sip of Rand's homemade wine. "I hope I'm not getting you drunk," I said internally.

I was shocked when a voice answered, the voice from the River Tins. "Your body is a vessel of energy. It has its own wisdom and way. The soul that chose you is safe and sound, no matter the circumstance. Rest easy, child."

My heart was emanating gratitude. From the moment I'd come out of my blissful state after consummation, all I could think about was that we were conceiving a baby in the middle of a war. There was no way to avoid my part in the battle or bloodshed, but this reassurance gave me peace.

"What is making you so happy? I must know." Elias took a seat beside me and put his hand on my belly. "Are they already moving about?"

I laughed. "No, I just got some validation that you are wise beyond words and our baby is safe."

"Validation from whom?" He kissed my left temple.

"From the River Tins voice."

Elias nodded. "Who do you believe that is? Honestly, tell me the truth."

I didn't hesitate. "The painter. I believe it's the painter himself speaking to me."

"I agree." I was slightly surprised by that admission.

"Why didn't you tell me?"

"I trust that you know better than me." He got to his feet and leaned over the sofa to grab my bag. "There is a way we could test that theory."

"How is that?" He handed me the bag.

"Do you feel Moira's writings were Martian or from Chitchakor?"

"The note she gave me!" I rummaged through my bag and found the folded piece of paper. I couldn't open it fast enough. Five markings that had looked like gibberish now read plain as day:

THE HIGH PRIESTESS HAS RETURNED. The time has come to forge the only weapon that can reshape the circles. The thread will repair the bridge that brings the world back together.

"HOLY SHIT! I CAN READ IT."

"What does it say already?"

"The High Priestess has returned. The time has come to forge the only weapon that can reshape the circles. The thread will repair the bridge that brings the world back together."

Elias looked at me expectantly. "What does it mean?"

LUCAS

The banquet hall was nice. They put me and Yesi up in toddler-like seats, so we could reach the massive table. Most of the giants were speaking in their native tongue, a language I was completely unfamiliar with. Emperor Calt was on the other side of Fetzle. He was conversing with a giant who was bald and had a long grey beard, but kept stealing glances at the queen.

Fetzle leaned in. "Giants talks a lot, Fetzle thinks. Whens will we needs to tell them?"

I understood Fetzle's impatience. I was getting antsy myself. Suddenly, a large crystal glass was set in front of me, filled with a golden liquid.

"I think this is the famous wine, baby girl." I almost squealed like a schoolgirl.

"You are correct, Master Healey," the emperor confirmed. "We giants are exceptional vintners."

"Your reputation goes far and wide." With that, I took a sip and was not disappointed. It was like honey, not sweet, but fresh like spring flowers and with notes of creamy butter, complete with a crisp finish. "That is dangerously good."

Yessica agreed. "Oh, my. I could be in trouble if this is what you are serving all night."

The emperor was pleased. He smiled and said, "Be careful, dear friends. This drink is fermented with giants in mind."

Duly noted.

Fetzle didn't say much as she drank her glass. One sip turned into a long chug, and when her large cup was empty, she burped. "Fetzle thinks this is pretty tasteys." We all laughed as the closest server filled her cup once more. She smiled a toothy grin and leaned down to whisper in my ear. "Fetzle has somes silly tingles in her bellys when that emperor keeps lookings at hers. Do you thinks it's magics?"

"If you like this, you will love the food. It pairs very nicely," Grey Beard interrupted us before I could respond. Then he leaned around the emperor to introduce himself. "I am Ropen, brother of the emperor. It is a pleasure to meet you."

I was already feeling the wine, and for that reason, feeling pretty friendly. "Do you all speak Asagi?"

"No. In fact, it's a fairly new occurrence that we speak anything other than our tongue. But recent events, particularly the reappearance of our High Priestess, stirred some changes in preparation for what is to come," Ropen clarified.

"Fetzle thinks this is a good times to explains our arrivals."

"Good queen, we have the rest of the evening to converse in private. For now, let us feast. Enjoy the sentiment of good company and fine drink. Merriment brings a special kind of magic to the world," Calt insisted, and I couldn't argue with the man, but there was something in his words. More to it than just a good time. My brilliant wife caught the same drift.

"Is there an ulterior motive to these festivities we are partaking in? To build a strong relationship, we must understand each other's motives. Wouldn't you agree, Emperor?" Yesi winked at me, and I had to hold back the urge to smother her in a glorious kiss. She was sexy as hell when she was assertive.

"Alas, your suspicions are warranted, dear Yessica. Our High

Priestess has an unveiling she wishes to divulge here at the banquet. And consequently, jubilation is a beautiful fuel for her abilities. By enjoying ourselves to the fullest, we may allow her to tap into her greatest potential." He took a drink of his wine. "I assure you that no harm is in accordance with the merriment that fuels her, and more so, what she intends to reveal will explain why we have been waiting for the arrival of the queen."

"We can participate in this ritual shit, but there is more that you need to know. We came across some information about Princess Chaness." I tried to whisper, but it was difficult with how noisy the room was. It was obvious both men heard me when their faces went ash-white.

Ropen spoke first. "It has been the span of over ten rules since last anyone spoke of Chaness. What news?"

"I don't know if you want me to tell you this here."

Fetzle took the lead. "Fetzle knows she's alives."

ESTHER

*J*illian was unconscious on the small bench. I considered whether I truly wanted her more lucid. She was an optimal tool when she was not entirely coherent. When she woke, there was no way in the strokes she would choose my company. I have been wicked to the woman, *very wicked.*

"Do you think she'll run when we give her her freedom?" Claudia was watching me watch her. I didn't like it at all.

"Why must we give her her freedom?"

"Because we all deserve to have that one single thing, a choice."

I ignored her response. I wasn't sure what I thought choices were anymore. *Have I been making choices this entire time, or only been manipulated into thinking I was?* I looked at the dark stairwell that led to the Oracle's vision chamber. Something in me knew there were answers down there.

"You keep looking at that passage like a monster may emerge from the shadows. I hate to break it to you, Esther, but you're the only monster here. Whatever ghost haunts that room, it is the very reason why we've come. So get on with it, because I don't think we have much time to linger anywhere for long. They will hunt us down and kill us."

"Have you always been this astute?" I looked at her with disdain.

"Have you always been this frightened?"

I growled under my breath. She was right. I knew she was right. *Why am I letting fear weaken me? Who is this shell of a woman I am becoming?*

"I could've used your insightfulness months ago," I said as I got to my feet.

"No, it would have been wasted on you. We both know that. You wanted servants motivated by the very thing you are avoiding—fear. I'm not afraid of you, nor do I waste my good sense on those who won't listen."

Claudia was antagonizing every nerve I had, and for the first time in thousands of years, I could not simply physically maul her to release my tension. I had to be composed to maintain the only alliance I had. This was perhaps the most infuriating position I'd ever been in. I walked to the dark stairwell and began to descend. Whatever monster was down here had to be better than facing the torment of her presence.

The stairs spiraled into a damp cave below the temple of Apollo proper. Centuries ago, it was lit by torches. Clearly, no one had been down here since my father and I abandoned the Haven thousands of years ago. When Di and her party arrived to free the Oracle of her imprisonment, there was no reason left to stay. We fled to avoid persecution. I remembered that day vividly. There was massive confusion at first.

***

YANNI BARGED INTO OUR ROOM, announcing Di's arrival. "She is here with a small army, my beloved. What are we to make of that?"

"Have they assaulted you or Father? Where is Apollo? The Oracle?"

"The Oracle is already in their custody. They are escorting her as though she were here against her will."

"She was here against her will?"

"Was she?" Yanni's face was contorted in confusion, when he asserted, "We have detained her against her will, yes."

We both just looked at each other blankly. It was as though I could not confirm or deny the notion. *Have we been holding her captive all this time?*

My father entered the room. "We need to run, children! Our friends have decided we have committed atrocities here in Delphi. And I am afraid I cannot convince them otherwise, unless you can?" The same look smeared my father's face when he asserted, "We held Aurora here against her will."

Di shouted as she came down the hall towards my chamber, several other feet in tow. "You will be held accountable for the crimes you have committed!"

My mind was trying to catch up with what was unfolding. In a fog of memories, thousands of memories, I felt guilt for mistreating Aurora. I sensed that my motivations were nefarious in nature, and clearly so did my father and Yanni. The confusion was only making it infuriating. "We must go!" I agreed. And we leapt from the window of my chamber one at a time, barely missing the vigilantes that were seeking justice.

For weeks after, the three of us tried to piece together our story for the last eight hundred years. Some moments were clear as day, but more often they were murky. Together, we concluded that we were in a fog. We blamed the vapors from the cave, *the very cave I was now approaching in the dark.* We blamed each other for not holding one another accountable or questioning the goings-on between the Oracle and her callers. *Why have we never asked her if she wanted to be here?* My father seemed to blame himself most of all, explaining that it was he who went to Aurora, he who lured her to Delphi, to his temple. He concluded that in his state, he held her against her will and didn't have the mind to release her from this gilded cage. What was worse yet was that he blamed himself for our exile, for coaxing us into joining him at Delphi.

❈

My head throbbed as I did my best to recall that time. I peered down into the abyss of darkness that swallowed the entrance of the cave. There were no vapors. It was clear and cold today.

"Why don't you go down there and meet your boogie man?"

"AAAHHHHHHHHH!!!!" I shrieked like a baby. Claudia had scared the hell out of me. "Claudia, what in the fucking strokes are you doing down here?"

"I thought you might like the support."

"When have I ever asked for your support?" I hissed.

"Sometimes we don't know how to ask for what we need," she said matter-of-factly as she put her hands on her hips.

"I need silence right now."

"Suit yourself, but it will only lose its power if you face it completely."

I knew there was truth in that. But there was more to it for me. I was facing the acceptance that I'd been a pawn in a plot that changed the trajectory of my entire life. A path that had my father executed, made me thirsty for revenge, and resulted in the death of my beloved Yanni. *What emotions were mine? What choices were mine? I was nothing but the sum of a series of programmed reactions.*

Claudia wasn't speaking, but she was still standing there, staring at me.

"Does silence mean something different to you?"

"I don't need to speak to help you get into that hole. You're going to want my assistance, trust me. If not getting in, getting out."

"Very well." There was no use in arguing. "Just be silent."

She rolled her eyes but said nothing more about it. I knew there was a rope down here somewhere. We'd used it once to hang a young Greek king by his feet for two days, to make an example of him. Finally, another patron paid his toll to the Oracle and we released him. *Whose idea was that?* My head hurt as I tried to outline the circumstances that led us to those violent measures. It was Aurora's. I could see the rage in her eyes when the king explained he didn't have her fee with him, after he'd already received a reading. The pain turned into an intense shooting sensation that split my head in two. I dropped the memory, and the pain quickly subsided. I rubbed my temples as I shuffled over to the wall where the rope hung, a reminder of what failure to comply would result in. *I wasn't always wired for violence?* It had been so long, so many centuries of torture and brutality, that I could hardly fathom an existence without it.

The rope was heavy. I threw it over my shoulder. Claudia took it where she stood, at the mouth of the cave, and she gently began to lower it down. The rope was nearly thirty feet long by my estimate, and when she was finished, it still did not appear to touch the bottom. I grabbed a torch from the wall, lit it with a flint, and threw it in the hole. We could see a very dim glow from the mouth where we stood, so there was a bottom.

"Is there more rope somewhere in this Haven? In case I need to extend the line."

"Somewhere. Pull this one out while you go in search of an extension. I will holler when I am ready to be hoisted up."

"Alright." Claudia quickly pulled it up, and then she was gone. Now it was time to do the one thing everything in my body was screaming for me not to do. I jumped into the mouth of the cave, to face something I didn't even know I feared until now. The truth.

LUCAS

I've got to give it to the troll Queen—she tells it like it is.

"You have proof of this?" Ropen asked.

"Fetzle does." She tapped at a pouch she was carrying on her belt.

The giants looked at each other, sharing a silent exchange. "Festivities have already begun. We will see to your proof once our High Priestess has completed her ritual and shared her visions."

Fetzle shrugged and took another long swig of the wine. Calt put his hand on her shoulder. The queen lit up a little from his touch. "I am so grateful for your visit, lovely queen."

I wondered if Fetzle had ever been called lovely before. By the way she was batting her eyes, I guessed not.

"How long does this ritual take?" Yessica inquired.

"The more merrymaking, the less time."

"Well, then pour us another." I raised my glass. "Let's get this fucking show on the road."

Yessica smiled a knowing smile at me. She knew I was going to get a little tipsy tonight. The way I saw it, we deserved a little lightheartedness after the heaviness of the last weeks. It wasn't good for anyone to constantly be wound up and on guard for the next attack.

That shit got old real fast, and it took a toll on the nerves, leaving you less cautious and more reactive. I should know better than anyone. I'd lived that way for centuries when I was working with the Nebas.

I cheers'd my wife again, and a moment later, a nice server was placing an enormous plate in front of both of us. The plate was literally the size of a dining room table, and it smelled amazing. When the emperor waved his hand, the servers removed the cloche. I was looking at an entire pig.

"I hope you won't be offended if we don't finish what's on our plates." I winked at Calt, and he just nodded in return as he dug into his own meal.

Yessica was mortified. "What in the strokes am I to do with this?" She looked around at the giants who were already eating. "They are eating with their hands, Lucas."

"Then, grab a handful." I reached over and pulled at the skin of the pig, tearing it, and proceeded to reach in and grab a fistful of meat. It was as good as it smelled. The emperor wasn't lying about the wine pairing. It was delicious.

Yessica reluctantly did the same. The look on her face confirmed that she, too, found it tasty. She may not have appreciated the manners, but she was enjoying the experience.

Just then, a beautiful giant wearing a black cloak with gold inlays threaded throughout, accompanied by two other female giants with similar clothing, entered the room. All three women had long black hair woven in an assortment of thin and thick braids. They looked like sisters. Maybe they were. Their skin was bronzed, sun-kissed. Their high cheekbones and petite nose structure was what made them look alike. The one in front gave off a different vibe, like a mystic power, and I knew she must be the High Priestess. The hall got quiet and I noticed Fetzle was instantly enthralled by the spectacle as well. The three of us adjusted ourselves to face her better.

The Priestess moved seductively to the center of the room, where no tables had been set. It was a circular space, and now that my attention was drawn to it, I noticed the carvings in the floor—several overlapping circles, some small and some large. The design was impressive, very intricate. I followed the gaze of a few giants that looked up, and then I realized that the ceiling was made of a massive mirror so you could watch the Priestess' movements from above. Her sweeping gestures were even more captivating from this vantage. I pointed it out to Yesi. There seemed to be gold sparks that flew behind her cloak as she traced some of the circles with her feet.

"We introduce our High Priestess. Isn't she incredible?" Calt whispered. "Almost as impressive as you, dear queen."

Fetzle giggled, then tried to brush off the compliment. "Fetzle knows the trolliage Pythoness doesn't looks like that."

The gold sparks turned into flames as the Priestess skipped faster along the lines. Her movements were fluid, graceful, sensual, like a dance without music. Smoke began to fill the room. It wasn't normal smoke, though. It was sweet and tasted like caramel. The Priestess sped up again, and the flames stopped chasing her. The fire remained in the etched markings, and the woman danced through them. This was the most entrancing magic I'd ever seen.

"Fetzle sees her aura grows as she does her rituals. It tastes likes nothing Fetzles ever tasted before."

The other two Priestesses began to chant, quiet at first but gaining in volume as their leader moved faster. "Aho, hum ta ho, heh tum ho." I had no idea what the language was. Louder and louder their voices rose, and when the chanting was basically at a volume I would describe as yelling, they stopped everything and the High Priestess fell to the floor. Flames engulfed her cloak, and I thought we were going to watch her be burned alive. I got to my feet, as if there was something I could do. Suddenly, she lifted herself from the ashes, naked, with her eyes closed. I took my stare from the ceiling to the voluptuous bare body in front of me. The room was so quiet you could hear a pin drop.

"The time has come to forge the weapon that will transform the strokes forever. The circles must be restored to balance. The painter has returned to earth to guide his children home. But their fate is not certain. Time is running out, and if the courage cannot meet the shadow with grace... this world will dissolve into darkness for all eternity. No stroke will go untainted. All that were painted will be lost to the abyss." Her voice was soft, but her message was fierce. She opened her eyes and directed them onto Fetzle. "It begins with you."

ELIAS

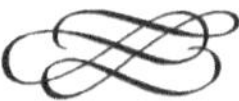

"It must be the Staff of Banishment, the weapon that must be forged," I quickly concluded.

"It does seem highly likely," she agreed. "But what is the thread? And where do we find the other blade and the staff?"

"It seems the likely place would be where we have friends. The trolls, and then we may extend our search to the giants."

"What if they don't want to reassemble it? I mean, it was the giants who disassembled it to begin with, right?"

"We have to trust, Olly. If this is the will of Malarin, surely it will be done." I meant what I said, but a part of me quivered at that statement, "The will of Malarin". *Do any of us know the will of our creator? And if we presumed we did, then death and destruction were just as much a part of his will as resurrection, along with all that is good and kind in this world.*

"Trust. I trust you and your intuition." She smiled and pulled me in and kissed my nose. "Look, we aren't leaving here tonight, we've already agreed. But we can check in with Lucas and let him know we are coming to see him in Listy at daybreak."

We tapped into our Rune and then I initiated a broadcast to

456

Lucas through the bidding tether. "Lucas, we must come to Listy and speak with Fetzle at first light."

I waited to feel the tickle that was associated with the tether communication. It was like a tickle in the ears, then Olly and I would hear a confirmation or another standard reply. But there was nothing.

"Where is he?" There was panic in Ophelia's tone.

I reached for the hairsy charm. It was still intact, but not where I expected it to be, in the Bermuda Triangle. I followed it further south to the Solomon Islands.

"He is with the giants."

"The giants? I mean, I told him about their message for Fetzle. Try him again."

I repeated the message, this time adding, "Or wherever you are."

The familiar tickle tugged at our ears, and a very inebriated reply funneled through. "Alright. We are with the giants, and man, they know how to drink. See you soon, but not too soon, I hope. Fuck it. I mean, whenever you guys want to come, that's cool."

Ophelia and I looked at each other before erupting into laughter.

OPHELIA

$\mathcal{W}$e were all packed and waiting for Itzlee, Fetzle's troll friend who was kind enough to agree to transport us down to the Solomon Islands at dawn. We'd spent most of the night making love and soaking each other up in the few precious moments we had alone. Nothing like the primal lovemaking we had enveloped in earlier in the day that led to an inexplicable absorption of Carissa's gifts, this was sweet, soft, and sensual. It made me wonder if we had to reach some heightened peak of ecstasy to recreate what happened the afternoon before.

"Are you ready for this?" I asked as I kissed the back of my husband's neck.

Elias was putting the box with his father's note in his bag.

"Hey, we didn't look at any of the other papers in there. We have a minute."

Elias shrugged and pulled out the box, lifted the lid, and sifted through an assortment of maps and random notes from his father. "I have many of these clippings from my dad. I will place these with the others I discovered over the years."

As he shuffled through them, I thought I saw a shimmer of light or a flash of movement.

"Wait, there is something to these. Show me the other ones your father collected."

"They are just here, I gave Ruit back his journals when he admitted they were his. But I kept the maps from Alistair's and the other clippings my father acquired and bequeathed to me. Some of the information was very useful and in fact was integral to seeing the Katuan Trials realized, while other pieces might just be rubbish." Elias explained as he pulled out a large stack of assorted papers.

I saw the glimmer again, a sheen wave across the paper. It moved like it was alive. I started unfolding the ones I could see with the effects. "These ones, there is something special about these ones. Can you see it?"

He shook his head. "Those are the very clippings I assumed to be rubbish."

"They aren't trash, but I can't tell you what they are yet." I tried to match up the lines. "It's a puzzle or a symbol." I reached for the box and began pulling out the pieces in there, when something else caught our attention.

"It is something for both of us." An envelope with both our names.

Miss Ophelia and My Dear Boy Elias

"It must be from Rand. I would know that penmanship anywhere."

"Well, open it."

He gingerly unfolded the sheet of paper and read the contents aloud.

To the charming Miss Ophelia and my dear boy Elias,

I write you this letter on the eve before I depart for The Cathedral. Thanks to your clever transmission and a genuine friendship I've developed with Rajaheesh, the Key Keeper, I can steal you away before the summit begins and share my secrets.

In the event that something goes awry, I am capitalizing on the likelihood that Caleb will convey the message that Cane left important informa-

tion for Elias here in Innsbruck. Without further ado, here is my admission. I killed Alistair. I identified him as one of the villains at your parents' murder. I followed him for three years, and when you showed up at his door, I knew I could wait no longer to get to the bottom of his treachery and discover his accomplice. He didn't cave, and refused to cooperate. When I realized he was communicating with monstrous allies while I interrogated him, I had to kill him to save you, Elias. Then I distracted Yanni in Chicago when he discovered you, Miss Ophelia. It was the fate of the strokes that I was there.

When we entered Hafiza, I had to see what you'd ascertained about Alistair before I came without proof and revealed my crimes. I knew you would not understand the lengths I took any other way. The day you found me in your room, Elias, I had discovered the other ingredients to the Loktpi. I did not know what they were for, but I had seen the other pieces in Alistair's study before you came in and collected what you could. I passed the pouch onto Ophelia during the siege of Hafiza in the hopes that they would help you in your search for answers.

I hope you can forgive me for my crimes. They were always with the truest intentions. This brings me to an important discovery I made. Alistair communicated through his Rune with his accomplice. It is the very same marking he had on his right hand, between his finger and thumb. Find the Conduit, other than the Talluses, who bears this mark and you have found his accomplice. Your parents' murderers will finally be brought to justice.

In an entirely different vein, it recently came to my attention through a fae acquaintance that Lucas has met his demise, and for that, Miss Ophelia, I am so sorry. I have never much cared for the chap, as you well know. Yes, it has everything to do with my protective nature around Elias, but more than that, I found him reckless and dangerous. When his Yessica died, he lost his compass, and people without a way can put everyone in their wake in danger. I never wanted that for you, either of you, but I dare say I didn't want this outcome. My heart hurts for you, Miss Ophelia, no matter mine and Lucas' differences.

I truly desire to share all of this in person, but should I fail... I know this letter will eventually find you.

I love you both,

Rand

TEARS BEGAN to fall for the friend that neither of us had been able to really mourn. He was what was strong, courageous and good in us all. Elias and I held each other in respectful silence. It was all we could do for him now. I was more grateful than ever that I got my goodbye on the bank of the River Tins.

Itzlee arrived and our moment was interrupted. We quickly gathered the papers up and stowed them away. Another mystery to be solved on another day.

I welcomed Olly and Viraclay at the grand entrance with Fetzle and the Emperor—I was seriously hung over. Yesi couldn't even get out of bed. Aside from the foreboding prophecy from a seductive High Priestess, I'd say it had been one epic night.

"How are you feeling, Lucas?" Olly teased as she approached the steps.

Elias was admiring Calt. It was strange to see how the giant dwarfed Fetzle. I wondered if the newlyweds would notice what Yesi and I had, going on between the emperor and the queen.

"I'm cool. Don't worry about me." I gave her a hug. "Let me introduce Emperor Calt. Emperor, meet Ophelia and Elias Kraus."

He bowed slightly and they returned the gesture. "Are you the son of Sorcey and Cane Kraus?"

"Indeed. Did you know my parents?"

"Very well, actually. I was sad to hear of their passing." Calt had more to say but he paused. We all waited. "Did your mother give you the Dirk of Inverness?"

"That is precisely why we are here."

Relief flashed across the emperor's face. "Your timing is impeccable. There is one problem. We cannot find the staff."

I was lost now. There were too many moving parts, and I was significantly slower than usual.

"You have the other blade?" Elias asked. "But not the staff to unite them?"

"Yes. Let us take this conversation inside. There are more ears that require attendance, and more mouths that have additional answers."

Calt put his hand down. I jumped on and gestured for Olly and Elias to join me. They took one another's hand and shook their heads in disbelief.

"Another day, another magical creature in the books," Olly said as she playfully nudged me with her shoulder. "You don't look so hot."

"Shut the fuck up."

Fetzle chimed in from behind. "Fetzle says Stinky Ophelia Banner is rights. Oh waits, Fetzle has corrections. Ophelias no longer stinkys and is now a Kraus. Fetzle says Ophelia not stinks. Kraus is rights."

"My aura doesn't stink anymore, Fetzle?"

The troll took a big whiff of air through her mouth. "Nopes. Fetzle thinks it smells likes grass and earths with a little glimmer of lights. No mores smells like sour and sweets and rust and oceans."

"Wow! Well, I am glad it smells better than that." Olly turned to me and Elias. "Why do you think my aura changed?"

I hadn't noticed that the High Priestess was waiting to greet us at the threshold. "Because you consummated and the strokes that were around you as an Ulus were not your own. Now that you have funneled them to the proper vessel, the Sulu," she nodded toward Viraclay, "the Queen can actually smell your genuine aura."

The High Priestess only wore a small black pelt between her thighs. Her breasts were bare, and her hair was braided and stacked on top of her head. She had several gold chains around her neck.

"I am the High Priestess Maia. We have much to discuss."

The fall was briefer than I expected, and the cavern below was larger than I imagined it would be. In fact, it was vast, and there was a tunnel that fed into the cave. I picked up the torch and propped it against a rock. Almost instantly, I realized it was not a rock at all, but rather a stone throne.

"What in the strokes is this place?"

There were strange markings all over the walls; they were oddly familiar. It occurred to me that they looked like the markings on the Katuan stones. The stones that had killed my mother. Beside the markings were images etched throughout the room. A particular image caught my eye. It was one I knew well. It was my birthmark. I walked over to the wall and traced it with my fingers.

Suddenly, a holographic scene manifested in front of me, like an old movie. It was of Clive. He was in this place, sitting on the stone throne. The vapor was rolling off him and dancing its way up to the surface through the hole in the Oracle's chamber. There was an energy exchange occurring that I'd never seen before. Whatever Clive was giving off was in exchange for an essence that he was summoning above him.

I watched as the image seemed to skip ahead in time. Aurora was down here with him. She was irate about something. There were no words exchanged between them, but the tension was palpable. "It's not enough, Clive. We can do better."

Then she stormed out of the cave through the tunnel. I grabbed the torch. I needed to see what was on the other end of this outlet. I ran, eager to have answers but afraid I would only find more questions. Ahead, a small light was coming into focus. I ran faster and was met with a wall with cracks of light shining through. I pressed against the stone and realized it moved. I pushed hard, and I watched in amazement as the stone rolled to the right, exposing the valley of Mount Parnassus.

This had been here all along. Clive was coming and going in Delphi the entire time, performing a magic exchange that created some mysterious fog. To what end, I did not know. But what appeared abundantly clear was that the Oracle had never been a captive. *She was the engineer.*

The emperor carried us through the palace and into a chamber below sea level. It was large, as it would have to be to hold an assembly of giants. There was an enormous viewing window into the ocean. It was rather breathtaking. The deep blue light gave the space a fluid cool ambiance.

"This is amazing," Olly observed.

"I wish Yesi was feeling better. She would've loved to see this."

"Fetzle thinks it's nice too." I noticed the troll queen follow the emperor with her eyes. *Peculiar*, I thought. *Could she be infatuated with a giant?*

My attention was averted when Olly nudged me with her elbow and pointed at the window. A silhouette appeared in the distance in the ocean. "Is that a whale?" I asked, straining my eyes to see the creature better. A moment later it was at the window, and it was clearly not a whale. It was iridescent blue, with scales that glimmered like the belly of an oyster, but with teals, blues and soft hues of greens. The creature's body was slender like an eel's, with dozens of fins. The eyes were all white with specs of deep blues. It was magnificent in every way.

A stammering voiced echoed behind us. "T-t-t-h-hat is my s-s-sister, Adanc." I turned around to see an enormous squirrel. "I-I-I am Ratatoskr."

"Thank you for the introduction, brother," Adanc's voice echoed into the room. Emperor Calt put us down on a long, tall bench, as he took a seat beside another giant who was bald but had a long grey beard. "Calt, Ropen, it is a pleasure to see you. The High Priestess said the assembly was urgent."

"She will be with us in a moment. She assured me as much. The High Priestess is collecting the Tapestry of Fate. Have you brought the items you've been so gracious to protect?"

"R-r-ratatoskr has." He pulled out a large golden spool of thread.

"As have I." Adanc turned, exposing her belly and a small knife in comparison to her size.

The giant referred to as Ropen unwrapped a parcel he had on his lap, revealing a crown.

"We have all come bearing our parts," the High Priestess said as she entered the room followed by two beautiful giants that could have been her sisters. The females behind her carried a large roll of fabric. "Mr. Kraus, would you be so kind as to share your Dirk with us?"

I pulled the Dirk from my bag and lay it on my lap.

"We are missing the staff?" Adanc noticed.

Olly tapped into our Rune. "I am confused. Why do they have a spool of thread, the other blade, and a crown, but not the staff?"

"We know where the staff is," the High Priestess admitted. "But before we divulge that information, we must bring to light some other truths."

Maia was in the center of the room, and her acolytes were preparing the roll of fabric to be displayed behind her.

"To some of you, this will be knowledge that you have had for many centuries, but for our guests, I must share long-since-lost facts. I am Maia, a star in corporeal form. I am one of the Seven Sisters. Do you know of us?"

I nodded, but Lucas immediately responded with a "No."

"Very well. We are the guardians of the thirteenth timeline. This means we oversee the balance of each planet within that timeline. The painter created this world, but this world is one of many. As a guardian of this timeline, where you exist, we sometimes take form in the flesh to assist the evolution of the planet back into harmony. The last time I took form in this world was during the time of Queen Peozleo and the death of the great Niffler. The Conduit world was approaching the imminent fall of Atlantis."

"Fetzle was just borns."

"Yes, sweet trolling. Your birth changed the course of the world."

I could not tell if that made Fetzle feel proud or ashamed, but it certainly left a mark.

"I gave my life force to assist in the dismantling of the Staff of Banishment. I did my best to avert another cycle of self-destruction within the strokes that be. Much has transpired since then, and this creation is now facing its greatest challenge, on the brink of utter annihilation."

Just then, the two other priestesses unrolled the tapestry.

"This is the Tapestry of Fate, woven by the Golden Spool of Thread bequeathed to the giants by the painter. Every Rittle used to have a sacred place with the creatures of this masterpiece, but during this circle of the strokes, the Rittles were stolen from their keepers. See here on the tapestry?" She pointed to a massive jumble of thread in a cyclone of circles. "This was the last extinction of the Conduit world. An entire generation of consummated Conduits disappeared into the ether five thousand years ago."

Ophelia and I looked at each other, knowing this was what Ganesha told us about.

"As guardians, we do our best to steward the creatures of the thirteenth timeline, but sometimes they cannibalize themselves. Conduits have done this many times, more than any other strokes created by Malarin. She pointed to another mass of circles, and another. "But this time, your destruction will obliterate every stroke ever painted. Because this time the Sulu and Ulus have emerged together."

I took her hand in mine. It was shaking—we were both shaking.

The Oracle's prophecy was true. Our fates are locked with our potential doom.

"You two are the reflection, a microcosm of what the world could transform into, harmony between the dark and light. The power your connection brings to the strokes is like ten thousand atomic bombs. One misstep and the entire world will cease to exist."

"What is the misstep? What are the choices we're facing that could cause us to explode?" Olly asked, her panic escalating with each word.

"That, dear one, remains to be seen." Maia pointed at the bottom of the tapestry. "Do you see this?"

It was a severance in the stitch. Everything after it was jagged. The continuity was gone.

"This was what we saw just before we used the power of the Golden Spool of Thread, the Crown, and my life force to dismantle the staff. I did not know then that this was the moment of your consummation. You created a Paradigm Tremor, and it was felt across all timelines, in all worlds. What has happened cannot be undone, and what will transpire is completely up to the strokes."

I was holding my breath. *This was so much bigger than I had imagined.*

"Your world will be the only one that faces annihilation, thank the stars, but I have a personal stake in this game. My sister has gone missing, and the last trail of her stardust led us here. If this planet dies, she will die with it. Any star trapped in a dying world is consumed in the vortex that is created. That is why I have returned to reassemble the staff. The weapon that defiled the first strokes is the very one that may redeem them. Then I will find my sister and trust that the strokes are in your favor."

The weight of it all was crushing. I searched Olly's face looking for hope, but found none. She was sinking, just as I was.

Lucas broke the silence first. "You said you knew where the staff was. What are we waiting for? Let's go get it."

"If only it were that easy, ever-eager one! The staff was given to my mother, the Star Seed, when it was dismantled. I felt it would be safest to have one piece of the Rittle completely out of reach. The Star Seed came to Earth seven hundred years ago to grant the wishes of your great Alchemist. She offered him the Pierses paper he sought. My twin sisters Tauri and Taura shared their Opus with great jubilation with the original Ulus Lorif many, many generations ago, at the near-dawning of your timeline. From that gifting has followed many incredible magics, including the Alchemist's Old Channels."

"Fetzle saws your mother once. She's most beautiful."

"Thank you, Queen. I agree. As she ascended back among the stars, she felt a calling to leave the staff with a particularly virtuous soul: Nandi—the daughter of Ruit. The Star Seed knows that nudges are the insights of all creators, therefore they cannot be ignored, and I could never blame her for honoring her intuition."

"I've seen the staff. Nandi used it to fight Vivienne. She saved my life with it."

The High Priestess nodded.

"But Nandi died that day, and the staff was..." Ophelia's words trailed off.

"The staff is now in the hands of Esther."

My mouth went dry and the back of my neck pooled with sweat. The staff we needed to save the world was in the possession of our greatest enemy.

OPHELIA

$\mathcal{I}$t was a lot to take in.

"Esther has a role to play in all of this yet," the High Priestess continued. "I can feel it."

Apollo felt that way as well. That his daughter, my aunt, could be the key to ending this war.

"Can you tell us more? There must be more than just a gut feeling," Lucas prodded.

"There is more. The Queen and the Emperor have a massive role to play in ending this tyranny. Princess Chaness is a captive. Her blood fuels the army of darkness. She must be saved, or there is no hope of a victory. The rightful Queen that wears the Crown of Thorns," she pointed at the gold ornament on Ropen's lap, "holds the key to all that was lost."

"What key, and what was lost?" I looked at Fetzle inquisitively. She shrugged.

"They were the final words whispered to me the last time I gave my essence to dismantle the staff. Queen Fetzle was destined for this moment. She is only here because of the sacrifice made by her grandmother that ultimately led us to this point."

"Fetzles feels nervous." Her body posture caved inward, and my heart hurt for my dear friend.

I saw Calt reach over and comfort her with his hand on her shoulder, and I was touched.

"There is nothing to be nervous about. This is your destiny." Then the priestess turned to me and Elias. "You two are the wild card, the unknown. There has never been a Sulu-Ulus in existence together. There are no records or histories to pull from, to anticipate what may come of this union. One thing is clear. You are already fracturing the paradigms that have been in place since the painter created this world. That is terrifying, because new rules must be forged in their place. The only solace we have is that Malarin has returned to his children. He is here now, as we speak."

"How do we reach him?" Elias asked.

"Through her." Maia pointed a long, slim finger at me. Instantaneously, the River Tins voice chimed in my head.

"I am never far away."

My mind was racing with the possibilities of what I'd just witnessed. *What kind of Covening creates that sort of holographic magic?* It was powerful and like nothing I had ever seen before. *Is it hobgoblin magic?* More and more, I was realizing that I had no idea what Clive was capable of. *Where has he come from really?*

I walked up the mountain back to the temple in a daze. It was time to collect my thoughts. *What do I know about Aurora and Clive?*

They shared a special bond through telepathy. Clive was the last of his clan, the last of the hobgoblin strokes. Besides being telepathic, hobgoblins seemed to syphon or extrapolate power from other beings. Aurora wanted to build a Super Sulu, so that she could have the ultimate dominion over this world. For her plan to work, she needed other Conduits to lock arms with and amplify her gifting. Many of her captives were now gone, but they also were in cahoots with the powrie King OAD who had a giant-troll Princess captive below the Orb Forest, whose blood they were using to energize the Orbs. When I put it all in perspective it, was clear there was more to this agenda than a Super Sulu, but I did not have enough information to understand the larger end game.

What else do I know? The Oracle was having gaps in her vision. They no longer had the poison they required to sedate captives or the antidote required to wake them. The earthquake had terrified both of them. Aurora had cut a child from her womb. I had some affiliation with Nestor and Ophelia. And now it seemed more likely than ever that I had been a cog in Aurora and Clive's wheel of domination. That the true villains of my story had been the Oracle and her henchman, all along.

LUCAS

"Let me get this straight. Olly is the painter?" I shook my head in disbelief. *This is fucking crazy!*

"No, she is not the painter. Chitchakor is personally communicating with her. She is the direct line to the creator of this world."

"Because I dipped my toe in the River Tins while fighting with Yanni."

Maia was sizing up Olly with her eyes. It made me uneasy.

"The Ulus is the greatest amplifier ever created in this world. You, dear Ophelia, take all that you absorb and reflect it back into the world through him." Maia looked to Viraclay. "He carries the power and keeps it safe. He is the container. But it is your gifting, your antenna rather, that is a direct line to the creator—to Malarin himself. Your encounter with the River Tins likely only strengthened that connection."

"Then the painter has come to help the Pai Ona win this war, to stop this carnage?" Elias asked excitedly.

"That is not so."

"I don't understand. He isn't here to help?" I looked at Olly nervously, wondering what this meant for her.

"Dalinkas created you all with free will. There is no wrong or right here. That is the problem with you earthlings. You have spent the entirety of your creation trying to separate yourselves, denying your whole nature by denying the nature of the creature beside you. We are all right and wrong, we are all dark and light. When you shame or judge the other, you lose your own power that can only come through true acceptance and alignment."

"You're saying that it was okay for the Nebas to kill thousands of Conduits?" Ophelia heightened the pitch of her voice. She was noticeably agitated.

"I am saying the truth is not black and white. The painter is not here to choose a side. He is here to dissolve the lines."

The three of us looked at each other, not knowing what to think of this revelation.

"Fetzle thinks this maybes goods?" The troll shrugged. "Fetzles is readys for her parts."

I had to hand it to the queen. She got straight to the point.

The emperor stood. "And we stand with you, Queen Fetzle, from now until the day they rest my bones."

Ropen looked at his brother skeptically because he was sensing the same thing. We all were. Calt definitely had a thing for Fetzle, and that was all but an admission of love. Olly looked at me with wide eyes and a huge smile. Fetzle looked just as admiringly up at the giant. These two were finding love in the darkest of places, and it was fucking adorable.

ELIAS

There were so many questions, but the one that seemed the most relevant was how we would acquire the staff from Esther.

"If what you say is true and Esther has a crucial part to play in all of this, how in the strokes do we reason with her? We need the staff to restore the Rittle. What would you have us do?"

"You will go to Delphi. She is there, but there is not much time. The Oracle hunts her too." The High Priestess got to her feet. "The queen will take you. We have other preparations to make before you return."

"You expect her to cooperate with us because she's on the outs with Aurora?" Lucas asked.

"No, but I expect the truth will set you all free." Maia looked over her shoulder one more time before sweeping out of the room with the other priestesses. "It is time you all embrace the dark," she said. Then she was gone.

"I guess we better get going." Olly got to her feet.

"That's it? We're just going to go strike up a conversation with Esther?" Lucas argued. He and I were in accord on this matter. I did not like the way this was unfolding.

Olly squared her shoulders and let out a big sigh. "Look, guys, I don't like it either, but the truth is we have two days before we prepare for the final battle, and we need that staff intact to save the world. I would like to invite Ruit to join us at Delphi. Reinforcements are good. But not going isn't an option. We have an Ulus, a Sulu, the great Alchemist, a troll queen, and my best friend, who is kind of a badass. It's time we start acting like the superheroes we are and save the damn world."

It would not have been my pep talk, but my wife did have a way about her. I took her hand in mine and her shoulders softened. "You are right, we do not have a choice. And we are all pretty badass, not just Lucas."

That got me a chuckle and a kiss from her. Lucas was shaking his head, but it was not out of defiance. It was more from a thread of disbelief. "Let me go get Yesi," he relented, and we were alone with the Emperor and the Queen.

"I wish I could go with you." Calt was gazing into the queen's eyes. "Alas, there is work I must assist the priestess with. But I will send my brother in my stead. I want you to feel supported, Fetzle."

The troll looked down at her feet sheepishly. "Fetzle thinks that we's be okays withouts any giants." She gently caressed the emperor's leg because it was the closest thing she could reach. "The Emperors is bests heres, and so is alls the giants. Fetzle bes backs soon."

Calt wanted to say more but did not. He leaned down and awkwardly hugged the troll before excusing himself.

It was obvious the queen was feeling emotional, so she turned to us. "Fetzles be getting hers shuttles readys, I thinks." Then she was gone.

I pulled Olly in for a hug. She nestled her head into my chest. "We are crazy, aren't we?"

I nodded.

"But we've been through worse, right?"

I pulled her back to look at her face. "Worse or not, we can overcome anything." I instantly pulled her back to my chest.

"My grandfather felt Esther could be reasoned with. The priestess has just said the truth will set us free. Esther just needs to know the truth."

We both knew it was not going to be that simple. But we had to try. We stood there in silence for a long moment.

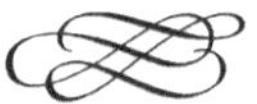

e were nearly at the shuttle when we heard the High Priestess calling for Fetzle. "Queen!"

We all stopped and waited for her to take one step and catch up with us. "I consulted the Divination Wands. I am afraid we need you here, helping the Emperor plan for the Princess's rescue. Once they have acquired the staff, Lucas can call on you to retrieve it, along with the Dirk of Inverness." She nodded toward Elias, who patted his hip where the Dirk was sheathed and cloaked in magic.

"Fetzle must takes her friends to Delphi."

"Yes, of course, but please return promptly." The queen nodded, and I wondered how much she liked taking orders from someone else. She had been on her own for so long. It didn't appear to bother her.

Then the priestess turned her attention to me. "I also received a message for you, Ulus. In time, you may make sense of it. Your strokes are of rare origin. The collaboration of what has always been and what was not meant to be allows you to bridge the two fates."

Another cryptic message. I internally rolled my eyes, but did my best to show the priestess the respect she deserved. "Thank you, High Priestess."

"I know that you absorbed the energy of that Vixen." *How could she know about that?* We hadn't even told Ruit yet. She narrowed her eyes. "You absorbed some of the essence of the Sorcerer stone as well. It is why you can understand dragon. Only an Alchemist should have been able to utilize that gift. Sorcerer's strokes were created that way. And although your Atoa, the Sulu, manifests these gifts effortlessly, he can also share them with you willingly. It will just take time for you two to learn to collaborate. Time is unfortunately the one thing you do not have much of."

She turned her attention back to the Queen. "I will see you shortly." Then she was gone, nearly out of sight with only a few steps.

Elias spoke through our Rune. "How are you?"

"I'm fine. Just another day, another cryptic message. But no, really, I'm fine. Can you please contact Ruit and see that he meets us at Delphi."

"Indeed." Then he signed off and was presumably in the Alchemist's head.

We all entered the shuttle, and I took a seat beside Yessica. I wanted to ask her a question. While Lucas was preoccupied asking Fetzle what magic she had that could make sure we detained Esther without any bloodshed, and Elias was busy briefing Ruit, it seemed like the right time.

"Can I ask you something?" Yessica turned to face me. I immediately wanted to kick myself for choosing to ask her, of all people, about her Soahcoit connection. The priestess mentioning the incident in Austria made this question all the more relevant. *If anyone can understand limited time and immense passion, it has to be her and Lucas—right?*

"I'm an open book. How can I help?"

I cleared my throat awkwardly. "How is the... I mean, do you and Lucas have good...? What I'm trying to say is..." Yessica's expression didn't give anything away. She just looked at me, patiently waiting for me to finally pop the question. "Do you and Lucas have mind-shattering sex, even after consummation? I mean, the kind of lovemaking that feels like you're one with the universe and you can hear each other's thoughts?"

She looked at me inquiringly, probably wondering why I would bring this question to her.

"I feel that Lucas and I have mind-blowing sex. I certainly feel the connection to love in our union, and if love isn't the foundation for all, I don't know what is. If you're asking if my husband is a good lover? The answer is absolutely."

I put my hands up. "No, sorry, that isn't what I was asking, but I can understand why it would seem that way. I feel really silly now." I shook my head with regret. She was handling this as well as could be expected considering the weird love triangle between me, Yessica, and her husband and my best friend.

She put her hand on my thigh. "I am sincerely asking what you are concerned about with this inquiry. Did I answer your question?"

"You... did. This isn't your fault. I'm making this awkward."

I stood up to leave.

"Can you sit down for a moment?"

I quickly sat back down. It was the least I could do.

"This wasn't exactly what you asked, but I would like to share something I have noticed since you and Elias' consummation and the Paradigm Tremor. When Lucas and I are in union, it feels as though the entire timeline is suspended. At first, I wanted to explain it away as passions after such a long separation. But the sensation of weightlessness and the full intoxication of love appears to be strengthening."

Relief saturated my shoulders and they relaxed.

"That does answer my question. Sorry about the stupid way I asked it."

"It seems reasonable to me that the couple that created a fissure in time may still be impacting how the world is engaging with ener-gy." She took my hand in hers. "But if I had an assessment of your impact, I would say you seem to be aligning us all with the expansiveness of love. I will happily take that influence."

I smiled at Yesi and put my other hand on top of hers. "I knew you would have the answers I needed." I pulled her in for a hug. "I'm so grateful that you are the woman that Lucas loves."

She squeezed me back. "I am also grateful that you are the woman Lucas loves."

Just then, Elias approached. "Sorry to break up the moment ladies. Ruit has just informed me that Stalt is at Delphi with his wife Claudia, who has been behind enemy lines as an informant since their daughter was abducted."

Lucas came up behind him. "Claudia is strong. She has been at this for a long time. I met her when I was trying to find Yesi." He put his hand on his wife's shoulder.

"Claudia told Stalt that Esther is weakened and will not be challenging to detain. It might be the perfect circumstance for reasoning with her. The Alchemist is meeting us there by way of a teleportation incantation he has devised."

Yessica stood up next to her husband. "The strokes are in our favor."

Elias communicated within our Rune. "Are you certain you are okay?"

"Yes. In fact, she kind of gave us some good news. You don't get to hog all the powers." I leaned in and kissed him.

ESTHER

"We need to go, Claudia," I demanded when I got back to the main chamber of Delphi. Jillian was slightly lucid and abruptly tried her best to scuttle backwards on all fours, out of my reach. "I have no use for you right now. Calm yourself, Jillian."

Claudia looked down in the hole and then back up at me. "I guess you didn't need my help." She dropped the rope. Claudia got down on her knees by the disheveled captive. "Don't worry, she isn't going to hurt you."

I sneered at them both, but didn't have the energy to argue any differently. "We need to go. I got the answers I needed." I didn't want to know anymore. I wanted to get out of this horrid place.

"What answers are those? Can they help us against the Oracle?"

I shook my head. Hopelessness surged through me. There was nothing that could help us defeat Aurora, and eventually the Pai Ona would hunt me down and execute me just like they did my father.

"Then we need to look a little harder, don't you think?" Just then, I heard something move in the shadows behind Claudia. I crouched down, ready to attack whatever came next. I would not die without a fight. Claudia stepped in front of me. "Calm down, Esther. It's my husband, Stalt."

"You called upon a Pai Ona? Here? You sentenced me to death!" I said the words but didn't feel the sting of betrayal. You can only be betrayed by someone you love or respect. Any other underhanded dealings are only to be expected in this world.

Stalt took his place by his Atoa. Jillian scooted herself to be behind both of them, and Claudia put her hands up in a gesture of peace. I hissed at her through bared teeth.

"My time with the Nebas was always about finding our daughter. I know they have her, but it will do her no good if I am slinking around in the shadows. I need the Pai Ona to know what I know, and if you're smart, you will do the same. It's the only way you will be shown any mercy."

"You believe the Pai Ona will show me mercy after all I have done? After all the lives I've ushered to the River Tins? You are a bigger fool than I thought." I crouched again. "So, I will just kill you both now and be done with this nonsense of mercy..."

Stalt moved in front of his wife as I reached for the staff behind my back. He would be a worthy opponent, but all I needed was one graze of a fingertip to end this brawl swiftly and victoriously. Claudia tried to lock eyes with me. I kept my stare on her brawny partner. I felt the earth move below my feet, and I lifted the staff above my head, when a gust of wind came out of nowhere and pinned me to the wall. I no sooner thought the thought than the Sulu and Viraclay entered the dark chamber, accompanied by the Alchemist and the man who killed my Yanni. My skin crawled with rage. I howled into the space between. I was ready to die. There was nothing left to fight for or against.

Then I heard a faint whisper on the wind, "Mercy." Ophelia looked at me with pity. The gusts of wind parted to let her approach, while still pinning me to the wall. She reached for the staff and easily took it from my grip, tossing it behind her to Ruit. Tears streamed down my cheeks. It was the abundance of anger that was spilling over from my soul. The realizations of a life lived in the dark. "Mercy." She said it once more. The wind stopped and my body fell to the floor. I didn't bother getting up. I didn't bother moving. I could feel Ophelia hovering over me. I was waiting for the blow. She knelt down and pulled the hair from my face. She was shielded. I could sense it even without touching her. "We have some things to discuss. I have a message from your father."

Only then did I look up into her eyes.

OPHELIA

This was surreal. I was staring at Esther and there hadn't been a single drop of blood spilt—yet. Ruit approached Claudia and Stalt with caution.

"May I?" He was gesturing to Jillian, who was nearly lifeless. "I have the antidote."

Claudia answered, but I saw the glint of interest in Esther's eyes as she watched him. "You have the tonic that can cure her?"

"I do, and if it pleases you, I would like to restore her."

"Please." Claudia took hold of her husband. "This means that they will be able to heal our baby when we get her, Stalty."

"Yes. Yes, it does, my sweet wife." He pulled her in for a long kiss.

Stalty? Not the cutest pet name. He proceeded to kiss her face all over. One thing about war—you suddenly feel like there is always enough time to tell people you love them. I'd never be the person to cut short a reunion. Esther, on the other hand...

"Enough!" She got to her feet. "Don't toy with me. Kill me and be done with it."

It was strange, but I had empathy for my aunt. She was going to learn that she was the greatest pawn of us all, when she'd spent thousands of years believing she was the orchestrator.

"We aren't here to kill you, Esther."

She scoffed.

"Although some of us would love to, given the chance," Lucas chimed in.

"Lucas Healey," Yesi scolded.

"I'm just keeping it real, you guys. The High Priestess said the truth will set you free. And this piece of shit, truthfully, deserves to die."

Esther cackled. "I would still beat you in hand-to-hand combat, Lucas."

"That's what Yanni thought."

She growled and tears streamed down her face.

"Stop it, Lucas." I shot him a glance that could kill. "Esther, I met your father on the banks of the River Tins, while Yanni possessed my body."

She wanted to ignore me, but I could sense her curiosity.

"He tried to tell you himself." She locked her eyes with mine. "He told me that you could be reasoned with, that you needed to know the truth." I had the urge to reach out and comfort her, but restrained myself. I was still acutely aware of how dangerous she was. "Aurora has been manipulating you with hobgoblin magic and lies for centuries. Everything you know about her is a lie. She and Clive were the ones who destroyed Atlantis and ultimately killed Shatki, the woman you called your mother."

I felt the rage ripple off her. "A dragon destroyed Atlantis, and my mother died because of the vow of the Katuan Stones."

"Clive and Aurora were trying to take the dragon captive. That is why Gwenora was there. They wanted her blood to sedate the Conduits they intended to abduct. They did eventually capture Gwenora and used her blood for centuries to drug their prisoners." A flash of recognition crossed her face. She knew I was telling the truth. "But your mother didn't die that day."

Esther's eyes got big.

"Your mother… is the Oracle."

She laughed hysterically. "This is how you intend to sway me with the truth? With ridiculous lies?"

"Your father and Aurora had a love affair before he met Shatki. It is why he was so against diluted blood and children before consummation. It wasn't for power. It was because he knew how catastrophic it could be to have children before you met your Atoa. When he left Aurora for Shatki, she was pregnant, and he didn't know. When she realized she would never have him back, that she was alone with a baby and had yet to meet her partner, she became hopeless. Then she ended up having twins, leaving her even more at a loss. She decided to separate you two."

"My twin brother?" Esther reached down to touch her inner thigh, and I knew she was putting it together. "Nestor."

I nodded and let that sink in for a moment.

"When she lost Apollo, something in her snapped."

"My father."

"You were sent to him. She commissioned someone to leave you at his doorstep with a note."

"Then she called on my mother to heal her," Elias chimed in. "Aurora told my mother that she only carried the one child, the boy Nestor, and that she wanted him to be sent away. But that my mother was to tell no one. This secret would be the secret that would ultimately kill her, as Aurora, the great Oracle, could never be connected to the atrocities of the Incubus Nestor."

I watched her face intently, looking for the moment the truth really sank in. The moment of acceptance.

"She hexed you and your father, probably Yanni as well. The hex looks like a small welt."

She reached under her arm to her side. I assumed that she knew exactly what I was referring to. "That's why my head hurts every time I try and remember what happened here. That's why my father acted so strange when we arrived. We were always being manipulated. We were hexed. Until my own vengeful nature swept me away. But she would know that she would be able to see how I would evolve into this monster." Tears streamed down her face. "I saw that she and Clive had been accessing and influencing anyone who came to Delphi with some smoke from the throne chamber, below the divination room, but I never could have imagined…" Her words trailed off.

I looked up at Ruit and Elias. "Can you show me this room?" I asked.

"My whole life… Yanni's life… Everyone I love has died by the hands of this beast, this diabolical duo, transforming me into a pit of violent despair."

"Esther, we don't have much time. The Oracle and Clive are hunting you as well. We need to see what may give us answers here in Delphi, then we must go." I kept my voice stern but quiet, hoping to alert her to the importance of what I was saying. I could tell she was in shock.

Something flashed across her face, but I couldn't discern what it was.

"I want to know all that you discover. I deserve to know. I will show you, but I must be present."

I'm sure most of us could agree *deserved* was a big assumption on her part. But there was nothing left to hide. Whatever we discovered would likely only validate all of Aurora's treachery. I nodded, and Elias did too.

Ruit handed Jillian over to Claudia and Stalt. "She is coming back slowly. Tend to her gently." They both nodded.

Lucas, Yesi, Ruit, Elias and I surrounded Esther, though I could sense there was no fight in her right now.

She looked forlorn, like she knew the truth was only going to get more challenging to swallow. And once again, I was struck by how much I empathized with her.

We walked down a dark staircase into a damp, dimly lit room. Only a single torch hung on the wall. In the center of the space was a hole in the ground. Esther grabbed the torch and flung it into the abyss.

"There is another way to enter the cavern, but this way is the quickest. Then she jumped in." My stomach lurched as my recurring dream of killing everyone I loved in a cave flooded back to me.

"Are you okay?" Elias noticed my unease.

I shook it off. "Yeah. I thought I was having déjà vu."

"Should I be worried?"

I shrugged. "I guess we will see what's down there and go from there." Then I jumped in, and the rest of them followed.

Esther stood in the furthest corner, holding the torch and touching the wall.

Ruit was examining the symbols. "These are the same at the markings in Sorcerer."

"And the Katuan Stones," Esther said. "This is the one I touched earlier, and it unlocked a story that played out right in front of me."

"It's our birthmark."

Esther nodded.

"What did you see?" Lucas demanded.

"See for yourself."

I popped into our Runes. "I can read them, but it's weird, because unlike the Martian writings, the language appears to have a film over the top. If we can peel that off, I think I will be able to read all of this."

"Like a ward?" Ruit asked.

"You can't see it?"

"No, I cannot."

Ruit shook his head.

"What are you waiting for?" Esther hissed.

"Shut up. You are lucky to be breathing right now," Lucas shot back and stepped forward. Yesi grabbed his arm. He stopped. "Just give me one reason."

"I have given you a thousand," Esther toyed.

"Now is not the time," Elias scolded.

The voice manifested in my head. "Clive did not wish for this truth to be revealed. He has concealed it with a spell of his own making. These were some of the original wisdoms I desired to share with my children. This place was built so that my creations could come convene with me whenever they needed to. The creation stories were shared here, then written down by one of my beloved strokes before Clive came and defiled this place. Sit in the throne, sweet child. You will know how to absorb and transmute the rest."

"You said we were in a hurry," Esther snapped.

I spoke to Elias and Ruit, "The painter said I must sit in the throne and absorb and transmute the energy. How do I do that without making love to Elias?"

Both men looked at me with bizarre expressions.

"And no! I am not suggesting that's what we do here."

"Take a seat, my love. We will be here to keep you safe."

Then I knew that was what I needed—to feel safe, to surrender to the flow of what was going to pass through me.

I took our conversation out of our heads. "Each of you, please circle me. Elias, stand in front, and Lucas, please stand behind the throne and in front of Esther."

Everyone took their places, Yesi and Ruit on either side. I hesitated for just a moment more before sitting down and feeling an intense rush of energy swirl about me and then immediately flooding every cell in me. My eyes were fixed on Elias. His confidence and strength fortified my sense of safety, and I fully surrendered, becoming an open channel, absorbing, transmuting, and gifting whatever was coming through to my Atoa. The film on the markings began to dissolve away, and simultaneously, Elias started projecting a tale that was coming through.

❁

TINDLE APPROACHED the meadow trepidatiously but was pleasantly surprised when both of his brothers greeted him with enthusiasm. If Fih was upset, Tindle could not sense it.

"We have missed you, brother," Priloc said as he pulled Tindle in for a hug.

"Cataphet has never kept you for so long. You must have helped her build a fortress," Fih teased, and it made Tindle happy to see his brother so light for the first time in many moons.

"I was busy but I'm grateful to be back. I have missed you both very, very much."

"Brother, there is much to share, but nothing greater than the truth that Lorif's grief has subsided and she is once again joyous." Fih hooked his arm over Tindle's shoulder. "It is as though her light is back. She cooks and plants and sings. Is she not magnificent, Priloc?"

Priloc nodded excitedly. "She has hosted us with food and drink almost every night since your absence. She insists she host us tonight, so you will see the great progress she has made."

Priloc looked at Tindle with genuine appreciation, knowing that it was his brother's courage that had restored the sweet woman back to balance. He was eager to hear how Tindle's time with the sisters went, since Priloc had expected them to return with his brother, and hoped this would not set Lorif back.

"You can share your ongoings at dinner, with all of us," Fih crowed. Tindle observed he had never seen his brother so happy, and for a moment a twinge of something tugged at his heart... Jealousy.

The day was bright and the brothers enjoyed creating strokes of contrast in the cacti realms of Hulip. Giant cacti scattered the horizon, each with a distinct shape. Tindle usually loved this type of creation with his brothers, but today he was eager to see Lorif and to give her the charm he had created for them to share. Tindle knew she would love it.

The sun began to set, and as the brothers walked back toward the Tonglin forest, Fih and Tindle both grew more alive with anticipation. Priloc noticed the oddity in Tindle that he had come to expect from Fih, and it worried him. What had happened to his brother on his journey? As they got closer to Fih and Lorif's home, the smells changed. Savory and sweet odors wafted in the air.

"That is Lorif's cooking. She is the most creative and amazing cook, brother. You will see," Fih boasted. Priloc noticed Tindle playing with a new trinket on his wrist. It was a delicately woven bracelet. He reached to touch it, to tell his brother he liked his new jewelry, but when he got close, Tindle quickly pulled his wrist away and covered it with his sleeve. Priloc could not hide his hurt. Tindle had always been very gentle with his brother.

Fih stopped when he realized something had happened between them. "Is everything okay?"

"Oh yes," Tindle assured them both. "I just realized the seam of my jacket is loose and I did not wish to pull it any further. Sorry, Priloc. Excuse my abruptness."

Priloc's eyes welled with tears. His brother was keeping something from him. Never had Priloc felt such betrayal. He wiped at his eyes but dismissed the exchange. He would bring it up to Tindle in private.

Lorif's face lit up when she saw the brothers approaching. Now that she was able to feel her sisters through the magics of the Pierses, a huge weight had been lifted. She owed Tindle so much for his courage and kindness. She hoped she would get to tell him so someday. When she saw him approaching, relief washed over her. Surely, he would have a message from her sisters.

The night was beautiful. The moon was full, and the air gently danced around them. Lorif had made all of Fih's favorite dishes, and the four of them laughed and sang until it was nearly dawn. Tindle had hoped to steal an opportunity to give Lorif the charm, but the moment did not present itself when Fih was not nearby. Lorif had hoped to sneak a word with Tindle and learn the message her sisters must have sent. Priloc watched on wearily. Although none seemed the wiser, he was afraid of what he was witnessing with the three people he cared for.

When the night was through, Tindle and Priloc walked together out of the forest. "May I come to Cataphet tomorrow? I want to hear all that transpired on your journey."

"There is not much to tell, brother. I went to the sisters' settlement and they were not there."

"What? Where were they? Are they okay? How is it that Lorif is okay?"

Tindle put his hand on his brother's shoulder. "It is all as it should be. I feel the sisters could not bear to stay where their sister was no more. I am certain they are safe."

"What will you tell Lorif?"

"I will not worry her with this. I have found other ways to still her pain. She is happy, as you can see."

Priloc was in disbelief. He began to weep, for something in his heart knew things were amiss. "What is it that you wear on your wrist?" He reached for his brother's hand once more.

"I was restless on the journey. I wove a charm during my nights by the fire. Nothing more."

But Priloc sensed it was something more.

"I will see you at dawn, brother." Tindle waved goodbye to Priloc and disappeared into the night. Priloc arrived at his ocean and wept for his brothers, for Lorif, Goyta and Orail. Tindle did not rest that night. He returned to Cataphet dismayed and also elated. Glad to see Lorif so happy but sad he did not get to give her his gift. When she arrived at the mouth of Cataphet, just before the sun was to rise, his heart swelled with jubilation.

"Lorif, what brings you here so late in the night and early in the day?"

She had a basket full of fruit. She dropped it to the floor and threw her arms around Tindle's neck. "Thank you, thank you, thank you. I have felt my sisters every day since you delivered the Pierses. I sense them sifting through the pages and I feel peace once more. But I must know—what did they say? Surely they have a message for me."

Tindle looked down at his hands. He was not prepared for this question. He improvised. "Your sisters miss you dearly. They send their blessings and are so grateful for the Pierses that I delivered. So grateful, in fact, that they helped me create this. Tindle showed her his wrist with the Gattilak charm. One for me and one for you, an incantation straight from the pages of the gift you bestowed. It will keep us both close and safe."

Tindle pulled the other one from his pocket. Lorif was taken aback. It was not what she envisioned, but a kind gesture, nonetheless. "Wow, thank you." She held her wrist out for Tindle to put it on her. He beamed at her as he felt the charm infuse their connection. Their strokes would forever be bonded. He searched Lorif's eyes to see if she felt it too. He could not say that she did because she said nothing.

She picked up her basket of fruit and handed it to him. "Thank you so much, Tindle." Lorif kissed him on the cheek again, and he felt tingles erupt in his entire body. "I am so grateful, but I must be getting back before Fih wakes and becomes worried." Then Lorif escaped into the shadows of what was left of the night.

And so, the days melted into nights, dawns into sunsets, and the four children of the painter danced around the strokes in magnificent and evasive ways. Where once Priloc felt his brothers were his closest companions, he now perceived a distance between them. Fih spent his moments enthralled with Lorif, which Priloc saw as beautiful. But he coveted her, and there was a looming secrecy about him that rejected Priloc's love in a way he could not describe. Tindle, who once told his brothers everything, was deceptive and protective of his private moments. He no longer invited his brothers to Cataphet's caves. Priloc witnessed how his brother hovered over Lorif as though his hope was to swoop in at any spare moment. Priloc detected how his brother continually erected walls to hide behind and away from Priloc's love. Lorif was purely genuine in every way. She lived out her days in service and gratitude for the strokes they were given. Priloc found her to be the safest place of them all because he knew she shared herself with vulnerability and he could do the same.

So it was that when Lorif came to Priloc with tears, drowning in an ocean of despair, he knew something was terribly wrong.

Priloc was sitting by the ocean on his favorite log, communing with the waves, when she approached. He heard her sobs before he saw her face. Priloc stood to comfort the weeping Lorif with open arms.

"Dear Lorif, what in the strokes ails you?"

She could not form words. Her body shook with agony. So Priloc held her still, without words, without expectation, simply with presence. When her tears dried up, she still could not speak, but together they sat on the log and stared at one another in silence. Hours passed and still they sat. When Lorif spoke, her voice broke and she nearly whispered truths she wished had not needed to be spoken.

"Priloc, I have had subtle correspondences with my sisters through a book gifted to me by the Seven Sisters themselves. It is called a Pierses. There are two volumes. One is in my possession, and the other is with Goyta and Orail." Priloc's stomach turned. He anticipated what was coming next. "I received these books the eve before Tindle came to me and offered his services, to go to my sisters and share my sorrow and give them this token to keep our connection alive. But in the pages are many incantations, and I got curious. I performed one where I should have entered the dreams of my sisters. But they were not here. They were not of this world. Instead, I hovered over a pool of rainbow colors and I knew their essence was no longer within the strokes." She put her face in her hands and wailed. Priloc wailed with her.

"How did Goyta and Orail's strokes pass beyond the River Tins? I am faced with two dreadful truths: Fih did something to harm my sisters, or Tindle did. Because both your brothers claim to have received blessings from my dearest of kin, when I have not heard them myself. What will I do?" Lorif hurtled herself into Priloc's arms, and together they shook with disbelief. Because what was to come next would forever change the strokes, and they both knew it.

At dawn, Lorif and Priloc entered the meadow. Fih was furious.

"What is this treachery?" he growled as they approached.

Tindle was quick to get ill-tempered as well. "This is horrendous. You spent the night with Priloc? That is where your allegiance goes when you are not with Fih? You choose him?"

"I choose truth. Which of you will tell me the truth?" Tindle and Fih looked at each other, confused.

"What truth do you seek, Lorif? What lie could send you into the arms of my brother?" Fih accused.

"I want to convene in the caves of Cataphet," she demanded.

"Why would you soil my home with your betrayal?"

"I did not betray you, Tindle, but your lies will come to light in the shadows of Cataphet. That, I am certain."

"How have you deceived my dearest love?" Fih accused.

"Do not pretend to be innocent, lover. I feel you are both on trial for your deception. And where I have been fooled, Cataphet will not be, as Priloc assures me."

Both brothers turned their venom toward Priloc.

"Coward."

"Fiend." They threw insult after insult at Priloc, and all he could do was weep. His heart was breaking into a million pieces, because he no longer knew the brothers he adored. Lorif and Priloc began to walk towards Cataphet. Tindle objected wildly but they persisted. Fih tried to push, pull, and command that they stop this onslaught of accusations, but still they persisted. When the mouth of the cave was in view, Fih and Tindle grew more desperate, but still Priloc and Lorif persisted. Cataphet welcomed them openly, and it was clear that her virtue was intact and she would get to the truth.

Lorif was determined to understand what had happened to her sisters at all costs. She knew for certain that one of the two brothers had the answers she sought. Tindle caught up with Lorif and grabbed her arm, spinning her around. "You cannot think the worst of me, Lorif. I have only ever done what I felt was best for you."

She ripped her arm away. "With lies and deceit? I will learn the depth of your treachery indeed."

Fih came on Lorif's other side. "This is not becoming, accusations and threats… We have been so happy, have we not?"

"You cornered me into a bargain I was not prepared to make. I always thought it was queer my sisters never even bothered with a goodbye on the day I left. It was not in their nature to be cruel. I should have trusted what my heart said to me on that day—go to them, hug and kiss them farewell." Lorif began to cry. The emotions were overcoming her.

Cataphet sensed their arrival. "I told you that your actions would have significant consequences, Tindle."

Priloc noticed the strokes about them were beginning to act peculiarly, vibrating, pulsating, and around Lorif they began to spiral into a funnel, like a vortex. Priloc also saw a tether from Tindle to Lorif, and then another bond between Lorif and Fih. They were different but both extremely powerful connections.

Cataphet then addressed Fih, "You are a monster. I see it so clearly. You do not honor the strokes the painter has created. You desire only to defile and destroy.

"Tindle, where once was a child who honored the strokes and created beauty, you covet and create chains."

"Your words are lies, Cataphet! You know nothing of what you speak," Tindle argued. Priloc watched on as his brother Fih grew in rage.

"Brothers, we must calm ourselves. The truth may be revealed by you, and you can right this wrong," Priloc pleaded, but in his heart, he knew nothing could right this wrong for Lorif. Her strokes were still spiraling, creating a cyclone of energy about her.

Lorif was afraid she was going to explode with pain. She could feel everything moving in her and through her, as though a gate had been opened inside her. She was absorbing every sound, emotion and thought. Suddenly, she knew what neither of the brothers would tell her. She saw how Fih stabbed her sister Goyta in the belly and watched her strokes melt into a pool of color. Lorif saw how he did the same to sweet, accepting Orail. Both of their strokes left without essence as their souls passed to the River Tins.

Then her awareness turned to Tindle's deception. She saw how he coveted her. Lied to her about the state of her sisters, burned their homes and pretended to be them as he engaged with the Pierses. She saw his intentions with the Gattilak charm, how he desired to hold her close without her knowing.

It was too much.

Cataphet spoke once more. "I will expose the truth, so that if you are fortunate, your strokes will be made right."

What Priloc witnessed next is hardly describable in words. Fih and Tindle both reached for Lorif's arms, each grabbing hold and attempting to sweep her away from the truth. But Lorif stood strong for she already knew the truth. The brothers pulled at her in either direction. The hurricane of strokes that Lorif had become began to tear down the center, like a leaf may be torn. It was as though the world stood still as Priloc watched his brothers tear the one thing they both loved apart, trying to evade the evil things they had done, trying to escape the truth.

Lorif screamed but she could not stop the dismantling that had begun. She was caught in the middle of destruction and creation. For Fih, who valued destruction above everything else, and for Tindle, who had always created with purpose. Priloc tried to stop them when he realized they would destroy her in their war for her affections, for her love. He jumped in, attempting to hold the pieces of Lorif together, but alas, he felt her strokes dissolve in his arms. Then the vortex around her stopped, everything got eerily quiet, before a cacophony of sounds erupted from the space that was once Lorif, sending shockwaves in all directions, shattering the strokes of both his brothers simultaneously. It was only Priloc's strokes who were spared.

Priloc got to his feet in absolute disbelief, destitute. He looked around and could not believe what he saw. Everything had turned to shades of grey. The color was gone, the strokes were muted, and nowhere in this dull landscape was there even a particle left of Fih, Tindle or Lorif. They were gone, and he was alone.

❀

SUDDENLY, bile crept up my throat, and before I could manage to warn anyone else in the room, I was vomiting all over the floor.

Elias was instantly at my side, pulling my hair from my face. I communicated through our Rune. "I think it's the baby."

"Indeed? Morning sickness, already?"

I just nodded as another wave of nausea twisted in my belly. Ruit's voice filled both of our heads. "Are you okay? Surely that is not your fate, Ophelia."

"I know. I feel sick, perhaps from my condition."

"I see. That is a rarity for a Consu, but not impossible. Let's get you to a quiet chamber where you may lie down."

Elias agreed and helped me upright as I did everything I could to suppress another upheaval. He turned to Lucas. "Detain her while we determine our next course of action."

"With pleasure." Lucas promptly walked over to Esther.

I looked around the room before we made our exit, and I saw that the film was gone and the writings on the wall were vast and brilliant. I could spend lifetimes down here learning directly from the painter. "No need, my child," the voice said as we gently floated up into the Oracle's divination chamber.

"This way." Ruit pointed at the stairs, and in a few moments my sweet husband was sweeping me into a room with gold curtains, a large mirror, and an elaborate four-poster bed with a creamy velvet cover and several throw pillows. I instinctively knew this was Aurora's room.

The two men hovered about me for a minute. Elias cleaned up the vomit from my hair and clothes, and Ruit assessed what tea he would make.

"I will return with a concoction to help ease your stomach."

Elias took a seat beside me and gazed down at my belly. "Already creating a stir, little one." He placed his hand on my stomach, and I noticed something that I hadn't before. I had a baby bump. I counted backwards in my head. It had only been three days since we conceived. Elias noticed it too. "May I?" He lifted my shirt to expose a clear baby bump.

Ruit's voice interrupted our moment of shock. "It has only been a few days!" It was the first time I had ever heard the Alchemist sound alarmed, only adding to the anxiety of the anomaly.

"Is it because of the Paradigm Tremor? Or because I'm Ulus?"

"Or because I am Sulu?" Elias added.

Ruit handed me the tea. "Drink this." His hands moved toward my belly. "May I?"

"Of course," I said as I took a sip of the tea, and instantly the nausea subsided, replaced with the uneasiness of anxiety.

Ruit palpated my stomach gently as we both watched him expectantly. "I will consult Sorcerer," was all he said before promptly leaving the room.

We stared at each other for a long moment, both of our hands cupping my womb space and each other. "I feel she is safe," Elias said assuredly.

A big, toothy grin spread across my face. I couldn't help it. Because he had simultaneously validated my sense as well—that the baby was perfectly healthy, and that she was a girl.

Ruit returned a few moments later, and with him Lucas and Yessica. Lucas was tossing Nandi's staff around, and it irritated me for some reason. It was too casual a gesture for the significance of the item.

"Can you just set that down, please?"

He put his hand up in surrender. "Who am I to challenge the pregnant Ulus?" He set the consolidated staff on a nightstand beside the bed.

Ruit read something from the pages of Sorcerer. "It appears the time spent in the Solomon Islands likely sped up your gestation process. The strokes move differently in the depths of the world. Your ability to absorb all of the strokes around you, including Giant strokes, has sped up everything. Not that different from how Viraclay's parents sped up his process."

Lucas nudged Elias with his elbow. "There is some irony here, don't you think?"

Elias just shook his head.

Yessica took a seat beside me and placed her hand on my shoulder. "Is that bad? Will Ophelia and the baby be okay?"

"I believe so, except that we are preparing to enter a battle and I have no idea how accelerated this pregnancy will be."

Lucas took his place behind his wife. "Another plot twist. It's nothing these two can't handle." It was a comment meant to make light of the situation, but it only aggravated me more. Apparently, pregnant Olly lost her sense of humor. I refrained from saying anything, but Elias could feel the tension.

"We will navigate this." He kissed my forehead. And of course, he was right, but damn the strokes, I was ready for a stroke of luck and a little less challenge.

"Perhaps I can create a tonic to slow the growth," Ruit suggested, and although I appreciated the thought, I was not going to take anything that further interfered with my pregnancy.

"Let's talk about that later. Right now, I think we need to discuss what we've just witnessed in the cave and figure out how we want to handle the Esther situation." I needed the spotlight off my baby for a moment, and these were very important things to consider as well.

"I, for one, am grateful that Viraclay and I aren't fighting over Olly's affections anymore. That would've been eerily similar."

Yessica elbowed her husband. "Can you please focus?"

I was grateful for her interference, because the mommy hormones were stretching my patience.

"The Gattilak charm is the same as the hairsy charm. What are the odds of that? That I would end up with the very same bracelet as Lorif."

"I have a theory about that. Just as the Sorcerer stone always makes its way to the hands of the great Alchemist of the age, perhaps the Gattilak charm is the same?" Ruit theorized.

Yesi agreed. "That resonates. There is truth in that."

I felt it too.

"I would agree with that assessment, but there is one thing that I struggle with in regard to the creation stories as a whole. In what order did these events occur? Did Fih stab his brother before or after he killed Lorif's sisters? When did the brothers create The Cathedral, since Cataphet was there since the beginning?" Yessica asked.

The painter's voice echoed in my mind. "It is all happening all at once. Time is another illusion of separation."

"What does that fucking mean?!" I shouted aloud, and everyone in the room jumped at my outburst.

Elias pulled the hair from my face and tucked it behind my ear, worry lines across his forehead. "What does what mean, my love?"

"Malarin answered Yessica's question." Everyone leaned in excitedly. "It is all happening all at once. Time is another illusion of separation."

"What does that fucking mean?" Lucas promptly echoed my sentiment.

LUCAS

*R*uit was waiting for me and Yessica in the hall as Stalt and Claudia approached. "Who is watching the wicked witch?"

"Jillian, and trust me, she won't let that woman move an inch," Claudia asserted. "Honestly, we might return to a beheaded Esther. Jillian deserves that retribution more than most."

I had to admit, I wouldn't be sad to stumble upon an Esther corpse.

"We need to leave this place. Fetzle's just contacted me. She is outside the Orb Forest, looking for where they are holding Princess Chaness, and she has reason to believe the Oracle is moving and it is in this direction."

"The High Priestess of the giants said we needed to be quick."

"Do you think Ophelia is up for the travel?" Yessica looked to Ruit.

"I do not believe she should travel by troll shuttle anymore. I suspect all the time spent in the depths is leaving a mark on the baby."

"I don't want to move Esther above ground. We need that bitch as secure as possible."

"I agree, Lucas. That is why you will escort Esther with Stalt, Claudia, Jillian and your wife, while I will get Ophelia and Viraclay somewhere safe until we can reconvene at The Cathedral. I've just received a transmission from Aremis. He has his own findings he would like to share from his excursion with Napitae."

"That was fast," Yesi read my mind. I was also grateful for Olly's sake. This would help her feel a lot better. One less person to worry about.

"Apparently, since the Originals are standing with us, they asked Napitae to make his errand brief."

Claudia was looking around at each of us like we had lost our damn minds. "Stalt, you have a lot to catch me up on. But let me tell you what I know before we part ways. Aurora and Clive are in cahoots with the powrie King OAD. They have been creating the Orbs from some super battery that the king has underground in Russia."

"Princess Chaness," Yesi and I said at the same time.

Claudia just shrugged us off. "Yeah, maybe. I don't know what it is, only that creepy Clive was able to recharge his personal batteries really quickly with the Orbs. I can also say with almost absolute certainty that they still have at least fifteen captives. One of which is our daughter." Claudia looked up to her husband. "I'm so sorry, Stalty. I tried."

"We will get her," he assured his Atoa, and I hoped for their sake that he was right.

"Whatever Aurora is up to requires the power of the Orbs and several Conduits to succeed. But the alliances within the Nebas are tenuous at best. They are all confused by the change of leadership, and although they despised Esther, they knew the agenda. They grow suspicious of what the Oracle's desired outcome is. Aurora was right to be concerned about Esther's absence. It will create more dissension. Plus, they don't have any more poison to keep the captives sedated, and I'm not sure they have any antidote either. The attack on Chernobyl really fucked up her plans. Her visions seem to be failing."

"What do you think she is trying to do?" I asked.

"The strokes if I know, but I will say this. Our daughter Aurelia is the most powerful Varon of our time. Stalt is the most powerful of his faction, and they tried to abduct him. It seems to me that she was attempting to create a super weapon of some sort."

I internally chuckled at what my dear old dad would think of that assertion.

Ruit looked behind at the long, dark corridor that led to the Oracle's prophetic chamber. He spoke so quietly I had to strain to hear him, even with my super-hearing. "Three or more present in her chamber, and she expressed the powers of a Sulu."

Elias and Ophelia stepped into the hall. "She is creating a Super Sulu," Elias stated as plain as day. A revelation that was the equivalent to an atomic bomb in our world. "But to what end? And what these Orbs have to do with the mechanism she has coined a Sulu Wheel, I dare not speculate."

ESTHER

Jillian stared at me, pure hatred in her eyes. None of it mattered to me anymore. My life was for nothing. My strokes were forsaken since the moment of my inception. The only beings I ever loved had been ripped away from this world while I obediently catered to their annihilator. I don't even know when or where the hex was woven into my timeline.

I wished they would just kill me. But that would be far too merciful. I would be some sort of bait for them in this war. In this case, it was no less than what I deserved. My only shred of solace was that perhaps I would be the one who would kill the Oracle. I could not fathom them giving me a weapon or the opportunity, but by the strokes, if I was ever given a single measure of grace beyond all this misfortune by Dalinkas himself, it would be this answered prayer.

That I may be the hand that slays my mother.

ELIAS

*R*uit had transported me and Olly via an incantation he found in Sorcerer, teleporting us to the Haven that Aremis was staying at outside Boston in the United States. It was quaint, a perfect place to catch our breath.

"I'll be back, my love. Please rest." I tucked her in gently and kissed her forehead. Her belly had swollen even more, nearly doubled in size. It was taxing her. I could feel it, although she put on a good show. Still, we also sensed that our baby girl was safe.

"Tell him I want to see him straight away. I need an Aremis hug."

"Indeed. He will get the message." I was nearly to the door.

"Baby?"

"Yes?"

"Something is bothering me about what we saw in Delphi."

"What is that?"

"Why would Clive want to keep that truth hidden? It didn't even mention hobgoblins."

"You are so brilliant. We must be missing something. Can we revisit it after my meeting?"

"Yes. Sadie and I will be here, waiting for you."

I turned around and looked at her with what must have been a ridiculously goofy grin. "Sadie?"

"Do you like it?"

I considered the name. Let it roll around in my head and off my tongue. "I love it! Sadie Mae Kraus. It has a ring to it."

"Mae, huh? I love it."

I skipped over to her and kissed her on the forehead once more, then her belly. "Rest." Then I was out the door.

"Where is Miss Ophelia?" Aremis asked as I met him in the hall.

"She is resting. Her condition is peculiar." It was the best I could do to describe my poor wife's accelerated pregnancy, as if bearing a child in the middle of a war was not challenging enough.

"Her condition?"

"The baby appears to be gestating at an accelerated rate."

"Like father, like son." Aremis patted me on the shoulder. "Are mother and child safe?"

"Indeed, and she wishes to see you just after we are done." I loved Aremis so much. He was family in every way. "I hate to break it to you though." He looked at me inquisitively. "Ophelia and I have both had the sense that she may be carrying a darling daughter who will take after her mother."

"A little girl? Like father, like daughter it is, then." He patted my shoulder with pride. "How is it that this miraculous conception is growing with acceleration?"

"Ruit believes it has to do with our travels through the troll lines and the Solomon Islands. As an Ulus, Ophelia absorbs all the energies she encounters. Only the strokes may know how that affects a pregnancy. The timing is not ideal, and the unknown creates a distraction."

"There will always be distractions; this I have learned well. It's good that she rests. I will share my news with you and Ruit. You can decide what to make of it and how to relay it to your wife."

Just then, Sparkle came from around the corner. "Aremis!" she shouted, and jumped into his arms, kissing him all over his face. I had to turn away from the intimate moment. I had not realized their relationship had progressed to kissing.

"Sparkle, I'm so glad you got my invitation to join us here in Boston." From the corner of my eye, I saw Aremis gently kiss her forehead and put her down. "I was just going to share my findings with Elias and Ruit. With his permission, perhaps you can join us?"

Sparkle had become one of Olly's greatest friends. I knew that whatever was shared would make its way to her ears, either through Aremis or my wife.

"Indeed." I gestured toward the study. Ruit was already there. "Shall we?" We entered the room, and I shut the door. The three of us took a seat in the center, where there were two large chase lounges. Sparkle plopped next to Aremis, getting as close as she could without being on his lap. I would need to ask Aremis about this transformation of their relationship later. It made me happy to see both of them enamored. They were two of the kindest people I had ever known. I took the lounge across from them, and Ruit joined me. "Out with it. What have you learned about the Ulus and about your own anomaly?"

Aremis appeared uncomfortable, and that made me anxious. "In the beginning, there were six strokes. Six colors. The original strokes were indeed the dragons. Cataphet was the first of her kind, and she alone possesses all the aspects of the elements that the dragons manifest. She harnesses earth, wind, fire and water effortlessly. All other dragons align with a single element.

"The second strokes were those of the trolls. They are able to reflect the gifts of all living strokes and the magics they actualize. Trolls are not just vessels in the way that they shuttle around the earth, but also in how they demonstrate other creatures' gifts.

"Next to be painted were the Keepers, Ratatoskr, the Niffler and Adanc. Together they could watch over the water, Adanc, the land, the Niffler and Ratatoskr, the trees. The siblings were charged with skills to move seamlessly through each layer of the world.

"Fourth to be created were the powries. The painter saw that not all of his creation would be peaceable, because he gave them free will. To absorb the potential pain, he painted a stroke that would flourish, even in the midst of strife.

"The family of fae was the most diverse of all the strokes, branching out into a million variations of magic from nymphs to faeries and everything in between. Before Conduits were created and before humans, the fae were the shepherds of the world, charged with overseeing every plant, stone and flame. To bear witness to the beauty that was ever evolving in every moment.

"Giants were the sixth to be painted, demonstrative in size and intellectual in their nature. The giants were created to weave kinship and harmony into the relationships of all the beings that dwelled on the earth."

Aremis was looking at me for recognition. There was something he said that he wanted me to pick up on.

"Where did you hear of this, and how does this pertain to Viraclay or Ophelia?" Ruit asked.

"It pertains to the entire Conduit world, rather."

"How so, Aremis?" Sparkle's sweet voice had a touch of angst in it.

"We are all descendants of the original six strokes."

"What? Are you trying to tell me I am part dragon or fairy?" Sparkle asked in disbelief. My thoughts mirrored hers.

"It is true. I have seen it."

"Where?"

I answered for him. "On the walls of a cave?"

He nodded solemnly. "How did you know, Elias?"

"We encountered something similar in Delphi. I suspected then that it was not the only place of its kind. Remnants of stories, of our histories that have been forgotten, left by Malarin himself, so that one day we may remember where we came from."

"This was one such place. This cave was regarded very highly by the fire dragons as a womb of origin for their creation. Curiously, it was literally beneath the Tartar village you and Miss Ophelia visited, the very one she asked me to drop in on."

"Curious indeed." Nothing was ever a coincidence. It was always divinely orchestrated. We had all experienced enough of this world to know that.

"The Tartar man, Wailee, greeted me with great hospitality. He somehow seemed to know I was traveling with a dragon, although Napitae never showed himself. I felt that Wailee could somehow see the strokes. Even if he did not know that was what he was witnessing. His account of the Ulus appeared to verify my assumption. Wailee explained that he gave Ulus Ophelia the Blessing Way because his lineage had been instructed by the last dragon to perform the rites should another Ulus manifest. The instructions were passed through his ancestors for thousands of years. After his grandfather shamed the family by failing to protect the Loktpi, he knew he had to do better."

This village was charged with two magical rites, from two different sources. What were the odds of that, I wondered.

"When he saw Ophelia, he knew exactly what she was. He performed the rites anchoring her to this world and all that is within it and without."

My mind was racing with potentiality. I, too, had had a blessing from Tulaswaga, and if it were the same rites, it would anchor my being to this world as well.

"That is why we created a Paradigm Tremor. The Blessing Way anchored our fates to the fate of the world."

"What?" Sparkle looked at me, aghast.

"Both Ophelia and I were anchored to the world by the Blessing Way rites."

"I'm so confused. What does this have to do with the original six strokes?"

Sparkle had me there. I had gone down a rabbit hole in another direction. I looked expectantly at Aremis for the answer.

"I am a descendant from the fire dragon stroke. My sweet Sparkle, you are likely a descendant from a fae family stroke. But the Sulu and Ulus, they have very unique origins. The Sulu is a descendant of Cataphet's strokes, and the Ulus was not created by Chitchakor, but a manifestation of his painting."

I put my hand to my mouth. By Malarin's brush, *what does this mean?*

LUCAS

While the others went to meet up with Aremis, Yesi, Claudia, Stalt, Jillian and I were transporting the prisoner. I would have rather killed her but, upon Olly's insistence, I had agreed to taking her somewhere safe and secluded. I knew just the place. The Garden, a troll prison located in the heart of Listy and impenetrable. Although Fetzle was busy with the mission of finding and releasing Princess Chaness, she still insisted on being our shuttle and taking us to the Garden. Plus, we needed her to get the Staff of Banishment and the Dirk of Inverness to the High Priestess.

I handed both weapons to the queen as we entered her shuttle. Something was off. I noticed it right away. Fetzle's digs were cleaner than usual. I looked around and was surprised by how tidy it was. "Hey, Queen, are you expecting company? This place looks nice."

Fetzle looked up at me like she had been caught red-handed in the cookie jar. I was pretty sure trolls couldn't physically blush, but if they could, she would've.

"No! Fetzle just moves things a littles for her friends. Thats all Fetzle do's, Lucas!"

My eyes got wide and I looked at Yesi to get validation that there was clearly more here. I wanted to press it. Yesi shook her head. I wished I could read her mind. *Did she know something I didn't? I bet this had something to do with the emperor.*

"Well, thanks," was all I could think to say, and I walked away. Stalt and Claudia were taking their job very seriously and holding Esther encased in a dried lava bubble. I was impressed. I knew they could get her to Listy just fine. I wanted to make sure the troll prison was as fortified as it was rumored to be. It was for trolls, after all, not sneaky Conduit villains.

I took a seat by my wife. "So, you know something I don't?"

"Yep. As a matter of fact, I do."

I looked at her inquisitively. "Well, Mrs. Healey, I didn't know our terms and conditions policy had changed to include secrets and tomfoolery."

"You should read the fine print." Yesi didn't look at me. She only smirked, staring off into the distance. She was sexy as hell.

"Touché."

"Fetzle says we are heres, at the gardens." The shuttle immediately came to a halt. Which was a strange sensation, because it wasn't exactly obvious we were moving either. "Fetzle thinks her friends be's carefuls. The gardens ares very brights."

I took Yessica's hand in mine. "I think the queen forgot you are as bright as the sun." I kissed her cheek and pulled her in front of me. "After you, my tricky little lantern."

"Don't worry, I will elucidate soon enough."

"Was that a punny joke you just made?"

She giggled over her shoulder, and I had to bite my lip to fight back how badly I wanted her right then and there. We exited the shuttle into a cavernous courtyard full of light. From what I gathered, it was actual sunlight, but it was so bright it was hard to tell for certain. There were no trees, but mounds of green grass were strewn throughout the landscape for miles. I looked up at Fetzle. She was basically translucent in this light. I had only ever seen her in the shade of a tree during the day. But here and now, you could nearly see through her.

"Fetzle told yous, Lucas. It's a nastys place, this Gardens."

Again, I looked around, and this time I found it hard to believe this was a prison sentence. The Garden was lovely, lush with flowers and an endless meadow.

"Overs heres, Fetzle thinks, Stalts." She pointed to a spot between two mounds. "This spots be good."

Yesi and I followed the couple, while Esther said nothing. *What could she say?* I'm sure she was expecting to be killed at any point. One wrong word, and if Claudia, Jillian or Stalt didn't do it, I might. Stalt moved some earth and quickly submerged the lava bubble into the ground and buried it, so that only Esther's head was in view. Fetzle put her hand on the dirt, and I saw a million roots crawl all over the tomb that encased Esther's body. *Cool trick.*

"My Queen," a male voice coughed behind me, and I nearly jumped out of my skin. One of the mounds had spoken.

Fetzle moved quicker than I'd ever seen her, pouncing on top of the mound directly behind me. There was a cracking noise, and a moan of pain. "You cannot speak to Queen Fetzle, yous disgusting betrayers, Pladzal." Then she spat, and I only then realized the mounds were trolls. The bodies of trolls that had slowly turned to stone. Pladzal's eyes blinked ever so slowly, and I saw the tiny roots were covering every inch of him, plastering him to the ground, where he sat hunched over.

"This is Pladzal? The asshole who betrayed your parents and took your queendom?"

Fetzle spat again. "Ugly Pladzal."

I guess I forgot that part.

"He is already turning to stone," Jillian observed.

"Fetzle knows time is different in the Gardens, and the sun makes our bodies to stones quickly."

"Will I turn to stone as well, Troll Queen?" Esther scoffed.

"You should be so lucky!" Now I was the one spitting. Esther rolled her eyes and looked away.

"Fetzle doesn'ts knows about nasty Conduits, but Fetzle thinks that stones would be nice. Fetzle is readys to go. Calt needs Fetzle in Russias."

The other three quickly followed the Queen without another thought. I was uneasy about this. It looked secure enough, but Esther could talk to this Pladzal asshole. *Is that a good idea?*

"What do you think, baby girl? Does this look like it's secure enough?"

"Once we leave, there is no way for Esther to get out. That's why there are no trees."

I looked around. She was right. "How do you think Fetzle gets in and out, then?"

"Fetzle has the only keys theres be," she shouted from inside her shuttle. "Lucas and Yessica, it's times to go. Fetzle doesn't wants to be late of the giant kings. Fetzle's needs to get thems the weapons and finds the Princess. Hurrys, hurrys!"

I raised an eyebrow at my wife. "Oh, now I see. That's why the shuttle is clean."

Yesi nodded dubiously.

"Are we going somewhere?"

"I will leave that decision up to you."

*R*uit, Aremis and Elias sat across from me, waiting for my reaction, I suppose. I couldn't muster up a reaction that would have adequately represented the astonishment I was experiencing.

"Why do you think Wailee's village was visited by two separate Conduits and given two separate missions?"

Elias looked at me like maybe I had not heard the punchline of the joke, but Ruit didn't miss a beat.

"My theory is that it was because the village is above the womb cave of the fire dragons. It seems to me that the more magic beholden to a place, especially in its origins, the more magic is drawn there. I certainly felt the pull to that village, and I did not know why at the time. But just like the great Alchemist Yilliana appreciated the power that vibrated through every blade of grass in Atlantis, I too was drawn to the power imbued to the Tartar land."

"I like that theory. It resonates."

"Olly, did you hear the part about being a stroke that was not created by the painter?"

I turned to my husband while trying to keep my tone neutral. "Yes, dear, and I also heard you're a descendant of Cataphet. Which kind of explains why your eyes are the same shade as hers, as well as that incredible mosaic window in The Cathedral. You are all blessed with that golden green charm."

He looked at me curiously.

"That is an incredible observation, Ophelia," Aremis validated.

"Thanks. I can be pretty sharp sometimes." I'd noticed the resemblance after my first encounter with Cataphet. Her eyes were so entrancing, and I'd been obsessed with Elias' eyes for nearly a year and a half of my life. It was nice that I could now connect the dots. "I am also sharp enough to follow the details of Aremis' story." I was being snarky, but the mommy hormones were keeping me on edge, and finding out your lineage is even more mysterious than you thought is a bit of a downer. I was not feeling at my personal best.

"Of course you are. I am sorry if I offended you." Elias kissed the back of my hand and I immediately softened. The poor guy was going through the same revelation rollercoaster as I was.

"Sorry, baby. It's the damn hormones."

He just nodded.

"Honestly, I'm not that surprised. Remember the High Priestess said, 'Your strokes are of rare origin. The collaboration of what has always been and what was not meant to be allows you to bridge the two fates.' Now, I don't know what that means, but it seems to coincide with this new fun fact."

Ruit nodded and continued. "Knowing what we know about the origin of the first Ulus, we could surmise that the strokes Olly is descending from manifested during the demise of the brothers and Lorif."

"But how can I be a descendant of someone who died before having children?"

"That, I do not know," Ruit admitted.

"It's not a lineage that is inherited, dear Miss Ophelia. I believe it is present in the soul," Aremis explained. "They were described as splinters."

"Well, how did we inherit splinters? How did the energy splinter to begin with?"

"All excellent questions… that I cannot answer," Aremis said.

"For the time being, I say we focus on what we do know. The Blessing Way ceremonies that Olly and I received have anchored us to this world. Should we attempt to sever them?"

I was following my husband's train of thought. "Could that stop the Paradigm Tremor we've caused?"

"I do not believe so. I feel that these events have been set in motion with a greater purpose. We need more information before we attempt to change anything. For now, the best we can do is pursue a victory against Aurora and the Nebas," Ruit maintained.

Everything that had led us to this moment seemed divinely orchestrated. Including the Blessing Ways. I had to believe that what was unfolding only needed patience and trust. We would understand it all when Malarin was ready to reveal it. That didn't mean waiting around for the answers was any easier.

ESTHER

I looked around as best I could from my tomb in the ground. Nothing but troll remains for miles. Honestly, I didn't care. The silence was welcome. My thoughts were jumbled with regrets and waves of realizations. The Oracle had betrayed me. My mother was the true villain of my story. My beloved and I had been manipulated and discarded. My father had been abused and left to pay for her crimes. There were no greater fools than the ones she kept closest to her chest.

"What are your offenses?" a raspy male voice spoke in Asagi and interrupted my torment.

"No worse than yours, I assure you."

"You betrayed your kind while in a haze of a hex and destroyed everything you may have held dear."

"What?" Was this monster reading my mind? Trolls had many tricks. They could express all kinds of creatures' gifts in a multitude of ways. There was no way of knowing what trickery he may have up his sleeve. "How could you have known about the hex?"

"You were hexed too?" The voice laughed. "You are mocking me, aren't you?"

"I am not. I don't find pleasure in being toyed with, troll." I was not going to entertain this charade.

"Who are you?"

The troll couldn't see me. I was behind him, his back hunched over, his head hung in the opposite direction. He might not even know I was a Conduit.

"What is it to you? You only need to know I will not be toyed with."

"I have no reason to toy with you. I am slowly dying in the most excruciating way possible while identified as a traitor and murderer of my people. Games are for the folly, and I have nothing but sorrow. Nevertheless, I will leave you be."

I exhaled loudly. My curiosity was piqued. If he wasn't toying with me, then we had an eerily similar story to tell.

"How were you hexed?"

"How, I do not know, but by whom appears to be obvious."

"Obvious to who? My patience grows thin, troll," I hissed.

He laughed louder than I expected from his voice. "What will your impatience do here, woman? Will you storm off in a fit?"

"You are unlikeable."

"That makes two of us, which is probably part of what got us here to begin with. I have never been the most congenial of trolls. Perhaps if I had been, I could have won the hand of Queen Fetzle without dealing in the underhandedness that put me in the grips of a plot to destroy the world."

"You destroyed the troll world? You must have failed, because you are now in prison and the queen is back on her throne," I scoffed.

"I did heinous things to the troll world, but my undertakings stretch far further than that. What I remember is foggy, but what I know is that the fiend who kept me hexed is in coterie with monsters extremely worse than me or you. These monsters will see the whole world burn. It all started when the Rittles were stolen from the kings and queens of old. Now, all of us are sitting ducks, and the final act will take everyone by surprise."

"Be plain, male troll, and stop speaking in riddles. Who hexed you?"

"Why, the hobgoblin Clive, of course, and his mistress, the Oracle Aurora."

LUCAS

essica and I decided to go back down to the Solomon Islands with Fetzle. We didn't know how we could help but there had to be something. The giants were reassembling the Staff of Banishment and organizing the efforts to free Princess Chaness. Plus, it was cute watching the emperor and the queen awkwardly flirt.

Yessica and I followed Fetzle as she carried the Staff and the Dirk down to the chamber. *We collected them only a day earlier? Or has it been less than a day?* "How long has it been since we were here?" I was suddenly acutely aware of how discombobulated I felt.

"Time moves differently below the earth, Lucas Healey," the High Priestess answered my question as we entered the room. For a giant, she was awfully stealthy. "I am not simply a giant."

And apparently, she can read my thoughts.

"As one of the Seven Sisters and keepers of the Thirteenth time-line, my abilities are vast."

"So why don't you just snap your fingers and make this all go away?" I asked as Calt and Ropen entered the room and Adanc came into view.

"We are keepers, not manipulators."

I looked at her skeptically.

"Then why are you helping us now?" my wife took the words right out of my mouth.

"We can be called to action, as long as the action resonates with our core essence and does not make direct changes to the timeline."

Fetzle cocked her head. "Fetzle thinks this is directs changes be. We's getting the Staffs and the Princesses."

"Dear Queen, both of these tasks could be achieved without me. It is yet to be seen whether you will be successful in freeing Princess Chaness, and it will remain to be seen if you will indeed triumph with the Staff of Banishment or ultimately relinquish it to the other side."

"You mean the bad guys." I asserted.

The High Priestess looked at me in such a way that I knew I wasn't going to like what came out of her mouth next. "Are you a *good* guy now, Lucas Healey? Is good or bad that easy to define or label? You murdered many people who were on the good side. Does that not make you bad? Or is it a certain number of bodies one must collect to be categorized as bad? I see your heart and it is neither pure, nor tainted by your deeds. You love fiercely and have hated just as passionately. We are all a collaboration of dark and light. Thank the creator for it. Without the darkness, you would not recognize the light in yourself or others. You were designed with a divine duality, as was every other being. When you Conduits finally realize this unshakeable truth, you may finally stop this endless cycle of conflict." She took her eyes away from me and began to walk toward the tapestry. "Now, the Oracle is an entirely different stroke. But there is no need to dissect that anomaly at the moment."

I felt chastised and also a growing curiosity. But we had more to do than talk about the good, the bad and the ugly. Calt came up behind Fetzle and touched the top of her head. I could've sworn her whole body blushed. She handed him the Dirk and the Staff while he passed her the Crown of Thorns, her crown. It was not very impressive. The crown needed a good polishing at the very least. It was huge, built with a variety of random stones, and looked like a ten-year-old might have designed it, not Fih.

Fetzle started to lift the crown above her head when the Priestess stopped her. "Not yet! When the crown adorns the true Queen's head, the assembly of the staff commences. We must be careful. It took the power of two Rittles and my essence to dismantle the staff. But the energy exchange did not stop there. The power in these Rittles, the Golden Spool of Thread, and the Crown of Thorns are the wedge that has kept the Staff of Banishment disassembled and hidden. Without their powerful strokes, the staff would have been found, or worse—reconstructed itself."

"So this thing has a mind of its own? And if so, why didn't the Dirk of Inverness find its way back to King OAD?" Calt asked.

"Alas, I do not know what was done to enchant and detach the Dirk because that was done by another. I am only hoping to circumvent it. And yes, just like all the other strokes ever created, the Rittles prefer to be whole," the High Priestess explained while she situated the Golden Spool of Thread meticulously in a circle near the center of the room. I noticed the etchings on the floor. They must be specific for this ritual.

"Fetzle wants to knows what's this sillys crowns do?"

That was a good question.

"Your grandmother never told you?"

"Fetzle doesn'ts thinks shes knews."

"Well that would explain why she gave it up so easily. It is the second most powerful Rittle, next to the Staff of Banishment. The Crown of Thorns fortifies those who serve it with their allegiance, no matter the stroke."

"Fetzle does nots understands fortifies."

"Those who vow their allegiance to the Crown become significantly harder to kill. The only weapon that may smite them down with absolute certainty is a Rittle."

Fetzle's eyes got big and then, immediately, gelatinous tears began to fall. "Fetzle knows this coulds saves her people." Calt began stroking the top of her head affectionately. "Fetzle knows this magics could haves saved hers parents." Calt picked the Queen up and comforted her in his arms.

I pulled Yesi into my arms. It was such a touching moment.

"I dare not cut your grief short, Queen, but time is valuable." Just then, four more priestesses entered the room, Ratatoskr behind them. He waved at his enormous sister and took a seat beside Ropen.

Yesi and I took our seats. "Something is nagging at me," I leaned in to tell my wife.

"Can it wait?"

I nodded because I couldn't quite gather exactly what it was. The High Priestess looked at me with a sideways grin, and it dawned on me. She knew what I couldn't quite grasp. There was a piece of this we were missing, a very obvious piece of what was about to happen.

"Let us begin." All five Priestesses sang in unison. Calt stood with the Staff and the Dirk, ready to place them with the other knife. The Queen stood patiently waiting for instruction with her crown. Two more Priestesses entered through an adjacent door. They promptly walked over and adjusted Fetzle to be in one of the other circles opposite the Spool of Thread.

I wondered if this was safe for my friend to be participating in.

The pressure in the center of the room was heavy, similar to the sensation of humidity, but dry. "Place the final elements of the Staff of Banishment in the center, Emperor," the High Priestess ordered before taking her position in the third circle on the ground.

The Golden Spool of Thread was picked up by a second Priestess. She held it above her head. Then the remaining five Priestesses danced in and out, weaving around the three circles, chanting words too quickly for me to decipher, or maybe in a language I didn't know. Then they moved out of the interior circles, now dancing around the perimeter and chanting even louder. The air in the room buzzed with energy. Faster and louder, faster and louder, and I thought about how this ritual was created. *Who would know this type of magic?* I quickly concluded that it must come from the Seven Sisters.

The room suddenly appeared foggy and my skin felt hot. I glanced around to see if anyone else was suffering from the weird sensation. I could tell that my wife also looked uncomfortable in her seat. I touched the small of her back, but she was fixated on what was happening. The five Priestesses stopped dancing. Their bodies elevated from the ground and continued rising as they resumed the chant. They raised the pitch, and the sensations took over my body again.

I wanted to make sure Yesi was okay, that this wasn't too unbearable for her. Before I could ask, the chanting stopped. The bodies rose higher still. They hit the ceiling then burst into ash, sparkling iridescent ash.

"Now! Put your crown on now, Queen."

Fetzle didn't hesitate. She placed the Crown of Thorns on her head. Her posture immediately changed. It was like she was stretched out and straightened up. The next thing happened so quickly that I almost missed it. The Priestess holding the Thread sang a brilliant melodic note and burst into the same shimmering ash as the Golden Spool of Thread fell to the floor. All eyes shot to the High Priestess, who was gyrating and vibrating, humming and moaning all at once. It was bizarre, yet somehow erotic. Her voice echoed in the wind. "All must pay allegiance to the Crown." Then she burst into ash, a cacophony of sound erupted from the center of the circles, and the Staff of Banishment was restored.

Everyone seemed to come out of the magical daze all at once, getting to their feet. A swarm of Priestesses came out of nowhere and began to weep openly, sifting through the sprinkle of ash that had scattered around the room. I watched as Fetzle picked up the Staff of Banishment in amazement, admiring it with an inquisitive look on her face.

"I feel different. I feel whole," Fetzle spoke eloquently, and my jaw dropped. "It feels like my entire lineage now lives inside me." She still had her bell voice, but she now articulated like the Queen.

hat did I know about the fall of Listy? My mind was searching for whatever facts I had about the troll wars. Of course, the powrie King OAD had led the assault on the troll shuttles. Simultaneously, the troll defector Pladzal aligned with the Nebas to enable us to manifest in multiple open battle locations at once, surprising the Pai Ona and ultimately turning the tide in the last open battle in our favor.

I'd had nothing to do with that strategy. Aurora had surprised me with the execution. I was just so excited for the turn in the tides that I hadn't ask questions. Up until that point, the battle had been looking bleak. I thought we would fail, but in one stroke, everything changed.

Once again, I was gripped by shame. My naivety had left me blind. I was never a leader, only the face to a secret charade, like a common politician.

"You are Pladzal?"

"Shamefully so."

Now was the time to get answers, if there ever was one. "How did you come into the company of Clive and Aurora?"

"That is an unhappy stance indeed. A fated moment I would never forget but live to regret." Pladzal cleared his throat, and it occurred to me that I didn't know how much time he had left. Perhaps he was moments away from death. He certainly sounded weak. "I was a young trolls-man in those days, full of pride and enthusiasm for life. I wanted to explore the world, meet every manner of strokes. I worked my way up into leadership quickly for my age. Two thousand years old, and I already had my own line."

"Your own line?" I tried not to let my annoyance drip into my tone. I was certain I failed.

"My apologies. It has been many decades since I had to explain the comings and goings of the trolliage. Female trolls are stronger and more superior in many ways. Therefore, they are the shuttle operators. Male trolls manage the shuttle lines. We create the lines and keep them clear. If you were lucky, you worked your way up through the trolls-man line and created a name for yourself. I had high aspirations of meeting the queen someday, so I kept my head down and worked my way up through the ranks."

He paused, and it occurred to me that perhaps he wanted validation for his accomplishments. But the moment passed quickly, and he continued.

"I was working tirelessly on a line that was stuck below the eastern land mass when Clive manifested just ahead of me in the darkness. He was a wonder to behold. I had never met a hobgoblin. They were among the rarest of the strokes, even then. They do not communicate like other creatures, but I sensed he was distressed. He carried a blade sheathed under his arm, and when he noticed I saw it, he attempted to hide it under his cloak. Then his demeanor changed entirely, and he approached me swiftly, placed his cold hand on the back of my right calf, and everything went a little fuzzy. Because we trolls manifest all forms of magics, I could sense I was bewitched, but there was nothing I could do. Clive was animating my body. I remember being so terrified that first time because he ordered me to navigate a vacant shuttle. Male trolls do not operate shuttles. It is forbidden. I was certain all of my hard work would be lost, and I would be caught and demoted." He chuckled. "Can you believe that was all I was worried about? I had no idea what had truly begun that day. This would turn out to be one of many shuttle rides I would facilitate for the hobgoblin. I dropped him off somewhere in Mesopotamia for that first errand. Our first two engagements left the greatest impressions, first because I tried to fight the hex and it hurt. It was aguishly tormenting to the head when I attempted to fight the fog. Then I grew to welcome it, because part of me didn't want to remember all the ways I was breaking the rules of the trolliage. I was just grateful we were not getting caught."

I stretched my neck, considering my own headaches that I only recently paid mind to.

"The second reason was because the blade he carried slowly transformed, and for the longest time, that was the only trinket he had on his person."

"What do you mean, it transformed?"

"As a troll, I see the strokes differently. I smell auras and sense magical properties. Most creatures and items move effortlessly together, meld and move with ease in the in-between spaces of collaborating energies. But the blade from that first sight was different. It did not collaborate. There was stillness around it. The second time he carried it, the stillness was infused with the manifestation of covetousness. It vibrated subtly and with wanting. The third time he carried the blade, it frightened me. It was imbued with rage. It reeked of destruction. But what left the greatest impression of that third visit was that the blade was in such stark contrast to the little life the creature Clive held in his other hand. One arm held the embodiment of death, and the other arm cradled the impetus of life —a newborn child."

My whole body went cold and goosebumps travelled up my neck. "Where did you take the child?"

"I cannot be entirely certain. But I believe I picked up Clive beneath what is now Eastern Europe, and he delivered the baby to a location near Morocco.

This was no luck of the strokes. This troll was the very one that had transported my discarded soul to the doorsteps of my father's home.

532

LUCAS

I remembered what had been eating at me, but it was too late to bring any attention to it. I knew in my gut that the High Priestess was going to give her worldly essence again, just as she'd done to dismantle the Staff. The thing was, I was pretty sure she had some valuable information that we all could've used before —POOF!—she was sparkly ash. I was internally kicking myself for not calling this out before we lost her.

In the aftermath of what had just happened, there was a little bit of a frenzy. Adanc and Ratatoskr was beside themselves, consoling one another through the glass. Emperor Calt and Queen Fetzle were in deep conversation. Ropen was instructing the remaining Priestesses that they needed to get to work on the tapestry. He hoped that now that the Golden Spool of Thread was restored, we may have a window into our fates. The Priestesses were grieving but eager to do their leaders' bidding.

I stood there holding Yesi, feeling eerily unmoved.

"That was the thing that was bothering you, wasn't it?"

"You read my mind, baby girl."

"She knew what she was doing, and she warned us that she was not really intervening."

"She could have said, 'By the way, if you have any questions, now's the time.'"

"Yes, she could've done that, I suppose. What would you have asked?"

"Fuck, I don't know. Maybe ask for a strategy to get the Princess back?"

Just then, a giant I didn't recognize entered the room. There was evident urgency in his demeanor. He whispered something in giant to his emperor and waited for the response.

Calt addressed the room. "The powrie king has left the Orb Forest."

Ratatoskr spoke first. "W-w-where does he go?"

"This is the time to strike," Adanc insisted. "We must save the Princess."

"Clive and Aurora are still there. She may see us coming," Yessica reasoned.

"What if we had a distraction?" I asked.

"An army of giants and trolls will be quite the distraction, my dear friend," Fetzle suggested, and I had to shake off the drastic change in her speech. It was discombobulating. She was my Fetzle, but all grown up.

"No, I mean bait. Then the army of giants and trolls could enter the grounds and search for the Princess."

"What kind of bait would lure the Oracle and hobgoblin out?" Ropen asked skeptically.

"I have just the right kind, and it's waiting for us back in Listy."

"How do you feel?" Olly was the size of a woman who was six months pregnant, easily.

"Honestly, I'm fine. I'm just a little tired, for a creature that shouldn't need sleep."

"Indeed." I watched her stomach like a hawk. We had already seen Sadie Mae moving multiple times in her mother's womb. It was magical to witness. I imagined this was what it was like for my parents.

"She's special, Elias."

"Of course she is."

"No, I mean, I feel it in my bones." Olly closed her eyes, as did I.

"As though she is what caused the Paradigm Tremor." We said it in unison. I just stared into the depths of my wife's beautiful hazel eyes, knowing that what we said was true.

LUCAS

Calt was the last to enter the shuttle. Good thing Fetzle had tidied it up. "OAD is coming here. The tapestry foretold it. He felt the assembly of the Staff."

"You must stay with your people," Fetzle insisted.

"No, my Queen, I am staying with you."

My Queen? This is getting serious fast.

"My brother Ropen will prepare our defense and we will lure him away by hiding the Staff once more. If he truly is sensing where the Rittle is, perhaps we can send him on a wild goose chase." Calt raised an eyebrow.

"Yes! We will have the trolliage shuttle it around the globe until we can safely get it to The Cathedral."

"You are brilliant."

I had to admit they were cute, but the ooey-gooey-ness of it all was starting to make me nauseous. I cleared my throat to interrupt the awkward intimacy.

"Let's go." Fetzle took my cue and started maneuvering her shuttle. We arrived at Listy moments later.

"I wonder what the trolliage will think of our queen's new presence?" Yessica whispered and then kissed my cheek just as the shuttle door flew open and Fetzle and her new armpiece stepped out. I was not always great at reading the room, but apparently excellent at reading a city, because the entire joint shut the fuck down and took a long gaze before slowly returning to life.

Yessica spotted the Khan, who was instructing a small legion of the Sholl-guard with Thracian and Dari. She wove through the queen and the emperor to greet her father. I stayed behind Fetzle. I wanted to get Esther and get out of here. A troll I recognized stepped in line with the Queen and waited for instruction.

"Take this to the Pythoness." She handed her the Staff. "Tell her to divine who of our trolliage should handle the Staff and where they should take it in order to keep it safe until it can be harbored by The Cathedral."

The troll was rendered speechless for a moment.

"Was I clear in my instruction, Itzlee?"

"Uh, uh, um, yes, my queen. Very, actually." Then she took the Staff and ran off.

"Your city is stunning, Fetzle," Calt admired.

"Thank you, dear emperor." She reached up and touched his gargantuan arm.

Oh fuck, more of this. "Hey, can we get Esther and get out of here?" Now that we knew the powrie king was chasing the Staff of Banishment like a homing device, I wanted to get my wife as far away from that thing as I could.

"Of course, Lucas." She turned to Calt. "Please wait here. We will be just a moment."

He touched the top of her head. "I don't wish to impose, but perhaps you should request that your trolliage make a vow to the crown? It will fortify them, keep them safer."

"You are magnificent! Collect them. Tell Itzlee that the trolliage must amass. I will be addressing them. Thank you." She smiled a toothy smile and then ushered me toward the Garden gate.

"So, you and Calt?"

"He is wonderful. Is he not?"

"I like him enough." I really just wanted her happy. "That crown suits you, you know."

"You are making me blush, Lucas. I feel like I matured into an entirely different she-troll when I placed it on my head."

Does that mean she didn't realize she was talking differently and standing taller? I would have to inquire about that more later. She was opening the prison gate. The light was shocking, even though I was expecting it. We quickly walked to where we'd left Esther to rot.

"Back so soon?" she sneered. "Miss me already, Lucas?"

The smile in her voice made me want to spit on her. *How could she be so smug even when she was a prisoner?* I got down on her level, and when I looked in her eyes, I was surprised to see something I knew well. Despair. I had a bizarre twinge of empathy. She was wearing the mask she wore well during a time when she was absolutely not. I could relate. I shook off the feeling. Empathizing with the bitch right now would do nothing for any of us. The High Priestess's words echoed in my head. *Who was I to decide what was good or bad?*

"Cat got your tongue, Lucas? Why are you staring at me?" Esther hissed.

"We have a job position for you to fill."

ESTHER

"You must love this." Fetzle had tied my hands with the Indra net. I was completely incapacitated. "You will leave me to die with the Oracle."

"You don't think your dear old mommy will spare you if she captures you?"

"No, I know she won't." I was replaying in my head the story I'd just been told by the male-troll in the Garden. *She never wanted me. I was a painful reminder of losing my father. Until I became a useful pawn.*

"Don't worry, I am not handing you over to her. I don't want you taking charge of the Nebas again. I just want to use you as bait."

"Does Ophelia know about this?"

Lucas stopped and glared at me, and I knew that Ophelia didn't know. "Olly has her hands full with other matters."

I laughed. "You better hope she doesn't find out. I have a feeling she would not be happy if she discovered you lied to her, again."

He growled and lunged at me. I expected an actual attack. I would welcome an opportunity to put my hands on the man who killed my Yanni.

"Fetzle, do you have something to gag this bitch with?"

"Yes, Lucas."

I didn't see what she grabbed, but I could feel it around my mouth. An attempt to say something confirmed I was incapacitated. Just as well. There was nothing to be said among enemies. We entered the city center and I was astounded by what I saw. Hundreds of trolls were waiting to see off their Queen and one huge giant. It was a sight to behold.

"My fierce trolliage!"

Only then did I realize she was articulating differently, and that she had her crown on her head.

"Today I call on you to vow your allegiance to the Crown of Thorns. That we may stand and fight alongside our friends and reclaim the strokes that are right in this world." The crowd cheered. "Take a knee."

Lucas let me go to make his own vow. *How odd! It was also arrogant of him. What if I ran off? Where would I go?*

"To the crown, I vow to serve."

The giant had also taken a knee, and he along with the others repeated the vow. A strange haze moved through the space, and I realized there was more to this than I knew. I looked up at the queen. There were so many transforming strokes, it was difficult to know what to expect next.

"Rise."

Everyone got to their feet.

"Let's go, Fetzle," Lucas urged, just as Yessica took her place by his side and he gripped my arm once more.

We all entered the shuttle. Yessica kept stealing glances at me, and I wondered what she thought of this plan. Her innocent heart would most certainly reject live bait, even someone who has been as wicked as me. She surprised me by scooting closer to me.

"I see you, Esther. The pain. The torment you are navigating right now."

Emotions flooded my eyes, and I rejected the urge to cry.

"You still have a choice to do it differently. Your strokes have not been wasted. I see that most of what has driven you is love. Don't let that stop you now."

Then Lucas came up behind her and she stopped. I closed my eyes and let her words wash over me. *Does she really see me? In some strange way, I actually feel like she does.*

OPHELIA

"*L*ucas is meeting us a day late? Can that man ever be on time?" I fumed.

"Baby, I believe it is because he is helping Fetzle and the giants rescue the Princess."

I scowled at my husband. Then quickly changed my attitude as I slowly got off the bed and headed toward the door. "It's these hormones."

"I know."

"Are you two ready?" Ruit asked through our Runes.

"On our way," my husband promptly replied. I was moving slightly slower than I would've liked. I was excited to leave the Haven in Boston and be back in The Cathedral. So much had happened in only three days, and I really hoped that Cataphet would be willing to meet with us.

Aremis and Sparkle were waiting in the hall, along with the rest of the Tallus family.

"You know where we are going, Almus?" Ruit turned to his son.

"Certainly."

Then we all locked arms, and the familiar buzzing feeling of tele-portation tickled my body from the inside out.

"Are we literally in the center of the French Quarter?" I looked up at the three-story grey building skeptically. "This is ridiculous."

"It looks better than the last time I was here," Inca admitted. "Nicolas has kept it in good condition." She looked at me expectantly. "Nicolas Cage."

"Really, Inca? Are you going to tell me he's a Conduit?"

"Well, either he can tell you or I can."

I could tell by Elias' expression that I had made an ass of myself. I mouthed the words. "Is that him, behind me?"

Elias smiled and nodded.

Aremis reached over my shoulder. "Good to see you, man."

I turned around slowly. "Nice to meet you Ophelia," he said. "You can call me Nick."

Nicolas reached around and fist-bumped Sparkle's awaiting hand.

"Uh, it's... well, thanks, and good to meet you, Nick." I jetted my hand out for a shake and he pulled me in for an awkward hug.

"The pleasure is all mine." Nicolas Cage let me go and I still stood there, starstruck.

"I wish I could say I still owned the place, but I don't know if anyone can really take ownership once The Cathedral moves in with a gang of dragons." Then he pointed at my belly as though he'd just seen it. "Expecting, eh? Not exactly the best time to pop one out."

My face contorted into an entire range of emotions in a minute, but before I could spout something out of this mommy brain of mine, my husband intervened.

"The greater the haunted signature of a place, the more powerful the Haven. This building must have one intense signature to lure Cataphet here."

Suddenly, the rod iron gate creaked open.

"Home, sweet home." Nick stepped in first. We all chuckled at his remark. "Ladies first." He gestured for Sparkle and me and the Tallus women to enter. It was 4 a.m. here in New Orleans, which meant nothing for the city that never sleeps. I looked around before

I ducked in. The drunk people on the street weren't paying any attention to a small mob of visitors entering the city's most notorious haunted house that was never opened to the public.

544

LUCAS

"This place gives me the creeps." I turned to Esther. "Why would you Nebas want to live in a hole with a bunch of balls?" She rolled her eyes but didn't say anything, and I remembered it was because she was still gagged. "Before I take this convenient little muzzle off, we need to have a plan." I looked at the barren landscape and found few markers to identify how large this Haven was, which would make it even more challenging to determine how many Nebas had arrived. There were no humans around, which was convenient for the giants and trolls to surface. We would need to attack from above and below to find the Princess and limit our casualties. I returned to the shuttle with Esther.

I looked at Fetzle and Calt, who were eagerly looking back at me. It dawned on me that I was probably the most qualified to form our strategy.

Stalt and Claudia insisted on joining us, in the event that they could save their daughter. They now seemed like the most reasonable candidates for co-strategizing, aside from our bait.

"Alright, Claudia, what do you know about this Haven?"

Relief flashed across her face. For a second, I think she thought we were just going to run up to the door and knock.

"The Orb Forest Haven is a long tube with a few rooms off-shooting from it." She placed a log on the ground to represent the tube. "I think we are here." She pointed to the northwest end.

Esther mumbled and shook her head, placing her foot to the east.

"We are at the east entrance? You're sure?"

Esther nodded and Claudia shifted gears.

"Hold on, are we going to base our strategy on Esther's honesty?" Yesi grabbed my arm to make me take pause. "Sorry, dear, I just need to get this straight."

Stalt interjected, "We cannot go in blind."

"Or based on intel from the enemy," I argued. Calt and Fetzle looked at each other but didn't say a word.

Claudia began rummaging around in her bag. "I have something for this." She pulled out two items—a crystal ball and a compass. "Take the gag off her, Fetzle."

"Wait one fucking minute!" I put my hand up in protest. "I need to understand what the hell is going on before we unleash the queen bee this close to the hive."

"These are two Rittles."

Jillian came up from behind me. She had been so quiet I had forgotten she was even here. "This one," she pointed at the globe, "detects deceit, and this one will take you anywhere you desire to go with simply a thought." Jillian sneered at Esther. "I was paying attention. Now, are we at the east entrance of the Haven?"

I stared at the ball expectantly and nothing happened.

"She's telling the truth," Jillian and Claudia said in unison.

I waved on at Fetzle and she took off the gag. Esther adjusted her mouth but said nothing. I was surprised.

"They were holding the comatose captives here." Claudia pointed at the end of the long tube. "Aurora and Clive were up in these rooms. King OAD came and went as he pleased but generally was hanging around this end of the Haven." Claudia got on her feet. "Before we fled, I heard an order from the Oracle that all remaining captives be brought to this Haven. That means there will be more Nebas than there were before, and at least fifteen sedated Consu."

"What about the Princess?" Calt looked down at the miniature diagram. "Nowhere on here do I see where they may be holding Chaness."

"May I?" Esther asked and looked around to see who would object to her contribution. I wanted to, man, I wanted to, but instead I picked up the crystal ball and held it tight while she spoke, looking for even the faintest flicker. "Can I have my hands?"

"Lucas?" Fetzle asked.

"She isn't going anywhere," Jillian affirmed.

I nodded for Fetzle to take Indra's net off.

Esther picked up handfuls of pebbles. "These are where the Orbs are placed throughout the forest and in the Haven." She quickly scattered them about, and it was obvious once they were in place that at the core of their placement was something central and huge. "The powrie king said they are using Chaness like a battery, so she must be in the center of these Orbs. Powries don't like the surface of this earth, so they will be buried deep, and if this Princess is as big as you say she is, they will be deeper than usual. The king may have mobilized, but there is no way he left his supply unattended, so you should be prepared for vast numbers of powrie infantry. The Nebas numbers are far less staggering, but I wouldn't worry about attacking the Nebas at this point since that isn't the mission here. If I were planning this assignment..." Esther looked at me sideways before continuing. "I would place the bait here, as far from the captives as possible. Drawing the Nebas army out, and the Oracle and Clive. Send Claudia, Lucas and Jillian into the Haven to retrieve the captives using the compass, sneaking them out silently, while the bait keeps their attention over here." She pointed outside the Haven completely. "How many giants and trolls do you have waiting to strike?"

Calt answered. "A hundred male-trolls, thirty she-trolls, fifty giants, and the keeper Ratatoskr."

"Good numbers." Esther nodded in approval, then turned to Stalt. "How many lava tubes can you manifest at once?"

"Six easily."

"Perfect. Do one here, here, here, here, here, cutting off supplies to these Orbs, and then a direct tube into the center until you hit the hollow. Where you will transport the Lantern," she nodded at Yesi flippantly, "as your first line of defense and signal for the trolls and giants to attack."

"Wait a minute!" I objected. "You had me up until..."

Yessica grabbed my arm again. "I can do this, Lucas."

"Baby girl, I know you can do anything, but you are not built to be in the center of a battlefield. You are light and love..."

She put her hand on my mouth. "I was built for this moment. I know it in my bones." Her eyes pleaded with me to see her, to hear her, and to trust her.

We all sat in silence for a long moment. I was trembling. I wanted to rage against this plan. But the honest truth was that it was a good strategy and it was the most likely to succeed. *And the fucking crystal ball didn't flicker, not even once!*

E L I A S

e were settling in when I heard a knock on our door. "Who do you think that is?" Olly asked.

"Whoever it is, I will be sure to tell them to bugger off," I teased. I just wanted her to smile. There was a heaviness about her as the battle moved closer and her belly grew bigger. I understood it. I just wanted to relieve her of it as often as I could.

"Please keep your buggers to yourself. We are expecting a whole lot of nervous Pai Ona arriving to support us very soon."

"Indeed." I was surprised to see an unfamiliar face when I opened the door. "How can I help you? I am Elias, and you are?" The woman was striking, with charcoal skin and bright blue eyes. Her hair was kinked, curly and long, down to her waist. She wore a forest-green jumper and gold, sparkly tennis shoes.

"My name is Daniela. Of course, I know who you are, Viraclay." Daniela had an American accent and a charming smile. She jetted her hand out to make a formal introduction. I gladly took it. "I'm here to honor my bidding." Suddenly, the confidence she was transmitting a moment ago faltered. "I-I-I I don't know how to say this."

"Trust me, Daniela, there are very few things that can surprise me these days."

549

"I am a Ramalan, and I spoke to your baby, Sadie."

My mouth went dry and I had to eat my words. Daniela had managed to catch me off guard. Once I gained my composure, I stepped aside and invited her in. "This seems like a conversation my wife would also like to hear. Please come in."

Olly was sitting on the couch. She greeted Daniela with a smile. "Hi! My name is Ophelia."

"I know who you are, Mrs. Kraus. Please pardon my intrusion." Daniela took a seat beside my wife, and I half-sat on the arm of the sofa behind Olly.

"Daniela here has something to share with us about our daughter. Please, we are all ears." I prayed to Malarin it was good news. Olly needed good news.

Daniela looked between the two of us for a moment and then at Ophelia's bulging belly. "Sadie came to me in a dream."

Olly quickly interjected in our thoughts. "Did you tell her our daughter's name?"

"No, I did not."

"In a dream?" Ophelia was fully invested in the conversation now. "What are your gifts?"

"I am a Ramalan. But I primarily speak to the souls waiting to enter this plane, through the portals of creation."

"Babies? You speak to babies that have yet to be born?" I clarified. Then I felt a tug at my senses and an intuition to use one of my inherited gifts—Berty's ability to see the strokes. So I switched lenses and opened myself up to watch the interactions happening between the strokes in this exchange. It was magnificent. Swirls and swarms of hues of greys, blacks and whites were weaving and twirling about the room.

"Yes, I speak to the souls of those either waiting to be invited into the portals of creation or the soul that is already in the process of creative manifestation. Sadie Mae is very well on her way to emergence into this world."

I examined Daniela's strokes closely. They were mostly white, with slivers of light grey. Her strokes felt very ethereal, and they seemed to originate from a space above our heads, yet there was no point of origin specifically.

"What was your dream about? What did our beautiful Sadie Mae say?" I looked at my wife, and it was as though I was seeing her for the first time. She was everywhere, all at once. Her strokes were every shade of black, grey and white. Chaotic, smooth, pulsating, still, swirling about her essence and into her being. This must have been what Berty was talking about when he said her strokes were different. I could sense that this vortex of strokes fed directly to me. I got dizzy and had to shake it off. "Elias, are you alright?" Olly touched my leg.

"Sorry. Indeed. I just got a little dizzy."

She gazed up at me with concern. One hand on her belly, the other on my knee, and I saw that in the center of her womb was complete stillness. A sanctuary. I continued to stare into the void of her womb while Daniela explained.

"First, Sadie wants you to know she is safe. That this accelerated growth is doing nothing to hurt or harm her."

Olly squeezed my leg. "That's a relief." I squeezed her hand back, but I was mesmerized. I could not take my eyes from her womb.

"This next message is a little more complicated."

"We can handle complicated," Olly assured her.

Daniela cleared her throat. "Sadie's soul comes from the Paladiens. She is entering the thirteenth timeline right now, when this world needs what she has to offer the most."

"Wow. This is amazing. What a gift." Olly squeezed my leg again. I tried to shift my focus, but I could not. I thought I saw something in the void. *A flicker of light?*

"Her message to you is this, if this world is not ready for her light."

I put my hand up to stop Daniela, because that was it. I definitely saw a flash of light. "Pardon me. Please. Just one moment."

"Elias, you're scaring me." Olly put bother her hands on her belly and I moved in closer to examine her womb. But whatever I had seen was gone, and I could feel the concern rolling off my wife. It was enough for me to switch back to my normal lens and come home to the present.

I resumed my position behind my wife and began massaging her shoulders. "Sorry. I got distracted with one of my gifts, and I apologize. Continue, Daniela."

"If this timeline is not prepared to witness her light, she will not walk through the final portal of manifestation into the gates of consciousness."

"Wait. What?"

"She wants you to know that, if that happens, it will have nothing to do with you two. She chose you as her parents because it is only the two of you who could be strong enough to carry her light into this world. This war, the violence that lies ahead, is not what will determine her viability in this timeline. You both have done everything right by your daughter."

"Wait. What?" Olly repeated. "She will not walk through the final manifestation portal?" "Are you saying that there is a possibility that our daughter will just vanish?" I held my wife a little tighter.

"She would not vanish. She would be delivered stillborn." Daniela looked incredibly uncomfortable. "I did not want to share this message. But Sadie insisted. I have had this dream for three nights. She needs you to know, there is nothing you can do to change her path. Sadie will not know what she may choose until the portal opens and her path will be made clear."

"Elias..." Then Ophelia began to weep. I took her in my arms and Daniela sat there, holding space for us with her own tears.

LUCAS

"Are you sure you're up for this?" I wanted to demand that she reconsider. Actually, I wanted to command her to sit back on the sidelines. But I had never seen her so resolved.

"Lucas, my gift has very rarely given me an opportunity to fight for those I love. I wouldn't change my strokes. They are mine to bear. However, I deserve to get to defend, fight, and just plain rage on those who have imprisoned and taken years of my life. Let me do this! Because I will, either way, but I would prefer your blessing."

I drew her in for a long, hard kiss. When I pulled my mouth away, I stared into her brilliant eyes. "Consider yourself blessed."

"Thank you," she whispered softly.

Just then, Fetzle called everyone's attention to the firepit in the center of her shuttle. "I have confirmation that everything is in place to execute the plan, and what's more, Itzlee has spotted King OAD in pursuit of the Staff of Banishment halfway across the world. We know the time to strike is now."

Calt stood by the queen proudly. "My giants are ready."

I turned to Esther. "Don't fuck this up." I held the crystal ball, still looking for any signs of deception.

"I may end this war for you tonight. I will kill her if I have the chance."

"Yeah, that's all fine and good, but will you then turn around and kill us?" Esther opened her mouth to object, when I had a thought. A quick Blood Bidding would give us all the reassurance we would need. We all already had the extra protection by paying allegiance to the Crown of Thorns. This would seal the deal. "Does someone have a knife?"

Stalt quickly handed me one he had sheathed on his leg.

"Lucas, we should go," Yesi insisted.

"It will take but a moment to make sure Esther can't really betray us. Pen and paper, please?"

Claudia scrambled to find them and handed them to me. Everyone looked on impatiently, most of all Esther.

"This is ridiculous, Lucas. The Rittle has shown you I have no intention of double-crossing you."

"With all due respect, Mistress of Satan, I don't know how this thing works. But I do know how quickly you change your mind." I saw a flash of that wicked smile and I knew I was doing the right thing. "What the fuck is your last name?"

She looked at me like a screw had worked loose. "Bonice."

"Hmmm, not what I would have expected." I handed her the piece of paper. "Read it."

"I, Esther Bonice, honor the Bidding before me with my life and the life of the Bidder that I will not act outside of the good of all who are present. I will not betray confidences or allegiances to the enemy Clive, the Oracle, or OAD, no matter the torture I may endure. I cannot kill the Bidder or anyone he loves. If I attempt to betray anyone who is witness to his Bidding, I will take my own life."

"Give me your hand." I quickly cut mine and then promptly sliced Esther's palm. As I made a deal with the devil.

OPHELIA

"I need an audience with Cataphet, now," I said to my husband as soon as Daniela left. "Can you please arrange it? I have had enough of this cryptic bullshit. I want more answers. I want to understand what we are fighting for. What kind of world has this painter created? That he could make me indestructible, assure me that our baby is safe, and then I find out Sadie may not survive? The Sovereign of the Dragons knows more."

I was pacing. I suspected this had something to do with my abnormal origins. But I was no longer going to have this information spoon-fed to me. It was time to understand who I was, and then perhaps I would know why Sadie would decide not to come into this world.

"I will find Ruit and we will arrange an audience."

"Soon," I asserted.

"Indeed."

Elias kissed me on the forehead and left our apartment.

ESTHER

She would see me coming the moment I stepped out of the shuttle. I adjusted my shoulders and fortified my spirit. Aurora had been the hand that killed everyone I loved. She orchestrated every assassination, murder, or accident. My strokes were defiled from the day I was born to that monster. This may be the only moment I ever got to seek justice. I didn't need answers. Her crimes were enough for me to know what she deserved.

The stone felt good on my bare feet. The crunch of the ice followed by seconds of searing freezing pain. I welcomed the sensation. What was to come would be far more painful. I was confident of that.

I heard them circling me—her minions. I needed to make my capture believable. I had to put up a good fight. Calypso stepped into my line of sight first.

"You have returned, Esther?"

I could smell Astrid before I saw her just over my right shoulder.

"Did the Pai Ona generously chase you back to the Nebas den?"

"What? Am I no longer considered your Mistress?" I crouched and they both flinched. *Good, they were still afraid of me. They should be.*

Several other Conduits stepped out from the woods. I counted ten in total. *I liked these odds.*

efore I could knock on Ruit's door, I heard Cataphet's voice in my head. "You needn't seek the Alchemist to arrange a meeting with me. You need only ask."

"My wife is in a state and she would like some answers."

"The answers she seeks are here in the throne room below."

"The throne room? Like the one we encountered in Delphi?"

"The very same."

"Olly wants to understand her origins and why we are here in a world full of so much pain and hardship."

"There is also much love. We cannot have one without the other."

"I reason you are right, but—"

Cataphet interrupted. "Bring the Ulus to the galley. But know this, Sulu. The answers are not simple, nor are they easy."

Just then, the door opened. Ruit was staring at me expectantly. "I would like to escort you both down to the galley if I may. And Cataphet informed me we should also invite Sparkle and Aremis to hold space for Ophelia."

I just nodded.

LUCAS

I had to give it to Esther; she knew how to fight. Once I saw her take down the first three Nebas in three minutes, I knew she'd give us all a real chance at succeeding. I hand-signaled that it was time to attack. Fetzle, Stalt, Yesi and Calt disappeared. I had a moment of wanting to throw up, just knowing what kind of danger she was putting herself into. But Fetzle promised me she would protect her.

"Lucas, we have to go now," Claudia reminded me, and the three of us locked arms. Claudia imagined the room with the sedated captives, and instantly the Compass took the three of us to the chamber. There was one guard. Claudia caught him with her gaze and had him stupefied in anguish while I shielded us and the captives and Jillian amplified it. I quickly counted fifteen bodies. All of the remaining prisoners were here.

"Is she here?" Claudia whispered.

"I don't know. But I can only move two at a time while you and Lucas keep the space secured." Then Jillian was gone, her hand on two Conduits and the Compass, transporting them directly into Fetzle's shuttle.

559

"Do you see her, Lucas?" Desperation was dripping into her every word.

"Honestly, I don't know, Claudia. But they are all here. So, if she's alive, we will have her."

Jillian flashed in and out again and I was having a hard time keeping my shield secure with the movement. We heard shuffling down the hall.

"More Nebas to detain Esther?" Claudia asked.

Hopefully they weren't coming here. I felt another intrusion into my shield by Jillian.

"Just stay focused." I was saying it to her and me too.

Then we heard the Oracle's voice ring through the hall. This was it. She either suspected something happening in her Haven or she was going to get Esther herself. Or worse, they discovered what was happening beneath us.

"Clive, we have to get her ourselves. These Nebas are incompetent!"

Thank the strokes.

Jillian entered the room again. "Move quicker."

Once they detained Esther, I didn't know how much longer we really had before all the other alarms would go off.

Two more groups of captives, and I was really struggling to maintain the integrity of the shield. We heard a huge ruckus down the hall. Screaming and howling. It was Esther. They had gotten her.

What will Aurora do with her defiant daughter? Does she already know her treachery? Do I really care?

"Claudia, we can all go in this final transport."

She promptly walked up to the Nebas scum and broke his neck. "Don't make me regret not killing you later, Sven."

Jillian blinked back in. I held my shield strong. We locked arms, and transported out with the remaining three captives.

OPHELIA

ataphet escorted us to the throne room beneath The Cathedral, beneath this land. I was shaking as we approached the stone chair. I wanted the truth, but I would be a fool if I didn't admit I was terrified of it. The markings were on every surface of the walls. I read snippets as I maneuvered my way to the center of the room. Elias helped me. I was so heavily pregnant, it was getting harder and harder to walk. *How was I going to go into battle like this? Focus, Olly. One obstacle at a time.*

"Do you want me to lift you onto the seat?"

I shot him a look that could kill. "I still have dignity, dear husband." Simultaneously, my mind shot back to the mountains outside the Haven Hafiza, when Di hoisted me up like a child on her hip. It felt like lifetimes ago. But it brought a smile to my face.

Aremis, Ruit and Sparkle took their positions around the room, Aremis at my back, and Sparkle and Ruit at my sides. Cataphet was not visible but I sensed her watchful eyes.

When I sat down, Elias stepped back to face me, just a foot away. I immediately felt the surge of energy move about me and then through me. It was less invasive this time. The whole process seemed to work quicker, and Elias was already projecting the story in front of us.

❋

LORIF'S BODY shook and trembled. It was all too much, and still the brothers pulled at her. Priloc dove into the vortex, pulling at Tindle, then grabbing at Fih, but none of them would listen. Lorif's body began to flake into crystals, colorful and sparkling into the air like glitter. The vortex of wind around her swept it up, and for a moment it was the most beautiful thing Cataphet had ever seen. Then it exploded, and the noise that echoed from the space where Lorif had been was bone-rattling. It felt like a thousand shards of projectile glass. Then, it was immediately followed by a vacuous shockwave ripping through every stroke mercilessly. There was nothing left of the two brothers, nothing left of Lorif, and the intensity of the shockwave was raking and ripping through what was left of the world around. Priloc covered his head and body as best he could and prayed to Chitchakor for grace.

The entire desert looked different. The colors had lost their vibrancy and you could see where they had once swirled and melded together, the textures were beginning to change. Some things solidified, other objects became more ethereal, clouds formed in the horizon, and sand seemed to waft away in the wind. The landscape of the world was changing into the familiar landscape most of the painter's creation would know it to be. Trees were trees and mountains were mountains. The strokes were dividing.

Priloc lay nearly lifeless in the center of the crater. Cataphet wept openly at the mouth of her cave. The ground shook with her grief. Her golden-green eyes glistened with tears as big as waterfalls. She howled in anguish. Her heart was broken. She'd just lost her only friend. The Original looked weak, physically exhausted. She slowly began to crawl toward Priloc. She desired to comfort him. A sliver of dragon's blood streamed down her back just as the wound began to heal.

Dazed and confused, Priloc rose to his feet. He looked around at the devastation. The entire landscape of his world was marred. The colors were gone. Only hues of greys remained. Just then, he saw something move at his feet. It was a small creature, lying where his brothers and Lorif had just stood. It had dark hair and long, spindly fingers, sharp teeth and beady eyes. Small in stature, like an infant. So Priloc swooped it up into his arms, ripped a piece of his cloak, and swaddled the creature. While holding this bizarre creation, he noticed the bracelet his brother Tindle gave to Lorif, still intact, on the ground in front of him. He picked it up and put it on his wrist. There were also etchings in the earth that Tindle did not recognize, but he paid little mind to them. The creature in his arms and the charm on his wrist gave him some semblance of comfort, as though he still held pieces of his torn family.

"Priloc," Cataphet said. In her weakened state, she could not reach him in time. He began to walk away toward his beloved ocean. "That creature will be the end of us all. It is spawned from covetousness. It is not of the painter's creation."

"Dear Cataphet, has there not been enough pain for one day?" said Priloc. "This stroke was created by Lorif and my brothers. Surely it cannot be all bad." Then he walked away, all the while looking adoringly at what he affectionately named Clive.

Priloc and Clive lived happily on the beach for many moons. As Clive grew in size, it became clear that he did not speak like Priloc could. They developed their own language, and when Clive was big enough, Priloc gave him the charm bracelet that Tindle once created. Over the years, the landscape of the world changed, and the nature of the strokes evolved to include more Conduits who expressed different extraordinary powers.

Priloc and Clive decided to venture out into the world and experience new and exciting things.

"First, we must delegate where the Rittles must go," Priloc explained to Clive as they collected Fih's creations from below the Toglin trees. "I will entrust you with Lorif's volume of the Pierses because I know you will be responsible with it, Clive." Priloc bestowed the powerful book of spells to his trusted companion. "The volume Tindle had is still in the depths of Cataphet's caves, where it will be safe."

Clive nodded in agreement. "These weapons and trinkets are very dangerous and powerful. It is only you or I who may enchant them so that others may wield them. This is a great responsibility, Clive." Clive nodded enthusiastically. "We will see to it that they end up in the hands of this world's leaders. Evenly distributed, so that no one stroke may feel greater than another. If they should ever fall into the hands of a single being again, it will be only you or I who sees to it that they are unmanageable, cursed rather, until we deem it otherwise. This is a great responsibility, Clive." With that, they set out on a mission, slowly and methodically delivering the Rittles to an appointed leader. The Staff of Banishment went to King OAD of the powries. Clive handed it to the king with pride.

During their travels, more of Clive's unique gifts began to emerge. Clive could absorb energies around him and generate something entirely new.

"That is quite extraordinary, Clive. I am so proud of you," Priloc would rave over his companion. They journeyed far and wide, laughing and communicating in their own special way. When they delivered the last Rittle to the giants, the Golden Spool of Thread, they did not know what to do next.

"Where shall we venture to next?" Priloc asked. Then he got quiet. "I think we should search for another of your kind, my friend. Surely there are more of you, just as the strokes have painted many more Conduits."

So, they set out to find more of Clive's kind. The search lasted centuries, but to no avail. They were unable to locate another of Clive's kin. One day, Priloc looked at his friend and said, "It seems you are the only stroke of your kind. That is magnificent."

But Priloc could tell from the look on Clive's face that he did not feel that it was magnificent at all. In fact, unbeknownst to Priloc, something was stirring in Clive. He was growing angry. Angry at the painter that there was no other being such as himself.

Priloc tried to cheer Clive up. "What shall we call you, then? Besides Clive, what would you like your strokes to be called?"

Clive took a stick and wrote out the word *hobgoblin*. "Hobgoblin?" Priloc exclaimed. "I love it! It is very adorable and fitting for an astonishment such as yourself. Clive the hobgoblin has a ring to it."

And so the companions continued on their way. Until, one day, Priloc met someone who would change his life forever. His Atoa, Laosay. He first saw her in a bazar, weaving through the crowd, smelling spices and tasting fruits. Priloc was awestruck. He had never seen such a beautiful stroke. "Do you see her, Clive? Is she not glorious?"

But Clive did not see what Priloc saw in Laosay. She looked like every other Conduit woman he had met. "I must go meet her," Priloc insisted, and then, without another thought, he was bouncing through the crowd to catch up to the beauty that captivated him. When Clive caught up to them, he knew something was different. Clive could feel that the bond between them was already stronger than anything he and Priloc shared.

"Clive, this is Laosay. Is that not the most stunning name you have ever heard?" Laosay reached out to embrace Clive in welcome, but he sensed her unease with him. She feared him. Clive smiled at her, and she shuddered. Priloc barely noticed. He was already absolutely infatuated. Clive knew that his days with his only companion were numbered.

Within a week, Priloc and Laosay consummated and were consciously conceiving a child. Priloc told Clive of the excellent news. "Clive, we are expecting. The strokes are in our favor! I have never been so happy." Every word felt like a dagger into Clive's heart. Clive knew the day would come when Priloc would ask him to leave, so instead of facing that rejection, he fled in the night the day Priloc and Laosay's daughter was born.

From that moment on, Clive's disdain for the world he did not belong in began to fester and grow. He hated Conduits most of all because they naturally came in pairs. He tried everything—living with the fae, convening with dragons. Nothing soothed his lonely heart. During one season in time, he transmuted energies to create an entire community of hobgoblin strokes from an incantation he found in the Pierses. He had hoped that by duplicating himself he would find comfort, yet still he did not. The minions became a drain on his energy, so he eventually annihilated them all.

Clive studied the Pierses tirelessly, hoping to find something that could change his strokes. He memorized every page, every spell, until he could begin to create his own magics. He sketched symbols that would come to him in his dreams, fractals of a language that lived in him. Between the Pierses and the unique symbols, Clive began transmuting the goodness of spells into the darkness of hexes. When his rage and hatred finally erupted, he vowed to destroy the Conduit strokes by any means necessary. Clive undid the good work he and Priloc had done, he stole all of the Rittles back from their keepers and soiled the memory of their existence so that the keepers had not even realized they were gone. Clive hid the stolen artifacts in an enchanted sack beneath the ground, he felt the Rittles would offer the power he needed to see the worlds undoing. However when they were stolen by the Niffler, he had to reconsider. He discovered the key to Conduit extinction was in the Sulu's power of each generation. But every time he fulfilled his mission, the Conduit strokes would return yet again, only fueling his abhorrence and deep desire for destruction that much more.

THE PROJECTION STOPPED. The last image lingered, the hobgoblin Clive holding the Staff of Banishment, covered in blood and a wicked grin smeared across his face.

No one said anything for a long, tense moment. I knew what they were all thinking. *I am the Ulus, the spawn of that thing.* I remembered what Maia had said, I am the collaboration of what has always been and what was never meant to be. *No wonder Sadie Mae is not sure she wants to choose me as her mother.*

ESTHER

live stood guard. He had me in some sort of invisible cage. Aurora was circling me, predator-like. She was wearing a long white gown. Her hair was tied up in knots and braids. I looked for a resemblance between us, and all I could see was wickedness and rage.

"This is inconvenient, Esther. I wanted you to be cooperative, and alas, I have no more dragon's blood to keep you detained and Clive's hex was disengaged when the world shook. We learned that the hard way when you slipped through our hands before. Now, I need Clive's abilities to delegate other duties. What am I to do with you?" I was certain she did not actually want me to answer that question, so I stayed silent. "I am intrigued by your return." She walked over to where I hung suspended in Clive's prison and examined me more closely. "You will be a valuable addition to my Sulu Wheel if I can manage you." She turned to the hobgoblin, and I knew they were having an exchange. "We tracked you down, and it appeared you got abducted by the Pai Ona. Why would you circle back here? For asylum? Oh! This will not do at all, Clive! You are needed to move the Orbs into place." Aurora paced in front of me.

"I know you are my mother."

She stopped but didn't look up at me.

"How could you do this to me? Make me the monster I am, kill everything and everyone I ever loved! You haven't a soul! You don't know what love is!"

"You are more correct than you know about my soul. But you are wrong about love. Love. Love made me this way!" she snapped back. "I loved your father deeply, and this is what love has done to me. It created such pain that only tyranny can fill the void."

"This has nothing to do with love or my father. You killed your Atoa. There is no love deeper than that. You abandoned your children... poisoned their souls."

Her eyes narrowed in on me, sharp and cold. "You do not know the half of what I am capable of."

"How could you do this to me and my brother?"

She laughed maniacally. "Oh, you cry for Nestor now? Of course you do, you disgustingly weak child. If you must know, I tried to spare you of this life!" Clive moved ever so slightly, and I realized he was trying to stop her from continuing with her tirade. If she noticed, she did not take the hint. "I met Clive while I was wandering, lost, in the Atlas Mountains just after Apollo had left me for his precious Shatki. I walked aimlessly, broken and alone—not only had my beloved left me, but I discovered shortly after his departure that I was with child. Pregnancy is different for a Conduit. Consu or Unconsu, your womb becomes nearly impenetrable. You become the fortress for the life growing within you. Chitchakor made us in such a way that not even the mother may choose death while she bears life. Why would the painter do such a thing? We have choice our entire existence, until we create life. Clive feels that it is because that soul chose you. Now you are in an accord, and neither soul can eliminate the contract until it is fulfilled. And in this case, that is giving birth. Whatever the reason, it is no matter. But Clive gave me hope. He knew of a blade, one half of the Staff of Banishment. He had stolen it for the Conduit Ureshikigal during the war of the sisters. Surely the blade that stabbed and nearly killed Tindle could end my life and the life of this child. So, my greatest ally took me to a safe place while he left to fetch the blade and bring it back to me. When he returned, I was nearly to term and desperate for a solution to my condition—my broken heart. All I did was weep, every moment of every day. When Clive handed me the Dirk, I knew there was something different about it. Clive's only request was that he be there to receive the essence, absorb the power that expelled when the blade took the life of me and my child. It was the least I could do for his mercy."

My face began to contort with disgust. I anticipated what was coming next and it was making me nauseous.

She laughed when she realized how appalled I was. "Get off your high horse, Esther. You have been useless since Yanni died."

I growled. *How dare she even say his name!* It was because of her that he was gone. It was because of her that we ever got tangled up in this war. I wanted to scream, claw her face. Do something to avenge my beloved, but there was nothing to be done in this moment.

"I took the blade and, without hesitation, plunged it into my swollen belly. But something odd happened once the knife was in my womb. An explosion of colors spilled from the wound. Some sort of Haven magic occurred, an imprint of gifts and powers from the blade and from what I had just done. Clive looked on and witnessed how one soul was severed into two—Esther and Nestor— while at the same time all the pain I had been wallowing in disappeared. I had not only split my baby's soul into two beings, I'd also cut my own attachment to this existence. I detached my soul cord, the essence that anchors us to our hearts. I freed myself from my own torment. There was no more broken heart. I felt nothing at all, nothing but a desire to exist and pursue my power. Whatever melding of the strokes had occurred had spared my life from a blade that was certainly powerful enough to take it. But I needed to be healed. So, Clive left with you, and I called on Sorcey to heal me."

"You cut us in half? We were one child?" I was muttering the questions, not expecting answers and mortified by the confession. "Your soul cord?"

She ignored the first two questions and continued with what pleased her. "That is what I have grown to call it. All beings have one. I have developed an ability to see others' soul cords. The only other Conduit I have encountered who doesn't have one is your brother, Nestor. I'm afraid you must have gotten that little nugget when I accidentally severed your soul. It makes him quite unlikeable, but far less weak than you. Nestor has no conscience whatsoever."

The bile rose in my throat. This entire testimony was deplorable.

Aurora began to fiddle with her gown, exposing her belly, and there, in the center, just below the navel, was a scar that looked just like my birthmark.

"All of you have it." She laughed and looked at Clive. "He doesn't approve of my admission, but I have been waiting to tell someone, to bask in the glory of centuries of preparation and strategy." She walked over to Clive and stroked his cheek. "Besides, my dearest friend, the tale is almost through. What began with the fall of Atlantis will finally conclude with the annihilation of all Conduits once and for all ridding this world of the Conduit stroke."

Rage was consuming me. Every cell was on fire with deep loathing. "Why did you destroy Atlantis? You killed Shatki. You killed my mother."

"Atlantis… Oh yes, that was our doing. I thought you knew when you said I killed everyone you loved." Aurora giggled. "Ultimately, we needed a dragon to begin our pursuit of captives, and I wanted Shatki dead. The fall of Atlantis was an exceptionally brilliant way to accomplish both." Aurora brushed her hand across Clive's cheek once more. "Clive does not see any use for the Conduit population in this world. We will keep those of you who will fuel my Sulu Wheel, and the rest will die."

"What is power if you have no one to dominate over?"

"The rest of the strokes will suffice. All will bow to us." She circled me once more. "The moment I plunged that blade into my belly I altered the strokes forever." She leaned in closer to my face. "I created my own lines, just as Fih had."

"Surely you know what became of Fih, then?"

She raised her eyebrows inquisitively. "You saw the story in the caves below Delphi. Clever little girl." She pinched my cheek.

"Then you know he is destroyed by his own covetousness."

"Aw, but you see, I killed my Tindle many, many years ago, in Atlantis." She smirked. "I also killed my Lorif."

"But what you covet is no longer love. What you covet is power and destruction." I looked at Clive. Something was stirring in me, a knowing that even Aurora was unaware of Clive's true motivations.

A flash of rage splintered her smug demeanor. "There will be no one left to contest me." She turned on her heel and headed for the door, then stopped. "Something is wrong. They have infiltrated the depths!"

It was my turn to smile.

ELIAS

"Why here?" Sparkle asked. "Why is it the place where the world ends?"

"Sulu, please translate." Cataphet directed and I obliged. "Vira-clay was correct. The greater the haunting, the more powerful the energetic signature. When I came into contact with this land over 5,000 years ago, I knew it was powerful. But memories fade, even for dragons, and the façade of the earth had changed immensely. This entire city is saturated with hauntings. Voodoo incepted here, one of the last known variant strokes. It would not be until the Ulus was born that the memories came back. This was the land of the three brothers, and this very spot is where Lorif lost her life. The spot where Clive was born. The place where the world ends, because it is where it began."

When I finished my translation Sparkle spoke again. "The first strokes were here?"

Cataphet's voice grew with agitation and I was grateful that my sweet friend was getting a kinder version from me. "No, the first lines. Did you not see the story? The world as we know it was incepted here, where Lorif was literally torn in two by the brothers, thus splintering all because she was the divine Ulus."

572

"Please explain more, Cataphet. I don't understand, and I need to. My daughter's life depends on it." Desperation poured from Olly. It made my heart ache.

"It is simpler than what you are making it out to be. It is all about harmonizing what has long since been out of balance. You are the key, the Sulu is the key, the Staff of Banishment, this place, the Gattilak charm… They are the elements that led to the undoing. Therefore, they are the very elements that will repair our world."

I interjected. "I didn't see a Sulu there when Lorif splintered the world. What is my part to play in all of this?"

"Your part is bigger than you know. And you are correct. The Sulu wasn't there when the world shattered. Nor was the Ulus there when the Sulu annihilated entire generations of Conduits over and over again through Clive's manipulations. There was no balance. Everything perishes without balance, without harmony between the duality of it all."

Ruit inquired about a thread that many of us have discussed in detail. "Which lines were the first lines? Which trespass happened to lead us all to our doom? Was it when Fih stabbed Tindle or when Fih killed the sisters? How can you be certain it wasn't one of those episodes that began the fractures that you're talking about? Couldn't it have been when The Cathedral was created or when Tindle began to covet Lorif? If we get it wrong, do we destroy the world? Each of those tales implies they were the first lines."

"They are all the original lines that broke the painter's heart. Each time Fih injured another or lied to his brothers, each time Tindle coveted or manipulated Lorif, when the brothers created The Cathedral, they separated us all from the whole. Time is not linear. Nor does destruction bubble up from a single choice. More often, it is the smallest decisions that begin to shape the world. Without an intended compass, like harmony, too easily do the seemingly unimportant decisions begin to create monstrous discontent. Because time is not real, it is all happening all at once, which is exactly why different beings have come and gone on this planet, but the insidiousness of the lines continues. It is in the DNA of every being born, until we are made whole once more. Just as a monarch butterfly migrates over generations through the same journey as its predecessors, so too will we ultimately migrate toward our doom until this is made right. Until the misshapen strokes of the hobgoblin are integrated back into the painter's original masterpiece."

"What about the Originals? How have you been injured by this fracture?" Olly asked.

Cataphet quickly rose to her feet, and the whole city must have shaken. "How dare you ask such an ignorant question!" she roared. "Is it not enough that we have been hunted, murdered for power? Is it not enough that my sister lay captive in a Haven for thousands of years, tortured and maimed? Is it not enough..." Her voice cracked through the rage. I did not have to translate the fury for it to be felt.

"It is more than enough. But the truth is only you dragons understand the true defilement of what happened to you when Lorif splintered the world," Aremis empathized.

Suddenly the dark cave lit with a million little flames. No, not flames. Fiery lizards. Towering beside Cataphet appeared the flaming monstrous dragon Napitae.

Aremis took the dragon's appearance as an opportunity to speak about their travels. "When Napitae and I travelled to China together, we shared much along that journey. He told me that on that day, every dragon, every stroke, every being that existed forfeited a splinter of themselves. Not by their own admission, but by the force that came from the Ulus when she was torn apart by love."

I do not know if I would call that love, I thought to myself, but then I considered how Lucas and I had nearly torn Olly apart in the name of love. As much as I attempted to be neutral, to lead without condition, I saw the pain it caused her.

Cataphet cleared her throat. "We recognize our splinter when we see it in corporeal form. Like all energies, they are cyclical, and they move in and out and all around the planet, coming to the world in a variety of different creatures and strokes. But mine is always the Sulu. I knew when you were born what you were. We sense our splinter, we can not create or destroy each other, we are one in the same." She nodded at me. "Aremis is Napitae's splinter. His has always been a Phoenix. But you, Ophelia Banner, the likes of you have not walked this planet since Lorif."

That explained why Olly could not fend Clive off in Chernobyl. He is impervious to her assault. I wonder if he knows that?

"Why? What's wrong with me, and what do hobgoblins have to do with it?"

"The hobgoblin is the only creature the painter did not imagine before its creation. It does not come from the strokes, its inception came on that day, when Lorif the Ulus splintered the world, she opened something that allowed Clive to manifest here. And he is the only creature that is whole of its own right. Because it was born in the shards of the rest of us. That is why it toils its time keeping us divided. In one war after the other, after the other. We had no hope that it would ever end its campaign of discord. I could not change anything. Whenever I attempt to thwart it with the power of the Sulu, the entire population is wiped out because there is no balance to counteract the expansiveness of the Sulu's power. I watched many Conduit friends die. But then the painter gave us you. The only being who can balance the Sulu and match the vortex of power that is the hobgoblin Clive."

"Is there anything we must do to ensure the balance is realized?" I asked.

"You and the Ulus have the capacity to collaborate your strokes in a new, profound way. As you do, you open up the possibilities for other Soahcoit pairs. It will take time for you to both truly surrender to this co-creation. Time is not on our side. Therefore, much is in the hands of Malarin."

When I completed the final statement from Cataphet, Sparkle noted what only Sparkle would. "What lucky strokes we have, that the Sulu and Ulus are you two! I feel the odds are in our favor."

LUCAS

Jillian was administering the troll tears to the sedated captives. While Claudia was crying and holding her daughter, who was still slowly coming to, I was pacing.

"What's taking so long?" I mumbled under my breath. "I should've gone with them. What if the Nebas have been tipped off by now?"

Then, all of the sudden, the shuttle got really crowded. It was a miracle that the Princess, Queen and Emperor did not squash any or all of the rescued captives.

"Yesi! Yessica!" I couldn't see anything around the enormous bodies.

"I'm here. I'm safe."

She sounded exhausted.

"Where is Esther?" she asked just as we made eye contact around Princess Chaness' gargantuan thigh.

"She's in there. They got her." I pulled my wife in tight for a hug, kissed her face, and thanked the strokes she was okay. "I need to know everything."

"You need to know nothing until we go get Esther," Yessica said firmly.

"Look, baby girl, I don't know how we are all in one piece, but we cannot go back in there now that they know they are missing one giant asset." I gestured up to the Princess. The emperor and queen were tending to her very gently. "We need to get out of here."

"I will tell you how we all got out of there in one piece. It was Esther's plan. She is a better ally than enemy. We go back and get her now."

I looked beyond my wife to see who else was listening to this and what their take was. By the look on Stalt, Claudia and Jillian's faces, they felt Yesi had a good point.

I waddled into our apartment. Elias had been watching me warily since we left the throne room. He knew me too well. For all I knew, he was reading my thoughts. Therefore, there was no point in hiding how I felt.

"Why is it me? Why do I have to be the spawn of something evil? I mean, I thought it was bad when I was Nestor's offspring. Now I'm the sliver of the only thing the painter never intentionally made and that is hell-bent on keeping the world shrouded in chaos and then destroying it." I threw myself on the bed, and Elias climbed on beside me, brushing my hair from my face as he lay his head on my chest. "No wonder Sadie is having second thoughts about her choices."

"I feel you are miraculous. In many ways, but in this way as well."

"Okay, I'll bite. How is this a miracle?"

"Well, first, not all miracles are obviously good, nor can they be inherently bad."

"That's a big disclaimer, Mr. Kraus." I held back the scoff I wanted to make. My husband deserved more respect than that.

"Hear me out. You, and the sliver of hobgoblin that resides within you, ultimately came from Lorif and her ability to stand for what was right. To demand justice for her sisters. Lorif stood for the love of her sisters, not to defile or create discord in the world. She used her voice, and it transformed the world forever, but her intentions were never bad. You are a spawn of that. Perhaps the drive that propels Clive comes from the other aspects of the incident that slivered the world... the brothers and their desire to covet. Or his own eternity of solitude and inability to connect with the other strokes."

"But I'm from that too."

"Indeed. But what if you only absorbed the good parts?"

"You're such a positive penny." I ran my fingers through his hair.

"When it comes to you, always." He propped himself up and looked at me. "Seriously, I see Lorif in you. I see how you stand up for what is right, no matter the cost. I see how you love your family, chosen and blood, fiercely. I see loyalty, commitment, strength and love... Mostly, I see love." Elias kissed me and I surrendered to his words, to the mirror he reflected back to me. It was likely truer than any angle I could ever see for myself.

When he pulled his mouth from mine and I stared into his golden-green eyes, the very eyes that haunted me upon our first meeting, I chuckled.

"What? What is funny?"

"Your eyes."

He looked at me expectantly, waiting for an explanation.

"It makes sense, the golden-green hazel color. I noticed before but didn't understand the correlation. The stained glass window we once encountered in the great hall of The Cathedral—it was that color." He sat up higher on the bed. "The first time I saw Cataphet's eyes, I noted the color. How does it feel to be part of the greatest dragon that ever existed? Part of The Cathedral itself, because Cataphet and The Cathedral are one? How does it feel to be that fucking awesome?"

Elias turned beet-red with embarrassment, and it made my heart smile.

"That feels like a lot of pressure."

"Yeah, now you know how I feel."

We both laughed and entangled ourselves in one another's bodies in every way we could, enjoying the peacefulness of this quiet moment.

"I was also thinking about what Cataphet said. How all the elements that created the splintering have returned to its origin. That can't be a coincidence."

"No, my dear wife, I do not believe it is a coincidence at all."

The painter's voice echoed in my head. "Everything has been brought back to its origin to be repainted. This time, dear one, the strokes created are already steeped in love. They already stir in you."

I started to cry.

"What? What's wrong?"

"The painter. He said the strokes we are creating are already steeped in love." I put my hands on my belly and Elias kissed them.

"Speaking of no coincidences, there is a Conduit I think we should speak too. He seemed to have first hand experience with Clive."

I sat up more abruptly. "Why are you just telling me this now? Yes, please go get him." Elias raised his eyebrows. "Like right now."

"Very well. I'll be back shortly."

Something else dawned on me, another "coincidence" slipping through the cracks. "Where is your box with all the remnants from your father?"

"Are you certain you are up for this much commotion right now?"

"I am fine." I asserted. "Let me make busywork for myself."

He shook his head gently, but didn't argue any further. A moment later he placed the box on the nightstand and kissed my forehead. "I will return shortly with Ramy."

I got straight to work. I splayed out all the pieces with the shimmer effect on the floor and albeit slow and awkwardly, began piecing together the puzzle before me.

ESTHER

"The Princess is gone! How can the Princess be gone?!" Aurora shouted. "What did you do?" She came up to me in my invisible cage and clawed at my face. I just laughed. I welcomed the pain. It enraged her.

A powrie manifested out of nowhere. The Oracle stopped her onslaught long enough to hear him say that four of the Orbs had disappeared into the earth and they were sure more were in danger of the same fate.

"Clive, make her unconscious."

Suddenly, I was on the floor, and Clive's boot was at my neck. I reached to remove it but I heard a breaking in my spine and all went dark.

LUCAS

I can't believe we're doing this.

"I just took two more Orbs into my lava tubes. If that does not create panic, I do not know what will," Stalt said.

"Let's go!" Claudia commanded as she locked arms with Yesi, Jillian and I, using the compass to take us back into the Orb Forest Haven. We were back in the captives' room, and we could hear chaos in the hall.

"What do we do now?" Jillian asked.

"Can you amplify my shield so that no one could see us?"

"Maybe."

"You heard her being dragged down this way. She can't be far."

"If the camouflage doesn't work, we can blind them with Yesi's light, or I can stupefy them with their fears."

"Fuck."

Yesi grabbed my hand. I swung open the door as soon as I could feel my gift amplified. Nebas were all around us. We narrowly missed a couple of collisions, but they didn't seem to see us. I hadn't spotted Aurora or Clive yet. There were three rooms at the end of the long hall. Assuming Esther was down here still. Two of the three doors were open. I pointed at the closed one and Claudia shrugged.

Good enough, I guess.

Jillian reached it first and tried the knob. It opened. She nodded vigorously. *This silent communication shit is impossible.*

I looked up to make sure no one was watching us, and I saw Clive at the end of the hall. His eyes were set on me. I could sense he could see straight through my shield.

A toothy grin spread across his face. "Hurry! They know!" I pushed Yesi through the door just in time to feel a body barrel against it. This room would be swarming in seconds. I dug my feet into the ground and barricaded the door. Jillian picked up Esther's limp body, and Claudia quickly made fast use of the Compass just as Yesi took my hand and the door splintered open.

*R*amy was easy enough to track down, he was once again in the library.

"Viraclay, we have to stop running into each other this way. Or perhaps, do I sense it right, when I say, this was an intentional meeting?"

"You are correct. I would like to invite you to share what information you have about Clive the hobgoblin with my wife and I. You implied there was more to the story and Ophelia and I would appreciate all the information we can get about this enemy."

"It would be a pleasure. When would you like to meet?"

"Now?" I tried to sound nonchalant, but Ramy was astute.

"No time like the present." He put the book he was looking at back on the shelf and gestured for me to show him the way.

I paused. Formulating what I wanted to say. "My wife is in a fragile state. Please be gentle with her."

"Of course, I would think of doing nothing else."

Olly would kill me if she knew I just asked him to use kid gloves on her, but she also wanted to believe she could handle the weight of the world on her shoulders. Moments later we were manifesting in front of our door. I gently knocked as I entered, to warn her I had returned with company. She was hovering over the floor in the most awkward position, sliding the scraps of paper into a circular formation.

"Look Elias, it looks like the faction diagram, the one you showed me before the Katuan Trials. The one that represents all the various giftings of the Conduit world."

We walked over to her and I looked at what she had puzzled together. It did in fact look like the diagram she spoke of. Ramy examined it over my shoulder.

"It is actually a Blessing Way. You're just missing the key." He pointed to the top right corner. "That piece, that piece completes the blessing."

We took the conversation into our heads. She said it first. "Blessing Way? That can't be a coincidence."

"Indeed, it cannot." I agreed then I reached down to help her off the floor.

"What do you know about the Blessing Ways? Ramy? Is that your name? Let's take a seat." Olly gestured to the couch.

Ramy sat in the chair across from us on the sofa. "My family used to be the keepers of the Blessing Ways. They were ancient blessing rituals that were said to be written and performed by Priloc himself. I was told a story as a boy, in the tale it was said that while the great Rittles were bestowed to the kings and queens of the original six strokes, it was the Conduits who received the Blessing Way. The rites that connected the strokes to this world. But you must have known my connection to the Blessing Way and Clive? That is why you asked for an audience with me, is it not?"

"In truth, we did not know they were connected." I admitted.

"Wow, well Chitchakor has his ways, does he not?"

"Indeed."

"Apparently." Olly said aghast as she rubbed her belly gently.

"The Blessing Way was created by both Priloc and Clive. But when Priloc left Clive to wander the world alone, Clive returned to the lands where I grew up and he demanded the rites back. It was said that my great great great grandparents watched in horror as he ripped the sacred way to shreds. I used to have a remnant like these, that you have collected. Alas Clive discovered it and nearly killed me to retrieve it. When I hunted the beast down to demand my family's legacy be restored, I stumbled upon the creature Clive syphoning the life force from Walthrup until he was made dust, then robbing him of the Gattilak charm that he wore. I was a coward, I could not save Walthrup and I did not demand my legacy restored."

"No one would blame you, I can't imagine what that must have been like." Olly empathized. "Forgive yourself."

He nodded and continued. "My family shared all that they could remember about the Ways verbally from generation to generation. I decided to maintain the legacy by educating the lineage of the Tartar people and the Cabecar people in the Blessing Way rites. For generations they have performed the rites, when called to."

Olly gasped.

"What?" Ramy asked.

"We have both received the rites." I explained.

"Without the key?" He pointed to the papers on the ground.

"No, from your legacy." Olly said. "I received it from the Tartars and Elias received it from the Cabecars."

"Astonishing." He rubbed his forehead. "Then where did you get these remnants?"

"My father."

Just then I felt the tug of the bidding tether. "It is Lucas, excuse us Ramy, we have been expecting this contact with an update."

"Well, he better be saying he's on his way. We have a lot to fill him in on." Olly crossed her arms expectantly.

The transmission was coming in patchy and staticky. I projected what I was getting onto the wall, so Ophelia could be included. "Olly. Man, Viraclay. We gotta make a plan or set up a defense while we make a plan. Because they are coming! The powries, Clive, Aurora and the Nebas. We poked the bear, and the bear is coming!" Then Lucas signed off.

"What in the strokes happened in Siberia?" My wife asked aloud.

We both looked at Ramy, who was still in shock about the revelations that just occurred.

I took the conversation into our Rune channel. "I do not know what transpired with Lucas and the rescue mission for Princess Chaness, but I feel we should take this to Ruit and see how many Pai Ona have arrived. Perhaps he can set up a clearer correspondence with Lucas and his comrades." I paused, still waiting for Ramy to say something. "What do you make of all of this?"

"He seems credible."

I touched Ramy's shoulder. "Are you okay?"

"Yes, I am sorry. I can see you two have much more on your plate then this. I hope I was helpful. Please let me know if I can be of further assistance." Then he was up and heading toward the door. "It was a pleasure." Then he was gone.

I was helping Olly with her shoes, so we could find Ruit and fill him in.

"There is something Ramy said, it makes me want to get in touch with Fetzle."

"What was that?"

"The High Priestess prophesied that, "The rightful Queen that wears the Crown of Thorns, holds the key to all that was lost.""

We said it in unison. "Fetzle must have the key."

"Fetzle, I just need you here for a quick strategy meeting and a debrief of developments."

"Very well Lucas, but I must get back to Princess Chaness as quickly as possible."

I side-eyed Yesi, because we both knew she really meant Calt. The room was full of the usually suspects now.

"Thanks for gracing us with your presence." Olly joked, but I sensed some pregnancy sass leaking into the tone.

"Right! Let's get to it then." I explained what happened in detail. The faces got paler and the jaws slacked lower as I described how Esther essentially saved us all. I would've paid a million dollars to read the minds in that room. When I was finished, no one said a word.

"Why didn't you ask me if you could use her as bate?" Olly finally cracked the ice.

"Because you would have said no."

Elias put his hand on her shoulder to calm her. "Where is Esther now?"

"Claudia and Jillian are watching her."

"We have had some developments too." I somehow dodged her

fury. Olly explained what she found in the paper remnants that Cane had collected and left for his son. Then described the incredible timing of Ramy's admission. Just as she finished Fetzle spoke up.

"I gave Cane those remnants. I didn't know what they were. I received them from the same poppit that gave me the hairsy charm. The poppit was also carrying a bag of enchanted paper and your father was on my next shuttle. Cane seemed intrigued by the bag of scraps and I had already received all I needed for my fare with the charm. So, I gave him the bag of paper."

"Why would a poppit have two extremely powerful magics and be so willing to give them away?" Ruit asked.

"They are incredible thieves. Not very bright though." Fetzle concluded.

"Do you have anymore of the remnants? We need the key." Elias looked doubtful. But he had to try.

"I do, it's the piece I wrapped the hairsy charm in for safe keeping. I know exactly where it is."

The whole room exhaled.

"I'll bring it straight away." Then she was gone and the room erupted with a buzz of conversations.

ESTHER

I came to, but waited to open my eyes, listening to what was happening around me, trying to get a feel for where I was. How mutilated my body would be. But there was no pain. There were no loud or recognizable sounds, just a humming of drums in the distance. *This couldn't be the River Tins?*

"We know you're awake," Claudia's irritating voice observed. "You're not dead yet."

"Quite the plot twist," Jillian teased.

My eyes shot open. "You?"

Both the women were at my bedside. Presumably watching over me. There were no shackles or binds, and if I wasn't mistaken, I might have been bathed.

"Yes, Esther, me." Jillian was sewing something, and she set it aside. "Do you know who was among those last captives?"

I shook my head.

"My Atoa and my mother. I know what kind of monster you are firsthand. I have also heard what has made you this thing that you are. If it were not for you and your strategy back there, I am confident we'd all be dead. Life is precious. I don't have the energy to waste it on hate. I'll choose grace. Especially if that grace has proven to reward me with love." She stood up. "I wanted to make sure you woke. I will take my leave and prepare for mobilization with the others."

"Mobilization?"

"We are in Listy. The Sholl-guard alongside the giants are mobilizing for the final battle."

"You aren't a prisoner, but I'd be lying if I said we were going to just let you go." Lucas stood in the doorway. "Thanks for watching her, Claudia. I got this."

Claudia nodded at me and left. Lucas took her seat.

"How are you feeling?"

"We don't have to do pleasantries."

"Oh, thank the fucking strokes."

I sat up and looked around the room. It was plain. It must be a troll chamber.

"Where is the final battle?"

"Will you fight with us?"

"What is your plan?"

"There are many strategies at play."

"Is this a standoff?"

"I supposed it is," he admitted. "Look, we couldn't have done what we did back there without you. It's that simple. We probably can do what we're going to do here without you, especially since we took all the Conduits she could use to maximize her Super Sulu thing."

"She still has a fleet of Nebas." Moreover, those Orbs were what gave Clive power, and *I was certain his motives were more sinister than hers. Did I keep all of this close?*

"You're right. They also have a legion of angry powries, and Clive, plus a surplus of Orbs."

"It sounds like there are more unknowns on their side, which is risky business for you guys. I might as well just take my freedom and let you burn each other out." But I knew that wasn't true because if Aurora won, Conduits would be gone forever. I wondered if that meant I wouldn't even see my Yanni in the River Tins.

"I know you know more. With your cooperation, we could finish this once and for all." He leaned in a little closer and whispered, "I know you well, Esther. I know you want vengeance for Yanni, Apollo and Shatki."

"Arrogant of you to say, considering."

"We have a Blood Bidding. I'm not worried about me, sweetheart." He leaned back and crossed his arms over his chest in a cocky, arrogant way, and I fought back an urge to lunge at him.

We sat there in cold silence for a long moment. "Can you promise me I can be the one to kill her?"

"I don't think Olly would even promise you that."

OPHELIA

"Update me with our numbers. Have the Ancients arrived?" Elias asked Winston and Ying, who sat across from him.

"All of the Ancients have come. Our numbers are impressive. Hundred strong."

"Indeed. One Ancient is the equivalent to thirty Consu. This is powerful," Aruna estimated.

"All who performed the Bidding and many others have appeared to take the oath at The Cathedral's gates," Helia said.

Lucas grabbed my arm gently. "I don't know how relevant it is, but Esther mentioned that the Oracle spoke of a Sulu Wheel. I thought I should share."

A seed of a thought was trying to bud, Sulu Wheel...the faction diagram...circles...the Blessing Way. But then Elias interrupted my process and it vanished.

"Excellent. Sounds like we are ready to congregate and give a general briefing."

"Uh-uh," Medusa interrupted my next point on the agenda. "There is someone who needs to speak with you in private, Olly."

"I don't think I need to be giving anyone private audiences right now, Medusa." I was already stretched too thin, and we had no time.

"This one is special, and she won't want to see him anyway." She pointed at Ruit.

"Really, I don't have the time for trivial—"

"It's Molpe. She's here, and I think you might want to convene with her in private. Or at least not with that guy in the room. Hell hath no fury like a Siren scorned."

Ruit attempted to look ashamed, but he more or less looked smug.

"Right. Elias?"

"Indeed." My husband and I were escorted into the hall by Medusa, where she quickly transported us to a meadow somewhere in The Cathedral. Molpe had her back to us when we manifested on the grassy lawn. Several of her Tendrils were on guard around her. There was a tension in the air, almost like the feeling just before a climax, and I wondered if that was because of her unease or the mixture of imminent battle and the seductress Siren's energy.

I popped into our Rune. "Is it appropriate to hug a Siren?"

"I haven't the faintest. Let her take the lead."

She turned around, and her long black hair danced around her voluptuous form. I'd thought she was sexy the first time I'd seen her, but whatever she'd been doing since Merr was suiting her. She spread her arms, and that answered that question. "Ophelia." I walked over and gave her a hug. "You are with child?"

"Oh, you noticed?" I teased. She looked at me peculiarly and I realized I didn't know Molpe's sense of humor at all, so perhaps shooting straight from the hip was better. "Yes, I am very pregnant. Due any moment."

Molpe nodded at Elias, but didn't offer him a hug. "Congratulations, Father. But the timing is poor, is it not?"

"Very. We didn't know that time in the troll shuttles and Solomon Islands would speed up gestation as it has."

"I see." She examined my body more thoroughly. "Did you know birth can be an orgasmic experience?"

"I'm sorry… Repeat that."

"In the olden days, my Tendrils didn't just seek the Siren's song during sexual exploits. In fact, we were midwives for many women during their orgasmic birthing portal. Pleasure takes much more surrender than pain. It widens the birthing portal significantly more, allowing all of the souls gifts to accompany them into this life. Pain is constrictive, pressured and forceful. The portal opens either way. But a mother giving birth, surrendering to the wide orgasmic waves of cosmic pleasure, is truly an open vessel." She leaned into whisper, as though Elias wouldn't hear her. "That is why those who cannot experience birth have changed the birthing story to labor, pain and hardship. The power of a woman embracing her ability to bring life into this world through orgasm is too frightening for them."

Admittedly, I had heard of women who had pleasurable labors. But this was something beyond that. It resonated with me, but I didn't have the time to think about it.

"My Tendrils and I could be your midwives?"

"That is an incredibly generous offer. Does that mean you intend to fight with us in this war?"

She laughed. "What is a Siren of Pleasure to do on a battlefield, Ophelia?" She had a point.

"Why, then, have you come?" Elias asked.

"To warn you. Many of the fae have chosen to align with the Nebas and the powrie king. Their numbers are vast and they move in force. They will reach the gates of The Cathedral by nightfall."

We expected them to arrive soon. That is of no surprise. But what does an army of fae consist of?

"Why would the fae side with the Nebas?" Elias asked the obvious question.

"The strokes will reveal themselves in due time. They also travel with golden Orbs of power. Those must be destroyed if you have any chance of winning this war. No matter who fights beside you."

Elias and I looked at each other. We knew the Orbs were important, but we didn't know to what extent.

"Do you know anything else about the Orbs?" I hoped for something that could help us understand how to destroy them.

"They are not of Malarin's strokes. They were created by Clive."

"Does that make a difference?"

"It does."

It's like pulling teeth here. "How so?" Elias asked.

"It is thought that only Clive will have the power to destroy them."

I brought the conversation into our heads. "Or what about his splinter?"

The painter's voice filled my head. "You must bring the Blessing Way with the key, to the place where the world ends. When the time is right and all the pieces are there. The Queen must place the key as the portal opens. Clive will be returned to the timeline from whence he came."

He is from another timeline?

"Yes, the ninth timeline."

I let out a big sigh, not really sure what any of this meant. But grateful for the instructions.

"Well at least the voice is being helpful and less vague."

"Pardon me?" Elias looked at me for an explanation.

LUCAS

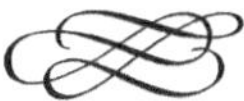

"She was impressive, Vosega," Stalt boasted about my wife. I looked over at Yesi, and she was glowing.

"You give me too much credit."

"Esther's plan executed perfectly. I created six lava tubes instantaneously." My dad high-fived his once-adversary. "Then this little lady was shuttled in by the queen. She dropped in and shone her light so brightly that the entire place lit up like a breaking dawn. The powries were stunned, then panicked. The trolls and giants barely needed to lift a finger to free Princess Chaness. It was powerful."

"I'm so proud of you." The Khan beamed at his daughter.

"Where is the Princess now?" Oya asked.

"Recovering on the Solomon Islands," I answered.

A moment later, Fetzle entered the room. "We need to prepare the Sholl-guard, Mr. Khan."

I still couldn't get over her transformation.

"I want to arrive to The Cathedral before the battle, to invite our allies to take the oath to the Crown of Thorns, offering them the extra protection."

"Good idea," I agreed. Yesi came up beside me and took my hand. "You impressed Stalt." She nudged me with her elbow.

"Stop it."

"You always impress me." I kissed her on the forehead.

"Ophelia and Elias have been informed that the legion of powries and an army of fae will reach The Cathedral by nightfall."

"The fae?" Thracian sounded as bewildered as I felt.

"They have joined the other side," Fetzle asserted.

ELIAS

"Everyone has been briefed, and everyone has taken the oath, except for the dragons." Ying came up beside me and Olly as we walked into the arena. It was a sight to behold. Ancients alongside dragons, beside trolls, locking arms with giants.

"Did you ever imagine?" My wife looked at me with disbelief. Ruit and his family were already center stage. They greeted us with hugs and took their seats just to the left of us. I saw many familiar faces. Conduits I now considered family. Ophelia waved at Lucas and Yesi. I nodded, and Lucas nodded back. The stadium was so quiet you could hear a pin drop.

I put my hand at the small of Olly's back and gave her a gentle nudge, letting her know I was here. But they wanted to hear from her.

"The day has come. The final battle begins tonight. The moment of justice for those we've lost has arrived." The congregation got to their feet and roared. "Our enemy is cunning, and for this reason, Viraclay and I have decided to deliver proof of the Oracle's treachery. Let there be no doubt that she cannot be trusted, that should you, any of you, get the opportunity to destroy the Oracle, there will be no hesitation."

A murmur rippled through the crowd. Curiosity, fear and astonishment.

I spoke to Ophelia with our Rune. "Are you prepared for this?"

"As much as I will ever be."

I nodded at Lucas again, and he, along with Fetzle and five Shollguard, stepped in front of the stage while Aremis escorted Esther out. The audience of Conduits quickly escalated into a mob.

"Esther is here to set the story straight. Between the three of us, you will see with your own eyes what we have discovered to be the truth."

I took the hand of Esther with my right, and the mob got louder and more outraged. Olly gripped my left. I began the projection and attempted to amplify the volume of the interactions above the rising voices. I was not certain they could hear a thing until the room got deathly quiet when Aurora made her admission to me of killing my parents. There were gasps when they witnessed Olly's interactions on the banks of the River Tins. Then there were several guttural screams when the Oracle described her choices and intentions to Esther.

When the projection was finished, I released Esther's hand and stood there for a long, pregnant pause. Deciding what I would say next.

"Tonight, we shall fight for the very existence of our stroke. If the Oracle and Clive prevail, Conduits will cease to exist. If they succeed, the world will fall into ruin. We are the only thing standing between them and the utter annihilation of Chitchakor's creation. The hobgoblin Clive would see everything burn. We cannot hesitate. We cannot hold back. We will not give up. We do not stand alone. Tonight, we fight for truth above all else. Let the truth lead you. Let your truth guide you. Let truth set us all free from tyranny once and for all!"

The stadium stood in unison and exploded with a cacophony of cheers.

LUCAS

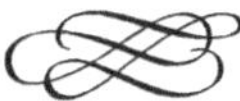

"The waiting is awful," Yesi said as she nuzzled into me.

"Yes, it is, baby girl."

We were literally at the front door of the LaLaurie Mansion, the first line of defense. Just like during the last open battle, we would attempt to drop into the in-between, into the veil, when the combat began. A space among the world and the humans, but not in the world. Sometimes the entry didn't happen smoothly, and the violence would pour out into the streets, but Cataphet said she would personally escort each squad into the veil. As far as I knew, we had never had the help of a dragon's stroke's before, so I thought our odds seemed pretty good. Olly was adamant that we avoid hurting innocent bystanders. I didn't think that was really possible. It was but a small price to pay for saving the world. *But what do I know?*

I looked at our assembly. There were hundreds of squads ready to strike around the French quarter when the enemy made itself known. Our group was primarily made up of familiar faces. Fetzle and ten of her Sholl-guard, Emperor Calt and four of his soldiers, Shiva and Baset, Ophelia, Viraclay, Esther, Aremis, Sparkle, Lilith, Winston, Lucia, Ying, Aruna, Ruit, Jezebel, Inca, Almus, Thracian,

Dari, Genghis, Borte, Claudia, Stalt, Aurelia, Jillian, Medusa, Tete, Helia, dear old Dad, Oya and Friedrick. Plus a couple dragons—Franky and Gwenora.

I knew some of these Conduits really well. Others were new acquaintances, but the one thing that tied us all together was our love for Olly. *And there was the impending apocalyptic end of the world.*

Ruit waved at me to come over. I saw him also gesture at Olly.

"I'll be right back."

Olly and I both got there at the same moment.

"I made these for you two." Ruit pulled out two bracelets that looked like the hairsy charm.

"You want us to do this again?" I looked warily at the Alchemist.

"No, the bond already exists between you two. I want you two to remember it." He placed the charm on Olly's wrist. "Cataphet said that it was of significance that all of the parts that existed during the first lines were here once more." He maneuvered the other one onto my wrist. "This bond you two share may very well contribute to the saving of the world. I want you both to remember that."

"Thank you, Ruit," Olly said graciously, and then her eyes got big. "They're here."

PART IV

ESTHER

J was ready. I had never been more ready for a battle in my life. I wanted to kill her myself or die trying. The ground shook beneath our feet. Never in my wildest dreams did I imagine I would be fighting beside Viraclay and the Pai Ona. I turned to my left, where Lucas was crouched, ready to pounce. The hands that ripped my Yanni from this world. *Can I really fight beside him? Will I defend him if the opportunity arose?* The earth shook again.

I could ponder my standing with Lucas at another time. Tonight, we were aligned. Tomorrow was another matter entirely.

I could feel it as we moved into the in-between veil. Elias told me it would be a weird sensation at first, and he wasn't kidding. It felt like being in shifting sand, like you're moving but not. I had to orient myself. I reached for my husband's hand. He quickly put the Staff of Banishment in his other hand and took hold of me. I thought I might be sick. The ground shook again. I grabbed my belly. *Hold tight in there, Sadie.*

Suddenly, the door was blown off its hinges. *Is that in the veil or in the human plane?* There was very little time to think about it before a tall, lanky figure's silhouette filled the doorway.

"I will be taking that." He pointed a long, spindly finger at the Staff, and I had to assume he was the powrie King OAD.

"Of course she would send you on the frontline, OAD," Esther hissed. "You're a minion, like the rest of them."

"Esther. So, it is true. You changed sides." The king laughed maniacally. "I would not have believed it. If I did not see it."

"Pleasantries are over." Esther was flying through the air at the powrie like a missile. "It's time you die."

ELIAS

I dispatched the rest of the squads through the Bidding tether, simultaneously informing them that we did not have eyes on the Oracle or Clive yet. A flood of powries entered through the main gate of The Cathedral. Cataphet had left it open on purpose to funnel the enemy into our location. The goal was to surround the enemy and direct them into the Haven, where we could dictate the landscape and end this where it all began.

Ophelia communicated through our Rune. "Here they come."

"Stay between me and Lucas." I handed her the Staff of Banishment to defend herself. Ultimately, Ophelia's skills were limited with how pregnant she was. We did not have enough time to learn how to collaborate our gifts yet, but she still funneled everything she encountered to me. It was integral that she be here, with me.

"And there is no way in hell you could convince me to be anywhere else."

"Did you just read my thoughts?"

"Baby, look out!" I turned around to see three powries and a centaur charging my back. I quickly summoned a fire ball to incinerate the onslaught.

Lucas came around to my right. "We need to get deeper into The Cathedral."

"Indeed." I signaled to Ying for he and Aruna to take her Thunderbirds up and see how the other squads were faring. Tete and Medusa would follow. Fetzle and Calt were to assess where Clive was with the Orbs.

Aremis came up on my flank. "We will cover your retreat and handle this first wave." He and Shiva were in position so that Olly and I could safely run to the next location, the place where we intended to make our final stand.

lmus tapped into our Rune. "Ying and Medusa returned to report there were no sitings of the Oracle or hobgoblin, and the powrie and fae armies are not operating as we expected. They will not advance any further than a few hundred feet into our line."

"She saw our first strategy." We expected that.

"Yes, we did," Elias answered my thoughts.

"What?" Almus understandably got confused.

"Sorry, Almus. Let us move to strategy B and see if we can get the funnel to work by pushing them into the gates."

"Certainly." Then he signed off.

"What? What's going on?" Lucas asked just as Esther showed up.

"The powries and fae have stopped storming the gate, and OAD retreated behind his frontline just before I could finish him off. He will restore his strength."

That's it. They are staying out of The Cathedral. They will be cut off once they enter her strokes. They are retreating to stay closer to their power source. The Orbs are close. We need to dispatch those first, then they will be forced to come after the Staff.

"You are brilliant, my wife." Elias was reading my thoughts

I opened my mouth to explain what I'd concluded when I felt crippling pain seize my lower back and down into my pubic bone. *Not now.* My knees buckled and Yesi caught me.

I held my breath until the pain subsided. Elias was rubbing my lower back gently. "Was that…"

"My first contraction? Yep." Lucas found me a chair and I took a seat. "Want to explain what we need to do next Elias?"

"Shouldn't we get you somewhere safe first?" Lucas looked between me and Elias, exasperated. But we had already had this conversation. I had to be here. I would give birth on this battlefield if that was how the strokes fated it to be. All of the elements that were here when the lines were drawn needed to be here for the battle to be won. Elias and I were a unit, and we were stronger together, always. And something in my bones knew that I would be the one to destroy the Orbs.

"We have to find the Orbs."

"Elias, Olly is going into labor." Yesi put her hand on her husband's arm. She understood the pact we had made. "She can't have this baby in the middle of a war."

"She can and she will."

Esther laughed. "I thought I would stop at nothing. You have me beat, pet."

Lucas shook his head in disbelief.

"We find the Orbs and we find the Oracle and Clive," Esther agreed.

Aremis, Sparkle, Winston and Lucia came running up. "They are retreating. They are attempting to draw us out," Aremis explained.

"We can't fall into their trap either," Yesi stated exactly what I was thinking. This was too calculated. They had somewhere they wanted us.

The Tallus family approached. "The trolls and giants are easily handling the line. We have to shift gears."

Helia approached, "We have to amplify the Oracle's blind spots."

"Lucas, you do something to Aurora's visions. She confessed as much during my captivity. I think you have to create the strategy."

"Well, that explains why they didn't see the rescue mission of the Princess coming." Lucas ran his fingers through his hair. "I'm sure I can come up with something."

"Be quick about it," Medusa shouted from on top of Tete. "Some of the violence has spilled into Bourbon Street."

No, no, no, no. I don't want any innocent bystanders harmed.

Just then, another contraction hit.

LUCAS

"This is fucking cool! You guys do this all the time?" I said to Elias through the Rune. He agreed to share his with me so that I could make last-minute battle strategy changes to avoid Aurora from seeing them in advance.

"We can all hear you, Lucas," Inca informed me. "You have to be more specific with your communication."

"Okay, okay. I'll do better."

"Good, because we don't need distractions on the battlefield," Olly added.

"Shit, I got it. More specific." I honed in on Viraclay. "How about now?"

"Yes. I can hear you exclusively."

Olly stood up. "I know how to detect the Orbs. Elias, use Berty's gift. He saw the strokes. Molpe said that the Orbs are of Clive's creation. They won't look the same. Clive won't look the same."

"I don't know how far I can see, Olly."

She waddled over to Elias, and whatever she shared was enough for him to agree. "The rest is up to you, guys. Once you have created the strategy, I will get it out to the squads. Ophelia and I will handle the Orbs. You must get them in here, no matter what."

"We got this. Did I say that out loud or in my Rune?"
"Out loud," Aremis, Ruit, Almus and Sparkle declared.
I turned to Esther. "I know you can throw something together."
"Lucas, I thought you'd never ask."

ELIAS

e were nearly up to Gwenora and Franky. "Are you certain you are up for this?"

"Please don't ask me again. We've already talked about this."

"Indeed."

"Ophelia, mate! Looks like we are heading them off."

"I heard that! I heard you, Franky!"

"Right. That's good, right?"

"She had lost the ability to hear dragon when we consummated. But today, she has heard my thoughts, and now, she understood dragon. That is good."

"That is great!" Then she bent over in pain from another contraction.

"Blimey! She is about to pop!"

"Indeed, but we need your help."

"How can we help, Viraclay?" Gwenora asked. "Anything."

Olly recovered. "We need a ride from you, and if my intuition is right, we will need some dirt moved by you. I believe the Orbs are underground. I want them moved into the catacombs of The Cathedral. Do you think you can do that?"

"I reckon these Orbs are a bit tricky, or you wouldn't need my help."

"They are something Clive created on his own. They will not be easily manipulated. You will likely only be able to manage the earth around them."

"I am your dragon!" Frankie said. He looked at Gwenora. "But I will not be flying. We learned the hard way that I need my four feet on the ground. Gwenora can tell me whatever I need to know."

"I love you." The large purple dragon leaned in and nuzzled against Franky's tiny frame.

"I love you more than rocks, and blimey, that says a lot." He nuzzled her back.

Ruit was examining me. I could feel his eyes. "What is between you and Lucas?"

"What in the strokes do you mean?" If he was implying we were somehow infatuated with one another, I may have to kill him.

"There is some sort of bond. I think it may also shield you from your mother's sight."

"The Oracle," I corrected.

"I made her take a Blood Bidding to ensure she didn't double-cross us when I was using her for bait."

"Brilliant, Lucas. By tying your fates, you are intrinsically creating blind spots with Esther as well."

"Lucky strokes, I guess." Lucas shrugged.

Lucky strokes indeed, I thought. This could be the advantage I needed to get to Aurora and kill her.

"With this in mind, I feel the rest of us should take our leave while you two form the strategy. As soon as you are ready to have us implement the first steps, communicate it through your Rune, Lucas, play by play, and we may have a fighting chance of staying a step ahead of the Oracle."

Yessica kissed her husband, and she and the others left toward the frontline.

"Do we still have that compass?"

"No, we gave it to Elias and Ophelia," Lucas admitted. "Why?"

"Never mind." I wanted it to complete my own mission. "How many squads do we have?"

"I think somewhere around seventy-five."

"Wait. What?"

"I can get an exact number."

"They need to move! Now!"

ELIAS

*I*n the veil, things were peculiar. The strokes were less vivid. Therefore, it felt harder to notice if there was an anomaly.

"Do you see anything? They would be underground," Olly insisted.

"I know, baby, but I do not see anything." I could see our squads strategically placed around the French Quarter, surrounding The Cathedral, ready to funnel the enemy into the front gate. I could see the swarms of powries and fae buzzing around the pockets of allies. They would advance and then retreat, like a yo-yo. I could see the variations in each creature. If I was not on a mission, it would be fascinating work to dissect the differences.

"I think I am seeing the strokes too," Olly announced. "Wow, what a menagerie." Then a contraction came on and she seized in pain, gripping my back harder.

"Is she okay?" Gwenora asked. "She should not give birth in the sky."

"I'm okay. And you're right, Gwenora. I don't want to give birth on your back. We need to find these Orbs, love."

Just then, one of the squads began to mobilize, and I saw something beneath them. It was hallow, void of all movement, circular and huge.

"The Orbs are under the squads. She knew our plan all along. We have to get them out of there!"

"Gwenora, tell Franky the Orbs are under each of our mobilized units. The enemy wasn't avoiding entering The Cathedral. They were keeping our men where they wanted them. The Orbs need to move now!" Olly commanded.

Just then, the strokes shuddered wildly around one of the pods of our allies on Frenchman Street. Then the powries and fae swarmed in. It was like the Conduits were frozen in place. They were just lambs for the slaughter.

"Gwenora, we have to help them!" I shouted, and she swooped down. Simultaneously, I summoned a wave of destruction from Shiva's gifts and incinerated the first wave of powries that were slicing through the Pai Ona. Thankfully the oath to the Crown was offering some sense of shielding, but a few of the enemies were wielding Rittles. It would not be long before they slaughtered everyone.

Olly shouted down to the Sholl-guard. "Get the Conduits out of there. It's a trap!"

They immediately mobilized, and when Gwenora elevated back into the sky, we saw that the other squads were also retreating.

"Look, Elias. Now you can see the Orbs in the strokes, clear as day."

She was right. But the one thing we still could not see was where the Nebas, the Oracle and Clive were.

LUCAS

"There are seventy-five Orbs. She knew. She saw this strategy, long before we even knew we had made it. The squads are full of the strongest and most courageous Conduits. There are more than enough of them to fuel her Super Sulu. They need to move, now!"

I tapped into the Rune and relayed the command to Ruit. "Every squad needs to retreat to The Cathedral. We played right into her hands. They have to move now!"

I saw Ruit running to the queen to notify her to mobilize her Sholl-guard.

"How will we get them to funnel into The Cathedral now?"

Just then, Gwenora flew in and landed in front of us. Viraclay jumped off the dragon's back. His wife threw the Staff of Banishment down to him. He tossed it to me so he could catch her.

"They are going to come to us," Olly stated confidently. "Franky has just commandeered all of the Orbs and transported them into the Throne Room in the depths below The Cathedral.

Instantly, the land of the final stand was filling with Conduits and trolls. The giant army came out from their positions, as did the dragons and the rest of the Pai Ona allies, all buzzing with curiosity, realizing the plans had changed. Then there was a thunderous knock on the door.

The Cathedral's front gate morphed into a majestic door with a beautiful stained glass mosaic of green and gold above it.

What the fuck is this about?

"Watch your thoughts, Lucas Healey. Your Rune is open," Inca reminded me.

"Right, sorry."

The knock shook the door again.

"Is someone going to answer that?" I looked around at all of us who had been guarding the front gate only a short time ago.

Olly took the Staff of Banishment from me in one hand, and her husband's hand in her other. Ruit took Jezebel's hand, and the two couples walked toward the door. The rest of us followed behind, prepared for whatever came next. I had Esther on my left and my wife on my right. Vosega and Oya were at my back. The queen and her guard were poised, as was the emperor and his army. Above us, Gwenora floated beside a flock of Thunderbirds and Tete.

The door opened, and there stood Aurora and Clive. Behind them was King OAD.

Gwenora immediately got agitated, and I wondered what she could see that I couldn't.

"You have something of ours," the Oracle hissed. "And we want them back!"

The purple dragon growled in the air. King OAD moved to the front. He had the small furry dragon in his wiry grip, something binding its neck, but I couldn't make out what.

"Do you know what kills a dragon?" Aurora toyed.

"Do not harm him," Olly demanded through bared teeth.

"The very thing they can't live without is the very thing that kills them." Aurora came up behind the dragon and stroked his hair. "This is an Earthen Dragon. The depths will suffocate him in seconds."

Cataphet roared behind us, and Gwenora snarled and snapped above us.

"Give us what is ours and we will return him to you."

"Give me my Staff, girl!" OAD sneered.

Olly was shaking. She was muffling sobs, and I knew she must be having a conversation we couldn't hear with the dragons.

She entered my head with the Rune. "They will kill him no matter what. We've seen it. In a moment, I will throw you the Staff. It's up to you to draw this army as deep as you can into the land of the final stand. We will be right behind you."

"We will not back down. We end this tonight!" Olly asserted, then threw the Staff to me. Immediately, I turned to run, and everyone but Yessica and Esther stepped forward to fight.

King OAD's eyes grew even more crimson with rage.

Franky's voice rang in my head for what I knew would be the last time. "You did well, mate. Take care of my Gwenora for me."

Then the king disappeared into the depths of the world, where the rock was dense or molten and from where Franky would never return. Gwenora wailed in anguish, and my heart broke open into a million pieces just as a contraction seized my body. My husband jumped in front of me to shield me with fire as I hunched over in pain.

I screamed, not from the pain of the contraction but from the throbbing of my shattered heart. I heard Aurora's wicked laugh over the commotion as the Sholl-guard stepped in to let Elias and I get to safety.

Gwenora's rage was in my head. "Why?! Why?! He was everything good in this world. Why in the strokes was he taken from me?" She began to swoop down and consume two or three powries at a time with a single bite. "I will kill them all."

"Olly, can you move?" Elias was holding me, and I needed to get to the land where the final stand would take place. I tried to take in what was happening around me, but it was overwhelming. Some powries were dying, while others were rising from the bloodshed. I saw centaurs and fairies. *Is that a mob of sasquatches?*

I tapped into our Rune. "I feel dizzy. I think the contractions are getting closer."

"I do too," he agreed. "We need to get you to the location. Beyond that, I can feel that murdering Franky was not a wise move. The Originals are enraged."

I adjusted myself to be fully upright. I saw what Elias was referring to. Cataphet, Gwenora and Napitae were in a flurry of carnage, directing everything they could at the powries that just continued to flood in through The Cathedral's gates.

Then the painter's voice came in louder and clearer than it ever had before. "Clive is not of this timeline. He is not of this stroke. When the Ulus was created by the brothers' covetedness, a portal was open for a brief moment. The portal between the ninth timeline and yours must be open once more. It is up to you, sweet daughter, to make this world right."

"How the fuck do I open a portal between two timelines?"

Elias looked at me like I might be losing it as he fended off another barrage of powries.

We reached the center of the land of the last stand, and as soon as the Staff of Banishment was put into place, the entire Cathedral transformed. It became a vast landscape with a canyon on one side and a delta that led into the ocean on the other. I could see the silhouettes of Adanc and the dragon Rothlan in the waves. Princess Chaness climbed from the canyon floor and took her place, towering over the whole panorama, waiting for her chance to have justice. I didn't truly belong to this side, but I also never belonged to the strokes that manipulated me. I am a monster, created by a monster, and today that legacy would come to an end. Everyone here was seeking their own justice. Some of them would be seeking it from me. I was very aware of that. That despite what seemed like an alliance or acceptance, the crimes I committed would be accounted for someday, and today may or may not be that day for me. But it would be that day for Aurora.

"Esther," a familiar voice said from behind me. I turned to see Ramy and Mikkel. Both of these men had every reason to kill me. *Will they?*

I nodded in acknowledgment. "Gentlemen."

Lucas turned to face them too. "Not today, guys. We have a swarm of the enemy coming this way."

"She is the enemy," Mikkel asserted.

"Olly went over this," Yessica interjected. "Esther saved your lives today. She was the one who realized the squads were under attack."

"Thank you, Yessica, but these men are correct. I am the enemy. I have taken your loved ones. I have murdered your Atoas. Nothing I do will change that. If killing me brings you peace, at least wait until after I kill my mother." Then I turned around to face the mob that was approaching.

Her contractions were definitely getting closer and more intense. We designated a location in the final stand location that would be heavily guarded so that she could give birth above the throne room, with the Blessing Way and maintain her presence in the final battle until we achieved victory.

But with this latest revelation from the painter, I hadn't the faintest idea what to do. *How did I keep my wife and child safe and lead this brigade?* Olly gripped my arm and clenched as another contraction took her.

"We are almost there, baby."

"This is a good sign, right?" she said through gasps. "Sadie Mae must be choosing us."

"She already chose us."

Olly looked up at me curiously.

"She chose us. Whether she will choose this world is not up to us. We are doing our best to make it safe enough for her."

Olly's eyes welled up with tears, and another contraction seized her body. *Definitely a lot closer contractions.* Out of nowhere, the Siren Molpe swept in beside her and swooped her up.

"Where is she to be?" A legion of her Tendrils swarmed in beside her.

"There." I pointed to the flat jetty we created that overlooked the battlefield. "Keep her safe."

"A hair on her head will not be harmed."

I reluctantly let go of my wife.

"I love you."

"Lasteea," she replied, and I kissed her before the Siren and her harem carried her up to the place where she would give birth.

LUCAS

"She is safe?" I asked Viraclay as he approached without Olly.

"Indeed."

"Is she going to give birth right now?" Yesi asked.

"Soon enough."

"This is insane," Medusa exclaimed from atop Tete in the sky. "Let's finish this shit so that you can welcome your baby girl!"

Tete crowed.

On the horizon came a swell of powries. There had to be millions. Their numbers were far greater than ours. OAD had been building his army for a long, long time. In between beady red eyes, you could see a Conduit and some other fae creatures sprinkled in. We needed them to flood into the flat land. This would sandwich them between Chaness and our allies in the ocean.

Ruit and his family, along with Winston, Lucia, Helia, Jillian, Claudia, Stalt, Aurelia, Aremis and Sparkle came sprinting up. My dad, Oya and the in-laws with Thracian and Dari were behind them. Friedrick and Shiva took a place next to Mikkel and Ramy, while Aruna and Ying rode on the backs of Thunderbirds in the sky.

"Didn't see this one coming," I said to Elias and Esther.

"Nor did I," Viraclay agreed. Esther said nothing.

Above the plethora of noises, I heard Olly scream in pain. Her contractions were getting worse.

The sea of the enemy parted and OAD, the Oracle and Clive came to the front of the line. It was now or never. I handed the Staff to Elias. "Let's do this!"

Viraclay sang out a piercing war cry, and it was just the thing to beckon the enemy a little closer. They came at us in a running charge.

"Y ou have to surrender. You are fighting it. To invite life into this world is a pleasure."

"You think this is a pleasure?" I gasped through waves of pain.

"It is if you surrender to it. You are a portal."

"I'm a what?" The painter had said I needed to be a portal between timelines.

"I said you are a portal to bring life into this world. When you surrender, the gates open and the soul can enter with ease and love."

Well, that sounded much better than pain and anguish, I had to admit.

"What do I do? Show me."

"I wish it were that simple. The next time you feel the contraction taking your body, become curious. Explore the sensation until you get to the root of it. Realize that it's a door that's opening within you. You wouldn't fight the door as it opened. You would welcome it."

Another contraction gripped my lower back and abdomen. I instinctively wanted to fight, but I paused. I imagined that on the other side of this door within me was Sadie. This was not a cramp in my body but a knock on the door from my daughter. She was ready to meet me. Love immediately swelled in my heart, and I felt my body soften.

"Yes, yes," Molpe affirmed. "That thread, follow that thread."

I got curious with the tension I was feeling, and it released ever so slightly. Underneath the tension were anticipation, excitement, joy. I leaned into the root of my body's visceral reaction and the fear dissolved, leaving only love and pleasure. Another contraction came but it felt orgasmic. My legs began to shiver with sensuality. I surrendered some more. I knew this feeling. I had experienced it with Elias. I surrendered deeper. My womb began to vibrate, and rhythmic waves of bliss circulated my entire core. A rapturous snake of energy was moving up my back into my breasts and exploded out of my mouth.

ELIAS

I raised the Staff to strike the first Nebas that met the end of my blade. It went into his torso with ease, then I lit his body on fire with a flick of my wrist. A powrie came at me from the left, I swung the Staff and to my surprise he shattered into a million pieces. Furthermore, his body did not duplicate more powries from the bloodshed. It would appear the Staff of Banishment killed powries instantly. This will be of great consequence, but for the time being my eyes were set on Aurora. I meant to end this now, once and for all, when a euphoric moan shook the entire Cathedral and every creature stopped in their tracks.

"That's some kind of labor," Lucas teased, and when I turned back around, I had lost sight of the Oracle again. She was bobbing and weaving in and out of her army. Princess Chaness was making fast work of every powrie she could reach. Drowning them, dismembering them, crushing them.

Adanc and Ratatoskr were working together. He would chase the enemy, bring them close to the water, and his sister would make quick work of dragging them to the bottom of the sea. Rothlan was all but out of the water completely, besides the tip of her tail, eating entire swarms of powries whole.

But no matter how efficiently we were fending them off, they were manifesting just as quickly, if not quicker. We needed to cut the head off the snake. I looked up at Ying on the back of a Thunderbird. I raised my hand to the sky, and a massive talon dropped down and swept me up. I needed an aerial view. Aruna and Ying came beside me.

"Where is King OAD?"

"I don't know. We've lost him in the crowd," Aruna confessed. I looked down at the group of Conduits I would consider my closest friends. I was alarmed when I realized they did not see the band of beastly boggarts coming up from behind. They had somehow snuck past Fetzle and her guard.

"Look out!" But my warning came too late. Three boggarts had already swarmed Lucia. Her tiny frame could not fend them off quick enough, and they were tearing her to shreds. I lit one on fire, incinerated another with a glance, and sent a gust of wind. There was nothing left of her body. They had consumed every bit of flesh. I held back the bile that crept up my throat and the tears that welled in my eyes.

Winston howled as he fell to his knees, clawing at the place where his wife had just been. Fifteen more boggarts were circling the perimeter of the group. Winston got up and, within seconds, the beasts were writhing in pain as their blood boiled. Jillian touched his shoulder, and the boggarts melted into pools of goop.

Another orgasmic moan from the place where my wife lay giving birth stole my attention for a moment. Death and birth were happening side by side, and my heart was torn.

OPHELIA

The waves of pleasure had their own momentum. I felt my being expanding. Creating space for Sadie to enter this world. I was open. I was vulnerable. I was just about to truly let go—and I heard a sinister voice.

"I can feel that they are here, beneath us. I will annihilate the Conduit strokes now and forever."

The voice pulled me out of my state of surrender. I needed to get to the Orbs. I was the only one who could destroy them.

"Ophelia, you are almost there. The portal is almost open." Molpe looked at me, confused and concerned.

"It's Clive. He has the Orbs. I have to stop him."

I reached out to Elias with our Rune. "Clive has found the Orbs. We need to get into the Throne Room." Instantly, my husband was at my side.

"Can you do this now, in your state?"

"No, she cannot," Molpe answered for me.

"I must." I touched the Siren's hand. "I will be right back." Both of us knew we couldn't be certain that was true. Then Elias and I were using the Compass to transport into the Throne Room in the depths below The Cathedral.

LUCAS

esi and I had a pretty good system. She would blind them, and I would poke them with the sharp end of a blade. The thing about powries is that they multiply from bloodshed, so every time a good guy died or a Nebas or fae went down, poof, there were more powries to handle. *They were a fucking pain in the ass!*

Incineration or cremation seemed to eliminate the duplication. So Aremis was staying very busy. Therefore, he didn't see the changeling that showed up behind him as an enormous snake.

Yessica turned her light on to try and blind the monster, but it didn't even flinch. It came down with its fangs into Aremis' right shoulder, and he screamed in pain. Sparkle had been fending off a Nebas by the name of Curts who hypnotizes creatures with his voice. He'd been trying to sing something and gain the upper hand in the fight. Aremis' scream distracted them both. Suddenly, an axe manifested in Curts' hands.

"That's a Rittle!" Esther shouted. Sparkle was disorientated. She put her hands up to block the blow from hitting Aremis, and as the blade sliced through her body, she disintegrated into ash.

"No!" Aremis cried, and the basilisk came down again, this time piercing Aremis through the heart. The venom permeated his body immediately. A ball of flame came from the sky and incinerated his body. Then a second ball of flame came and incinerated the changeling. I turned around to see it was the fire dragon.

Ruit tapped into our Rune. "Basilisk venom would have killed him slowly and painfully. Napitae would not see him suffer."

Yessica's knees gave out. I grabbed her before she fell. "Aremis. Sparkle. They are gone."

I saw Curts turn his attention towards us, and just before he was about to swing the axe, Esther jumped on his back, taking control of his body and the Rittle. Esther had just saved our lives.

"Get her somewhere to recover. You are useless this distracted." Esther spat, and she and her animated Curts walked straight into the mob of powries, creating carnage in their wake.

I wanted Aurora. She was here. I knew this because she had just distributed the Rittles. She was close enough to put this weapon in Curts' hands and send him to harm Sparkle. I walked behind Curts as I commanded his body to sing and swing the axe wildly.

"Aurora! Stop running! There is nowhere to hide anymore!"

I thought I heard her laugh. Perhaps I just wanted to. Curts and I were approaching the line that the Sholl-guard was holding. I doubted anything could get past the she-trolls, so I turned to the left, thought we would sweep up the periphery line, when a brawny centaur galloped to a stop directly in front of Curts. He reared up, knocking the axe from Curts' hands. I scrambled to get to it and avoid the hooves that were bashing Curts' bloody little body to a pulp. I got hold of the axe and got to my feet just as the centaur pointed his bow and arrow to the sky, aiming at Aruna and her Thunderbirds. He got one shot off as I touched his back haunches and attempted to snatch his body. I couldn't, because there was already something occupying the space. *It is a hex.*

The fae were all under one of Clive's hexes. I could feel the haze of the hex and the confusion of the victim. There was a distinct disassociation from the spirit, the same as when I managed the faculties of a body. *What if I just challenged the occupancy?* I pushed a little harder, pressing alongside the consciousness of the centaur, helping him with his own internal resistance to what he knew was foreign—and pop!

I felt the hex lift.

"What in the strokes is happening?"

"I don't have time to explain. You've been hexed, along with all the other fae. Get somewhere safe and out of the way until I can help the rest of your people. It will do nothing to reason with them. They will kill you. Do you understand me?" He looked around at the carnage in disbelief.

"How did this happen?"

"I know this is unbelievable right now, but if you don't listen to me, you will likely die."

He nodded in a haze.

I had an idea that would save fae lives and turn the tides in the war, but my new moral compass was prompting me to get this centaur to safety.

"Follow me." With the axe, I carved the way up to the queen.

"Esther, there is a centaur behind you!" she shouted as I approached.

"Queen Fetzle, the fae have been hexed. I have an idea about how I can awaken them, but I need to find Jillian and Ruit. I just woke this one up. Will you secure him behind your lines?"

She looked at me, then the centaur, a few times before ushering him into her guard. "Are you certain he will not return to his state?"

I shook my head. "I'm going to act quickly."

ELIAS

e used the compass to get down into the Throne Room, where Franky had stored the Orbs, all seventy-five of them. The space was large enough to hold Cataphet and Napitae, so it was spacious enough to contain the Orbs.

"How am I going to destroy these?" Olly was examining the golden spheres up close.

King OAD's voice cut through the darkness. "You cannot destroy the Orbs, girl. You are audacious."

I had the Staff at the ready, but I did not see the king or Clive.

"I'm audacious? You killed a dragon in The Cathedral."

He laughed, and it echoed and bounded off the walls.

Olly gripped my hand. She was having another contraction. But this time it was not a wave of pain, but a wave of pleasure. I felt it pulsating off her. It reminded me of the moment we had in Rand's cottage in Austria. She breathed through it and refrained from making any noise.

Olly communicated through our Rune. "I can hear Clive's thoughts when I'm open in labor, and I sensed something during my contraction. I need more time. We need to keep them distracted while I formulate a plan. Can you do that?"

"I'll do my best."

Then King OAD's red eyes appeared in the shadowy space between two Orbs. "Lovely. You brought me my staff."

LUCAS

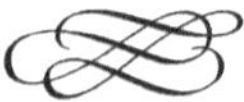

Stalt and Vosega had created a lava stream that encircled those of us who were still holding the central point, where we had always intended to funnel the enemy to. The lava slowed down the powries just enough for us to breathe between attacks.

"How are you holding up, baby girl?"

"I am..." She lifted her hand, and a massive ray of light beamed over my shoulder.

I turned to see Oya fry two powries with lightning bolts.

"Thank you."

Genghis stepped beside his daughter. "We cannot hold this line much longer, Lucas. The powries just keep coming." I knew he was right.

Ruit and Almus came up behind the Khan. "It's the Orbs. They give the army limitless power and regeneration," Almus reasoned, and it made sense to me because this was supernatural by all accounts.

All of the sudden, Esther leapt into the conversation out of nowhere. "The fae are hexed! I can break it. Ruit, can you create something to combat it and communicate with them all at once?" She pointed at Jillian. "We need her!"

"Father, how much time do you need?" Almus asked.

Ruit looked around at our exhausted faces. "I need to consult Sorcerer."

Gwenora swooped down and took out a brigade of powries that were just about to infiltrate the circle.

"Go now!" I shouted.

Jezebel came up behind her husband, and they disappeared into the halls of The Cathedral. Inca and Friedrick were creating pillars of redwood trees around the circle—one more deterrent. Winston was still inconsolable. He had not stopped melting every enemy from the inside out since Lucia was killed. I looked up and saw Tete and Medusa turning the trees to stone, fortifying the obstacles. *But where were Ying and Aruna?*

No sooner did I think it than a Thunderbird delivered Aruna's lifeless body feet away. Ying jumped off the bird's back. "It's a centaur arrow. She is dying."

Blood poured from the wound in her chest. I didn't know anything about fae magic.

Mikkel slowed down the space between and around us.

Ying held his wife in his arms. "Does anyone know anything about fae poison?" he screamed. "Please! Help her!" Tears streamed down his face.

None of us knew what to do.

Shiva came to Ying's side and put his enormous hand on Aruna's wound. He shook his head, as though to say there was nothing to be done.

"No! No, I will not accept that!"

Shiva used his waters to cleanse the wound.

Borte spoke for the Ancient. "This may give her a few more moments."

The time warp was disrupted by a swarm of arrows. Shiva easily destroyed them, then got to his feet. Yessica knelt down where he had been, and Medusa jumped off Tete's back to be there with Aruna as well. Her birds circled above.

"Carry her strokes. Bury her hopes. Let it be known that she's on her way home. The hearth is warm. The river flows. Her heart will know the way to go." Medusa sang a song I'd never heard. But others had. Yesi and Helia knew the words, and even Esther sang the tune. "Carry her strokes. Bury her hopes. Let it be known that she's on her way home. The hearth is warm. The river flows. Her heart will know the way to go."

ESTHER

*A*runa died in Ying's arms just as Ruit returned.

"I have the incantation." He tucked the journal behind his back. "Are you ready?" I looked at the wailing Ying one last time. It was too close to my own loss. I was shaken. But I had to pull it together. If we freed the fae, we would double our numbers, and maybe I could finally flush out the Oracle.

"Jillian!" She ran over. This was a strange moment. "I would like to ask for your consent to utilize your amplification to remove the hex from the fae."

She looked at me inquisitively and then laughed at my formality. "Yes, Esther, I concede."

The three of us locked arms, and everyone else, including Ying, took a defensive stance to keep us safe while we performed the Covening.

I felt Jillian's familiar amplification sensation. I reached my gift, stretched it to encompass every stroke of fae that I could find, then I latched on. For a moment, the sound on the battlefield quieted and buzzed with bewilderment. Even the powries paused, not sure what to make of their allies' peculiar behavior. I had used Jillian's gift often enough to know it was being maximized. I could only hope

Ruit was making fast work of his incantation. My own gift was beginning to tear at the seams. I'd never spread it so thin or held a fae stroke for very long.

A burning sensation started to sneak up through the soles of my feet. This was not normal. There was too much energy moving between the three of us. My body was collapsing from the inside out.

OPHELIA

"This will work just fine. I will eliminate the Conduit stroke once and for all at the place where it all began," Clive schemed. I still hadn't set eyes on him. Another wave of contractions came on, and I felt my spirit expand. My energy field encompassed the Orbs, and I understood how they were woven together. Molpe was right. They were not strokes, they were strings, like enormous balls of yarn. I just had to find the ends to begin the unraveling.

Elias moved behind me. King OAD was brandishing two large spears. "They are not the same as my Staff, but I assure you I am quite adept."

Clive's thoughts intruded my mind again. "I will disconnect from OAD, then the energy source will be exclusively mine and I can begin the extinction. This time I don't need the Sulu. My creations will achieve the explosive eradication. The Sulu Wheel I designed, inspired by the Blessing Way rites will bestow the power of the Orbs to me and instead of binding everything together, I will rip them apart."

That was the thought that slipped away a day earlier. Clive designed

647

the Blessing Way, that looked like the faction diagram and the Sulu Wheel required all the factions. They all overlap, like the overlapping circles. But I am the Ulus. I balance the power of the Sulu. I must tether to the source. I can transmute the energy and thwart his plan. Now, how the hell do I tether to these damn balls?

LUCAS

Something was wrong. I could tell. "Ruit! How can I help you?" I asked through our Rune.

"It is almost complete," he struggled to express.

"But it's hurting you guys." Jillian was about to pass out. Esther was internally writhing, and Ruit looked like he might waste away right in front of me. Jezebel, Almus and Inca looked on with tears in their eyes. They were going to lose him all over again.

"Stop them!" I demanded the Talluses do something.

Jezebel took the conversation into my head. "He always knew this was his purpose. To unite our people."

Esther let go of Jillian's hand. "My part is complete."

Jillian's eyes rolled back into her head and Esther caught her. Ruit still gripped her hand. His skin began to evaporate away like smoke in the wind.

"Ruit! We need you!" I screamed. "Don't do this!"

"No, Lucas. I have played my part. My strokes are satisfied." He made eye contact with me and nodded assuredly. "Remember your connection with Ophelia."

A fog filled the land of the final stand as Ruit's body dissolved into vapor. Cries from the fae indicated they understood how they had been betrayed, and they turned on the powries closest to them.

My heart cracked open as I realized Ruit was gone. *He was really gone.*

ELIAS

"*I* must transmute the energy," she said through our Rune. "Keep him occupied."

"What does that mean, Olly? You do not even know the power of these Orbs. How can you be certain you can do this?"

"Because I am. Because I have you. Because I know it in my bones."

Everything in me wanted to protest, but I could not. Everything that had brought us here was for this fated moment, to change the world forever. I could no sooner stop her from seeing her destiny realized than I could my own.

I squared my shoulders and faced OAD. "You want this Staff back, you will have to pry it from my dead hands."

"Challenge accepted." Then the king dove at me with lightning speed.

here was she? It was time for her reckoning.

Lilith came to my side. Last I'd seen her, I'd killed her husband and handed her to her personal monster, my brother. "Nestor and Aurora have been spotted. There." She pointed to a small alcove. Between where the trolliage was fighting and the giants. "To bring my daughter peace, I must kill him. Will you help me? I know I cannot do it alone."

"Yes. I promise you, we will kill him." It was the least I could do to atone for the sins I had committed against this woman.

Lucas saw we were up to something. "Where are you going?"

"We have spotted the Oracle and Nestor."

"You can't go alone."

Ying and Winston overheard the conversation. "We will go with you."

"As will I and Claudia. There is a small army of Nebas surrounding them." Stalt insisted.

"The rest of you are needed for when Olly and Viraclay return. This location must stay secure," Lucas reminded the others.

"We are plenty." Stalt cracked his knuckles.

I gave Lillith the axe. "You're going to need this."

Ying called down the Thunderbirds and we jumped on their backs. Within seconds, we were above the small army of Nebas that guarded their leader. Ying nodded and we all simultaneously catapulted into the mob. I landed on Astrid.

"I've been waiting so long to do this." I seized control of her body and sent a shockwave of electricity directly at Nestor. I wanted Lillith to have every advantage she could get. With Astrid's form now under my control, I could go directly for the source. Ying propelled metal objects into the crowd of Nebas, impaling them and making them easy prey for Winston, who quickly boiled them alive. Claudia stunned whomever she could make eye contact with, Stalt summoned a pool of lava behind them, and she gently pushed the enemy in. Astrid cleared the way as I made eye contact with Aurora so she knew I was coming. Without Clive or her minions, she was nearly defenseless.

Calypso jumped in front of me, and before I could react, Ying was on top of her. He stabbed her twice in the back before she elevated his body in the air and with one flick of her wrist, dismembered him, tossing his remains into a nearby fire.

Winston turned just in time to see the death of yet another friend. He directed all of his rage onto Calypso, but she met him with the same focus. His body began to elevate and tear. Her skin began to bubble and melt. I reached to take control of her, but before I could,, she collapsed into a pool of blood and bones and Winston was gone.

My moment of distraction gave Astrid an opportunity to relinquish her senses. She turned on me, and I felt searing pain grip my entire being as massive voltages of electricity surged through my veins. Aurora cackled. She was so close. I couldn't lose her.

My vision was starting to blur at the edges and go dark. The attack abruptly ended, and I saw that Lilith had sliced Astrid in two with the axe. The Oracle was caught off guard. I pounced on top of her, taking control of her body. The Nebas stopped fighting, not sure what to do, now that their leader was compromised.

Lilith was circling Nestor. She wasn't going to let this one go.

No trial could bring her peace or her daughter any true sense of safety as long as he was alive. Since I knew he had no soul, I believed she was entirely justified in her revenge.

Everyone backed up. The defeated Nebas just looked on. Nestor had no friends here. "You're a monster, and the terror ends today."

Nestor put his hands up in defeat with a wicked smile on his face. "My work here has been glorious."

Lilith didn't hesitate. She beheaded him with one swing of the blade.

OPHELIA

$\mathcal{A}$n expanse of pleasure and a wave of energy moved through me, and I knew that I had a very limited time before Sadie Mae would be arriving. It was now or never. I surrendered deeper into the pleasure, into the energetic field where I could see the strings woven together. I could feel Clive's essence. It was different. It too was threads, not strokes. I felt into my own being and found the thread amongst the strokes. The splinter that made me Ulus.

I could somehow see what Clive was doing although he was not in front of me. I witnessed him cut the line that tethered the king and the Orbs. He let go of the loose thread and began amplifying his power.

"Clive, I can hear you. I see you."

Startled, he paused for a moment, and I took the opportunity to manipulate the strokes around the loose end and quickly tie it to myself.

He laughed. "What kind of Sulu are you? You can speak in my head? No stroke has ever been able to communicate with me in any language."

"Because you aren't of this world, which is why you hate it."

"You are right, Sulu, I do hate it." Clive came around the back of an Orb, and for the first time, I had eyes on him in the physical realm. "But once I eradicate the Conduits once and for all, I might find it palatable."

"What about Aurora? You'll kill her too."

"She has no soul. She does not care."

"I know that Priloc broke your heart."

He laughed again. "You know nothing, and it was good of you to bind yourself to my Orbs. It will only make the extinction that much more powerful, Sulu."

I could tell he wasn't going to be reasonable.

Chitchakor's voice hummed in my head. "The time is now. When he activates the Orbs, you activate the portal. The Staff of Banishment and the Oracle must enter the River Tins. Clive must enter the portal. His threads will take him home. On the banks of the River Tins, Elias will utilize Moira's gift to enter back through the Gates of Consciousness, but your gate has been sealed, so do not find yourself on the banks unless it is your time to die. Do not hesitate, daughter. Deepen your surrender."

Clive began activating the Orbs. I had to move quickly. I tapped into the Rune and connected to Lucas and Elias simultaneously. "Have Fetzle standing by to place the final key of the Blessing Way. We also need the Oracle and the Staff at the place where the world ends. Do we have her? It's time for them to be returned to the River Tins."

Lucas answered, "We are ready for you."

I looked at my husband, who was in full combat with the powrie king. *I had to help him, but how?*

Then another wave of contractions hit, and Clive's eyes got large as he felt the surge of my energy.

"What are you?"

"I am an Ulus."

LUCAS

"*E*sther!" The powrie onslaught had slowed significantly a moment earlier. It was like they had run out of steam. Esther approached with the Oracle complacent and in her arms. "Olly needs the Oracle at the River Tins."

"But I will be the one who drowns her in the river."

"I can't promise that."

Esther growled and hissed, but she didn't protest. Vosega and Oya were now easily managing the perimeter of the lava circle. It felt like we might actually have a chance at defeating these assholes. I grabbed Yesi's face and pulled her in for an exhausted kiss. Then waved to the Queen to join us, where we stood waiting for every piece to fall into place. With three mighty leaps the troll Queen was in position and Emperor Calt by her side.

I threw a fireball and he dodged it easily. He was fast and agile. OAD swung at me with both of his spears, and just barely missed my left arm. Before I could anticipate his next move, he was nearly on top of me. I managed a gust of wind and sent him back ten paces. He smiled.

"Fun tricks." Then his smile disappeared and he looked around frantically. "Clive! What are you doing?" Something had changed around his strokes. His power was diminishing.

"Never mind the Orbs. I only need my staff." He dove at me once more. I maneuvered right and was now facing my wife. She was in some sort of trance. I saw Clive come out from around the shadow of an Orb. *What am I to do?* I remembered that Clive could not harm his splinter.

OAD darted at me again, more desperate and weaker still. I shifted to the left and easily missed him this time. Olly's voice came through our Rune. "Have Fetzle standing by to place the final key of the Blessing Way. We also need the Oracle and the Staff at the place where the world ends. Do we have her? It's time for them to be returned to the River Tins."

Lucas responded, and I knew I needed to get to Olly and use the compass to transport us to the appointed spot. I took control of the strokes around OAD's body and locked him to the ground. He was growing weaker and weaker by the second. I made certain he was secure and turned back to Olly to see that she was suspended in midair. The strokes in the room were vibrating feverishly. I tapped into Berty's gift and I could see that the strokes were erupting into billions of micro-explosions. *Is this what the extinction looks like?*

Holding Aurora and managing her gifts, I saw it all. It wasn't her memories, it was her visions that led her to make the moves she made, from the moment she killed Cadmael to her years at Delphi. She saw Yanni die and made sure my father's execution was realized. She murdered my mother while the Katuan Stones sent Alantis to bottom of the sea. The Oracle saw it all. Until she couldn't. Lucas fouled her vision, as did the Ulus, and ultimately the Paradigm Tremor left her blind in a multitude of ways and finally freed those of us who had been cursed by Clive's hex.

She was a shattered woman. It was time for her to enter the River Tins. I would be the one to escort her there myself.

OPHELIA

The thread got taut, and I could see that all I needed to do was pull. So I did. The nebulous of the Orbs began to detangle.

"What are you doing? How are you doing that?"

The stored power within the Orbs began to transfer into my being. I wanted to fight it, just like the contractions, just like I had fought the surplus of gifts before I consummated. A contraction took hold of my body, and I rode the wave of pleasure. The surrender opened my channel further, and I could sense the portal. I absorbed more of the Orbs' energy. It surged through me, and this time I didn't resist.

"Stop. This isn't possible," Clive pleaded. I took hold of his tether line, made sure he couldn't escape. I may not be able to hurt my splinter but I could send him back to where he came from.

"It's time for you to go home, Clive."

"Elias, Olly?" I reached out with the Rune. It felt like they should've been here by now.

Suddenly, a goddess-like creature with an entourage of exotic models manifested in front of me. "She is coming. I will help her with the labor."

"I'm sorry, who are you?"

"I am the Siren Molpe."

"I can vouch for her, Lucas," Helia said as she approached.

"Lucas," Elias' voice sounded in my head. "She is opening the portal to the River Tins and the ninth timeline simultaneously. I will bring the Staff to the banks. Promise me you will use your Gattilak charm to keep her anchored to this world, no matter what."

"I promise." I looked down at the bracelet that Ruit had made us and I held back tears.

OPHELIA

I'd absorbed all the energy the Orbs had held. My body was now the bridge between worlds. I felt Sadie's soul waiting to enter the thirteenth timeline. I could feel the portal opening across all timelines. Through me, there was a door cracking open. Suddenly, the painter's voice was in my head. "Dear child, you are finally surrendering to your truest potential. To the potential that all my children possess, limitlessness." Any resistance that was left in my body dissolved away.

I reached out to Elias with my Rune, "Now, my beloved. The moment is now." He turned his back on the king and came to my side just as my body returned to the ground. I held tight to Clive, while Elias used the Compass. Within seconds, Elias, Clive and I were in the very place where the world ends. Molpe and her Tendrils were there to support me. Relief washed over me. I nodded at Fetzle and she placed the key to the Blessing Way in it's position. I felt the surge of energy from the Orbs transfer to the blessing that would reunite all of Malarin's strokes, returning them to one single stroke, connecting us to all. At the same time the portal for the ninth timeline opened.

Molpe cupped my face with her hand. "You are ready." She smiled at me in a knowing way.

Esther held my grandmother Aurora's listless body. "Elias, take the Oracle." He slung the Staff of Banishment into a sling on his back and went to reach for Aurora.

"No need. I'll do the honors."

"But Esther..." I wanted to explain that I didn't know if she would be able to come back. But the look on her face told me she already knew the price she would have to pay.

I still held Clive close with the tether. With my next contraction, I would open the portal completely, and the remaining power I transmuted from the Orbs would send Clive back to his timeline. And once Aurora and the Staff were returned to the original strokes of the River Tins, the lines would be erased forever.

Molpe took one of my hands and Lucas took the other. If the last era was forged in covetedness and pain, this one would be birthed through pleasure and love. The contraction came on strong, and I surrendered completely and wholly to the bliss of divine connection between all that is. In front of us, at our feet, appeared a vast hole of swirling colorful strokes. I released Clive's tether, and he stumbled back into the abyss of the strokes, disappearing into the ethers from where he came.

"Farewell, pet. I have a sneaking suspicion I won't be coming back from this adventure." Esther looked around at the anxious faces of my comrades. "Perhaps next go-around, some of us will be friends." She laughed. "Or not." Just as Esther dove into the portal, her eyes got big. "Ophelia, look..." Her words trailed off as she disappeared. Everyone's eyes were on her, so no one noticed that OAD had snuck up behind me and Elias. I felt the blow to my left side. I couldn't tell what struck me, but the warm flow of blood let me know it was a blade. I stumbled forward. The shock was closing the portal.

My husband snapped around but Helia already had the king disarmed with one touch. She threw the weapon to Elias.

"Elias, you have to go now!" I yelled. He hesitated, not sure what to do. "Now!" I pushed him with all the strength I had left, and he fell into the abyss. "I love you." It came out as a whisper. The portal promptly slammed shut. Panic surged through me. *Sadie!* She was struggling. I could feel it. I looked down to see I'd been impaled. Blood stained all the way down my right side.

Lucas propped me up. I looked up to see OAD staring at me, his bloodthirsty red eyes piercing into my soul. Out of nowhere, Gwenora swooped in and took him in her talons. As she flew away, I could see she was dismantling him. She roared and aerobated around the night's sky, taking her rage out on the monster who'd murdered Franky. Somewhere in me, I empathized with OAD's darkness. I didn't truly blame him. It was part of all of us. *We all had shadow.*

Pain seared through me and into my womb, pulling me back to the terrible reality of my situation. Molpe's voice was calm but stern. "Your placenta has been ruptured. Sadie must come now, or she will die."

"Get her out! Get her out now!" I gasped. Now fully present in the moment, I realized something wasn't right with me either. "What did he wound me with? Something is wrong."

Lucas didn't say anything but I could tell by the look on his face that it was worse than I imagined.

Yessica came up beside me and took my hand.

I heard Almus' voice somewhere in front of me, but my vision was hazy. *What could do this to an Ulus?* "Get Sadie out." I wanted to scream it, but it came out like a whisper. It was like the life was literally draining out of me. "Lucas, get her out."

Yessica squeezed my hand tighter. "We will save you both." It sounded like she was ten million miles away. I realized my soul was being torn from my body. I knew this sensation. I had felt it before. *I am dying.*

LUCAS

*L*ucas "Molpe, she can't die." I fondled the bracelet on my wrist and looked at Olly's limp, bloody body. The fighting had stopped completely. "How did he stab her with the Staff of Banishment?" It had happened so fast. It was on Elias' back, and then OAD was behind them both. He moved so quickly Elias couldn't react. She was impaled before any of us knew he was there. The king must have calculated where the Staff was and assumed he could disarm Viraclay if he moved fast enough. And he'd been right.

"Lucas, your thoughts are loud and not helpful right now," Jezebel interrupted.

"Right."

"My husband felt your hairsy charm connection with Olly was integral. Perhaps that is the key to her survival?"

"Yeah, yeah, you're right." I took hold of Olly's wrist and searched for our connection. It was faint but I could feel it. "Where's Jillian?"

OPHELIA

 smelled the sweetness of the banks of the River Tins before I opened my eyes to see the vibrant colors of the stream in front of me.

"Olly!" Elias' voice was shrill. "I do not know how he was able to stab you with the Staff. I have failed you and Sadie."

I put my hands to my pregnant belly but Sadie wasn't there. A medley of pain, relief and grief hit me like a tsunami. I gasped, then let the sobs take over my whole being. I would never see my daughter's face. I would never hold her—these were my final moments with my husband. Elias ran to me, dropping the Staff to the ground and scrambling to meet me where I lay writhing in pain.

"I am so sorry. I failed you." He cradled me in his trembling arms. Our connection was so deep that everything that had transpired simply downloaded into his mind and he knew, without me saying a word, he knew all that I was feeling.

He wailed. "No! No! No! This is not how this ends! Malarin!" he yelled, fury escalating with each syllable.

Esther had paused, nearly to the water's edge. "We will all meet on the banks of the River Tins someday."

"This is not Ophelia's day!"

I pulled myself together, realizing that this was my day, and that Elias needed to finish what we started and get home to our daughter. I cupped his face in my hand. "Today is my day. Our daughter needs you." I gestured to the beautiful grey door. "That's your door, mine is sealed. The lines are gone, and the world will need a leader like you. I'll be waiting for you."

He just shook his head in denial. I started to pull myself up, knowing that the only way he would move forward was if I stepped into the river. I got to my feet, and just as I did, I heard a scuffle. Over his shoulder, I saw that Aurora had come to and had somehow scrambled away from Esther and was wielding the Staff of Banishment. Only then did I remember that our gifts didn't work on the banks, so of course the Oracle would no longer be manageable.

"How touching." She sneered at Elias and me as she swung the Staff toward Esther to keep her back. Her focus then went entirely to her daughter. "I am leaving here, and you, my daughter, should truly consider joining me." She gestured toward the door with a nod of her head.

Esther didn't say anything.

"Now that you know the truth, there is nothing left to hide. We can rule as equals. And with the Ulus and Sulu gone, there will be no one to stop us. Queens for eternity."

Esther's posture changed, softened, and I knew she was considering her mother's offer. Aurora saw it too, so she continued. "I was wrong to keep the truth from you. I was wrong to betray you. I only did what I thought was best for our mission. The world is full of weak and mindless fools. You have always been neither. You have been strong and resilient, fierce and loyal to me."

Esther moved toward her mother slowly, and Aurora didn't back away. I couldn't believe what I was witnessing. "What will you do with them?"

Aurora looked over her shoulder at me and Elias flippantly. "The girl is already dead. We just have to eliminate Viraclay. The miracle child who has been both the catalyst for my power and the thorn in my side. I felt Elias' body stiffen under my touch when she said I was already dead.

"Then you and I can waltz back through that door and finish this once and for all. It is time we won. It's time the darkness prevailed. No matter what you think of my methods, I always saw the dark in you. I only needed to coax it out. It's who you are."

Esther moved even closer to Aurora. "Do it, then. Kill him. I have no love for Viraclay or his pet."

Aurora chuckled under her breath. "That's my girl." She swung the blade around until it was inches from Elias' throat. "Tell your parents hello for me."

I felt the rage bubble up within him. He lunged forward, the blade barely missing his jugular as Aurora stepped sideways to miss his blow and keep the Staff from his grasp. I got to my feet and shadowed him, prepared to make my own stand. I was already gone, but Sadie needed her father.

I spoke through our Rune. "Flank her." I stepped to his left, ready to circle behind, when Esther took her spot beside her mother.

"You treacherous whore!"

"Now, now. Your language, pet," she said teasingly. "Is that any way to speak to your aunty?"

I spat at her. Esther dodged it and stepped around with her back to the Oracle's so they could see us from every direction.

"Are you really surprised?" Aurora taunted. "She is, after all, my daughter."

Elias darted toward Esther. She would be the easiest to eliminate, since she was unarmed.

"Mother! The Staff!" Esther commanded, and Aurora quickly handed it over.

"Elias!" I knew he was watching, but it was all I could do as he faced Esther once more.

She laughed as she whipped around quicker than I had ever seen her move before, gracefully maneuvering the blade of Inverness to Aurora's throat. "Who is the fool now?"

Elias quickly moved to my side.

"What game is this, Esther?"

"I am through with games, Aurora. You killed my father, you manipulated me for centuries, and you murdered my Yanni… twice." It came out as a hiss. "You are not my mother. You assassinated her at the Trials in Atlantis, along with countless others whom I loved." The blade began piercing the Oracle's skin. A single stream of blood trickled down her neck.

"Elias, look at her neck." No sooner did I say it, than the Oracle begin to jerk and twitch.

"Esther, we do not know what the blade will do here." Elias pulled me back behind him and started piloting me toward the door.

"There is no point, my love. I'm gone. You must get home to our Sadie Mae."

"Did you hear that, Mother? There is no telling what the blade will do in this hallow place." Esther looked crazed. "There is only one way to find out."

Aurora opened her mouth to object, but before she could utter a syllable, Esther drove the blade into her throat. Blood spilled out, then it was as though the Oracle imploded from the inside out. A cacophony of noises echoed in all directions. Esther was thrown back by the blow, landing in the flow of the River Tins. She was only up to her waist, when a blissful smile swept over her face. She looked at peace for the first time. "There you are, my beloved. I am home." Then she closed her eyes and lay back in the water. The stream gently engulfed her like a hug as she sank into the rainbow water.

They are gone. Esther and Aurora are gone. My body trembled with shock. I looked into Elias' eyes to see the same medley of disbelief and astonishment. *The Nebas war is over.*

Suddenly, another thunderous round of noises began firing off.

"What is that?"

Elias shook his head. "I do not know, but I do know we need to finish what we started." He pointed to the Staff that was now yards away from the door and the river. "I have to get the Staff into the water. It is the only way to repair the Paradigm Tremor. And you have to welcome our daughter into this world." He pulled me in for a passionate kiss. The ground shook beneath us and we lost our balance.

"Elias, this is your door. I'm already dead. This place is falling apart." I could sense the strokes that kept it intact were dissolving. It was a very strange sensation, a knowing that the banks of the River Tins were about to be washed away. Then, all of the sudden, I felt the sensation of the hairsy charm. Lucas was trying to pull me home.

"Sadie needs you. Our people need you to help pick up the pieces. No one knows what is on the other side of this Paradigm Tremor, but I do know with absolute certainty that you will be essential to rebuilding the world as it should be—from love and with love."

"I'm already gone," I said again, but it was no use. I could see it in his eyes. "Please don't do this. I can't live without you." Lucas pulled harder on the bond between us.

Everything shook around us again, and a strange light danced along the water. Elias pulled me in once more. "Lasteea." He pressed his lips to mine gently, yet with more ferocity than I'd ever felt before. The tears were streaming down my cheeks uncontrollably. I grabbed his arms, determined not to let him go, while everything began to dissolve around us. I felt the air shift behind me, a fierce tug from the hairsy charm, and then without warning I was falling. Elias had pushed me through his door. He was gone and I was falling into an abyss.

ELIAS

s soon as I shut the door, it disappeared. The ground shook violently and I fell to my knees. It felt appropriate to say a prayer. "Chitchakor, Malarin, Dalinkas and all the other names you have ever been praised by, make my family whole. My Atoa has served you in all ways, selflessly and with the purest of intentions. My daughter is innocent and deserves to know the love of her mother. I pray with every ounce of my being that you allow them this simple but profound gift. I give my life to you, for theirs."

Then, with no time left to waste, I was sprinting toward the Staff of Banishment. There was nothing left to do but offer it to the River Tins. I raced back to the shoreline, barely able to keep my footing as everything trembled under me and around me. If transformation had a taste, smell or texture, this would be it. I was engulfed in the belly of world transformation, and it was beautiful chaos. I got on my knees once more, closed my eyes, and gently placed the Staff into the water. It sank immediately, and I sat there for what felt like an eternity, wondering what was next, when a familiar voice trilled over the echoes of destruction.

"Stand up, my son."

"Mom?" I turned around and saw the all-too-familiar silhouette of my mother. The light had dimmed to a deep twilight, that dusky time of day when you are transitioning into the dark wonders of the night.

"Your father and I have missed you. We are so proud of you. Rise. Give me a hug, won't you?"

I could not get up fast enough. I dove into her arms, and they felt like a long-lost home that I had been searching for far too long. I have been a weary traveler. "I will be with you and father now. Have you come to take me to the other side?"

"You are on the other side, my sweet boy. You did it."

"I am dead."

"Far from it." She pulled me out of her embrace to look me in the face. I desperately wanted to snuggle back into her shoulder, to be done with waiting for the finality of death to take me. Her eyes beamed at me. "You did, it. You and Ophelia returned us to our original strokes of vibrant blues, golden oranges and bright purples."

I shook my head. I did not understand.

"Do you remember one of the first fables we ever told you? The creation myth of the painter and our world. How Fih drew the first lines, fating us all to wander around looking for our Atoa when the moon said hello and the sun said goodbye. Do you remember how the painter wept and a single teardrop fell upon the canvas that he thought was destroyed by separation and darkness. The blurred lines gave him hope and he spared his creatures, his children, giving them a fleeting moment at dusk to find their other half and make the world whole once more."

"I found her, but there is no way out of this place." I looked around, and only then realized the chaos had stopped. I was back in the sacred container I experienced with Olly when we consummated.

My mother gently pulled my face back to hers, searching my eyes for recognition, but I was still lost. "You and Ophelia were the teardrop that has led us to the dusk, so the cycle of pain, brutality and separation has ended and we are free, truly free to be whole again." My heart swelled and tears cascaded down my cheeks. Relief surged through all of my body. "We are free," she repeated. "Sadie Mae is a very special soul, and her decision to join our timeline is the true dawning of a new age."

"What does that mean for those we have lost? What does that mean for you and Father?"

"The washing of our colors in the River Tins has made our transformation final. But never again will we repeat the cycle of hatred, greed and power as our souls have done since the first lines were drawn. The war of the sisters is the same as the one between the Nebas and the Pai Ona. It is the same as the wars that plagued the world in every cycle. It is done. The love that you and Ophelia share was enough to bring back wholeness. We can all see and embrace the dark and the light, the sweet and the sour, the rage and the joy… There are no more lines."

"But then, where will you go?"

"Together, your father and I have already expanded our energy into a new, divinely led path where we are one. It is glorious, and it is all thanks to you." She brushed my hair from my face. "I like this look on you. It suits you."

I smiled. "But what about those who have lost their Atoas? Will they ever be whole?"

"My curious and compassionate boy, time is a strange thing. It does not truly exist. For those of us in spirit form, if you will, without the division of a physical body, we exist connected to all and, in many ways, never disconnected from those we love— because we are love. It does not take patience or cause anxiety because we are fully present in love. It is only when we are pulled to a moment like this, back into a shape we have inhabited before, only then do the memories and feelings of loss or a sense of longing occur. What I am trying to say is that those who have lost will reunite with their Atoas when it is their time to step into their next transformation. Thanks to you and Ophelia, the united Soahcoit will be whole and will get to choose where they desire their next birth to be. They are no longer anchored to this story."

I sighed. I had so many questions.

"I see your wheels turning. I wish I could answer all of your queries. Alas, we haven't the time."

"You just said time does not exist here."

"Time does not exist for those of us who have died, but you, my son, have not died."

I looked around once more. *Then where am I?*

"You're in the cosmic womb, and because you are a Sulu who absorbed the powers of a Phoenix, you will be reborn in your existing world. And just as you witnessed Aremis be reborn and age rapidly to resume his former life after the fall of Hafiza, so will you."

"I will... be reborn." I stumbled over the words. "I will get to be a father."

"You are already a father. That is why we haven't the time." She pulled me in for another long hug. "Your father and I always knew you would be the one to change the world. We had no idea that it would be this powerful. Please let those who have survived know that there is no hurry to reach the other side. Their loved ones are at peace. This new paradigm needs new leaders, and the survivors were fated to shepherd the new world in." She pulled me back and looked me in the eyes once more. "Besides, I heard the painter has some new tricks up his sleeve. There is more than one way to reunite with your Atoa." She winked playfully.

"What does that mean?"

"Trust me when I say you will learn to love surprises when you have an eternity to live." She kissed my forehead. "It is time. Lie down. I'll stay with you until the call comes."

I lay down instinctively in the fetal position. My mother stroked my hair softly, and my eyes closed. It seemed like the natural thing to do. My body felt like I was wrapped in the perfect blanket, weighted and warm. Then I just drifted to sleep.

PART V

OPHELIA

"*Mom!*" I pulled the swaddle wrap tighter over my shoulder, trying to cover Sadie's ears, hoping the ruckus would not wake her. I had only just got her to sleep. "Eleanor!"

I caressed Sadie's sweet ivory cheek with my finger. "If the boys don't wake you up, I will, huh, little one?" I turned around, ready to call for my mother again, when Lilith came from the hall.

"What is it, Olly? How can I help?"

"Where is my mom?"

My grandmother blushed and shuffled her feet. "She is otherwise occupied with her Atoa." Lilith played with a lock of her long blonde hair. "She deserves some happiness, don't you think?"

That was an understatement. My mom deserved the world after what she had been through. I was beyond grateful when she met Quinn. She finally got her happily ever after.

"Of course. I just thought she was here a minute ago, that's all." I swept past Lilith and pointed at the boys rough-housing in the yard. "I can't keep my eyes on all three of them at once. Aremis all but poked Elias' eye out a moment ago, and although these two may be Phoenixes, I have no idea if they are actually impervious to impaling's." I tucked Sadie in a little closer to my chest. "And I just got this one down."

Suddenly, there was another wail from the backyard. "That really hurt, Viraclay! I'm going to wreck you now!" Aremis screamed as he directed his large fencing stick at my seven-year-old husband and charged.

"I am on it," Lilith asserted, and was immediately out the back door.

I moved to the couch and plopped down. "I didn't see this one coming, Sadie. Did you?" My daughter's cherub face fit perfectly in the palm of my hand. Wild strawberry curls framed freckled cheeks and soft pink lips. *I am in love.* It was impossible not to be. "I didn't think I'd be a single mom raising three children." I looked out the window once more. Lilith had the boys cornered. They were giggling and attempting to get away from her by climbing a large olive tree. "Thank the strokes for your grandmothers."

Eleanor walked into the living room, and behind her was Quinn, tucking his shirt in. "Sorry ,Olly." My mom squeezed my shoulder as she passed me on the couch. "I'll help GG."

GG was short for great-grandma, an appointed nickname given to Lilith by my young husband a few months back. "Thanks, Mom." I smiled up at her. She was just about out the door when I reminded her, "You don't have to apologize. It's good to see you happy."

Quinn winked at me. "Thank you, Ophelia. I think happiness looks ravishing on her." Then he pinched her butt, and she playfully swatted at him as they joined Lilith in the hot pursuit of adolescent boys.

I played with a tendril of Sadie's hair affectionately as I considered the last month.

"WAIT! Wait! I have to open the portal!"

Lucas put his hand on my cheek. "Sadie is coming! I promised Elias I would save you and the baby."

Tears streamed down my face as a typhoon of emotions took my body, soul-searing pain beside the orgasmic connectedness to all and the soul I was shepherding into the world.

Molpe whispered in my ear, "She's coming. Listen to your body. Feel everything."

I surrendered to all of it. The pleasure, the anguish, the fear and the loss. At first it consumed me and then it expanded me into every color of every stroke. The entire world became void of sound, and an eternity happened in an instant. I don't know how long I was suspended there in the void, but the painter's voice was the first thing that gave me reference to life.

"You did it. You removed the lines. The world has returned to its true nature, a tapestry of colors."

I couldn't see Malarin, but I could feel his voice resonating in the cells of my being. "Sadie, is she okay?"

"Her gentle soul could only enter this timeline if you and Elias succeeded, and you have, and she is here."

Joy swelled inside me.

"My children have been creating lines and dancing too far into the shadow or praising to much of the light for eons. The circles have finally broken, thanks to the courage of two brave souls. You and Elias were determined to see love win, connection prevail, and beauty be restored. The two of you brought every element that was present during the drawing of the lines back to the very spot they needed to be integrated into to restore balance. This is a new age in the thirteenth timeline."

"How did we do that? You must have been orchestrating the whole thing."

"It is true I orchestrated some of the happenings to bring you here. But true transformation has to come from within. This world that I created has its own consciousness, its own will. For it to be restored, it had to come from within the strokes themselves. Just as the lines were drawn by the strokes themselves. We are all connected."

I knew that to be true. "What about my husband? What about the others who died here today?"

"Some of the strokes will never return, but that is their choice. Their energy will move to other timelines or dimensions, but rest assured, they will be restored to their wholeness."

"You're saying they will be with their Atoas?"

"They are their Atoas. Which is exactly why Elias will be returned to you and Sadie."

Relief surged through every cell of my being.

"Because of your sacrifice and birthing a new world from love and without the lines of separation, I have recovered the true place of the powries. Without their king and the Staff of Banishment, they have returned to the shallows of the earth to consume and transmute any turmoil that happens on the surface. We still need darkness and light, but they must coexist in harmony and with transparency. Do you understand?"

I searched within me, where I witnessed my own dark and light, and I knew what he said was a fundamental truth. "Balance."

"Yes, sweet child. The key is harmony and connection with all parts of ourselves and all beings. Feeling disconnected, feeling the lines of separation is what made Aurora and Clive the monsters they became. Every war was based on the illusion of separation. When we are isolated, we lose sight of our light and fall into shadow."

My heart twinged in empathy for Clive and Aurora, knowing it was their perception of the loss of love that had defiled their light.

"That feeling you just felt was exactly why you were the soul for this profound transformation. You can love the light and the dark in yourself and in others. You should know, Clive is with his kind now and he is whole."

The piece of me that was a splinter of him seemed to integrate a little deeper into my soul. "It is time for you to return to the world."

"Will I ever hear your voice again?"

"Sweet daughter, in the world you've just created, every stroke will hear my voice when they decide to. There are no more boxes to hide their hearts, from their creator or their magic."

Then I felt warmth swaddle my soul and I was instantly back in my body. The war around us had stopped. Every creature was looking on at us. Molpe helped me sit up, and I turned to Lucas, who was holding a beautiful baby girl with strawberry red curls.

"Sadie," I whispered. She looked up at me with a deep knowing in her eyes. I could tell her spirit was far wiser than mine.

"Here you go, Mama." Lucas handed me my baby girl wrapped in a pink blanket.

I took her in my arms, and every part of my body melted with her presence. She was liquid sunshine in a ridiculously cute form. "How long was I out?"

"But a moment," Yessica answered, as I looked up to see she was holding a child in her arms. Astonishing. *I had twins?*

Another cooing baby caught my attention. Helia was holding yet a third baby. I searched the vicinity for more babies, and that was when I noticed that the strokes looked different. The world looked different. It was like there was a strand of love connecting every living thing, and the colors were brilliant.

"Yeah, pretty fucking cool!" Lucas agreed. He watched my face as I tried to take it all in. "That's all on you, Olly. You did this."

"You changed the world," Molpe agreed.

"But you didn't have three babies," Lucas confirmed. "That one that Helia is holding is Aremis, and the one Yesi has got is your darling husband."

"What?" This time, when I looked at the baby in Yessica's arms, I really took him in. Sure enough, there was Elias. I would know those eyes anywhere, and now I could see them in our daughter's face too.

LUCAS

"What do you wear to this sort of thing? Really?"

Yesi adjusted my tie. "You look handsome, as always." She kissed my cheek.

"Okay, but what do you wear? The trolls are going to be naked, and the giants wear loincloths. This seems like a bit fucking much." I gestured to my suit. I grabbed my wife's luscious ass, and she squealed. "You, on the other hand, look hot."

"You could have simply asked the queen what she would've liked you to wear."

"She's too busy for that shit right now." I sat down on the bed while Yesi put on her gold strappy shoes to go with her nude sequined dress. The slit in the dress exposed her entire right leg, and it was taking all the willpower I could muster not to climb on top of her like an animal. "You look practically naked. Maybe I should wear something like that." I reached for her thigh and she playfully swatted at my hand.

"Eh, eh, eh... Later, Mr. Healey. I don't want to be late."

I threw myself back on the bed, trying to think of anything and everything that might kill this throbbing erection. "Do you think that a male giant's penis is too big for a she-troll's vagina?" *Yep, that will do it. Thinking of troll vagina could kill any mood.*

"Really, Lucas?"

I shrugged and sat back up. "Inquiring minds want to know."

"Please do not ask the bride or groom that question tonight. No matter how drunk you get, I repeat, please do not ask the bride or groom that question." My stunning wife walked over to the vanity and grabbed her earrings.

"I'm not the only one thinking it." *I promise you that.* "Okay, where will they live? In Listy or the Solomon Islands?"

"Probably the Solomon Islands, since Princess Chaness is happily reigning over Listy at the moment."

The Princess had acclimated nicely to leadership, and she was sincerely one of the kindest beings I'd ever met. The trolliage was loving her. Her sacrifice had endeared her to them in ways that bloodlines could never touch. Everyone still adored their Queen, but the Princess was cultivating something uniquely beautiful among the trolls.

"Are your parents meeting us there?"

"Are you nervous? Because that's the third time you've asked me that tonight." She concluded her final assessment of herself in the mirror and turned to me. "You are afraid you are not going to nail the speech, aren't you?"

"If I could win over the crowd at the Kraus wedding, this should be a piece of cake."

Yesi came over and brushed her fingers through my hair. "But you were still pretending to be the brooding, 'I don't have feelings or give two fucks' guy then."

"My wife doesn't talk like that. Who are you and what have you done with her?" I stood up from the bed and whisked her into my arms— *And the erection is back.*

"If Lucas Healey can have feelings, then Yessica Healey can have a potty mouth from time to time. Now, put me down and let's get going."

I reluctantly put her down, grabbed her hand, and we stepped out the door into the hall of The Cathedral and quickly teleported to the catacombs of the dragon den where the wedding was being held. Olly had told me about her journey down here, so I wasn't entirely surprised by the ambiance, but it was still a little unsettling to be surrounded by thousands of bones.

Yesi watched me look around, and before I could mouth off, she gave me a look that reminded me to keep my mouth shut. *Thank the strokes I had her.*

The first familiar face was the young Aremis. He had to be approaching his mid-twenties now. He looked good, but what was even more shocking was the hottie he had on his arm who looked vaguely familiar as well.

"Aremis." My wife had the warmest greetings. She leaned in and gave him a hug and kiss on the cheek. He let go of his date's arm, and I took the opportunity to introduce myself.

"Hi. I'm Lucas." I put my hand out to shake hers.

"I know who you are, Lucas Healey, but apparently I am unrecognizable."

I internally slapped my forehead. *Here for two minutes, and I'm already making an impression.*

She smiled and the familiarity connected, although I never knew her at this age. "Natasha?"

The way both of their faces lit up, I knew it was true. "But…"

"Apparently, when you are whole with a Phoenix, you get certain resurrection privileges."

Tears welled up in my eyes. I wanted to push them back, but how could I not be happy for a man like Aremis getting a second chance with his Atoa? I pulled him in for a strong hug. "Congratulations, man."

"Hey," a very familiar voice said from behind. "I don't think Aremis, Natasha or Elias have any idea what it's like to raise three infants at once. Resurrection privileges, my ass. Who knew Ulus stood for hectic toddler mom in Asagi?"

I turned around to see Olly holding Sadie on her hip. The little angel with her mama's wild fiery hair was beaming at me. She splayed her arms out and I scooped her up. "Lulu, Lulu!" she cheered. I kissed her all over her face while Yesi hugged Olly and the strapping Elias. Lucky Ophelia was getting to experience her husband through all his ages, and the early twenties were good to Viraclay. He looked just like Cane.

"Looking good, man," I said as I side-hugged him with his daughter in my arms.

"Thank God. It almost makes the teenage years worth it." Ophelia kissed me on the cheek.

"You mean I missed all the fun." I playfully punched Elias in the arm.

"Fun is a very sensitive subject in our home at present." He winked.

"We are in the final stretch," Aremis commented. "Elias will reach his consummation age in a month."

"I'm going to miss some things about the early twenties," Olly teased.

"Dear God, you two! Get a room. Tete thinks it's gross." Tete and Medusa came up along our left.

"So, we're getting the gang back together?" Medusa said as we all exchanged pleasantries.

"Apparently." Borte's sour demeanor brought its special flavor to the mix.

"Borte, Khan, I am sure that the Queen is very happy to have you here." Elias was always good at keeping the peace.

"She has become a dear friend since we worked so closely training her Sholl-guard," the Khan admitted. "We enjoy her company very much."

"Much more than we enjoy most Conduits'," Borte added. A smile spread across the old empress's face. "I did not say we enjoyed it more than the company of the Ancients, my friend."

I looked up to see she was communicating, as she often did, with Shiva, who was approaching with Helia. Helia had become the ambassador of the Ancients after Winston died during the final battle. The position seemed to suit her. More hugs and greetings all around before a very loud announcement echoed off the cave walls.

"Please take your seats. The ceremony is about to begin." Princess Chaness' voice was pleasant and firm.

"We better get to our seats."

Everyone agreed, and we followed the herd of some of the wildest variety of creatures I'd ever seen. We took our seats next to the Krauses, since I was still holding my niece hostage. "They are going to have to pry you out of my cold dead hands," I said as I pinched her nose.

"Lulu, Lulu," she chimed back.

"I'll take that as consent." Man, I loved this kid.

A gentle squeeze on my shoulder from Vosega let me know he and Oya were sitting behind us. "Happy to see you son."

I nodded reassuredly at him and noticed there wasn't an ounce of internal cringe from him calling me son.

Then the music sounded, and we watched a procession of giant men walk down the aisle. Emperor Calt was the last one, and he took his place at the altar where Princess Chaness was waiting patiently to officiate this shindig. The music changed, and it was apparent the bride was coming down the aisle. We all stood.

When I saw my dearest friend Fetzle approaching the altar, I had to stifle a laugh. My wife turned around to glare at me, because, apparently, I didn't do a good enough job. I had never seen Fetzle wear a single shred of clothing during our entire friendship, and she was sashaying toward her husband in a bright pink fluffy garment that made her look like a dahlia on steroids. I had to wonder if the Emperor was reconsidering his choices.

Pink ribbons, fabric and feathers were flying everywhere as she enthusiastically took her place and grabbed Calt's willing hands. The smile on his face said it all—he thought she hung the fucking moon. It felt good to know that.

"Thank you to all the attendees. You may be seated." The Princess looked around the room as she spoke. We all sat. I, for one, was excited to see what a giant-troll wedding would be like. "Per the request of our Queen, we are not performing a traditional trolliage wedding or a traditional giant wedding, because this is not a traditional union. Instead, the couple have decided to model their ceremony after a Conduit ceremony that the Queen once attended."

I looked beyond Elias at Olly and winked. That's got to be their big bash she's talking about. Ophelia sheepishly shrugged.

"As officiant, I am here to connect these two creatures." Okay, I thought... I might have phrased that differently, *but who was I to judge?* "Queen Fetzle, will you be with Emperor Calt forever and beyond?"

"Yes, forever and beyond." She was holding a big bouquet of palm fronds that had been painted pink to match the rest of the ensemble. She lifted it up above her head, as though to show her victory.

"Wooohhooo, Fetzle!" I cheered, and Sadie's face lit up with excitement too. "You wouldn't believe it now, but Auntie Fetzle used to talk funny sometimes," I whispered in the little one's ear. "But we always loved her."

"Fet, Fet, Fet!" That was toddler for Fetzle.

Chaness turned to Calt. "Emperor Calt, will you be with Queen Fetzle forever and beyond?"

"Absolutely, without question." His eyes never left the she-troll's face.

"By the power someone gave me, I now say that you two are married. You can kiss her if you want."

Fetzle threw her handful of palm fronds in the air and took a flying leap into her husband's arms. I was grateful we weren't seated in the front row. The kiss went on a disturbingly long time before Princess Chaness tapped Fetzle on the shoulder to break up the make-out session before it got inappropriate for the children.

"That's my girl." I smiled, and Yesi shook her head at my ridiculousness. "Hey, if it doesn't make a few people want to gag, is it really a kiss?"

She rolled her eyes.

"Give me my child back before you teach her such atrocities via osmosis of proximity." Olly playfully reached over and grabbed Sadie, who was nodding off without me realizing. "No, really, I'm going to pass her off to Eleanor so that we can have some fun."

"Big E is here? Where?"

I turned around and saw her a few rows back.

"She's late for everything these days... Not because she's doing her hair either."

My eyes got big as I realized Olly was referring to Eleanor spending way too much time getting frisky with her Atoa. I raised my hand and gave Eleanor a thumbs-up. I didn't care if she understood why or not. Olly rolled her eyes. *Isn't this sweet?* I'm sandwiched between two women who love me and also think I should shut my mouth.

Olly passed off a sleepy Sadie, and the rest of us got busy at the bar. It was a good night to have a good night, I thought. When the bride and groom approached, I was all too eager to join in their jubilation. They ordered a round of shots for all of us, and we cheered and toasted in all directions. I had a moment of sadness as I thought about how much some of our fallen comrades would have enjoyed this moment. Specifically I thought about Ruit and his poor family. The remaining Talluses were invited to the ceremony but apparently chose not to attend. My heart hurt for them. I swallowed to hold back the tears. I could talk to Yesi about it later.

"The Emperor and I would like to have a word with you and Yesi," Fetzle said discreetly.

I took Yesi's hand and we followed the couple into an alcove away from the noisy hall.

"Thank you both for attending. It means so much to us," Calt said.

"We wouldn't miss it for the world, man." If he was not gargantuan, I would have hugged him.

"My husband and I have a very important request for two of my closest friends."

"Anything for you, Fetzle." Yessica squeezed my hand as she

answered for both of us. And I agreed with my wife. There was nothing I wouldn't do for my old friend, but I was very curious.

"We have not yet announced it, but we are with child."

"Congratulations, you guys!" Again, a prime moment for hugs that just lingered in the size-deficit air.

"What wonderful news!" Yessica agreed.

"We would be honored if you would be our little one's godparents." Fetzle leaned down and got in Yesi and I's faces, really close. "Be honest, will you be this little bundle's godparents?" She stood up and put her hands on her belly.

A million things flashed through my head at once, and I wished Yesi had a damn Rune to share it all with my wife. Questions like, *How will we care for a giant-troll baby if something happens to them? The thing will be born larger than both of us put together. What does a giant-troll baby diaper look like? By the strokes, what does giant-troll baby poop look like? What do they eat? There aren't enough nipples on the planet to satiate an appetite of those proportions. What if they sit on one of us?* The list went on and on.

Fetzle was still looking at me pointedly, waiting for an answer, when my lovely and considerate wife pulled herself together enough to say what I was terrified of saying, "Of course, Fetzle, Calt. We would be honored."

GLOSSARY

Adfector~ A faction of Conduit that manipulates emotions.

Alalli~ The Asagi word for mother.

Amplifier~ A Conduit that can enhance any other Conduits abilities around them.

Ancients~ A faction of Conduit that is very old and has a variety of gifts.

Animo~ A faction of Conduit that manipulates consciousness.

Armorist~ A Conduit that creates shields.

Aromatic~ A Conduit that can manipulate smell.

Asagi~ Conduit Language.

Atoa~ A Conduit's other half or partner.

Aura~ A Conduit that can see the color of the strokes around another Conduit, because of this they can sense intents and truths.

Brilfalti~ The secret word that incited the Katuan Stones to rebuild the arena and manage the Trials.

Body Snatcher~ A Conduit who can manipulate others physical forms.

Bustany~ A faction of Conduit that manipulates plants or vegetation.

Circuitu~ A faction of Conduit that manipulates objects or elements around them.

Chitchakor, Malarin, Dalininkas~ The master painter and creator of all life in the world.

Conduit~ A semi-immortal being that expresses extraordinary powers when consummated with their other half, or pair. Upon consummation Conduits no longer age. Conduits are always coupled as a receiver and an imposer.

Consu~ A consummated Conduit

Conveyor~ A Conduit that can articulate any message, feeling or sensation to anyone within a certain radius.

Corpori~ A faction of Conduit that manipulates the body.

Covening~ The act of Conduits gathering to perform the ancient magic.

Dalininkas, Chitchakor, Malarin, ~ The master painter and creator of all life in the world.

Decimate~ A Conduit that can make anything explode with a single touch, including parts of the body.

Directorate~ The committee of Conduits assigned by the Katuan Stones to oversee the trials.

Elemental~ A faction of Conduit that can manifest or create the earth, wind, water or fire.

Epochus~ A Conduit that can distort time.

Eyok~ An ancient morning ritual that includes a guest and a host sharing stories. It is customary for the host to start the ritual with a story of their own choosing. The host can then ask their guest to share a story of the host's choosing. It is customary for the ritual to last the entire length of the guest's visit. The purpose is to share Conduit history and build each Conduit's legacy

Giant~ A Conduit that can grow in size.

Gilly Mead~ A breakfast mead produced by Vosega. It has less alcohol and is fermented differently than other meads. It is served hot.

Haven~ A place of ancient magic, often a safe house created by Covening.
Healers~ A Conduit that can heal.
Hillio~ The medallion used to communicate with Fetzle the troll

Illusionist~ A Conduit that can create things that are not there.
Incubus~ A Conduit that impregnates women.
Imposer~ A Conduit that can impose their will or energy onto another being or object.
Incantor~ A faction of Conduit that creates or manipulates magical elements/

Kata~ The language of the Katuan Stones.
Katan~ A team in the Katuan Trials.
Katuanak Arena~ The arena built with the Katuan Stones.
Katuan Trials~ The trials that take place in the Katuanak Arena. There are three, The Creation Trial, The Destruction Trial and the Transformation Trial.

Lasteea~ A connection and feeling deeper than love.
Lantern~ A Conduit who can absorb and reflect light.
Loktpi~ A magical key that can dissolve any wards and unlock any door, revealing the location and passage into any Conduit Haven.

Malarin, Dalininkas, Chitchakor ~ The master painter and creator of all life in the world.
Mapper~ A Conduit who can create maps to various locations or create paths to otherwise obscure locations.
Master Mason~ A Conduit that can build anything with anything.
Mekoninis~ The three Conduits who can defend and make mischief for the other teams during the Creation Trial.
Minerals~ An earth elemental that can command control of metals,

stones, salts, anything that is found in the earth in its most basic form.

Nebas~ Evil or 'bad' Conduits who most likely align with Esther and Yanni, either in secret or openly.

Pai Ona~ The 'good' Conduits, those fighting to unite and end the war.
Paksyon~ A small congregation of Conduits, who are usually participating in covening..
Pealatunic- The Asagi word for magic.
The Pierses~ Sister books that contain ancient magic spells.
Phoenix~ What Aremis believes he has become when he returns to life after being killed by his own flame. There is still much to discover about this type of gift.
Plitos, Milti, Damilton~ The phrase needed to transfer a Rune, it means 'mine is yours, ours is theirs.'
Poginuli~ A broken Conduit pair, an individual Conduit whose partner has been slain.
Projector~ A Conduit who can replay memories or project a scene into a larger capacity or screen.

Ramalan~ A faction of Conduit that can see the future.
Receiver~ A Conduit that receives or absorbs another object or being's energy.
The Rittles~ Weapons forged with magical poisons that inflict severe injury.
The River Tins~ The magical river where your colors can be cleaned, according to the creation myth of the Conduits.

Shape Shifter~ A Conduit who can take a different form.
Shield~ A Conduit who can camouflage or energetically guard against gifts or detection.
Soahcoit~ A consummated Conduit pair.
Sulu~ A beacon of energy, often in the form of a group of Conduits.

In rare occasions it is an individual Conduit that creates an energy vortex.

Swali~ A human that has some Conduit heritage, or a demi-god.

Tahwil~ A faction of Conduit that can manipulate their own form.
Taqa~ A faction of Conduit that manipulates energy.
Timbress~ A Conduit who can manipulate sound.
Truth Sayer~ A Conduit who can detect the truth or compel you to tell the truth.
Tulaswaga~ The Asagi word for gift.

Quakers~ An earth elemental that can shake the earth, move the plates within the earth's surface.

Unconsu~ A Conduit that is still mortal and has not been consummated.

Varon~ A faction of Conduit that influences animals.
Vulcan~ An earth elemental Conduit that has the power to control and manifest or create volcanic activity.

ACKNOWLEDGMENTS

First, I need to thank my readers! For their patience and their persistence. I know this book took the longest to produce, but I hope you feel like it was worth the wait.

I would like to thank all of my family and friends who have cheered me on throughout this process. I could not have done this without you, like literally, I would just be a puddle on the floor. So from the bottom of my heart I want you to know how grateful I am for you all. I see you! I hear you! I love you!

A special thanks to all my beta readers along the way. There have been many of you and I hope I don't leave anyone out. It takes a village to make this happen and you guys are my village!
Jen, Alicia, Michelle, Yvonne, Sheryl, Becky, Lynne, Stephanie, Darah, Rebekah L., Rebekah D. and Erika.

I cannot thank Ella Medler, enough! She and I have been through life along this journey. Not only is she an amazing editor that pushes me to grow and believes in my project, she has been a

guardian angel who has given me immense grace. Thank you
FOREVER!

I also want to show my appreciation for the incredibly talented
Cherie Fox, who created my covers. She brought my story to life.
Plus she is one of the easiest and most considerate people to work
with.

Lastly, I have to thank all of the furry friends who have kept me
company during long writing nights and the feathery friends who
brought me inspiration. Franky, Sparkle, Divina Eepa Kangaroo,
Balto, Nadja, Watson, Laila, Trucker (aka Larry), River, Ruger,
Guinness, Barry, Ace, Ryder, Bo and Rose.

I want to say thank you so much for taking the time to read the final book of the series, *FOREVER*. This has been a dream of mine, for many years. It was an honor to take you on this journey through The Conduit Chronicles.

And if you enjoyed the book, please take a moment to review it on Amazon.com. As authors, we like to hear what our readers appreciate about our stories.

ABOUT THE AUTHOR

Ashley Hohenstein lives in Northern California.
Ashley was a massage therapist and health educator for over twenty
years. She has owned several businesses and has found
entrepreneurship to be dynamic and fulfilling.
Currently she supports peoples healing journey's with a variety of
modalities that she has studied all over the world.